LANTERNS AND LACE

DIANN MILLS

BARBOUR
PUBLISHING

To my sister Debbie for all of her love, encouragement,
and sweet reminders of our daddy's sense of humor.

© 2006 by DiAnn Mills

ISBN 1-59789-356-0

Scripture quotations are taken from the King James Version of the Bible.

Cover Design: Lookout Design Group, Inc.

For more information about DiAnn Mills, please access the author's web site at the
following Internet address: www.diannmills.com

Published by Barbour Publishing, Inc., P.O. Box 719, Uhrichsville, Ohio 44683,
www.barbourbooks.com

*Our mission is to publish and distribute inspirational products offering exceptional value
and biblical encouragement to the masses.*

Printed in the United States of America.
5 4 3 2 1

A NEW HEART ALSO WILL I GIVE YOU,
AND A NEW SPIRIT WILL I PUT WITHIN YOU: AND I WILL
TAKE AWAY THE STONY HEART OUT OF YOUR FLESH,
AND I WILL GIVE YOU AN HEART OF FLESH.
EZEKIEL 36:26

CHAPTER  1

Jenny Martin would face a gang of outlaws in the hope of finding her sister's child. Over the past several days, she'd slept upright until her back throbbed, eaten beans as hard and dry as stone, and endured the humiliation of men eyeing her because she traveled the Union Pacific without an escort.

Now, as the end of her travels grew to a close, she couldn't help but sense an air of excitement despite the long, uncomfortable journey. She attempted to stand and walk about the car, but dizziness forced her back down onto the scratchy seat. Sleep tugged at her stinging eyes, and she closed them for an instant, but a painfully loud snore from an elderly man across the aisle kept her from giving in to the rest her body craved. Other womanly discomforts plagued her aching body, and she did her best to will them away. At least for the present.

I will never take my life as a proper lady for granted again.

The doors between the railroad cars slammed shut, and she startled. Nothing in Cleveland had prepared her for the primitive living conditions of the Wild West. A less than pleasant odor met her nostrils and threw her stomach into a whirl—no doubt from the elderly man who snored. Between that and a portly man's foul cigar,

7

the last few hours had been nearly unbearable.

Jenny glanced out the window and watched the countryside slip by. This trip was supposed to have been an exciting adventure, one she'd describe to her students once school resumed in September. She'd ridden the Northern Pacific Railroad to Texas and boarded the Union Pacific en route to Kahlerville with the enthusiasm of a giddy girl. Viewing the terrain across this vast land had given her a sense of freedom, but her sentiments faded as the hours moved to one grueling day after another. Still, at the end of Jenny's journey to Kahlerville, Texas, lived a little girl who needed her family.

She smiled despite her discomfort. The destination of her dreams was but a few miles away. Jenny resisted the urge to open the window and allow some portion of the sultry air to circulate. She wanted to disembark without a fine coating of soot darkening her face and traveling attire. Earlier, she'd changed into a clean traveling dress and a cape of slate gray lined in gray taffeta that could also serve as a mackintosh, but for her purposes it would shield her from smoke and dust. She sighed. Oh, how she'd welcome a fresh, cooling rain. The clear azure sky held no such promise. Instead, she'd think about her niece and how the child must be as beautiful as Jessica.

Within moments, it became increasingly clear that if she didn't permit some breeze to blow in from the outside, she would surely faint. Jenny lifted the latch on the window. Soon fine black dirt settled on her hat, face, neck, cape, and dress. How foolish to change into clean clothes. Perhaps her little niece wouldn't mind that her auntie was soiled.

She fanned herself as vigorously as propriety allowed and stared out the window. Tall pine trees grew close to the track and swayed slightly, offering a brief respite from the heat. They reminded her of the gaslights on the street corners of home. The trees passed, and an array of black-eyed Susans covered an entire field. How utterly captivating. Never had she expected such beauty in this desolate country.

The porter walked by, and Jenny lifted her gaze to offer a faint smile. "Sir, do you know what time we will arrive in Kahlerville?"

The elderly man, whose molted mustache bent below his chin, tipped his hat. "Late this afternoon, miss."

"Thank you." Sometimes she feared her constitution would not allow another minute on board the train. "Sir, can you tell me anything about the town?"

"It's quite pleasant, rather homey. Let me think. . . . I have an aunt and uncle living there, so I'm more familiar with Kahlerville than some of the other stops. I remember a newspaper, telegraph office, a bank, sheriff's office, law office, barber, livery and feed store, a general store, a church, and an undertaker." He pointed with his right index finger as though he'd memorized the businesses located up and down the street. "I think there are a few other establishments, too. A boardinghouse for one. I remember the food is especially good there. Are you visiting family?"

Jenny pondered how to answer the question. Her mother would have told the porter to mind his own affairs, except her mother's ways often sounded impolite. "My deceased sister used to live in Kahlerville." She promptly focused her attention on the cracked and split seat beside her.

"I'm sorry, miss. And I nearly forgot the reason why I'm here."

She turned her attention back to the kindly man.

"There's a gentleman sitting in first class who would like for you to join him."

Jenny sighed and fought the unsettling in her stomach. Sitting in first class had its advantages. Abruptly, her breakfast nearly made it to her throat. "I couldn't possibly. I feel rather ill, and I don't have a chaperon."

"I understand, and I'll give him your reply. I believe he's taking the train to Kahlerville, too. I would not have approached you with the gentleman's request, except he specifically asked for you by name and described your appearance. I thought perhaps you were acquainted."

A mixture of curiosity and alarm raced through her. "My goodness. I don't know anyone on board. What is the gentleman's name?"

"Mr. Aubrey Turner."

Jenny tilted her head. "Is he from Ohio?"

"He didn't say. Would you like for me to ask him?"

"Oh, no." She smiled and allowed the train's rhythmic hum to soothe her for a moment. "Please give him my regrets."

"Of course. Mr. Turner did ask that I relate to you that he'd been a close friend of your sister, Jessica."

She startled. How did this Mr. Turner know she and Jessica were sisters? The thought frightened her. Could he have been a part of Jessica's unmentionable profession? Perhaps Jenny should have accepted Oscar's proposal before she left Cleveland. At least she would have had a ring on her left hand to eliminate inappropriate advances. This Mr. Turner—what if he thought she shared her sister's livelihood?

She took a deep breath. *I do look like my sister.* Humiliation swept over her as though every passenger knew Jessica's disgraceful behavior had caused their parents to disown her. Jenny glanced down at her clothes, now wrinkled and soiled, but certainly not the attire her sister would have chosen. Even when Jessica had sought to please their parents, she chose brighter colors and a much snugger fit.

Why did he want to talk to me? Jenny's mental distress now matched her physical uneasiness. Poor Jessica needed to stay buried. Jenny had no desire to learn about the circumstances surrounding her sister's wayward life or her men friends. She settled back and closed her eyes in hopes the troublesome thoughts would dissipate.

The arrival into Kahlerville held no fanfare, and Jenny's expectations were only to find the boardinghouse. She'd grown very accustomed to Cleveland and all the finery a city offered, but she didn't expect anything more than the quaint country town that greeted her. For the present, a warm bath and a real bed with fresh linens would ease all the annoyances of travel. Weary beyond description, she stepped down from the rail car and onto the first step.

A mass of fiery air nearly suffocated her. She gasped for breath, and tears stung her eyes. A mixture of dirt, soot, and intense heat spun her into a coughing spasm. Bile rose in her throat. She tasted the familiar acridity of the past several days.

Please, no, I'm not going to be sick. I'd rather choke first.

Jenny dropped her small traveling bag and heard it hit the ground with a thud. Her right hand reached for the side rail, but her fingers refused to wrap around the metal. A wave of blackness enveloped her head and numbed her senses. She realized the brittle limbs that supported her body were about to give way, and there was nothing she could do to stop it. A pair of strong arms reached from behind. Darkness washed over her, and she felt herself falling forward.

Jenny woke to the muffled voice of a man calling her name. "Miss Martin," he said. "Miss Martin, can you hear me?"

"Must be the heat." She heard another man's voice and recognized it as the porter's. "It's a scorcher."

"Let's get her inside the train station," the first man said. "Doesn't this town have a doctor?"

She felt herself being swept up and carried as though she were but a mere child. *I'm all right. I don't need a doctor.* The words refused to come. She raised her head and gave into the blackness again.

When Jenny forced open her eyes, she blinked and swallowed the bitter taste in her mouth. Slowly the fog in her head lifted, and she found herself looking up into a pair of deep violet eyes.

"Are you feeling better, Miss Martin?" he asked, and she recognized the voice as the man who had been with the porter. "A doctor should be here shortly."

The doctor of this town was the last person she needed. She should be presentable. . .a proper lady in appearance and demeanor. "I'm. . .fine." Suddenly, she became distinctly aware of reclining in the arms of this strange man. She stirred and tried to move, but a dull throb beat across her right temple.

"You fell and hit your head." His deep voice reminded her of

Shakespeare and the reading of *Hamlet*. "I tried to catch you, but I wasn't fast enough. Please accept my apologies."

"Thank you. I mean, I'm sorry." Jenny noted the man's incredible good looks: handsome with wavy, straw-colored hair and a deeply tanned face. And it wasn't her imagination. His eyes were the same color as the spring lilacs that bloomed outside her mother's kitchen window.

"There's no need to apologize," he said. "Just rest until the doctor arrives."

"I don't need a doctor. Really. If only I could get to the boarding-house where I might rest."

"Nonsense. You have slept very little since leaving St. Louis and eaten even less. The journey from Ohio has been very difficult for you."

His accurate accounting of the past several days of train travel disturbed her. How did this stranger know these things? She swallowed again and fought the urge to be very ill. The train pulled away from the station, its deafening sound making her head throb worse than before.

"How do you know about me?" she asked after several moments of ordering her body to cease its churning.

"Excuse my poor manners, Miss Martin, and allow me to introduce myself. My name is Aubrey Turner. Do you recall the porter extending my invitation to join me?"

Jenny nodded and closed her eyes, feeling even more miserable.

"I feared you shunned my invitation due to my association with your sister," he said. "But now I wonder if I should have contacted you sooner."

Before she had a chance to consider Aubrey Turner's words, Jenny heard the sound of boots stepping across the wooden plank floor of the train station.

"You must be the doctor," Mr. Turner said. "I do say it has taken you long enough."

"Yes, I'm Dr. Grant Andrews." He paused. "I was tending to a patient when I received the message."

Jenny turned her head. Her stomach convulsed. Her head pounded, and her throat burned. Beads of perspiration trickled down her face and slipped beneath the fabric of her dress. Disgusting vomit covered her. She neither had the strength to wipe her mouth nor the ability to stop the sickness. *Whatever have I done to deserve this humiliation?* Not only did she feel wretched, but she also knew she looked awful and smelled even worse. She fought the tears. How could she ever face anyone in Kahlerville after the spectacle she had just made of herself?

I've fainted, fallen, hurt my head, and vomited. And I haven't been in town an hour. For the first time in her life, Jenny wished she could die.

CHAPTER  2

Jenny refused to succumb to another fainting spell. Dazzling sunlight shone overhead and blinded her, and huge drops of perspiration trickled down her face. Conscious of still lying in Aubrey Turner's embrace, she felt as though floating in his arms. Everyone at the train station viewed her humiliation.

"I'm carrying you to the back of the doctor's wagon," Mr. Turner whispered. "I hope his office is more accommodating than this primitive wagon. At least there are a few quilts back here."

Jenny didn't care what the wagon looked like. She simply wanted to be far away from onlookers. "Thank you, Mr. Turner, for helping me. This is. . .quite regrettable."

"Once you're out of this heat, you'll feel better," he said. "I do hope your condition improves very soon, Miss Martin."

Jenny couldn't construct a single intelligent word. She closed her eyes and reclined on the hard wagon bed.

"I apologize for the discomfort," Dr. Andrews said. "It's but a short distance to my home. There I can determine what has made you so ill."

She didn't respond to his kind voice either. *I'd rather be making my way to the undertaker.*

Dr. Andrews drove the wagon slowly. Must the whole town view her miserable condition? Once at his residence, he carried her inside to his office and onto an examination table. She glanced about at his equipment, very similar to what she was accustomed to seeing in Cleveland. The room smelled of a peculiar odor, not offensive, but faintly of medicine. On the opposite side of the room set a large desk and bookcase with two extra chairs. Neat. Tidy.

I shall not perish from filth here.

Her initial dealings with Dr. Andrews destroyed any preconceived ideas that she may have had regarding the man. She'd envisioned an elderly doctor with gray hair and stooped shoulders—not the young, good-looking man with the huge almond-shaped green eyes and hair the color of rich honey.

Dr. Andrews gently examined her while she fought the urge to be ill one more time. "You appear to be exhausted," he said.

"I haven't slept well or eaten properly in days."

"That confirms my diagnosis. I don't believe you are seriously ill, simply in need of rest and a change in diet. A few days in bed and some good home cooking should have you feeling much better. The lump on your head is minor, but it may cause a few headaches. In the meantime, I'd like for you to stay in one of my spare bedrooms so I can watch for signs of anything more complicated—just to be sure."

"But. . .I. . ."

Dr. Andrews took her hand in his and smiled. "I don't think you want to risk fainting again in the confines of a room at the boardinghouse. If propriety is a concern, my housekeeper lives here with me and my daughter."

"Thank you. I appreciate your kindness. I am normally quite healthy, not at all like this. I don't want to impose on your kindness." Jenny dabbed her eyes. Was she babbling?

"My job is to make my patients well." He opened the door of his office and called for Miss Mimi. A round, silver-haired woman stepped inside carrying a glass of water. She looked like a grandmother, not a housekeeper, certainly not the uniformed type to whom Jenny was accustomed. Dr. Andrews introduced the two. "Miss Mimi will help you bathe. She often assists me as a nurse, and she'll make you feel comfortable."

Jenny cringed from the rank smell meeting her nostrils and the way her traveling dress stuck to her undergarments and body. She bit back the tears, determined not to make any more of a spectacle of herself than she already had. Utter mortification lingered in the air as heavy as the odor of vomit. "I can take care of myself," she managed.

"I'll stay with you just in case you feel faint." Mimi smiled as though she understood Jenny's plight. "I have smelling salts in my pocket if we need them."

"This isn't really necessary."

But the woman remained inside the room after Dr. Andrews excused himself.

Turning from the sympathetic face of Miss Mimi, Jenny fumbled with the buttons around her neck. Trembling fingers couldn't seem to push them through the small loops. The longer she worked with them, the bigger the lump in her throat grew. A sob slid upward, and she couldn't wish it away.

"Let me help you, honey." Mimi moved closer and held out the glass of water. "Let's begin with this."

Jenny wrapped her fingers around it and shivered. "Thank you. My mouth tastes so wretched."

It had been years since anyone had helped Jenny undress or bathe, and her independent nature fought the idea of a stranger performing such a task.

"I'm so miserable." Jenny attempted to stop the flow of tears, but they flooded her eyes and rolled over her cheeks. "All those people at the train station saw me ill."

Miss Mimi draped her arm around Jenny's shoulders. "Let me help you. I know this must be difficult, but you are very weak. We can do this together. . .discreetly."

Jenny nodded. She had no choice. Miss Mimi offered her all the privacy she needed while tending to her needs. Once clean and dressed in a fresh nightgown that Miss Mimi had pulled from Jenny's trunk, she felt remarkably refreshed. Dr. Andrews helped her ascend the stairs to a bedroom.

"I'd like for you to get some sleep, and I'll check on you periodically throughout the evening hours."

"Yes, of course," she mumbled through closed eyes. All she wanted to do was rid her mind of this horrible ordeal.

Jenny stirred in her sleep. A nightmare clung to her hazy dream world, one in which she begged the gods of torment to leave her alone. Humiliation unlike she'd ever experienced, repeated sights and sounds no fitting lady should endure.

She blinked several times in an effort to clear her mind from sleep and usher in consciousness. Her nebulous gaze focused on unfamiliar surroundings. Bouquets of blue and yellow flowers dotted the walls, and an open window invited a welcome breeze from swaying tree branches. A marble and oak washstand, a stately armoire, rocker, and trunk were the only pieces of furniture except for the intricately carved headboard. She stroked the thin white coverlet trimmed in white tatted lace that lightly covered her, and she repeatedly ran her fingers over a pale blue and green embroidered basket of flowers on the pillowcase.

Somewhere she heard a piano and strained to hear the tune. It was a hymn, one her old piano teacher used to play. Jenny hadn't focused on religious songs for years. She concentrated on classical pieces as emphasized by her music professor at the university. But this particular song had been a recital piece, in fact her very first performance— "Amazing Grace."

Jenny sighed and recalled all those dreadful nights on board the train. Now she lay tucked in a feather bed inhaling the faint scent of roses from the linens, decidedly more pleasant than the smells from the night before.

She held her breath. The events of the previous day had been real.

Where am I? In the same breath, all the remembrances poured over her like a chilling rain on a cold winter day. Jenny painfully relived every embarrassing moment from the instant she stumbled down from the train until her stomach convulsed in the presence of Mr. Turner and Dr. Andrews.

"Oh." She moaned in memory of the torrid heat and how she'd fainted and hit her head. A dull ache still persisted. She gingerly touched a lump high on the right side of her forehead.

In the light of day, the embarrassment again burned her cheeks. The thought of facing Dr. Andrews and Miss Mimi seemed to be more than she could bear. Jenny buried her head in the pillow. How could she look at anyone in this town after yesterday? Dreaded tears threatened to flow, but she swallowed them. Mother and Father would be sorely disappointed in her behavior. Displays of emotion were not the proper manner for handling problems.

After several minutes her thoughts slipped back to Dr. Andrews. Why didn't his wife appear? And where was Jessica's child? He'd spoken of his daughter. Questions darted in and out of her mind. Of one thing she felt certain: the temporary living arrangements would allow her to become better acquainted with the doctor and his family. The whole nasty business with her illness could be a stroke of luck, and hopefully, she'd soon be on her way back home with her niece.

Her glance fell upon her trunk and bags. Dare she get dressed? Taking a deep breath, she threw back the thin coverlet and slowly moved her legs to the side of the bed. The room began to spin. When it refused to cease, she lay back down and closed her eyes. *I'll try again in a little while.* Sleep enveloped her senses.

Grant picked up his empty cup for the third time and attempted to drink from it.

"Why don't you let me get you some more coffee?" Mimi peered at him across the table.

"I don't want any." He stared into the cup, seeing nothing for the worrisome thoughts swirling around in his head.

"Oh, Grant. I do hate to see you so disturbed." Compassion laced her words.

A deep sense of melancholy threatened to overtake him. He set the cup on its saucer and gently pushed it back along with a half-eaten plate of scrambled eggs and buttery grits. "I'm worried about our new patient. Not her condition, but her reason for being here."

"I feel the same way. When I stepped inside your office, I thought I was looking at a ghost—the same big brown eyes and dark hair. Then she introduced herself as Jenny Martin." Mimi paused. "Is this Jessica's sister or a cousin? The resemblance is remarkable." She tilted her head as though an ear turned his way would cause her to hear better. "Do you know something that you're not telling me?"

His eyes narrowed. "I don't know any more than you do. But I've got to find out what this is all about."

"I saw you spent a long time in the study this morning."

"I needed to pray."

She picked up his cup and disappeared into the kitchen only to return with it filled with hot coffee. Her midnight blue eyes captured his gaze. "If we were drinkin' folks, I'd add something a little stronger."

Grant chuckled. "If I was a drinkin' man, I'd accept it." Taking a sip and burning his tongue, he set the cup down. He couldn't disguise his apprehension. "I remember two and a half years ago when Morgan helped me with Rebecca's adoption. I expected someone to appear and claim her or some citizen to object because I was single. Not that I wanted to give her up, but I anticipated it might happen. No one, not one single inquiry about Jessica's baby girl responded to the Dallas and Houston newspapers." He shook his head. "Like you, the instant I saw our patient upstairs, I knew she was a member of Rebecca's family."

"I wish you'd left her at the train station. Excuse me, I don't really mean that."

He raised a brow.

"Well, maybe I mean it a little."

He laughed, but his heart refused to be soothed with humor. Memories jumbled his mind. "I keep thinking about those uncertain times during Rebecca's adoption—the moments when I didn't know how to pray or what to pray for. I felt selfish in wanting to keep Rebecca and fearful of coveting a baby who might belong to someone else." Grant studied the dear lady beside him. Wrinkle upon wrinkle lay across her face. Love lines. Beautiful touches of God that reminded him of the power of His grace.

"But Rebecca is yours."

"Legally, but morally? I simply don't have any answers, and my mind won't give me a rest." Grant reached across the table and took Mimi's hand in his. "I apologize for my bad temperament this morning. And thank you for helping me with Miss Martin."

"I understand how you feel." She swiped at a tear. "She's a threat to all of us."

"So what do you suggest?" Grant asked. Mimi usually saw things from a different perspective: older, wiser, and with a female point of view.

"Right now I'm a little scared, confused. Maybe angry. I don't have any suggestions but to have patience. This could be an innocent visit. Perhaps Miss Martin wants to make sure Rebecca is well cared for or plans to visit her sister's grave. Mercy, she may not know her sister passed on. God has a purpose for all of this, but I wish He'd tell one of us what it is."

He nodded and picked up his fork, tapping it lightly on the table.

Several moments passed before he spoke again. "Did Miss Martin give any indication why she's here?"

"No. The poor thing suffered so that my heart went out to her. She cried the entire time I helped her bathe."

"I checked on her several times during the night. Most of the time, I wanted to look into the room and find her gone." He smiled. Confession was supposed to be good for the soul. "I also looked in on Rebecca each time I stepped from Miss Martin's room."

"I spent a lot of time last night watching our little girl sleep, too. It's a wonder we didn't pass each other in the hallway." Mimi laughed softly.

"I think I saw you leaving the nursery at one point. I should have called out. We could have kept each other company."

Mimi crossed her arms. "My questions are the same as yours."

Grant stared into Mimi's face. "I'm not so sure I want to know why she's here."

"That doesn't sound like you."

"Rebecca is my daughter," he said. "I never thought I could love anyone like I do her."

"It's a father's love." She leaned toward him. "I think we may be overreacting. God gave you Rebecca. You and I have confirmed His hand in her adoption. He will work this out. Like you said, Miss Martin may not know about Jessica's death or of Rebecca."

"True. I'm thinking the worst without the least concern for Miss Martin's health or even grief."

"Well, you'll have to ask her and get your questions answered."

"I intend to, just as soon as she is feeling better. But—"

"Grant, listen to an old woman who loves you and Rebecca very much. Worrying won't accomplish a thing but add gray to your hair and prove your lack of faith in God."

"My head is listening, but my heart is thumping like a scared rabbit."

"Mine, too, dear boy. Mine, too."

CHAPTER  3

Grant told everyone that the huge, oak-shaded area behind his home was the coolest spot in Kahlerville. He could always count on a breeze to lower the sweltering temperatures, and today proved his theory. Century-old trees waved to the sun perched in a cloudless sky. Life didn't get much better than this, because he knew there were days in which life buried him where the sun never shone. His brother Morgan called those times "stall-cleaning" days, but today Grant refused to even smell trouble. No matter what the reason Miss Jenny Martin had chosen to visit, she would not spoil this moment.

He rolled up the sleeves of his white shirt and eased down beside Rebecca beneath the leafy canopy of a wide oak tree. How very strange that being outside with his little daughter caused him to appreciate the poetry of life. Grant chuckled. He wouldn't dare repeat his thoughts to another human soul. *Poetry of life?* Maybe he should have embarked upon a literature degree instead of the Hippocratic oath.

Upon a red and white tablecloth sat fried chicken, sliced tomatoes, applesauce, and freshly baked oatmeal cookies. This was a special time of the day for him and his little daughter. The noon hour allowed Mimi time alone and Grant the opportunity to have Rebecca all to himself.

When the grandfather clock in the foyer chimed twelve times, he worked hard to finish up with his last patient. And unless an emergency arose, Monday through Saturday, father and daughter ate together and, on Sundays, joined his whole family for dinner at the parsonage.

Rebecca sat poised waiting for him to ask the blessing. Her dainty little hands lay folded in her lap, and her feet extended onto the grass. She rubbed her ankles together, and Grant could almost hear her say, "The grass tickles, Papa." When she gave him a big dimpled grin, he forgot any ill-tempered patients or those seriously ill. But today the reason Miss Jenny Martin had come calling plagued him worse than a bellyache after eating too many green apples.

He caught a glimpse of Rebecca's huge, nut-brown eyes curtained with long, thick lashes that innocently danced and sparkled to whatever whim intrigued her. Dark brown curls framed her impish face, and already she had thicker hair than most little girls her age. That morning, Mimi had swept up the front and sides of Rebecca's abundant locks into a green ribbon. It matched her deep green-and-white print dress. Many of Rebecca's little dresses were green. It was Grant's favorite color.

He smiled into the angelic face and planted a kiss on her forehead. He gathered up her tiny soft hands into his, and they bowed their heads for prayer.

"Father God, we thank Thee for this beautiful day and for all Thy gifts. Bless this food and the hands that have prepared it. In Jesus' name, amen."

"Amen," Rebecca repeated and peered up at her father expectantly.

"Very good. Let me fill your plate."

In between bites, they chatted about their morning. "And what did you do to help Mimi today?" he asked.

She sat up very straight and wiped her mouth with a crisp white napkin. "Me helped with washing."

"Wonderful." Grant gave his best approving nod. "How did you help her?"

"Hmm." She propped her forefinger under her chin just like Mimi did when she contemplated a matter. "Counted the pins."

"Clothespins?"

"Yes, sir." She dipped her spoon in a pile of applesauce on her plate and dragged it dangerously close to the edge.

He helped her scoop it into her spoon. "How many were there?"

"Fourteen ten."

"Sounds like a lot of them." He laughed softly. "I'm sure you made her very happy."

"Yes, sir. Mimi loves me."

He watched her eye the oatmeal cookie on her plate. "Why don't you taste that cookie and see if it's good?"

She picked it up and took a nibble. "Tastes 'solutely wonderful."

How he loved his daughter. He urged her to take a sip of milk, which she did obediently. Rebecca didn't care for its taste, and the task usually took some prodding, but today she didn't complain.

"I'm proud of you drinking milk," he said. "I must tell Mimi."

Rebecca finished her small glass, dabbed her mouth, and set the napkin beside her empty plate. Crawling up into his lap, she laid her head against his chest. Her eyes grew heavy. And as usual, she would soon be asleep. Right here in his backyard, life was good.

"Papa." She sat upright and pointed her finger to an upstairs window of their home. "Lady sick?"

Grant followed her gaze to the room where Miss Martin rested. To his amazement, the woman watched from the bedroom window. He wondered how long she'd been observing them. "Yes, sweetheart. She's feeling better."

"Good. No yike to be sick." She shook her head, her curls flying against her cheeks.

"I don't like for you to be sick, either. Do you want to wave at the lady?"

Rebecca sat even straighter on Grant's lap and wiggled her fingers. With an enormous gesture, she blew Miss Martin a kiss.

My dear sweet angel.

She planted a tiny rosebud kiss on his chin and snuggled back into her resting spot. He glanced up at Miss Martin, who still observed them from the window. When he waved, she didn't return the greeting. Alarm settled upon him like stepping on a rattler.

Other than Miss Martin's physical condition, Grant had attempted not to dwell on the woman until he had an opportunity to question her. He'd almost convinced himself that his fears were unfounded. Due to the number of patients this morning who needed his attention, he'd asked Mimi to check on her. Miss Martin had progressed rapidly with rest and a limited diet of broth and toast. By tomorrow, she should be able to eat boiled potatoes and oatmeal. Per Grant's instructions, Mimi encouraged her to drink small amounts of water at regular intervals and to report any nausea. At this point, his original diagnosis of her suffering from lack of good nutrition mixed with heat exhaustion appeared to be correct. He assumed she'd be moving into the boardinghouse soon.

Grant felt decisively uncomfortable with the young woman in his home. More so, he wanted to know why she'd come to Kahlerville. In the few times they'd talked, she hadn't mentioned the purpose of her visit or anything about Jessica or Rebecca. He met her silence with mixed emotions. Could it be she didn't know about her niece? How sad for her if this was a social visit, and her sister had passed away more than two years ago.

To the best of his knowledge, Miss Martin hadn't seen Rebecca's face close enough to note the similarities. Grant and Mimi purposely kept her at a distance until the danger of contagion had passed. Still, for his own peace of mind, he needed answers to his questions soon.

Miss Martin had told Mimi that she was a schoolteacher from Cleveland, Ohio, but he questioned if the school year had been completed. Maybe this was all the family Jessica had left. It appeared unusual and inappropriate for a young single woman to travel across the country alone, but that was none of his business. For that matter, who was the man who had assisted her at the train station? Hopefully Miss Martin didn't share the same profession as Jessica. After breakfast tomorrow, he must talk to her. She should be feeling well enough by then to engage in serious conversation.

The more Grant considered Jenny Martin, the more he felt her journey must be one of devotion. He'd gladly show her Jessica's grave and introduce Rebecca as his daughter. Any other connection to Jessica would have to be met with prayer and. . .more prayer.

Mimi approached the picnic area, interrupting his deliberations. "A gentleman is here to see you, a Mr. Aubrey Turner," she whispered. "I'll put her to bed."

He nodded and lifted the child into her arms. At least he'd had this hour with Rebecca in their private sanctuary before being summoned back to work.

Aubrey Turner, a tall, blond fellow impeccably dressed in a tan suit and deep brown lizard-skin boots, awaited him in his office. He shifted a matching top hat and gloves before rising to his feet.

"We meet again, Mr. Turner." Grant reached out to grasp the man's hand.

Turner's hand was smooth, not the touch of a working man. "Dr. Andrews, it's a pleasure to see you." His genteel words did not match the coldness in his eyes.

"Thank you, and do sit down." Grant motioned to a nearby chair. "How can I help you?"

Turner's broad smile revealed perfectly straight, milky white teeth. "I won't take up much of your time. I simply wanted to inquire about Miss Martin's health."

Grant seated himself at his desk. "She's doing much better. Would you like for me to see if she's feeling well enough for visitors?"

"That's very kind of you but not necessary. I'm sure she needs her rest." He glanced about. "I've never been in this part of Texas. You have a friendly town. Nice folks. Is it always this hot?"

"Always. This is central Texas. We have two temperatures, dripping and unbearable."

Turner laughed. "I appreciate your tending to Miss Martin. It's a relief to know she's recovering from that dreadful experience on board the train. I fully intend to file a report with the railroad company."

"I'll make sure she knows you inquired about her health. Would you like to leave a specific message?"

Turner appeared to contemplate the matter before speaking. "Yes. Please give her my sincere regards. She needn't fret in the delay. Her health is much more important. We can continue our search for information about Jessica when she's recovered." He tugged on his gloves. "Oh, and if she needs assistance moving into the boardinghouse, I am available."

"Of course. Is there anything else I can do for you?"

Turner stood. "Not a thing. Good day, Dr. Andrews."

Grant ushered him to the front hallway and opened the door. Turner had confirmed his suspicions. The two were traveling together, and Jessica and Miss Martin were related. But what kind of information were they seeking?

Grant watched Miss Martin steal another look at Rebecca. The two more than favored each other. Even the woman's facial expressions matched those of his little daughter. He had introduced Rebecca as his child and had stated that her mother had died in childbirth. Later, when Jenny and Grant found the time to talk, he might explain the situation to her.

Mostly he wanted her gone from his home. *I'm a grown man, and I'm threatened by a woman who is barely tall enough to reach my shoulders.*

Early that morning while the night sky still darkened the world, he'd spent over an hour in prayer. What happened to all the peace that had enveloped him then? He needed a heavy dose of it now—more like an injection.

Grant continued to study, as inconspicuously as possible, the comely young woman seated across from him. Her face had slightly more color than yesterday, and she'd made the effort to join them for breakfast. He noticed that she dressed very much in fashion—dark full skirt and a white blouse with a high lace collar. Why women insisted upon those hundreds of tiny pearl buttons was beyond him. Her hair had been gathered at the top of her head and pulled into a loose knot with strands of curls framing her face. *My Rebecca will be just as lovely.*

"You look much better this morning, Miss Martin," he said. "I trust your health is improving."

"Thank you, Dr. Andrews. I'm really feeling like my old self, and I do appreciate what you and Miss Mimi have done for me. Your excellent care is commendable." She sighed, or rather her thin shoulders lifted slightly. "Breakfast is lovely. I never thought oatmeal could taste this splendid."

She did have a musical quality about her voice. "You're quite welcome, and my name is Grant. We don't need formalities here." He wiped oatmeal from Rebecca's chin.

"And please, call me Jenny."

He gave her a genuine smile. "I'd like for you to eat soft foods for a couple more days, and you should be fine. Please rest often until you feel all of your strength has returned. You don't need another occurrence of the past few days. And I wouldn't drink milk. It might upset your stomach."

"No danger of that. I despise milk. . . . Goodness, I'm sorry. I forgot your daughter was sitting here." Jenny stiffened, and her eyes widened.

Grant laughed. "Don't concern yourself with it. She has her own views on the matter, and believe me, none of them are good."

"I don't yike it." Rebecca shook her head and tossed her curls.

"But Papa makes me drink a little."

"My sister didn't care for milk, either."

And Grant knew, without a doubt, that Jenny understood the relationship between Rebecca and Jessica. There would be no pretense. He must obtain some answers soon.

"Do you feel up to discussing a matter after breakfast? I'm free until about eight thirty." Grant pulled his pocket watch from inside his jacket and checked the time.

"Certainly. Do you want to talk now?" Jenny lifted her chin, but he detected a quiver of her lips.

This will not be amiable. I can feel it in my bones. This conversation would not be about Jessica's grave site. "I believe that is an excellent idea. I'll just take the coffeepot with us into my office, as long as Mimi doesn't mind keeping an eye on Rebecca."

With the housekeeper's consent, Grant ushered Jenny from the dining room, down the hallway, and into his office near the front door. Breathing a prayer for wisdom, he shut the heavy oaken double doors behind them. Two windows had been opened earlier, providing a pleasant breeze and lightly scenting the room with the fresh, lingering fragrance of roses. He needed something pleasant this morning to divert his gathering apprehension.

"Do sit down, Jenny." Grant pointed to one of the two chairs normally used by patients. Once she seated herself, he sat across from her. "I admit this discussion is of concern to me. Before I get started, is there anything you need to ask or tell me?"

Jenny paused as though contemplating his request. "I need to know the amount of my bill. I'm planning to move into the boardinghouse this afternoon, and I don't want to leave owing you money."

"There's no charge."

Jenny sat more rigid than the ladies he knew. She clutched her hands so tightly that her knuckles turned white.

"Why?" she asked.

"I don't charge family." He stared straight into her huge brown eyes, too much like his beloved daughter's. "I'm assuming Jessica was your sister."

She fidgeted, and Grant waited.

"I always pay my obligations," she said.

"Not this time."

"Did my sister?"

"She didn't have an opportunity."

"Are you Rebecca's real father?"

"The adoption papers state so." Grant fought to gain control of a slowly rising irritation with the woman before him. "Jenny, why are you in Kahlerville?"

Silence permeated the room—so quiet that Grant heard the wind rustling through the trees.

"Do I need to repeat my question?" He allowed a moment for her to reply. "My intentions are not to be rude. I simply want an answer." He leaned back in his chair and ignored the pounding of his heart.

She squeezed her hands together more tightly than before. "I came to see my sister's grave. . .and to escort my niece back to Cleveland. . .where she belongs."

CHAPTER  4

Jenny realized she'd spoken rashly the moment the words escaped her lips. Color rose in Grant's face. A twinge of fear twisted inside her, as though Father sat opposite her. She hadn't planned to be insensitive or cruel but logical. Surely Rebecca was a burden to him and Miss Mimi. Jenny pushed aside the scene of Rebecca and Grant sharing lunch yesterday. The memory tugged at her heart with a longing for someone to love and be loved as she saw with them. But sentiments were for another time. She'd come this far with the quest for her niece, and she must continue.

Grant cleared his throat. "Excuse me, Miss Martin, but Rebecca is my daughter. I would be more than happy to show you Jessica's grave and relate to you those final moments of her life, but you are not taking your niece anywhere." Grant spoke with control, but his gaze challenged her. "She is my daughter."

"I know she's legally yours. My parents hired a Pinkerton to locate Jessica after she left home. He informed us of my sister's social status." She lifted her chin. "And of her passing after she gave birth to an illegitimate daughter. Surely, Dr. Andrews, you can see that, as Rebecca's aunt, I am the proper guardian. Perhaps you need some time—"

"I don't need any time to consider your ridiculous, unreasonable request." The color in Grant's face now resembled a ripe tomato.

Deep inside, Jenny wanted to cease speaking. She sounded cruel, uncaring, not even diplomatic. "But you have no wife, only a housekeeper. Rebecca takes her meals in the dining room instead of in the kitchen where she needs to learn proper etiquette until age fourteen before joining adults." Perspiration dotted her forehead and trickled down the side of her face.

"Are you questioning my parenting abilities?"

Jenny caught her breath. She'd gone too far. "I said nothing of the sort. From what I've seen, you're a fine father. But think about Rebecca's future. She needs to learn the proprieties of society. Unless—"

"Unless what?"

"Unless you are her true father. Why else would you adopt an illegitimate baby from a woman who made her living in a brothel?"

Grant leaned forward. "I have no idea who fathered Rebecca. Jessica asked me to raise her as my own, and I gave my word."

"When did she make this request?"

"When she lay dying. . .moments after Rebecca's birth."

Desperation bubbled in Jenny's throat. "My sister did not have the capacity to make rational decisions. Anyone who saw the senseless things she did would attest to her irresponsibility. Our parents have suffered long enough. She disgraced them with her utter selfishness. They grieve her death. They grieve her mistakes. Let me have Rebecca. I beg of you. They need a glimmer of hope from the daughter they lost."

"And it took you more than two years to reach that conclusion?"

"I'm here now."

He shook his head and laughed. "A little late for afterthoughts. Is taking my daughter from those who love her for your parents' benefit or yours? Because I haven't heard one word about love for your sister or Rebecca."

"I'm basing my claims on reality."

"Am I to be enlightened by your argument?"

She heard the bitterness in every word. He'd been pushed to his limit.

"I'm sorry for the way I broached this subject," she said. "I want what's best for my niece, and I believe that is with her own family. You are right in stating a good bit of time has elapsed. I had to work and save the money to arrange transportation here." Jenny locked battle with her gaze. He had to see she was right.

"Posting a missive doesn't cost a cent. I'd have paid for it. And what about your parents? Were they not able to send a letter, either? I fail to see a display of concern over the welfare of Rebecca. Help me to understand your sudden change of heart for a sister for whom you obviously had little affection."

Jenny's head throbbed. She'd utterly failed in this endeavor. "I can't speak any more of family matters."

"But you have no problem prying into mine."

"I believe our conversation is finished, Dr. Andrews." Jenny stood on wobbly legs. "I will be moving from here within the hour. Please have my bill ready for payment. I do regret that I haven't been able to communicate what is in my heart. Perhaps we can talk at a later date."

"Our conversation is not over."

Grant moved to the door and blocked her exit. His presence loomed over her. She would hear what he had to say, whether she chose to or not.

"You may do as you wish, but first you will listen to me. How you feel about your sister is certainly your affair, but how you speak of her is another matter. She happens to be my daughter's mother. Moments ago, you made derogatory remarks about Jessica, and I would appreciate it for my daughter's sake that such comments never occur again." He appeared much calmer than she. "While you are in my home or in the presence of my daughter or any of us who love and care for her, you are forbidden to defame Jessica's memory. She died a good woman, and she believed I would be a suitable father for her child. I accepted the task. I am not a perfect man, but I love my daughter with all my heart. Neither you nor anyone else will ever take her from me. Is that clearly understood?"

"I've upset you, and I apologize—"

He raised his hand, and the gesture silenced her. "You can examine the adoption papers and do whatever else you feel is necessary. Yet understand this: Rebecca Faith Andrews is my child. She is not the fancy of an impetuous, demanding woman who has no more manners than to enter a man's home and declare his child her property. Good day, Miss Martin. As I stated before, there are no charges for my services. Jessica was family, and you are her sister."

Jenny's face grew warm. "I have not traveled all this distance just to turn around and go back home. We have matters to discuss and settle."

"When you are able to discuss things calmly, perhaps." He opened the door of his study. "Good day, Miss Martin."

Grant listened to the sharp click of Jenny's heels as she marched across the foyer's wooden floor to the stairway. He closed the door a bit more soundly than usual, repressing a deep desire to slam it until the whole house shook. And once the house shook and the window panes rattled, he'd do the same to Miss Jenny Martin. Anger invaded every part of his body, and he instinctively began pacing the floor to dispel its fervor. He'd gladly carry all of Jenny Martin's bags and that massive trunk down the stairs to his wagon and on to the boardinghouse.

So, Jenny Martin came to Kahlerville to whisk away my daughter! How perfectly virtuous of her. He pounded his fist into his palm.

Grant considered how Jenny had paid little attention to Rebecca at breakfast except to make a comment here and there. Not at all the actions one would expect from an aunt who had never seen her niece before. No tender, endearing looks or endless questions about the first two years of his daughter's life. Rather, she observed her cautiously, as though fearing something.

"Humph." She probably had been assessing his capabilities as a father and planned to make full report of it to some fancy city lawyer. Not one word of love or affection for Jessica—her own sister. The woman didn't even know how to respect the dead. He'd like nothing better than to follow her right up those stairs and escort her out of town.

She'd never set foot in this house again. And as far as visiting Rebecca—well, Jenny could see her from a distance with Mimi or him. Jenny should have stayed in Cleveland where she belonged. And what about her parents? Who would allow a single young woman to travel across the country in the company of that. . .that dandy?

He persisted in pacing the room, fuming with each reflection. His heart raced until his pulse thundered throughout his body. So intense were his emotions that he barely heard a faint knock.

"Papa," the little voice said. "Papa."

Taking a deep breath, Grant opened the door and bent down to his little daughter. Just seeing her soothed his vehement emotions. "Yes, sweetheart." He brushed a wispy curl from her face.

"Lady cry." She pointed to the stairs and searched his face for an answer.

"Did she say anything to you?" Fury threatened to take over his last bit of control. Rebecca shook her head, and her brown eyes grew even bigger. "Lady kiss me."

She pointed to her cheek.

"Miss Martin kissed you?" Grant asked, surprised at Jenny's display of affection.

His daughter nodded and reached for Grant to take her. Trembling, she wrapped her arms around his neck and rested her head against his shoulder.

Remorse for his burst of temper pricked Grant's heart. His angry words had frightened Rebecca, the one person he wanted to protect.

"Why lady cry?" Rebecca asked.

Shame needled at him. He could have handled the situation much better than this. Look what his self-righteous attitude had caused.

"Papa?"

Grant looked into his daughter's sweet face and kissed her cheek. "I'm sorry Papa's loud voice scared you."

"Scare lady, too."

Oh, Lord, out of the mouths of babes do we hear the truth. He lifted her chin. "Then I'm going to take you to Mimi and go see about Miss Martin."

"You kiss her and tell her you're sorry?"

Not in a million years. "I will apologize and see that she's fine."

He carried Rebecca into the dining room and set her in Mimi's lap. The older woman's eyes mirrored her curiosity.

"I'm going upstairs to talk to Jenny," Grant said. "Rebecca said she was crying."

"I saw." Mimi moistened her lips. "Rebecca, sweetheart, why don't you help me by carrying the spoons into the kitchen?"

The child smiled happily. "Yes, ma'am." Scooting off Mimi's lap, she gathered up the utensils.

"Walk very slowly," Mimi said, "and put them on the kitchen table. You can count them, too."

Grant watched Rebecca disappear. "Did you hear anything?"

"I'm old, not deaf. I heard more than I cared to."

"Didn't handle it well, did I?"

"Better than I would." Her dark blue eyes smoldered. "Left to me, you'd be calling the sheriff by now. I'd have given her more than a piece of my mind."

Grant sighed. "I wasn't a gentleman. Not only did my shouting upset Jenny and Rebecca, but it also displeased God. I'm going to apologize and hope I don't lose my temper again." He turned to leave, then glanced back into the woman's disquieting face. "Pray for me. I'm going to need it."

"Murder has crossed my mind."

He forced a chuckle. "That's the least of what has crossed mine."

Grant walked back into the front hallway where the circular staircase wound to the upper bedrooms. A rag doll sat precariously on the first step, its head touching its toes as though waiting for a tumble. Without a thought, he placed the doll upright, thinking he felt the same way. Resting his hand briefly on the banister, he slowly ascended the stairs. Each wooden step, each heartbeat brought him closer to another confrontation with Jenny. God needed to put barbed-wire across his mouth.

Taking a deep breath, he rapped on Jenny's bedroom door, still uncertain of what he should say. The fire of anger had slowly dissipated, but he could not forget the woman wanted to take his daughter from him.

"Who is there?"

Jenny's weak voice reminded him of her illness. He cringed at the thought. "I'd like to apologize for my outburst of temper." Silence met him as he waited patiently before speaking again. "Is it possible for us to talk without arguing?" At last the door opened. Her red swollen eyes heaped more coals on his guilt. What happened to his compassionate nature?

"I think enough has been said." Jenny's lips quivered.

"Maybe so, but I am sorry for the rude manner in which I spoke to you."

She swallowed hard, her gaze darting about. "I lost control of my temper, too. I should have considered the circumstances before I spoke so harshly."

For the first time, he noticed how the young woman couldn't weigh much more than a sack of feed. And in that brief moment she reminded him of a little girl recovering from a temper tantrum. "You've been ill," he said. "In fact, you're not fully recovered. As for me, I don't really have an excuse."

"You love your daughter." She dabbed her nose with a lace handkerchief. "I should have seen and understood how you felt."

"I love Rebecca with all that is in me. She's a special gift, more precious than my own life." He hesitated. "I'm sorry to have upset you. Please don't leave today. Spend another day or two recuperating. There's a great deal for us to discuss but certainly not now. Rest today, and perhaps tomorrow you'll see things differently."

Jenny continued to stand rigid, and he fully expected another battle. "I'm not so sure that is a good idea. You're aware of my reasons for coming to Kahlerville, and the tension between us will be noticeably uncomfortable."

"Not if we make a good effort to be civil to each other."

Her eyes bore into his, eyes too much like Rebecca's. "I would think you'd want to be rid of me."

Without hesitation, but the problem would probably get worse. Grant gave her a half smile. "Let's get acquainted for Rebecca's sake. Who knows? We may even become friends."

"I will not change my mind about why I came to Kahlerville."

He sighed and crossed his arms over his chest. "I realize that, but I think once you see how happy we are as a family, you will reconsider your plans." She didn't reply, and he wondered what she was thinking. "We could take Rebecca and visit the cemetery tomorrow, providing you are feeling up to it."

"Tomorrow is Saturday," she said, giving the impression that time played an important part in her venture.

"Does tomorrow present a problem?" Did she have plans with Aubrey Turner?

"Oh no. Not at all. I was thinking about my move into the boardinghouse."

"You could handle that matter on Monday. Sunday for us is a day of rest. Would you like to accompany us to church?"

She glanced at the floor, then back to his face. "I don't go to church. Haven't been there since I was a little girl."

"Then will you do us the honors?"

"I really don't know what to say."

Grant ignored the reluctance in her voice. "A yes will do."

She nodded slowly. "All right. I'll stay through tomorrow afternoon, because I do want to spend some time with my niece. I'll make a decision about Sunday then." She eyed him suspiciously. "Why are you being kind to me?"

"You are my daughter's aunt," he said. "But more so, you are important to God. Please think about waiting until Monday morning to move to the boardinghouse."

Confusion etched her delicate features. "You will not change my mind."

How right you are, Miss Martin. It will take God. "Rest now. Mimi or I will look in on you later."

CHAPTER 5

"Now tell me one more time why Jenny is staying in this house until Monday," Mimi asked. "I'm afraid you've taken leave of your senses."

He peered into the dining room, where Rebecca played with her rag doll. "To get acquainted with Rebecca, you, and me. I'd like to take her to Jessica's grave. And of course, she needs more time to get well."

The older woman's eyes narrowed. "I'm trying to be compassionate and loving, but after what she said to you? Really, Grant, think about this. She wants your daughter—*our* Rebecca."

He drummed his fingers on the kitchen table. "I know. A part of me thinks I've lost my mind, too, but I feel I'm supposed to give her another chance."

"You're wanting to accomplish a lot in the course of two days." Mimi bustled about. She wiped clean this and put away that in a frenzy of activity.

Grant took an armful of dishes from her and lifted them up into the cupboard. "Perhaps it will involve a few visits here after she moves into the boardinghouse."

"Oh? Won't that make it easier for her to snatch Rebecca from under our noses?"

"That won't happen. I'd never let her take Rebecca from the house. You or I will always be close by."

Mimi shook her gray head. "And how long does she plan to stay in town?"

"I didn't ask. But I will."

"Grant, why are you going to so much trouble when it's not necessary? You don't have to prove anything to this woman."

For a moment, he thought she might burst into tears. He wasn't sure he could handle one more emotional female this morning. Breathing a prayer, he paused and attempted to sort out his thoughts. "I understand how you feel, Mimi, but she's Rebecca's aunt. And I'm fairly certain she isn't a believer."

"Mercy me. The woman is a heathen."

Grant laughed. "Hadn't looked at it quite that way." He swallowed the humor in Mimi's tone. "I think if Jenny finds a relationship with the Lord, then she'll toss this ridiculous notion of hers aside."

"You've come up with all this since your argument with her?"

"Haven't had many patients today."

She shrugged. "Good thing. My dear boy, we all have plenty to pray about. I dare say I won't let our little girl out of my sight." She turned and watched Rebecca cradle her doll. "Just because she might become a child of God doesn't mean all of her thinking changes."

Grant felt his heart plummet to his toes. He'd been pondering the same thing. Some of the Christians he knew could be rather opinionated and stubborn. He was one of them, and a perfectionist, too. "I'll be careful, and I'll see what else I can find out about her and her traveling companion."

Mimi covered her mouth. "I forgot to tell you something. When I told Jenny about Mr. Turner's visit, she said she barely knew the man. In fact, she acted quite surprised."

We can continue our search for information about Jessica when she's ready, Turner had said. Why would Jenny lie?

"It will be difficult to pray for her when I'd just as soon direct her

41

to the train station. I don't like this, Grant. I don't like it one bit." Having voiced her final view on the subject, Mimi stepped into the dining room to play with Rebecca.

Hours later, Grant sat in his office and deliberated the state of the Andrews' household. Frankly, he found it difficult to concentrate on important matters before him. He'd gone from wanting to physically throw Jenny from his house to nearly begging her to stay. His idealistic approach bothered him, and now he wondered if he'd initiated more trouble when it came to protecting his daughter. Especially since Jenny had told Mimi that she barely knew Turner, but the man had claimed a relationship with her. Who was he to believe?

Dear Lord, what have I gotten myself into?

Sometimes Jenny despised the woman she'd become. All of her life, she'd listened to her parents and dutifully followed their instructions, and now she was behaving just like them. Something she'd never wanted. She should have felt some satisfaction in expressing her intentions to Grant. Instead, she wanted to crawl into a hole and never show her face again. How did he view her? Did he think she was capable of manipulating those who didn't see things her way? Perhaps so, since Jessica persuaded men with her charms. But she wasn't like her sister at all. Jessica had a stubborn strength that Jenny lacked. And her mood at this moment proved it.

Exhausted, she lay across the carefully made bed and closed her eyes. If only she were at home, then someone would tell her what to do. But here in Kahlerville, Texas, she had no one but herself. Back home, Mother was probably hosting a tea in which the ladies discussed the right to vote along with the latest gossip. Father was most likely planning his next speech on Darwinism and the theory of evolution or the corruptness of the government. Jenny doubted if either of them realized she wasn't in Boston with friends. After all, she'd lied about her destination. Yet once she returned with Rebecca, they'd be so very grateful and proud.

But I'm here, and I've insulted a good man who is raising my niece. He also helped me when I made a fool of myself at the train station. Jenny sucked in a breath. Maybe she had become just like her parents. For the first time, she clearly understood what had driven Jessica away.

What should she do now? Stay and attempt to work out a friendship of sorts with Grant, or leave and hope he allowed her to see the little girl in the future? Jenny never dreamed he'd refuse her offer to relieve him of raising a child. She had assumed it was a burden. A picture of Grant and Rebecca at breakfast settled in her mind. How she envied their relationship. Would Rebecca one day turn to her with the same adoring look in her eyes? Oh, how she hoped so. Her niece was such a captivating little girl, and thankfully not as impulsive and high strung as Jessica.

Jenny had wanted to reach out and draw Rebecca close to her, but she feared Grant and Miss Mimi's reaction. Or maybe she feared her own heart melting at the touch of such a beautiful child.

Jenny shook her head. She was doing this for Mother and Father. They'd be raising Rebecca, not Jenny.

Opening her eyes, she decided to forgo moving into the boarding-house until Monday. Many things lay unsettled about Grant, and the extra days would give her time to observe the good doctor—in hopes of finding a flaw.

Suddenly, Jenny sat upright. *Aubrey Turner.* Why ever did the man insinuate that she and he were more than brief acquaintances? His knowledge of Jessica confused and upset her. Being the sister of a prostitute wasn't the type of thing a decent woman claimed. She had originally planned to be a distant cousin, but she'd spoiled that concept at breakfast. She cringed. Surely Mr. Turner wasn't Rebecca's father or, worse yet, Jessica's husband. If he claimed the child, she'd lose her chance of ever pleasing Mother and Father.

Feeling decisively ill, Jenny chose to sleep away the disturbances threatening to destroy her journey to Texas. Once rested, she'd certainly have the answers.

~~~

After seeing his last patient of the afternoon, Grant seized the opportunity to stop by the general store and purchase a few licorice sticks. The children enjoyed the sweet treats, and he did, too. When Mimi and Rebecca weren't around, he swirled a good licorice stick in his coffee. If he was ever caught, Mimi would be horrified and Rebecca would want to try the same in her milk.

The warm afternoon had gathered intense humidity, and the scent of rain filled his nostrils. He picked up his pace and acknowledged the increased droplets of perspiration underneath his shirt and jacket. The dusty streets could use a dip in a water trough.

Inside the general store, Lester Hillman, the town banker, talked to Pete Kahler, the owner of Kahler's General Store. Grant stepped around them and studied the assortment of candy in huge jars lining the front counter. The voices of the locals captured his attention. Couldn't help but hear them when they stood so close.

"What's going on, Pete?" Lester asked.

"Our youngest boy, Frank, is getting married in a couple of weeks. I'm glad to be working and out of the womenfolks' way. The missus is frettin' over a family dinner tonight. Cookin' everything in sight." Pete patted his round stomach. "But it will be good."

"Who's he marryin'?" Lester asked. The banker puffed on a pipe, a rather unpleasant fragrance of tobacco.

"Ellen Smythe." Pete's voice was a near whisper. "I'm sure you've seen her helping out here at the store."

"Didn't she use to be one of Martha's girls?" Lester snickered.

"Yes, but she left Martha's more than two years ago."

"I remember." Lester shook his head and took another puff. "Her friend...what was her name? ...Well, anyway, she died in childbirth, and Ellen moved out of Martha's and started living respectable."

"Seems like you know a lot about what goes on at Martha's Place," Pete said.

"Just wondered how you felt about your son marrying a woman like that."

"Just fine, Lester. Just fine."

"How about the missus? How does she feel about her baby boy settlin' down with a soiled dove?" Lester took another puff on his pipe.

"I said just fine. She's having a big dinner, isn't she?" Pete's hands rested on the opposite side of the counter. His fingers curled up in his palms.

"Fancy doings doesn't mean she's welcome in your family. I wouldn't want a boy of mine marrying one of Martha's girls," Lester said.

"I'm not in the business of picking out my boys' wives."

"Well, if you were, I'm sure you wouldn't have picked her kind." Lester teetered on his heels. "Do you suppose Doc Grant is the father of that baby he took in?"

Pete inhaled deeply. "Frankly, I don't care either way. It's none of my business. Why don't you ask him? He's standing right beside you."

Lester startled.

"Something you want to ask me, Lester?"

Lester held up his hands. "I'm only repeating gospel truth." He nodded at Grant. "What kind of God-fearin' man adopts a prostitute's child unless—"

"Unless what?" Grant's integrity had been questioned enough in the past. He thought the town gossip had ended a year ago, but here it was again rearing its ugly head.

"Apologize to the man." Pete leaned over the counter and stuck his finger in Lester's face. "You may have a lot of money, Lester, but if I refuse to sell you anything, you'll have a far piece to ride for supplies."

"It's all right," Grant said. "No harm done."

Lester turned and left the store without his tobacco. Pete laid it aside. "He'll be back when he realizes his pipe's empty. Sorry about what he said, Grant."

"And I didn't like what he said about Ellen and Frank." Indignation simmered inside him. "Ellen's lived with the Widow Lewis ever since Jessica died. No point in dragging up the girl's past. Everyone has a right to start over."

"Well, Widow Lewis needed someone to look after her, and I understand Ellen does a right smart job," Pete said. "Besides that, she works hard here at the store. The only reason she isn't waiting on Lester is because the missus needed her to help with tonight's dinner. Fine girl. I'm proud of her."

"I despise gossip," Grant said.

"So did our Lord. I should have reminded Lester about that, too."

Grant laughed. "You can when he comes back for his tobacco."

"I'll take this hat and shirt," a voice said.

Grant whirled around to see Aubrey Turner holding a new Stetson and a blue shirt.

"I'm sorry. Didn't see you standing over there," Pete said. "Did you find all you needed?"

"I surely did." He handed his purchases to Grant and stuck out his hand. "Good to see you again."

Grant nodded. Something about the man bothered him. *I'm getting as judgmental as Lester.* He shook Turner's hand. "Are you enjoying our town?"

"Quite a bit. I'm relaxing and waiting on Jenny to recover."

"She's recovering nicely."

"And still at your home?"

Grant stiffened. The sarcasm in Turner's tone hadn't gone unnoticed. "As a matter of fact, she is. Were you planning to pay a call?"

Turner smiled. "Jenny and I will have plenty of time together in the days to come. She is most anxious to uncover Jessica's past.

LANTERNS LACE

However, you can give her my regards."

"My pleasure."

Jenny must have lied to him about her relationship with Aubrey Turner. This proved it without a doubt.

CHAPTER  6

Jenny's first impression of Piney Woods Church and the two-story parsonage beside it was of picturesque serenity. The church fairly glistened with white paint, and an equally sparkling picket fence separated the building and the house. Vines of deep red roses wound their way through the back portion of the fence, while bushes of yellow and white lantana cuddled against the side of the parsonage.

Directly behind the church, under a towering grove of pine trees, a narrow path led to Piney Woods Cemetery. Grant's wagon made its way past dense undergrowth, carrying Jenny and Rebecca to an open meadow of marked and unmarked graves. A few sites hosted large tombstones, richly engraved with eloquent epitaphs, but most graves held simple wooden crosses or modest headstones carved with only a brevity of words. Friends and family members of the deceased obviously added fresh flowers to the graves and kept the area neat and free from weeds.

Jenny smelled the fresh grass and the faint scent of some wildflower. If she'd felt more comfortable with Grant, she'd have asked him to point out the source. As it was, she chose to ride in silence, attempting without success to rid her mind of the prospect of viewing Jessica's grave.

Grant followed a well-worn trail, pulling the horse to a halt where it could graze. Stepping down from the wagon, he first lifted Rebecca from Jenny's lap. She carried a single rose with the stem wrapped in a cloth to protect her little hands from thorns. He then offered Jenny his hand. His smile sent a strange chill through her, and she instantly turned her attention to the cemetery. Perplexed, she wondered what it was about the man that caused her to feel so unsure of herself.

"I'm glad we came this morning before it gets too warm," Grant said, shading his eyes from the bright sun. "Rebecca and I are used to the climbing temperatures, but I'm sure you feel differently."

"I won't ever become accustomed to this heat." She wished she'd brought a fan.

He chuckled. "While studying medicine in Boston, I couldn't tolerate the cold. The other students constantly teased me about it—and my Southern drawl. But by the time I graduated, I'd settled in just fine to the cooler climate."

"I don't imagine I'll be here long enough to accomplish that." She glanced down at Rebecca and quickly back at him. A twinge of guilt laced her words. This all was becoming much too difficult.

Grant pointed to the right of them. "Over there is Jessica's grave."

Jenny's attention followed his gesture. She felt strangely solemn, uncertain, and afraid of her emotions. Over the years, she'd built a wall between herself and Jessica. Apathy seemed the safest, most secure stand, especially when she saw how her older sister's open rebellion affected their parents. She didn't hate Jessica, but she didn't think she loved her, either. Most of her sentiments were based on utter contempt for her sister's behavior. She honestly didn't know what she felt anymore. Certainly nothing in the past had prepared her for this moment.

"Would you like to visit her grave by yourself, or would you like us to accompany you?" Grant's voice sounded tender and soothing, as though he sensed her turmoil.

"I'd like for you and Rebecca to go with me." His startling sea green eyes searched her face and unnerved her. "Oh my, I didn't bring flowers. And I saw Rebecca with her rose."

"We can bring them another time."

"Flowers for Mama?" Rebecca tugged on Grant's pant leg.

"Yes, sweetheart. Miss Jenny is your mama's sister." He glanced up at Jenny. "What would you like Rebecca to call you?"

Jenny's heart raced. "Is Aunt Jenny appropriate?"

"I think it's perfect." He turned his attention back to his daughter. "Would you like to show Aunt Jenny your mama's resting place?"

The title of "Aunt Jenny" brought all the uncertainty to the surface. Jenny wrestled with the awkwardness of the moment and believed she'd won. Mother and Father would be proud of her control. Rebecca ran toward a secluded spot. In her eagerness, she tripped and fell headfirst into a clump of grass. Before Grant could rescue her, she jumped up, brushed herself off, and hurried in the direction again.

"Becca fine," she called to them, inciting a hearty laugh from Grant and a genuine smile from Jenny.

They strolled on slowly, and for that bit more of precious time, Jenny inwardly thanked him. "What was it like in the beginning with a tiny baby and your practice?"

"The hardest thing I'd ever attempted. The first night of feeding Rebecca every three hours opened my eyes to motherhood. Two ladies in town with new babies were a pure blessing, but I insisted on doing my part." He laughed. "I can be real stubborn, so it took a few sleepless nights to convince me I needed help. Actually, it took two weeks before I knocked on my mother's door. Even then, it was because of something she'd done instead of what Rebecca needed."

"What did she do?"

"She'd stopped by my home and stolen the mountains of soiled clothes. I was angrier than a riled up hornet."

"Where does she live?"

He pointed back from where they came. "At the parsonage. She's married to the reverend. After my initial cry for help, it was easier to call on my sister and sister-in-law for advice. Mind you, my medical practice continued on."

Jenny tried to form a mental picture of an exhausted Grant carrying a small bundle into his office. "Reality can be overwhelming," she said.

"I agree. I had no idea how to take care of Rebecca properly and tend to my medical practice. All of my fancy university training did not equip me for motherhood. And my own personal war with perfectionism didn't help, either. Rebecca was a good baby, but she did inform me of her needs through an excellent set of lungs."

Guilt washed over her. In Grant's shoes, she'd have failed miserably. "I admire what you did—have done." She started to add a comment about her taking over, but the memory of his anger the day before stopped her. "Grant, did any. . .did the father ever come forth?"

He hesitated, and she glanced up at him. "No."

How insensitive for her to ask such a personal question. Jessica probably had no idea who the father was. "When did Mimi join you?"

"When Rebecca was three months old. Mimi's a widow, and she just seemed to show up every morning. Later I found out that my mother had encouraged her. Before long, I realized I couldn't get along without Mimi. I purchased a larger home, and she moved in."

"I'm glad it worked out well for you," she said. The words sounded hollow, an afterthought to the sacrifices he had made for Jessica's daughter.

"Here we are." He stopped beside a grass-covered plot.

Jenny hadn't been conscious of where they'd been walking. She'd been too engrossed in their conversation. Suddenly, remembrances of two small sisters at play overcame her. In all of her preconceived ideas of what she'd experience when standing by Jessica's grave, none had alluded to the immense grief and tears. She bent to touch the withered roses lying in front of the headstone. Rebecca's contribution glistened in the sunlight as though it had been dew-kissed. Through blurry vision, she read the marker:

Jessica Martin
Died January 10, 1893
An angel at the feet of Jesus

Her fingers trembled as she traced her sister's name and the date of her death with a gloved finger.

"I didn't know her birthday or middle name." Grant kneeled beside her. "A friend of hers didn't know, either."

"It's January 22, 1870, and her middle name was Kathryn." Jenny lightly brushed the wetness from her cheeks. "Did you put the stone here?" She choked back a sob. "Yes, of course you did." When he failed to respond, a sense of wonder and bewilderment for this man arose in her. An enigma. A part of her wanted to understand him. Another part was afraid of him. "Why?"

"Why wouldn't I?"

"Aunt Jenny cry?" Rebecca stared up at her father.

"Yes, sweetheart," Grant said. "Aunt Jenny loved your mama."

"Me, too," Rebecca said. "And Jesus."

Have I really loved Jessica all these years when I believed I despised her?

"Jesus takes care of Mama in heben." Rebecca reached out and cradled Jenny's face in her hands. With a tilt of her head, she kissed Jenny's cheek. "Dat's a kiss from Mama."

The tears were harder to stop. This precious, beautiful child was a part of Jessica, and her views of Jesus and heaven sounded real—believable. Father would forbid a mention of deity. He'd insist Rebecca find her answers in science, and so would Jenny. She looked deep into Rebecca's face, as though seeing the child for the very first time. Images of a much younger Jessica danced across her mind. She and Jessica had been little girls the last time they expressed their love for each other. Closing her eyes against the disturbing reminder, sorrow and regret moved her to uncontrollable weeping. She felt Grant's arms encircle her shoulders, and a tiny hand patted her back.

"Thank you. . . .for everything you did for her," she managed. "I wish I'd been here to help." And the strange realization puzzled her.

The unbridled grief was not the way she'd been taught to handle life. How terribly disappointed Mother and Father would be. More than once since coming to Kahlerville, she'd felt their presence criticizing Grant, Rebecca, and their life. Mother and Father seemed so distant, but their values hammered into her very core.

Grant pulled a handkerchief from his pocket and placed it in Jenny's hand. "You might want to visit with Ellen Smythe. They were good friends. I think the only one your sister had. Jessica's death changed Ellen's life."

"I'd like to talk to her," Jenny said without thinking through the implications of how Ellen and Jessica became friends. She felt drained, weak, and filled with a deep yearning to make up for the closeness she'd missed with her sister. Reaching out to grasp one of Rebecca's rose petals, she swallowed hard. "I want to do something other than bring flowers tomorrow. I'm not sure what."

"Flowers are a beginning. We usually bring some from home or from my mother and Reverend Rainer's garden."

Jenny remembered the charming two-story home beside the church. Everything there looked peaceful, as though it depicted something from a book—not particularly real, but a fantasy. She smiled at Rebecca picking wild daises and running to place them on her mother's grave. The child appeared so happy. If she stole her away from Grant, could Jenny make her equally as content?

"Have you decided to attend church with us?" Grant seated himself on the grass beside her. "We have Sunday dinner at the parsonage every week, and I'd really like for you to join us."

"I question the logic of accompanying you. I'm not exactly here on a mission of goodwill."

"You aren't? Maybe you don't understand the real reason why you're here."

She startled. "Whatever do you mean?"

"God has a purpose for everything. I haven't any answers for you. But He does." He captured her gaze with his almond-shaped eyes. "My family is very loving, and you *are* family. We aren't without our share of problems, but we support each other."

She hesitated, deliberating her earlier decision to be agreeable coupled with the sadness and regret over her sister's untimely death. "Will others be there?"

"My brother and sister with their families."

She glanced back at the tombstone, the one Grant had erected for her sister. Maybe he was Rebecca's father. Maybe he had loved Jessica.

"I haven't said a word about why you're here," he said.

Jenny continued to study the grave while indecision raced across her mind. She shouldn't get herself involved with his family. It would only be difficult later, yet something about Grant moved her to comply with his request—not for selfish gain, but for a deeper need that she didn't quite understand.

"I'd really be nervous." She wrung her hands and ignored the doubts that dulled her better judgment. So many questions with so few answers.

"There is no need to be. All of them will make you feel welcome."

Maybe it was his gentle persuasion or the way he smiled or the sweet kiss from Rebecca. In any event, she ignored her inklings. "All right, I'll go."

Saturday night, alone in his office, Grant leaned back in his massive leather chair and listened to the grandfather clock chime midnight. More than just physically tired, he bordered on mental exhaustion.

Still, his mind continued to reflect on this morning's happenings. For the first time, he'd seen Jenny emerge from her shell. Not once did he hear a condescending word or a demeaning tone in her voice. She spoke neither tersely nor with reproach, and most assuredly, she had been pleasant company. Even the spillage of tears at the cemetery seemed surprisingly genuine.

Who is this woman who wants my daughter?

Rebecca adored her. She'd wiggled her way unto Jenny's lap and reached out to hold her hand. And the kiss. Something Mimi had done for her many times, but he'd never seen Rebecca imitate her. Grant smiled. His little daughter should develop a relationship with Jenny. She was her aunt. He still wondered why Jenny's parents had not made the trip with her. Wouldn't they want to see their daughter's grave and their grandchild, even if Grant had no intentions of turning over their granddaughter to them? Perhaps they were ill. This revelation had not entered his mind before this evening. Failing health could also be a motive for Jenny's desire to take Rebecca back with her. If this were indeed the case, he'd gladly travel to Ohio so they could spend some time with their granddaughter. Tomorrow he'd ask Jenny about her parents.

Grant wondered why she never mentioned Aubrey Turner. Obviously, Jenny didn't want it known that she'd traveled with the man. Perhaps that topic was better left alone. After all, Jenny's personal life had no bearing on his purpose of showing how Rebecca was well cared for and loved.

CHAPTER  7

Jenny willed her nerves to settle. Apprehension. Dread. Why ever did she agree to attend church and spend Sunday afternoon with Grant's family? She recalled the unpleasant times when an unhappy parent confronted her at school or when her parents displayed their annoyance over something she or Jessica had done, but not one unpleasant memory compared to the mounting anxiety of meeting Grant's friends and family.

Consider one problem at a time. Conduct yourself properly in church, then leave it behind for dinner afterward.

Grant may have changed his mind and told his family why she came to Kahlerville. How horrible—a whole family of Andrews ready to pounce on her! Not that Jenny could blame his family, for she still planned to take Rebecca home to Cleveland. Yesterday she'd been touched by a morsel of sentiment, but not today. Could her noble design be wrong? How could it be? The more time she spent with the child, the more she wanted her. At the cemetery, Jenny realized how desperately she desired to keep a reminder of Jessica alive. Rebecca could provide exactly that, but this time things would be different—and better. The little girl needed her real family.

Mother and Father will adore her. Rebecca will certainly bring laughter into their lives. And they will have me to thank.

Jenny struggled to keep her attention on the reverend. Normally, she paid the utmost attention to every word of a lecture, but today her mind kept slipping back to the incidents of the week. To make matters worse, Father had forbidden her from ever attending church. She glanced about as though Archibald Martin might be lurking in some corner. He contended that the weak and ignorant used God as a crutch. Odd, Grant didn't appear lacking in intelligence or strength. Quite the contrary.

With an inward sigh, she decided to listen to the message if for no more reason than that this was a part of Rebecca's life. Each time she found herself centering on an event or conversation with Grant, she'd quickly chide herself, for it solved nothing. The source of her distress sat beside her, his presence creating a sensation that she did not welcome. Distraction. That's what Dr. Grant Andrews was, and she had better tasks to attend to. She wished Mimi were nearby, but the older woman occupied a pew with her own family.

Rebecca seized Jenny's attention. The little girl nestled against Grant's chest, and as if on cue, she lifted her head and planted a kiss on his chin. Oh, how Jenny longed to be the recipient of Rebecca's devotion.

Music began to play on a sadly out-of-tune piano, and she realized she hadn't heard a single word spoken by the reverend. Horrified, she nearly choked. Would Grant or his family question her about the sermon?

Once the service was over, Grant politely introduced her to curious onlookers who blocked their path to the door. She warmly greeted little old ladies with cloud-colored hair peeking out from elaborate hats and bonnets and a host of women seeking information about the young woman accompanying Dr. Andrews to church. Then there were the poison arrows cast Jenny's way from a few young women. He chuckled.

"What's so funny?" she asked.

"I'm not so sure you'd find it humorous." His warm breath was dangerously close to her neck.

"I think I might."

"Glad to see you're perceptive."

My, she had flirted with him. She should be ashamed. Why, he was clearly the enemy, the one person keeping her from Rebecca. *Don't lose sight of why you've come all this way.*

A couple approached with three children trailing behind them. The man reminded her of Grant. He had turquoise-colored eyes, something she'd never seen before and found rather intimidating.

"Jenny, this is my brother, Morgan, and his wife, Casey." He finished the introductions. The striking woman was fairly tall with beautiful auburn hair. Morgan must be the lawyer who had finalized Rebecca's adoption. At least, that is what the Pinkerton had told her parents. Before she had time to think about the man being a threat to her carefully laid plans, she met nine-year-old Chad, seven-year-old Lark, and two-year-old Daniel. The youngest had inherited his mother's auburn curls and longed to be held.

Close behind them was a muscular man and a petite woman with flaxen hair. Grant introduced them as his sister and brother-in-law—Ben and Bonnie Kahler. Right behind them were two young boys: Zachary, age eight, and Michael Paul, age five. Jenny noted the couple also expected a third child.

For certain, she'd rather face Father during one of his tirades than the afternoon ahead. Would Grant's family confront her about her plans? Jenny shuddered at the thought of yet another argument. One episode with Grant had been more than enough.

She must have been insane to accept this invitation. Her thoughts juggled with whether she should endure dinner or politely decline. Already her stomach began to protest the ordeal ahead. Mercy, would the confusion ever end?

From the recesses of her heart, she recalled one of her father's favorite sayings: *Sentiments are foolish when there is a job to do.* She stared at her gloved hands and could almost hear his booming voice. *Nothing matters but the task at hand. Let no one get in the way of your goals.*

Father knew best. Jenny didn't dare question him.

Before they reached the back of the church, a woman approached Grant concerning her feverish son. "Can you take a look at him now? I'm sure it will only take a few minutes, and I live close by."

"I'll watch Rebecca," Jenny said and smiled.

He returned the gesture and motioned to a slender woman standing beside the reverend. She must be his mother. "Mama, this is Jenny Martin. Would you keep her and Rebecca company? I have a sick little boy to see."

"You didn't have to ask." The woman extended both hands to grasp Jenny's. "It's a pleasure. I'm Jocelyn Rainer, and I understand you are joining us for dinner."

Jenny nodded, wanting ever so much to run.

"Hi, Grandma," Rebecca said. "Can I stand by Granddaddy?"

"Of course, darling." She took the little girl's hand and wove through the crowd of people with Jenny following like a poor animal on its way to be slaughtered. This was going to be a nightmare.

With Rebecca deposited beside her grandfather, the two women stepped out into the bright sunshine.

"Did you enjoy the service?" Jocelyn asked.

"Yes, it was lovely." *What I remember of it.*

"Would you like to come ahead with me to the parsonage? The rest of the family is most likely there."

"No, thank you. I'd rather wait for Grant unless you need assistance."

"Heavens, no. Casey and Bonnie are all the help I need. The food simply needs to be set on the table."

At least they don't expect me to know how to cook.

With the sun perched at high noon, she soon felt a slow stream of perspiration slip down her face. Already, her clothes clung to her body, and dampness gathered around the ribbon and lace encircling her neck. At this rate, her jacketed dress would soon be drenched. Seeking a reprieve, she stepped beneath a tree.

After what seemed forever, Grant appeared on the road. His easy stride attracted her—far too much.

"The parsonage is much cooler." He offered her his arm.

"Your mother invited me, but I preferred to wait for you." She linked her arm into his but avoided his face.

He laughed low, a deep-throated sound that had not the right to unnerve her, but it did. "There's no need to worry. I assure you."

They walked silently toward the parsonage. Birds sang, and she wished the same lightheartedness enveloped her. "You are very dedicated to the medical profession," she began, thinking a change in conversation might pacify her nerves. "And I've seen a unique sense of compassion for others."

"It comes from my faith. I can't serve God without first loving people—and for me that means tending to their needs."

With the mention of deity, she grew more distressed. She knew medical doctors at home who by studying science believed in Darwin's theory of the origins of life, and her parents supported Darwin's theory, as well.

Reverend Rainer met them at the door of the parsonage and ushered them both inside. Jenny immediately noticed his thick white hair and soft gray eyes. She should have noted these things when he preached, but her mind had been a blur. The other family members were in lively discussion throughout the house, not at all what Jenny had expected.

Jocelyn Rainer waved from the kitchen. "Jenny, we're so very glad that you're joining us for dinner. Do come into the kitchen where we all can talk."

Soon, Jenny listened to Casey, Bonnie, and Jocelyn tease and laugh. She envied their affection and the way they sincerely cared for each other. At home they would have sat in the parlor while the servants served the meal. Conversation would have been intellectually stimulating, but she doubted if the arts and philosophy would be discussed this day.

"May I do something to help?" Jenny asked, not sure where that question had come from.

Jocelyn nibbled at her lip. "Umm, would you like to help Casey set the food on the table?"

"Wonderful," Bonnie said and eased into a chair. "I'll let you two do all the work. Between the heat and not being able to breathe, I feel as lazy as a cat."

"You've been lazy since the day you were born," Morgan said from the hallway. "Nothing new under the sun here."

The women laughed, and moments later Jenny, Casey, and Jocelyn crowded bowls and platters onto a huge circular table.

"So, you are our Rebecca's aunt," Jocelyn said. "She favors you, but both of you look like Jessica."

Jenny's eyes grew wide. "You knew my sister?"

"Oh yes," the reverend's wife replied. "She visited the church a few times and came to the parsonage once."

Jenny didn't know quite how to respond and turned her attention to adding serving spoons to the table. She felt the weight of someone's stare and realized Grant was watching her rather curiously. Realizing he would like nothing better than to see her gone from Kahlerville, she refused to meet his gaze.

"Grant told me that you teach school and piano," Jocelyn said. "And you tutor French."

"Yes, ma'am."

"We'd love to hear you play sometime," Jocelyn said. "The piano at church is in sad condition, but Grant has a splendid one. Mimi plays on occasion for family gatherings."

She slowly expelled a breath. That's who she'd heard play the first morning she awoke in his home. Grant's family treated her so kindly. Surely they didn't know her mission. "I'd be honored to play for you," she said. Goodness, had the bump on her head left her senseless?

The smell of fried chicken, mashed potatoes, gravy, plump biscuits, steamy hot vegetables, and blackberry pie was wonderful considering what she'd eaten for the past several days.

"I see you eyeing that food." Grant's tone held more than a little amusement.

"It's a feast."

"Don't overdo it," he warned, "but I think you could have a little of everything."

The sound of his voice sent a strange tingle up her spine. Again. This had to cease. She fought the sensation with every ounce of strength she could muster. After the reverend's grace for dinner, he promptly picked up the biscuits and passed them to Jocelyn on his right and on around to the entire family, including the children.

"Jocelyn and I have been married six and a half years, and I still haven't been able to teach her how to bake biscuits," he said.

Jocelyn placed one fluffy delight on her plate and passed the platter on to Morgan. "And you, dear husband, have never learned how to make coffee."

"Amen," Morgan said, "but Mama can sure fry chicken."

The conversation wasn't at all what Jenny expected. Neither did she expect the well-behaved children nor the merriment. After the meal, the children played, and the men ventured to the church grounds to survey the newly painted building. Jenny couldn't remember ever enjoying herself more. The children were polite and obedient, and the adults made her feel at ease. Casey made a point of inviting her to their ranch, and Jenny believed she really meant it.

The neatly kept two-story home held a certain charm that drew her to its warmth.

In the parlor Jenny sat and patted the edge of the blue and gold sofa while the other women continued to talk. The sofa and a pair of gold tapestry, overstuffed chairs obviously needed replacing. Several areas were threadbare, but the reverend's salary probably didn't afford many extras. Still, the older couple and their family appeared incredibly happy, and she wondered why. Maybe they didn't know what they lacked. She must ponder on that aspect later.

Along toward evening, they all moved to the Piney Woods Church for the evening service. Grant had come ahead of her with his stepfather. To her surprise, Aubrey Turner attended.

"Good evening, Miss Martin," he said, as she entered the small church holding Rebecca's hand. "Are you fully recovered?"

"Why, yes, I am. Thank you for checking on me at Dr. Andrews's home." Jenny wondered if she should introduce Mr. Turner to Grant's family.

"I hope we can share dinner together one day soon. I'm staying at the boardinghouse. Will you be seeking a room there, also?"

She took a deep breath. "Yes, I plan to do so soon."

"Wonderful. We shall have a long discussion about Jessica."

"How did you know my sister?"

"Why, we were engaged. Didn't she tell you?"

An icy chill attacked her body. Jessica engaged? Did Rebecca belong to Mr. Turner?

He knelt to face Rebecca. A strange look passed over his face. A hint of sadness attached itself to his handsome features. "Hello, little lady, and what is your name."

"Rebecca Faith Andrews, sir."

"You are very beautiful."

"Thank you. I look like my mama and Aunt Jenny."

"Indeed you do, Miss Andrews." Mr. Turner glanced up at Jenny. His eyes clouded, and he blinked. "How did I not know about this?"

"I'm. . .I'm not sure," Jenny said.

Mr. Turner stood and licked his lips. Clearly disturbed, his gaze darted about. "This changes things considerably. The good doctor has much to answer for."

Jenny chose not to respond. Something about Aubrey Turner frightened her, not for what he said but for the indefinable look upon his face and the hint of threat to his words.

CHAPTER  8

Something was wrong with Jenny. Grant saw the troubled look on her face the moment she turned away from Turner. The man smiled as though engaging her in a delightful conversation. Grant hadn't gotten to her and Rebecca fast enough before Turner approached them. Had they quarreled? In any event, he wanted his daughter away from both of them.

"I'll take my daughter." Grant bent to lift Rebecca up into his arms. "Now you two can talk without any disturbance."

"She's not a problem—" Jenny stopped her sentence in midair. "I'd like to join you." She nodded at Turner and walked alongside Grant.

Fury consumed Grant, and he recognized a mixture of protectiveness and jealousy. "I don't want my daughter in the middle of your personal affairs," he whispered.

"What are you talking about?"

"Your traveling companion."

She paled. "I do not know the man. He approached me on the train when I fell."

Grant grasped at a need to control his temper. He was in church, in the presence of God, his family, and friends. He sat on a pew with Morgan and Casey and placed Rebecca on his lap. He took a few deep breaths while he sensed Jenny's gaze on him. "I don't appreciate lies. Turner told me about your plans to find information about Jessica."

"And I'm telling you that I never met the man until I fainted a few days ago. But. . ." She hesitated.

"What?" If he didn't end this conversation, their whispers would arouse attention.

"He says he's a friend of Jessica's. Just now he said they'd been engaged."

Rebecca. Surely Aubrey Turner is not the father. "We'll talk later."

"I don't think so, Dr. Andrews."

Before Grant had an opportunity to question her further, the introduction to the first hymn of the evening filled the air. An off-key chord struck his bad mood. In the next instant, Jenny left the pew, and he had no desire to chase after her.

Jenny made her way from the church and down the road toward the boardinghouse. She'd not stay another night with the pompous, self-righteous Dr. Andrews. How dare he think she'd traveled with Mr. Turner? And how dare Mr. Turner tell Grant some absurd story about the two searching for information about Jessica.

Why did Mr. Turner make it a point to tell Grant such falsehoods? Alarm swept over her. The strong possibility of Mr. Turner following her from Ohio nearly paralyzed her. Could the man be a Pinkerton agent? Or was he Rebecca's father and wished to claim her? But that didn't explain the lies. Unscrupulous described Turner's tactics, yet he claimed he and Jessica had been engaged.

"Miss Martin, Jenny."

She recognized the voice, and it did not comfort her trepidation. "Leave me alone, Mr. Turner."

"You need an escort. It's not safe or proper for you to be out here alone. Put aside your distrust of me, and let me be a gentleman."

"It's not dark, and I'd rather be alone." Her heart pounded against her chest.

He made his way alongside her. "Can't we be friends? After all, we came here for the same reason."

"You have no idea why I'm here, and furthermore, it's none of your concern."

He laughed. "You have the same fire that attracted me to Jessica."

She stopped in the middle of the road and spun toward him. "If you don't leave me alone this instant, I will scream."

"No need to take those measures." He smiled again, rather sadly. "Tell me about Jessica's daughter. How old is she?"

"That is none of your business. I will scream."

He laughed again. "Please, I'm not an enemy. I understand you don't know me well, but I do want to be of assistance."

"No, thank you."

"We will talk in the future. You can rest assured of that."

She walked away, leaving him behind. Trembling took over her body, and she feared her legs would not carry her the rest of the way to the boardinghouse. Unless she had misunderstood, Turner had threatened her. Informing the sheriff offered no consolation, for Sheriff Ben Kahler was married to Grant's sister. And Jenny refused to leave town. This gave her no other choice but to take care of matters herself.

At the boardinghouse she registered with a shaky hand and paid a week in advance to the proprietor, Mr. Harold Snyder. Everything smelled heavily of fried pork, her least favorite of meats. Grant's home smelled of freshness with open windows and vases of fresh roses.

"How long will you need a room?" Mr. Snyder was a thin fellow with a long, pointed nose.

"I'm not sure," she said. "May I pay you each week until I make a decision?"

"Very well." Mr. Snyder seemed pleased. "The second floor is for the ladies. You will be in room four, up the stairs and at the end of the hall. Breakfast is served at seven, dinner at noon, and supper at six."

She followed the man upstairs. The establishment looked clean, and she heard no noise. Mr. Snyder proceeded to unlock a small room that looked a bit shabby in comparison to the charming bedroom at the doctor's home.

"Thank you, sir," she said as his long, bony fingers handed her the key. "This will do quite nicely." As soon as he left, she raised a window to air out the stale smell tarrying from the previous guest.

She considered the room's basic furnishings: a single iron bed, an oak washstand complete with a basin and pitcher, a dresser and mirror, a small armoire, and a well-worn chair in a faded gold fabric. A threadbare quilt lay across the bed, and blinds covered the window. But it was clean.

Jenny removed her hat and lay across the bed. Too many things wrestled with her mind. She must consider a new plan to secure Rebecca since the good doctor was not married, as she had originally hoped. Neither did he have a houseful of children and want to give her up. She shouldn't allow the kindness of the Andrews family or their love for Rebecca to stand in her way. Her niece deserved to be with her own family.

Just as she drifted off to sleep, a knock at the door startled her. "Miss Martin, you have a visitor in the lobby," Mr. Snyder said.

"Who is it?"

"Doc Andrews."

Jenny fumed. "I have no need of a physician. Not now or ever. You may give him that message."

Monday afternoon while Rebecca took her nap, Grant had calmed down enough to take his adoption papers to Morgan for his inspection and then to pay one last call on Jenny. His mother's words still rang in his ears: *You should have gone after her when she left church.* But when he whirled around to check on Jenny, Turner had followed her. Grant figured the two deserved each other. Although that wasn't much of a Christian thought for a man sitting in church, he had to confess to honest feelings. For some reason, Jenny Martin brought out the worst in him.

Maybe he wasn't a good father at all. Maybe Rebecca needed Jenny as a substitute for a mother. Maybe he was just plain selfish in wanting to keep his little daughter. He clenched his jaw. Maybe he needed to stop doubting himself.

Grant made his way down the street to his brother's law office. He had Rebecca's adoption papers in his hand and a heavy weight in his heart. Two people had interrupted his otherwise peaceful life— Jenny Martin and Aubrey Turner. Jenny wanted his daughter, and Turner—well, Grant prayed he was not Rebecca's father.

Moments later he observed his brother painstakingly examining each document in Rebecca's adoption file. The only sound came from the steady *tick-tock* of a mahogany wall clock mounted behind Morgan's desk. Grant checked the hour, then read for the third time his brother's law degree hanging on an adjacent wall. His attention moved across the room to the titles of law books stacked precariously on a bookcase beneath the clock.

His patience wavering, Grant studied the lines etched on Morgan's brow. He appeared so deeply immersed in the papers before him that he failed to acknowledge the pair of eyes scrutinizing him. Grant pulled a pen from inside his jacket and scribbled the name Jenny Martin on a pad of paper before him. Beneath her name, he wrote Rebecca Faith Andrews and her birthday. He drummed the pen on the top of the mahogany desk. His brother glanced up and shook his head.

"Must you always make some sort of noise?" Amusement flashed from Morgan's eyes.

Grant smiled and ceased the tapping. "Only when impatient,

nervous, or biding time."

"Which is it today?"

"Probably all three." He capped his pen and dropped it inside his jacket pocket in an attempt to soothe his battered nerves.

His brother peered over the pad of paper. "What is bothering you the most, Jenny Martin or Aubrey Turner?"

"Both."

"And. . ."

Grant chuckled despite his restless demeanor. The entire family knew he never revealed personal information unless coaxed and prodded beyond any logical understanding. "I have neglected to tell you a few things about Miss Martin."

Morgan closed the file and settled back in his brown leather chair. "I'm listening, Grant. I'll admit the past few days have been a bit unusual, and I've wondered why Jessica's family has waited all this time to seek out their daughter."

"She wants Rebecca."

"I wondered about that, but why now?"

"I've never gotten a clear answer other than she is the proper guardian and something about her parents grieving over Jessica."

"Don't you think you deserve a clear answer?"

"I'm heading over to the boardinghouse right now."

"Is that why you two were quarreling last night at church?"

Grant shook his head. "That had to do with Aubrey Turner."

"Would you just tell me the whole story? I feel like I'm trying to pry the truth out of a defendant—or worse yet, one of my kids."

"He and Jenny are traveling companions, although she denies it."

"And you're sure about this?"

"He told me."

Morgan leaned back in his chair. "I see. And you believe him over Jenny?"

Grant hesitated. "I'm so furious with Jenny's reasons for coming here that I guess I want to believe him."

"Are you thinking he might be Rebecca's father?"

"I was until this morning." Grant hesitated while he sorted out his thoughts. "He admitted never being here before, and Jessica worked at Martha's a year and a half before she died. There's no way he could be Rebecca's father." He blew out an exasperated sigh. "Unless he lied instead of Jenny. Last night seeing Jenny and Turner together with my daughter in the middle was a little more than I could handle."

"Don't blame you."

Grant pointed at the adoption file. "Are the papers legal and binding?"

"Yes. I did draw them up, remember? The documents were and are according to the laws of the state, and they have all been properly executed. Now, there's always a chance Miss Martin will hire a lawyer to obtain custody."

Silence prevailed, deafening silence over and above the incessant ticking of the clock. Grant paused awhile longer before speaking. "I think if she'd considered a lawyer, she would have made mention of the fact. The thought has crossed my mind—more than once—that Jenny might elect to snatch her away, especially with the way I made her furious last night."

"She'd be in bad shape with the law if she attempted that."

Grant laughed, the first all day. "Guess I needed reassurance. All right, big brother, I'll head over there now and face the lady."

"Do you mind if I share any of this with Casey?"

"Go ahead. I need all of the prayers I can get."

"Glad you came by for another reason. I have a request."

Grant knew what was coming by the glint in his brother's eye. "Does this have anything to do with branding?"

"Possibly." A grin spread over Morgan's face. "We could use you on Saturday. You could stay until Sunday morning. Rebecca loves the ranch."

Grant laughed. "So this is all for Rebecca?"

"Naturally. And it would give Mimi a break, too. Nothing like hard work to cure what ails you."

"I'm so glad you have other peoples' interests at heart. All right. We'll be there."

The idea of spending a day at the ranch sounded like good medicine. He could sort through the problems with Jenny and Turner, then have a better perspective on Sunday. Perhaps Jenny would attend church and dinner again. If not, he'd ask her the next week.

He startled. How could he want Jenny to leave town and want her to stay at the same time? Had he lost his mind? The woman had been nothing but trouble. She knew nothing about being a Christian, much less acting like one. Still, when she smiled and he saw Rebecca in her, he wanted to get to know her a little more. Suddenly, Grant felt the whole situation with Jenny was nothing more than a minor irritation.

❧⟳⟲❧

Early that morning Jenny had requested that Mr. Snyder send for her trunks at Grant's home. As she placed her personal belongings in the drawers and the armoire, she realized that Mr. Turner had become more of a threat to her plan than Grant. She understood Grant a little better than Mr. Turner. The latter frightened her with his knowledge about Jessica and the fact he must have followed her to Kahlerville.

She shivered in the rising warmth of the day. Her decision last night weighed heavily on her mind. As soon as she finished unpacking, she'd do what was necessary.

Midmorning, Jenny ventured downstairs. Telltale smells from breakfast caused her stomach to rumble, but she needed to tend to her errand first. After obtaining directions from Mr. Snyder and being introduced to his kind wife, Cleo Ann, she stepped out into a day filled with heavy clouds. The scent of rain replaced the aroma of bacon and eggs from the boardinghouse. Maybe the rain would lower the ghastly heat.

Once in front of Kahler's General Store, she studied the two large display windows. One had women's goods and the other men's. Neither window had what she needed. She glanced up at the storefront and thought the owner had done a fairly good job, considering the small town. Inside, a bell tinkled, and once again, an assortment of smells met her—coffee, leather, cinnamon, and an herb she didn't recognize. Any other time, she'd have browsed through the store.

"Can I help you?" A rather round man smiled.

"Yes, sir. I'm looking for a small revolver."

CHAPTER  9

Grant left Morgan's law office and headed to the boardinghouse, where he knew Jenny had taken up residence. The heaviness of dealing with her no longer plagued him. He imagined Jenny had gotten over her anger, and they'd be able to discuss their differences reasonably like adults.

He walked across the boardwalk in front of the general store and glanced inside the display window to see Jenny with Pete Kahler. He hesitated. Perhaps waiting outside for her made more sense than calling on her at the boardinghouse.

The moment she exited the store, he caught her attention. "Morning, Jenny. How are you doing?"

"Very well, until now."

Ouch. "I was hoping we could talk." She carried a purchase along with a drawstring bag draping from her wrist. "Would you like for me to carry your package?"

"That's not necessary. I don't want to talk, and I don't need your help."

A surge of anger snaked up his body, but he refused to let this little bit of a woman cause him to lose his temper again. "I think that if anyone should be angry in our situation, it should be me."

"Oh? I don't recall calling you a liar."

"Are you still insisting that you and Aubrey Turner did not travel to Kahlerville together?"

"Yes. I repeat. I do not know the man." A snippet of emotion edged her final word.

"Why would he tell me otherwise?" Grant almost believed her, or maybe he wanted to, which made no sense at all.

She drew in a quick breath. "Maybe he wants Rebecca."

"Jenny, he couldn't possibly be her father. He admitted never being in Kahlerville before, and Jessica lived here over a year and a half before she died."

Her eyes moistened. "I. . .feared he might be. Why else would he follow me from Cleveland?"

"I have no idea." Grant studied her a moment longer. "Are you frightened?"

Her lips quivered, and she pressed them together. "I'm not sure. The idea of Mr. Turner knowing things about me is a little disconcerting."

"Do you want to talk to the sheriff—my brother-in-law?"

"Maybe. But not today." She lifted her shoulders. "I must be going now."

"May I check on you later?"

She shook her head. "No. It's better this way."

"If you change your mind, I'd like to introduce you to one of Jessica's old friends."

She turned in obvious interest. "I think I'd like that."

"She knew Jessica better than anyone in this town."

Jenny tilted her head in a charming manner. "My goodness. We've talked for five minutes without arguing. I'll think about it all." She nodded and walked away. With a swish of her skirts, she faced him once more. "Will I be allowed to see Rebecca again?"

"I think we can do that, Jenny." He moved closer to her. "I'm very curious. Why didn't your parents come with you?"

"They don't know I'm here." Jenny stared off down the street.

"Wouldn't they worry about you? Or is that none of my business?"

She shook her head, fixing her eyes on the bank adjacent to the boardinghouse. "They think I'm traveling with friends in Boston."

"You traveled all this distance without telling anyone exactly where you were going?"

"You disapprove?" She faced him with a cold stare.

He arched a brow. "I just find it strange. What if something happened to you? Your parents would have lost two daughters."

The pained look on Jenny's face moved him. "My parents are difficult to understand. They never fully recovered when Jessica ran away from home. You see, when she deserted them and involved herself in. . .other activities, they grew bitter. If they had known about this trip, they would have disowned me." Suddenly, she stiffened, and a slight gasp escaped her. "I must be going now."

"Then exactly why do you want Rebecca?" Grant battled the turmoil inside him. The strength he found to contain his temper was certainly not his own. "Jenny, I want to understand you, and I want to be your friend."

Her face blanched, and he viewed an endless array of emotions in her face. For a moment, Grant saw a weakening in Jenny's otherwise stoic facade.

"Talk to me," he urged softly. "Tell me why you feel compelled to take my daughter away from the only family she's ever known."

"I'm neither ready nor prepared to answer your questions. Besides, it's. . .very complicated."

He wanted to believe this woman could be won over. Hadn't he observed her enough times to believe her crusty exterior masked something entirely different? "I have plenty of time to listen."

She focused on the goings-on in the street as though they held more fascination than their conversation. A mangy dog trotted past. "Not today," she said. "They are my parents. I owe them a life free from pain."

Grant heard the misery in her fragile voice. "That's not possible. Life will always have its hurts and sorrows. Everything in this world is temporary. Only God can give us true peace and contentment—"

"Grant, I must try. They are all I have."

Long moments followed. Grant realized he couldn't make any further progress at the present, but today had been a beginning. "I guess I'll be on my way," he said. "I need to see Mama and the reverend before heading home."

She forced a smile. "Of course. I'm really anxious to get settled. Thank you once more for the assistance and medical attention." Jenny extended a gloved hand.

He grasped it lightly. "You're welcome. And don't forget, Mama invited you to spend next Sunday with us."

"I'm not sure." Jenny's slender shoulders drooped momentarily. "I do appreciate the invitation, though." She reached inside her drawstring bag. "I did write her and Reverend Rainer a note for yesterday. Would you be so kind as to deliver it for me?"

"Most certainly, and I'll talk with you later on in the week about Sunday." He accepted the note and deposited it inside his shirt pocket. "Let me know if you need anything." He took a deep breath. "You are welcome to visit Rebecca as often as you wish, but she isn't to leave the house without Mimi or me."

He saw how his words cut through her like a jagged knife. Her lovely face visibly seethed with anger. "Are you merely being kind to me in order to keep my behavior under control?" She trembled. "Has all this talk about me being a part of your family just been a syrupy pretense?" She took a ragged breath and whispered, "Please, just leave me alone."

Grant obliged, comprehending that more discussion inevitably invited an argument. Watching her leave, he questioned what kind of relationship Jenny shared with her parents—and she certainly did not know the Lord. Her sister lay buried, and he'd heard enough to perceive remorse on her part. Without Rebecca, she had no hope at all. All that remained for Jenny was the anticipation of having for her own a brown-eyed little girl.

He shook his head and shuddered. *Oh, heavenly Father, it appears that Jenny is using Rebecca as her savior. Show me how to help her find You.*

Grant watched her disappear into the boardinghouse, bewildered at his response to her and frustrated that she'd ever come to town. But what role did Turner play in this? Could the man be a potential threat? Question upon question filled his head while he stood in the middle of the hot street.

He shrugged and thought he'd pick up a licorice stick or two inside the general store. The reverend shared the same fondness for the candy, and he wanted to make sure he had some in his pocket.

"Hey, Grant. How are you doing?" Pete asked.

"Good, I guess. If I started complaining, I'd be here all day." He lifted the lid from the licorice jar and pulled out a half dozen pieces.

"That little gal who just left here sure surprised me."

"Why's that?" Unless Pete had tasted Jenny's temper.

"She just bought a revolver."

Jenny finished unpacking and proceeded down the stairs to the boardinghouse's dining room. She'd worked through the rest of the morning, making sure her belongings were put away neatly. For the moment, she felt optimistic about the future. Grant would allow her to see Rebecca, and she had a weapon to protect both the child and herself from Aubrey Turner.

She heard laughter and someone humming a nondescript tune. The sound of music always soothed her. The smell of chicken and dumplings made her mouth water. Life could be good. This had to be a positive omen.

The dining room looked inviting, not formal and sophisticated, but homey. Odd how her preferences had changed since leaving home. Mother and Father would never lower themselves to eat here. She smiled. She'd become a bit rebellious of late. The blue and white gingham tablecloths and curtains were faded but clean like her room upstairs. Jenny seated herself at a corner table and requested the chicken and dumplings from a woman who wore a pale blue sun bonnet.

"Are you having a good day, Miss Martin?" Aubrey Turner asked.

Jenny's heart raced. She had the revolver in her crochet and beaded reticule, but it wasn't loaded. She needed someone to show her how to fill its chambers with bullets and fire it. "It's a fine day, Mr. Turner."

"May I join you?"

"Of course." She forced a faint smile. No point in refusing him when she didn't know his capabilities. *Surely he'll not harm me here. Or am I being foolish?*

"What an honor." He removed his hat and placed it on an empty chair. "Thank you for your company this afternoon. Are you satisfied with the boardinghouse?"

"So far I'm pleased with the services here."

"Archibald and Jeanette would not agree, I'm sure."

Did Jessica tell you our parents' names? What do you want from me? "You're quite right. They would be appalled." She leaned closer. "What do you know about my sister?"

His violet eyes sparkled. "A beautiful woman. My love. My life."

"You said you were engaged?"

He nodded. "We would have been married by now if she hadn't left me."

"Left you? Why? Excuse me if I'm prying into your affairs, but I need to understand how you met my sister and why she ended up here."

His face softened. He reached to take her hand, but she pulled it back. "I'm sorry," he said. "You look so much like Jessica that it's impossible for me to gaze upon your exquisite features without remembering the love I had for your sister."

"Can you tell me about her?"

He nodded. A young woman served their dinner and set two tall glasses of lemonade on the table. Once the young woman moved toward the kitchen, he gave her an engaging smile. *No wonder Jessica was attracted to him.*

"First of all, please call me Aubrey, and may I call you Jenny?"

"Certainly." Jenny lifted the lemonade to her lips. She needed to learn more about this man, and befriending him seemed to be the only way.

"Jessica and I met in Cleveland. She was with friends, and I was quite captivated with her beauty. I'd barely gotten to know her before she became ill. Do you remember when she caught the measles and your parents feared her face might scar?" Concern etched his brow. "I missed her so during those weeks."

Jenny cringed with yet another accurate accounting of her sister. She vividly remembered the two weeks Jessica lay in a darkened bedroom, tossing fitfully in a raging fever.

"Despite their worries, she only received a tiny scar below her left earlobe," he continued. "Ah, but you, my dear, are as perfect as a freshly budded rose."

Aubrey's lavish compliments may have pleased Jessica, but Jenny found them repulsive. In the next few moments, he repeatedly praised Jenny's beauty, her intelligence, her bravery for embarking upon a journey across the country alone, her resemblance to Jessica, and various other flatteries that nauseated her.

He is insufferable. It's no wonder Jessica left him. Only an ignorant ninny would place any value in his superfluous words.

"What is your profession?" she asked.

He straightened. "I'm an actor. That's how I first met your sister—at a cast party at the theater in Cleveland."

While sipping lemonade, Jenny willed the time to miraculously

79

slip by. Her parents would have forbidden Jessica to see Aubrey. She could only imagine the turmoil in the Martin house. Her stomach twisted and churned, as it often did when she felt distressed. He did not answer her questions about Jessica but changed the conversation to talk about himself. During a rendition of Aubrey's leading role in *Romeo and Juliet* in Cleveland, a yawn escaped her.

"Excuse me," she said.

"It's I who must beg your pardon." Aubrey said. "You asked me why Jessica left Cleveland. . .and me."

"This is very important to me."

He moistened his lips and glanced away. "I don't really know the reason. One moment we were happy and making plans for the future, and then she vanished. I was prepared to ask your father's permission to marry Jessica the very day she disappeared."

"She didn't leave you a note?"

"No. I was to meet her at noon that day, but she never showed up. I've been looking for her ever since. That's why. . .that's why I followed you. I thought maybe she'd contacted you. And the little girl—how old is she?"

Jenny remembered Grant's words earlier today about Aubrey. *He could not possibly be her father.* "She's two and a half. According to Grant, Jessica lived here for more than a year and a half before giving birth to Rebecca."

Troubled lines creased around the edges of his eyes. "How did she pass away?"

"Childbirth." When he indeed looked grieved, she feared her own frail emotions. "I'm so sorry."

"I had many hopes for our future," Aubrey said.

There were many things I wish were different, too. She attempted to suppress another yawn. No point in being excessively rude.

Aubrey pulled a gold chain from his trouser pocket and eased aside the cover to reveal a gold and diamond studded timepiece. "You are definitely Jessica's sister. She always insisted upon a nap in the afternoon and wanted to retire early in the evening."

Jessica never napped! Her ability to get by on little sleep usually got her into mischief. Jenny's thoughts raced with suspicion.

"The idiosyncrasies must be in our blood."

"Exactly, and I need to excuse myself so you can rest."

"And I am *very* tired."

"It amazes me how much you two are alike. I may fall in love all over again." He touched her arm.

"That would not be fair to you, Aubrey," Jenny said and placed both hands in her lap. "Jessica lived as your love, and I'm but a physical image of my sister. You must find an entirely different woman on whom to focus your attention, someone who deserves your individuality."

"Are you shattering my dreams?" Aubrey spoke barely above a whisper. "I have thought of little else but you since the train left Ohio. I feared deep in my heart that my beloved Jessica had met her demise, but seeing you is like being born again into paradise. I keep thinking that if you and I were married, we could provide a home for little Rebecca."

"I am expected to marry a gentleman in Cleveland," she replied, fighting the repulsion for Aubrey in the pit of her stomach. "A fine man by the name of Oscar DeHayes."

"Ah, yes, the wealthy entrepreneur—who is much older than you, I might add. I assume your father arranged it." He leaned across the table. "I can overcome your affections for him. All I want is an opportunity to court you. You know, my Jessica feared telling your parents about me because of my profession, but I can see you are much braver."

She vowed to change the topic of conversation. Her relationship with Oscar already plagued her without Aubrey's interference.

"Jenny, I beg of you to give me a chance to prove my affections."

"But I'm not the woman for you. Listen carefully to me, for I don't reveal my faults lightly." She hesitated and lowered her voice as though others might hear her undesirable characteristics. "I am much too independent and have a frightful temper."

His facial expression changed sharply, and the bitterness that met her eyes caused her heart to beat fiercely.

"Oh, I remember Jessica's temper. . . . She had her moments."

Jenny felt the color rush from her face. If she had doubted Aubrey's relationship with Jessica before, she certainly held no misgivings now. From his abrupt reaction, he must have encountered her sister's fury and vacillating mood discrepancies. Most assuredly, Aubrey knew Jessica, for only the immediate family ever experienced her unpredictable rages.

She rose from her chair, and he walked her to the staircase. With a nod, she climbed the staircase to her room. Her thoughts returned to Jessica. Whatever had drawn her sister to Aubrey Turner? True, he was incredibly handsome, and his violet eyes nearly hypnotized her, but his way of attracting the attention of those around him mortified her. Perhaps actors distinguished themselves in this manner. Jenny couldn't fathom Jessica enduring that facet of Aubrey's behavior. At least not for very long.

It's time I met Ellen Smythe. She may be able to answer some questions for me.

CHAPTER  10

"Papa?"

"Yes, sweetheart."

"Where's Aunt Jenny?"

"She's at the boardinghouse."

"Why?" Rebecca peered wide-eyed through heavily veiled lashes.

"Because she's not sick anymore and doesn't need my care." Grant played with a soft brown strand of her freshly washed and dried hair. It reminded him of silk—soft and priceless.

"What's boardinghouse?"

"It's a place for people to stay when they are away from home."

"Why?"

"Because sometimes people travel so far that they can't get back home to sleep in their own beds." He gently eased a stubborn tangle through his fingertips.

"Why?"

Grant kissed the top of her head. "Rebecca, you ask more questions than your papa can answer. Do you want to see more of Aunt Jenny?"

"Yes, sir."

"All right, little one. Tomorrow, if you take a good nap for Mimi, I'll take you with me to visit Aunt Jenny. Maybe she will go with us to church and dinner at Grandma and Grandpa's again on Sunday."

"I will. Promise. 'Cause I don't want to be ugly for you and Aunt Jenny. I wanna be sweet."

"I know you do. Right now you need a good night's sleep. Let's say your prayers before Mimi comes in to kiss you good night."

Grant kneeled with Rebecca at her bedside. Together they folded their hands and closed their eyes. "Heavenly Father," he began.

"Heabenly Father." Her tiny voice must surely echo across heaven's portals.

"Thank you for this day."

"Thank you for this day."

"Be with me this night."

"Be with me this night."

"And guide me through tomorrow."

"And guide me through 'morrow."

"God bless. . ."

"Papa, I know this part," she whispered, her eyes clenched shut. "God bless Papa, Mimi, Grandma, Grandpa, Uncle Morgan, Aunt Casey. . ."

He listened to Rebecca name each member of the family, knowing the longer she prayed, the more it delayed her inevitable bedtime. As she continued with each family member's name, including a stray dog that she'd suddenly grown quite fond of, he thanked God for the precious treasure entrusted to him.

"And bless Aunt Jenny," Rebecca said.

"Very good." He lifted her up into his arms and drew her close. "Now into bed you go."

"Becca not tired." She yawned.

"Oh?"

"A little," she said. "Papa?"

"Yes, sweetheart."

"I love you."

He kissed her forehead. "And I love you." Grant heard Mimi's footsteps in the hallway. "Ah, and here's Mimi. Good night, little one."

"G'night." In the shadows of the dimly lit room, he saw snatches of Jenny in his little girl's tiny features. It caught him off guard, and guilt needled at him for some of the things he'd been thinking about the woman. He needed to do better by her.

I'm a big part of the problem. I consistently look for shortcomings in Jenny rather than seeking out her finer points. He vowed to try harder, no matter how angry she made him.

Tomorrow he'd take Rebecca to visit her at the boardinghouse. Tomorrow he'd list all the good characteristics about Jenny Martin. Tomorrow he'd discover a more positive attitude about the present set of circumstances. Grant wished tomorrow were Saturday so he could relieve his frustrations through hard work at the ranch.

Life had been a whole lot easier before Jenny came into the picture—and Aubrey Turner. After much prayer and observation of Jenny, Grant now believed she didn't know Turner, and that indicated a real problem. A man who followed a woman across the country and lied about his relationship with her meant danger. Grant sighed. Another stop tomorrow would be Ben's office to see if Turner was wanted by the law. And while he was out, he should pose the same question to Morgan.

Jenny awakened early the following morning with a dull headache. A number of items needed to be handled today, one of which was to find someone who could show her how to operate the revolver. The Wild West had taken on a whole new meaning and certainly more than what the dime novels portrayed. Mother and Father had no idea that she read such shameful literature along with her favorite Jane Austen.

The thought of meeting Aubrey at breakfast nearly stopped her from leaving her room, but she was famished after picking through supper the night before. She'd wakened early and hoped Aubrey slept late.

The enticing smells of a delightful breakfast wafted up the stairs and into her room. She quickly dressed and hurried down to the dining area. Instead of meeting Aubrey, she spotted Morgan sipping coffee and reading through a stack of papers.

I surely hope those aren't Grant's adoption papers.

But her stomach rumbled louder than the alarm sounding in her head.

She seated herself at the only table available, which happened to be to Morgan's right. She requested scrambled eggs, bacon, a biscuit, and tea from Mrs. Snyder, and the moment she finished ordering breakfast, Morgan turned her way.

"Morning, Miss Martin. How are you doing this fine day?"

"Very well, thank you."

"We all enjoyed your visit on Sunday. I hope you plan to join us again."

She smiled. What a perfect gentleman when he and the rest of the Andrews family were most likely scheming how to run her out of town. "I'm considering the invitation." She turned her attention to a table of rowdy cowboy types and frowned.

"This is not Cleveland, Ohio," Morgan said.

"I'm becoming more and more convinced of that fact, Mr. Andrews."

He gathered up the papers before him. "I was just rereading the adoption papers for Rebecca." Morgan smiled. "Everything is in order."

She maintained her composure. "Sometimes the best environment for a child is a moral decision, not a legal one."

He stood. "I agree with you wholeheartedly, but in this instance the two are one and the same."

Jenny watched him walk away. She would not let a single Andrews spoil her day, her plans, or her future.

At the general store, Mr. Kahler was not in sight. Disappointment settled in at the possibility of not having anyone show her how to use the revolver. A young woman with strawberry blond hair arranged the shelves behind the register.

"Is Mr. Kahler available?" Jenny asked.

"No, ma'am. He'll be here in about an hour. Would you like to leave a message for him?" The young woman gasped and took a step back.

"Is something wrong? Are you ill?"

The woman shook her head. "No. I'm fine. You look like someone I used to know. A good friend who died."

Could this be Ellen, Jessica's friend? Jenny's heart pounded faster. "Do you mean Jessica Martin?"

"Yes. Are you by any chance Jenny?"

"I am. Are you Ellen?"

The woman's eyes grew larger, and it was then Jenny noticed a splash of peach-colored freckles across her nose. Surely this adorable young woman had not been a. . .

The woman responded by moving closer and hugging Jenny. "I thought I'd seen a ghost. The resemblance is remarkable."

"I've been told that."

"I know you came by to see Mr. Kahler, but is there anything I can do for you?"

"I don't think so." She tilted her head. "Is there a time when you and I can talk about Jessica?"

"I'd love to." Ellen paused. "Let me think a moment. I'm getting married in a little over a week, and there are many preparations yet to be completed."

"Congratulations. We can meet after your wedding."

Ellen shook her head. "I don't want to wait that long. I'm free on Thursday afternoon after one o'clock when I finish here."

"I'm at the boardinghouse. Shall we meet there?"

"Perfect. If you like, we can walk to where I live."

Jenny thought her blood must surely have frozen in her veins. Did Ellen still live in the—

"I live with a widow near the outskirts of town."

Jenny hoped she'd disguised her initial reaction. "That would be lovely." She bid the young woman good-bye and walked back into the sunshine.

Convinced her day had taken a definite turn for the better, Jenny decided to forgo asking Mr. Kahler about how to use the Smith & Wesson Pocket .32. She smiled. She actually remembered what it was called, even though she had no idea what the .32 meant. But the revolver fit nicely inside her reticule. In any event, Jenny feared Ellen might inform Grant that she'd purchased the weapon, since they were apparently friends. For now she'd go on back to the boardinghouse and look at the revolver very closely. Perhaps she could figure out how to load and fire it without any help. Pulling the trigger shouldn't be a problem, but aiming presented definite challenges. Suddenly, she perked. Mr. Snyder might show her how to use it.

What a splendid idea. And on Thursday afternoon she'd learn more about Jessica. Maybe, just maybe, Jessica may have told Ellen that Jenny would be a good mother for her child. That should satisfy Grant and his family. Then she wouldn't appear as an unscrupulous woman who didn't care about her niece.

A peculiar sensation warmed her from her toes to her head. The idea of Grant viewing her as a compassionate, caring woman mattered very much. But why?

Ellen watched Jenny cross the dusty street and step onto the board-walk leading toward the boardinghouse. In her haste, she failed to see a man on horseback, but he stopped for her to pass. Jenny's mind must be on other matters.

She and Jessica looked so much alike, the same dark hair and huge eyes in a petite body—and extremely beautiful. The unique resemblance almost frightened her, as though the two women shared more than sisterhood. And little Rebecca was but a miniature version of both women. *Three peas in a pod.* Unfortunately, Jessica possessed a few characteristics that she hoped never surfaced in either Rebecca or Jenny.

Why had Jenny decided to come after all this time? Jessica had said one day her sister would find her way to Kahlerville, but Ellen hadn't expected it. In fact, she'd given up. Surely this visit wasn't to cause problems for Grant. He loved Rebecca. His every word and action regarding the child proved it.

With their short conversation, Ellen didn't view Jenny as the troublemaker type, but Ellen recalled Jessica's stubborn and rebellious nature. As much as Ellen cared for Jessica and referred to her as a good friend, she had had her difficult moments.

Ellen shook her head, certain she was conjuring up needless notions. Suddenly, she remembered something Mr. Kahler had said: *A young woman, a newcomer to Kahlerville, came in and purchased a revolver. How odd when we have a good sheriff in our quiet little town.*

Ellen rubbed her palms together. She must simply pray that Jenny had good intentions for this visit, but the prayer didn't stop the incessant pounding of her heart.

Grant entered the boardinghouse lobby with Rebecca in tow. She wore a huge green bow in her dark curls and a matching green and white pinafore dress. But her smile was the most captivating. At least for her papa. He greeted Harold Snyder.

"Would you check to see if Miss Jenny Martin is seeing visitors?"

Harold lifted a brow and leaned on the registration desk. "The last time you asked me that, she wasn't happy. I want to keep my patrons on my good side."

Grant grinned and pointed down at Rebecca. "Please tell her that Doc Andrews and Rebecca request her presence."

Harold scratched a whiskered jaw. "I'll see what I can do."

Grant walked with Rebecca to the entrance of the dining room. Lester Hillman sat at a table with Aubrey Turner. Two of his least favorite people. From the contented look on Lester's face, he was very pleased with himself.

"Thank you for your business," Lester said. "I'm sure you'll be happy with our bank's services."

Turner nodded. "And I appreciate your organizing a little card game. Thursday night will be fine."

Grant whirled back around and led Rebecca to the parlor area across the hallway. Definitely not the conversation he wanted his daughter to hear. *So the man is a gambler. Another excellent trait.* Some folks had no problem with gambling, but Grant had seen too many families suffer because a man parted with his money at the poker tables instead of taking care of those who needed him. He helped Rebecca get seated on an overstuffed chair and smooth out her dress. A few moments later Jenny descended the stairway with Harold right behind her.

"Aunt Jenny." Rebecca jumped from the chair and raced into the woman's arms.

A twinge of jealousy stabbed at his heart.

"Rebecca, how good to see you." Jenny bent to the little girl's side and kissed her cheek. "You look beautiful."

"Thank you. Mimi said I was a prin. . .prin. . ." She glanced up at Grant.

"Princess."

Rebecca's shoulders lifted, and she nodded. "Yes, that's it."

"You are indeed a princess." Jenny laughed lightly, then lifted her gaze to Grant. "Thank you. This means so much to me."

The warmth radiating from her eyes nearly took his breath away. And this second response to her made him more furious than the first. He must be working too hard. His normal methodical life had gotten beyond his control.

"Is there a reason for you to visit me?" she asked.

"We want you to go to chuhch with us again," Rebecca said.

Jenny moistened her lips. "I'm not sure. I don't think it's a good idea."

Grant wondered how Jenny would talk her way out of this one. For a moment he felt sorry for her. His Rebecca practiced the art of tenacity.

"Please," the little girl said. "I'll be very good for you."

Jenny laughed. "Does it mean that much to you?"

Rebecca nodded.

"All right. One more time."

Grant swallowed a bit of humor. In the next breath, he remembered how having Jenny seated beside him this past Sunday had caused his mind to wander. "Would you like to take a stroll?" Perspiration dampened his back.

Jenny took Rebecca's hand into hers. "I'd love to."

"Oh, goodie." Rebecca slipped her other hand into Grant's. "This is how me, Papa, and Mimi take walks."

Grant avoided glancing in Jenny's direction. Anyone seeing the three of them together would jump to more conclusions than the clucking tongues last Sunday in church. He'd most likely read about it in the weekly *Kahlerville Sun* under the society column.

"Jenny, wait, please."

The irritating voice of Aubrey Turner splattered on Grant like walking under a tree full of blackbirds.

She turned to face him but didn't release Rebecca's hand.

"Did you forget?" Turner asked.

Confusion passed over her face. "Forget what?"

"Our stroll through town." He smiled at Grant and patted Rebecca on the head, right atop her perfectly tied hair ribbon.

"We had nothing arranged."

He laughed lightly. "You are so much like Jessica. She had problems remembering our special times, too."

It didn't matter that Jenny had chosen him and Rebecca over Turner. Grant simply wanted to be free of both of them.

"I'm sorry to interrupt your plans," Grant said. "We can do this another time."

"Absolutely not." Jenny's eyes blazed, and crimson rose from the neck of her high-collared white blouse. "Mr. Turner, we did not have anything arranged, and I do not appreciate the claims that we did." She met Grant's gaze. "Shall we continue?"

"Then will you join me for the evening meal?" Turner asked. "I am determined to have you accept my marriage proposal." He nodded at Grant. "We could provide a fine home for Jessica's daughter."

Grant fought the urge to lay a fist alongside Turner's face and toss him into a pile of horse manure. "You, sir, will never be a part of my daughter's life." He swallowed hard and took in the man's tan suit, white gloves, and ruffled shirt. He belonged back East or, better yet, on a leaky riverboat.

"I see you aren't in agreement with Jenny's plans." He turned to Jenny. "Dinner at seven?"

"No, thank you," Jenny said and proceeded to the door.

"You do not have to alter your plans for us," Grant said once they were outside.

"You don't understand," she said. "We had no such arrangement. I loathe the man, but he insists upon making these outlandish statements and humiliating me."

Turner's lying about his dealings with Jenny stamped upon Grant's mind again. "Why does he do this?"

"I don't know, but I'm beginning to feel frightened." She shook her head. "It's as though he's trying to convince me that I've lost my senses."

Maybe she was telling the truth. "Allow me to contact the sheriff and my brother on your behalf."

"I don't think it's necessary. I believe he's harmless, just persistent."

"Someone who is harmless doesn't follow a woman across the country."

"I can handle Mr. Turner. I know exactly what to do."

Can you? From the lines etched on her brow, he wondered if she spoke too rashly. Kahlerville had been birthed in the wilds with desperate men riding into town at whim. Grant's precious daughter and a bit of a woman were no match for a potentially dangerous man.

CHAPTER  11

Promptly at one o'clock on Thursday afternoon, Jenny walked down the wide oak stairs of the boardinghouse to wait for Ellen. At last she was going to talk to the person who knew Jessica best. The excitement had kept Jenny awake the night before and watching the clock since sunrise. So many questions juggled in her mind. Some were delicate and could very well insult Ellen. Jenny refused to pry into life at the brothel. Jessica's reasons for selling her body had to lie buried with her.

How could Jenny find the answers to her questions in fifteen minutes, the proper calling time for ladies? She sighed. Kahlerville didn't adhere to society's etiquette as rigidly as Cleveland. She'd allow Ellen to lead the length of their meeting.

No sooner had Jenny walked past the registration desk than she saw Ellen already seated in the parlor. The woman smiled timidly from a deep red overstuffed chair. Odd, she looked more like a girl than a woman who—well, lived like Jessica. But Jessica had the face of an angel and a smile that would have parted the sea—one of Grandma Martin's favorite sayings about her granddaughters.

Ellen stood to greet Jenny and extended a gloved hand. "You look so much like Jessica. Thank you for wanting to talk to me about her. I hope I can help you."

"I'm glad you came." Jenny sensed her emotions rising to the top of her throat. She swallowed a lump and hoped she didn't lose her composure.

"I'm a little nervous," Ellen said.

"So am I. Shall we sit down? Or would you rather talk over a cup of coffee or tea?"

Ellen moistened her lips. "Tea would be nice. Jessica and I used to drink tea together."

After being seated and placing their order with Mrs. Snyder, Jenny contemplated how to initiate the conversation. She'd written a few questions but left them in her room. As much as she wanted to know about Jessica's life in Kahlerville, not knowing the truth almost seemed the wiser choice.

"Where would you like to begin?" Ellen asked.

Jenny considered the ever-mounting concerns about Jessica's life. "How long did you know my sister?"

"I'd been working at Martha's about six months before she came." Ellen removed her gloves and fidgeted with a pearl button on one of them. "We became friends right away. The other girls tended to be loud, cursed, fought among themselves, and drank too much. Jessica and I thought we were better than that." She shrugged. "How very sad when we all did the same work."

Jenny rested her hands in her lap with her back perfectly arched. She couldn't imagine a life so sordid. How could Jessica resort to such low means? "You don't have to tell me uncomfortable things."

Ellen smiled. "My friendship with your sister was while working at Martha's. There is no other way to explain our relationship. I understand none of this is easy for a lady of your standing."

"I'm afraid my questions will sound as if I'm judging you."

Ellen leaned across the small table. Her hazel eyes radiated something Jenny didn't recognize, but she'd seen the same earnestness in Mimi, Grant, and his family.

"I know what I *was*," Ellen said. "But God has forgiven me and wiped free my past. Ask what you need to settle your mind about Jessica."

Jenny took a deep breath. This frail-looking, tiny young woman was the picture of innocence and beauty. How did religion accomplish that? Father insisted any obsession with deity was a foolish myth. Mother agreed with him, but Grandma Martin had talked about God even when Father forbade it. She said Jessica and Jenny needed to know about the Creator of the universe. Then she died when the sisters were barely in their teens.

"Jenny, are you all right?" Ellen asked.

Immediately she snapped back to the present. "I'm sorry. My mind wandered for a moment. One of my questions is about Rebecca's father. Do you know who he is?"

"No. She told me she had no idea, and I believed her."

Jenny took another deep breath. "Did my sister ever talk about home?"

"Sometimes. She must not have had a good relationship with your parents, because she was bitter. But she often spoke of you."

"What did she say? We. . .we weren't close as we should have been."

Mrs. Snyder set two cups of tea in front of them, and Ellen waited until the woman left the dining room. "Jessica said she had a younger sister named Jenny who was kind and good. She also said your parents treated you unfairly. Actually she said your parents were demanding when it came to you."

Jenny blinked back the tears welling in her eyes. "I thought she despised me. And I never thought she noticed how Mother and Father. . .dealt with me."

"Why can't you equal the academic achievements of your sister? Are you stupid?" Jenny shook away the memories.

"Jessica missed you, and she regretted not being with you."

"I never knew."

"She hid her feelings about many things."

Jenny couldn't stop the flow of tears. She reached inside her reticule for a handkerchief and felt the steel barrel of the handgun. A thought shook her senses. Had Jessica ever been afraid? Had she died alone and frightened without anyone to love her?

"Maybe we should talk again. This is much too upsetting for you," Ellen said.

"I feel like my sister was a stranger. I wish our lives had been different."

"We all have regrets, Jenny. Not a day goes by that I am not bothered by something from the past. Yet I am so blessed to have Frank."

Jenny glanced up. "That's right. You're getting married. When is the wedding?"

"A week from tomorrow. Would you like to come? It will be at Piney Woods Church."

"Yes, I would. Thank you very much. Perhaps we can meet again after life slows down for you."

"I will look forward to it." Ellen lifted the tea cup to her lips. "This brings back good memories with Jessica. I haven't had a cup of tea since she died."

"Then we will do this again. May I walk with you to your home?"

"Sounds like a wonderful idea."

The two made their way out to the boardwalk and into the un-bearable heat.

"I wonder if I will ever become accustomed to the sweltering temperatures," Jenny said.

Ellen laughed. "It gets worse in midsummer and on into August and September."

"I hope I will be home by then."

"How long do you intend to stay?"

Jenny deliberated her reply. "I'm not sure. I'm concerned about Rebecca."

"You shouldn't be. Doc Andrews is a fine Christian man. He adores her."

"I want to be sure." From the corner of Jenny's eye, she saw Aubrey Turner walking their way from across the street. "Oh, no."

"What's wrong?"

"Aubrey Turner. He's heading our way. The man claims to have been engaged to Jessica."

"The best way to ignore a man is to keep moving."

No matter how much Jenny willed the man away, he walked their way at a fast clip.

"Excuse me. Jenny, may I have a word with you?" he asked in that disdainful, overpolite manner.

"Keep walking," Ellen whispered.

"And you, too, Miss Smythe. I'd like a moment of your time."

Jenny stopped, realizing the insufferable man would not leave them alone. "How can we help you?" she asked.

"I'm searching desperately for more information about Jessica." He removed his hat and smiled at Ellen. "I understand you were her closest friend. Excuse me. My name is Aubrey Turner, and I was engaged to Jessica before she left Ohio."

"I know nothing about that," Ellen said. "And I don't recall her mentioning you."

Sadness passed over his handsome features. "Could we meet and talk about Jessica?"

"I don't think so, Mr. Turner. In another week I will be married, which makes your request inappropriate."

He lifted a brow. "I'm sure your fiancé would not mind."

"But I would. Good day, Mr. Turner." She nodded and proceeded down the street with Jenny beside her.

"You handled him quite nicely," Jenny said.

"If Jessica had ever mentioned him, I would have been polite. As it is, I think his fancy clothes and mannerisms are a mask for something else."

"You saw all of that in our brief conversation?" Jenny asked.

Ellen shook her head. "When you work in a brothel, you learn to see people for who they really are."

"Should I be afraid?" Jenny had inwardly answered this question the day she purchased the weapon.

"I'm not sure. Just be wary."

Grant wiped the sweat from his face onto his shirt sleeve and blinked back the stinging in his eyes. His back ached, and every muscle in his body screamed in protest. But he loved hard work. He grabbed the calf's tail, flipped the animal over, and held its front legs to the ground. Morgan slipped the rope off the calf's back legs and pushed the back legs down so one of the hands could lay a hot iron with the Double H brand across the calf's rear.

"Done," Morgan said and moved back on his heels to free the calf.

Grant did the same and watched while a rider herded the wailing calf back to its bellowing mama in the pasture. Before the two men could take a moment's rest, another hand rode into a small penned area designated for unbranded calves and lassoed a calf around its back legs.

"Are you in a hurry, Jesse?" Grant grinned.

"I'm taking my time," Jesse said. "I think city life is making you a weak man."

Grant grabbed the calf. "I'm as strong as I ever was. That's why I have to head out here every once in a while to show you fellas how it's done."

"We feel sorry for you and let you help," Morgan said, grabbing the calf and wrestling it to the ground.

Jesse laughed. "Yeah, afterwards we have to pick up the slack."

"Oh yeah? I'll remember all this fine talk the next time you or

Morgan play twenty-year-olds and try to break horses."

"He got us there," Jesse said.

"Right. Casey had to hold you both down while I set your arms." He released the calf he was holding. "So big brother and Mr. Ride 'Em Cowboy, you have me to thank that you two are able to help the rest of us today."

Morgan punched him with the arm that Grant had set. It felt good, real good to work the ranch.

Later on, Grant and Morgan took a water break and gazed out over the fence at a couple of mares.

"Did you talk to Ben yesterday?" Morgan asked.

"No. I thought he might be here today."

"He had a shooting to take care of from Thursday night."

Grant startled. "He didn't come after me to patch up anybody."

"That's because the man got shot in a card game and didn't make it."

A mare trotted to them and nestled her nose against Morgan's palm.

"Who was it?"

"Ivan Howe. Turner shot him dead in the heart."

Howe, a rancher, was known for his hot temper and weakness for liquor. "What happened? I overheard Lester planning a card game with Turner."

"Howe accused him of cheating and drew a gun on him. Turner was faster."

Self-defense. Grant shook his head. "Howe has about a half dozen kids and a poorly wife. Hate to see that." He hesitated. "Turner is trouble, Morgan. I can smell it."

The rain began in the wee hours of Sunday morning. Jenny stirred slightly during the brief prelude of crackling thunder and flashes of light, but the sound of summer rain drumming against the roof gently ushered her back into a dream world.

Deep in another time, two small girls shared a tea party on the front porch of their home, where a steady shower stopped them from carrying their festivities onto the lawn. Jessica properly poured the tea, and Jenny's Miss Suzanne, a blond, fragile beauty, politely asked for sugar and cream. Jenny smiled in her sleep. Now she could fill the cup for Jessica's doll, Miss Eloise—but the dainty china pot was empty.

Jessica began to cry. As the tears spilled down over her cheeks, flooding the tiny cup and lace-covered table, Jessica snatched up Miss Eloise and dashed out into the rain and disappeared into a misty haze. She ran so far that Jenny could no longer see her. Jenny called for her sister repeatedly, but she refused to answer. The unrelenting downpour left Jenny alone, frightened, and unable to move. She could only whisper Jessica's name.

A crash of thunder shook the room and startled Jenny upright. Groggy from sleep and shivering from the dream's intensity, she glanced about the dark room and attempted to establish some semblance of reality.

I guess I miss her more than I ever thought possible. Jenny wiped the dampness from her cheeks. *I wish I'd tried harder to understand her instead of being so jealous. It wasn't her fault that she was Mother and Father's favorite. I never tried to listen when she wanted to talk—not even when she wept. How heartless of me.*

Consumed with guilt, Jenny listened to the hypnotic sounds outside her window. Believing the steady rainfall would lull her back to sleep, she snuggled against her pillow, but rest eluded her.

Aubrey Turner's statement about Jessica requiring an afternoon nap still puzzled her. Her sister had never slept in the middle of the day, and she required only a few hours at night. Many a time Jenny had been shaken from her slumber by an impulsive sister who wanted a playmate and, as the years went by, a companion for her escapades. Sometimes she would go for three or four days without an hour's repose.

Jenny shook her head. Some memories were simply too painful. Merely recalling the high-pitched, almost insane exhilaration of her sister during those times brought back a flood of painful recollections that she'd rather forget: Father screaming for Jessica to stay in her room, Mother attempting to settle her oldest daughter, and Jenny hiding somewhere in the house until it all stopped.

Why had their firstborn been their favorite? Had it really been because she did better in school than Jessica? Jenny opened her eyes. What if Rebecca had difficulty in school?

Why had Aubrey Turner waited all this time to find Jessica? Had he been watching Jenny for more than four years in Cleveland? She shuddered. Her fears of him grew each time he approached her. Ellen was right. His intolerable mannerisms and his fabrication about Jessica's sleep patterns must cover something. Dare she talk to Grant about Turner? The idea of appearing like a helpless female shadowed her first inclination. If Grant had any thoughts of allowing her to have Rebecca, this could stop him.

She forced the thoughts from her mind. Grant and Rebecca would be there early to escort her to church, and she needed the rest. A vision of her brown-eyed niece soothed her like a warm, crackling fire on a chilly night. Oh, how she longed for the day when sweet Rebecca would be hers.

Just as she drifted off to sleep, a question from seemingly nowhere floated across her mind. How could she subject a child to her parents' views and criticisms? Would they truly treat Jessica's daughter with love and kindness? Or would history repeat itself?

CHAPTER  12

As dawn broke the night's darkness at Morgan and Casey's ranch, storm clouds rolled and tossed aside any notion of a beautiful day. Most of those sleeping at the Double H were aroused in the wee hours of the morning to rumbling thunder and jagged bolts of lightning. Soon it gave way to a summer downpour, pounding the dry earth like a stampede of wild horses. Shortly before sunrise it ended, but persistent leaden clouds threatened to repeat their earlier performance and showered a stream of doubt upon Sunday church attendance in Kahlerville. Although Morgan owned a fashionable surrey, one that could shelter them from the weather, no one wished to undertake a ride into town with blowing rain and an angry sky.

"If the storm doesn't move away in the next hour, we won't be able to go to church." Morgan leaned back in a ladder-back chair in the kitchen. "Wet weather is one thing, but it's foolish to risk the safety of the children."

"I agree," Casey said and refilled his coffee mug, then Grant's. "They were all awake during the storm and most likely as crabby as grizzlies."

Morgan laced his fingers behind his head. "I, for one, don't relish the thought of spending an afternoon cooped up with them at the parsonage. The good Lord might find me guilty of murder."

Grant shook his head. "And I'd be right there with you." He took a sip of coffee only to find it much too hot. He bit his tongue before clumsily setting the mug on the table. "Tempers would be flaring hotter than Casey's coffee."

Morgan laughed. "Looks like it's settled then. I'm sure Mama and the reverend won't be expecting us. Ben and Bonnie live close enough to possibly make it, providing this next approaching storm hits quickly and moves on. As for us, why don't I pull out the Bible for our own Sunday service?"

Grant stood and pulled back the kitchen curtain. "There's one problem." He studied the sky for signs of the storm's passing.

"What's that?" Morgan asked.

"I'm supposed to escort Jenny to church and the parsonage."

Casey's eyes widened. "Surely she wouldn't expect you to ride out in this storm."

Grant reached for his mug on the table. "She doesn't know Rebecca and I spent the night here. And the weather might get better."

Morgan joined him at the window. "What direction is it moving?"

Grant gave his brother a knowing look. "Right above our heads and on toward town. . . . I don't like to leave her there waiting for me, especially when I had trouble getting her to go in the first place."

"I'm sure she'll understand." Casey eyed him strangely and tossed a look at Morgan, who sat back down at the table.

Grant refused to question their silent exchange. Most likely, they'd talked about Jenny and had their own opinion of her and the situation. "I'm not certain Jenny understands much of anything that makes sense to us. Did Morgan explain why she came to this part of the country?"

She nodded with a sigh. "Yes, he told me the whole story. She really needs our patience and understanding."

"While she makes plans to kidnap my daughter?" He combed his fingers through his hair. "I pity her, then I despise her. I want to help her, and then I want to throw her out of town. I'd like for Rebecca to have a relationship with her, but I want her back in Ohio."

"Would you like for me to talk to her?" Casey asked. "Sounds like she needs a friend."

"Good luck," Grant said. "Just when I think I'm making headway, she runs in the opposite direction. And I don't trust Aubrey Turner, either. He claims to have been her traveling partner, but she denies it, and I believe her. Now that he shot and killed Ivan Howe, I'm real nervous about Jenny's safety."

"He's a peculiar fellow," Morgan said. "At least we've established he can't be Rebecca's father. What did Ben say?"

"He's looking into it."

"Are you sure jealousy isn't part of the problem with Turner?" Morgan asked.

"Absolutely not. I'm concerned about the welfare of my daughter and her aunt." Grant took a labored breath. "I'm sorry. If I don't lower my voice, our kids will be up. I assure you I have no feelings for Jenny other than wanting to see her gone from my life. Mimi calls her a heathen. Wants to tar and feather her." Grant forced a nervous laugh. "Most of the time I agree. The best way to end this mess is to be friendly and show Jenny that Rebecca is in good hands. Maybe then she'll give up her foolish notions and go home."

"Just checking, little brother." Morgan grinned.

"There are no sparks between Jenny and me except the ones igniting our tempers. But I still have to stay in her good graces. I prefer to look like a responsible man who keeps his word, not one who leaves her stranded at the boardinghouse. Guess I can drop by there later and explain the situation."

"Have you established rules for her visits?" Morgan asked.

"I told her she was welcome to visit Rebecca, but she could not take my daughter from the house without Mimi or me accompanying them. And she was furious."

"What's wrong with that? You have every legal and moral right to dictate who takes Rebecca from your home. You're her father, for pity's sake. I wonder about you, little brother. Get tough with this woman."

"Calm down, Morgan. I agree, and I have no intentions of backing down. But the more times I make her angry, the more times I wonder how desperate she may become in her scheme to have Rebecca."

Casey touched Morgan's arm. "Honey sweetens better than vinegar."

He gave his wife a quick kiss. "You might be right there."

Grant ignored them. They still carried on like newlyweds. Disgusting. "I also believe there's more to Jenny wanting Rebecca than simply keeping Jessica's memory alive with the grandparents. I want to help her—"

"You want to help everybody," Morgan said. "Don't be foolish. You can't save every unfortunate soul."

Grant sensed a ruffling of his own feathers, but Morgan was simply being the big brother—protecting those he loved. "But I must try."

"Or die trying," Morgan added. "Turner is not a man to tangle with."

Grant smiled. "You and I have tangled with a few bad guys in the past."

"The far past," Casey said. "And I prefer you leave it there." She focused her attention on Grant. "Jenny isn't a Christian, is she?"

"No. She told me her father didn't permit church attendance."

Morgan shook his head. "How did you manage to get yourself into such a mess?"

"I ask God that very same question. . .often."

"All right, here is some free legal advice. You can't throw Jenny out of town, even though you want to. Although if I were in your shoes, I'd probably lose my temper and tie her to the train tracks." He took a sip of coffee. "And you can't ignore her. So simply proceed as you've planned. Keep inviting her to church and dinner. Allow her to see Rebecca and whatever else you can come up with. I suggest you stay away from pressuring her about the plans to take Rebecca."

Grant reflected a moment on the advice. "I'll see what I can do."

The sound of wrestling boys caused Morgan to moan. "Let me see what I can do to settle our band of outlaws." He tugged on a strand of Casey's auburn hair.

She frowned. "They are *children*."

A crash caused her to jump.

"I'd better go with you," Grant said. "My little darlin' is probably the hardest outlaw up there."

"And I'll get started on biscuits and sausage," Casey said. "Don't be too hard on the children. Look at their fathers."

By late morning, Grant had made preparations to start back home. Bright sunshine and humid temperatures replaced nature's fury from earlier in the day, but the storm had snatched away a little girl's need for sleep. Rebecca hadn't rested well during the night. Neither would she give into a nap the day before. The excitement of branding cows and playing with her cousins had kept her busy and awake.

He smoothed a clean saddle blanket and an old quilt onto the back of the wagon for a makeshift bed. Rebecca climbed in without a single protest, and within a few moments, she slept.

The sound of the horses pulling against the reins and the creaking wagon wheels lulled him back to contemplate Morgan's words concerning Jenny and his own reaction to them.

Being a man given to precise thoughts, actions, and plans, Grant rankled at his brother's hint of an attraction to Jenny. But it also caused him alarm. In the back of his Bible, just before the map section, lay a neatly folded slip of paper stating the attributes of a godly wife. He'd compiled the list years ago after conceding his love for Casey in favor of Morgan, and he rarely looked at it now. When he wrote it, he was nursing a broken heart. He simply didn't have time for a woman. Without looking or calling all of those qualities to mind, Grant knew for certain that Jenny possessed few of those desirable traits.

The more he mulled over Morgan's implication, the angrier he became. Jenny was self-centered, proud, far too independent, and—

Whoa, he'd set himself up as a judge again. Concentrating on her good points, he tried again. She had a soft heart for children. She displayed grief for her sister. She was an attractive woman.

The image of her large brown eyes danced across Grant's mind and seemed to haunt him during the day and keep him awake at night. He attributed it to her striking similarity to Rebecca, except his daughter's eyes always sparkled as though God had set a matching pair of stars in them. Jenny's, on the other hand, reminded him of an incident years ago. . . .

When Grant had been barely twelve years old, Morgan had asked him to go deer hunting. This was the first time his older brother had ever invited him along, and Grant wanted desperately to impress him. He'd crouched low in thick brush for hours waiting for a deer to pass by. Suddenly, a twig snapped, and before him stood a young doe. Morgan mouthed the words for him to take advantage of the situation, and Grant lifted his rifle. His finger brushed against the trigger just as his father and Morgan had instructed.

Expectation ground at his nerves. He longed to squeeze it gently, expertly. Just then, the doe lifted her head. Huge brown eyes locked onto his gaze—enormous, pleading pools, silently begging him to spare her. In the next moment, she tossed her head as though flirtation and feeble confidence would save her.

He didn't take down a deer that day, and those brown eyes seemed to repeat themselves in the form of Jenny Martin.

Only a man who had no sense fell in love with a woman because she appeared needy or pretty. And he had more important things to do than get involved with a woman who didn't know the Lord. He'd seen too many folks saddle themselves with an unbeliever. The Bible warned against it, and he had no desire to go against God's Word.

He shook his head and tried to rid his thoughts of her lovely face and the sound of her musical laughter. Admittedly, Jenny Martin had a peculiar habit of causing him to think about kissing her. Once when Mimi wasn't angry with Jenny, she compared her to a porcelain doll, and Grant had to agree. He liked the way her dark tresses stubbornly slipped from her perfectly styled hair and the way her lips curved up when she smiled. Her tiny features made him feel protective, except when he made her angry. Then *he* needed protection.

He lifted the reins and quickened the pace of his horse. The sooner he made it to town and apologized to Jenny, the sooner he could tend to more important matters—such as finding out more about Aubrey Turner.

Once home, Grant carried Rebecca up to her bedroom and left her in Mimi's care. Impulsively, he snatched up a red rose from a vine that climbed up a fence post in the rear of his house. In his rush, he pricked his finger on a thorn. She'd better be worth this. He stepped around mud puddles and overflowing wagon ruts en route to the boardinghouse and rehearsed his apology for not escorting her to church. Providing Jenny talked to him, he'd like to ask her for a stroll to the parsonage. Maybe his mother or the reverend could get through to her.

Every dog in town seemed to be prowling around the streets, lapping the water in the mud puddles and scrapping with each other like naughty children. A mangy hound dog growled at his heels, but the moment Grant turned, the dog raced away. At least he was in control of something.

He wanted a pleasant afternoon to talk and establish a friendship with Jenny, certainly vital if he was ever going to understand her. Apprehension gathered about him as he neared the two-story lodging. Jenny could very well refuse to come downstairs, or she might be in the company of Aubrey Turner. Memory of the Thursday-night shooting alarmed him. Jenny needed to be warned.

Harold Snyder greeted Grant with a list of grievances. "The cook's not here today." He peered down the end of his long nose. "Last night's storm damaged their roof, and she's helping her husband repair it."

"Sorry to hear that. Anything serious?"

Harold shook his head. "Naw. Only thing serious is Cleo Ann trying to cook for the guests here." He leaned in closer to Grant. "She can't cook. . .never could."

"Well, I'm here to see Miss Martin. No need to worry about me getting sick."

Harold took an anxious look into the empty dining room. Normally, little vases of fresh flowers sat on each table. "Good. After folks eat Cleo Ann's cooking, they may need you."

The owner shook his balding head with genuine frustration, and Grant swallowed a laugh. "Did Miss Martin join you for lunch?"

He thought for a moment. "I don't believe I've seen her since breakfast."

"Would you mind letting her know I'm here?"

Harold disappeared up the stairs, and Grant waited, hat in hand. The rose in his other hand looked like a pathetic peace offering, and he felt as awkward as a gangly schoolboy. Maybe he should have brought Rebecca with him. That worked the last time, but he couldn't very well inform Jenny about Turner's actions with his daughter listening to every word.

The sound of boot steps on the stairway seized his attention. "She'll be right down," Harold said.

Shortly afterward, Jenny descended the stairway with the grandeur of a fine lady. Did she have suitors in Cleveland? Did she attend elegant plays and dine in fine restaurants? Of course she did. Every inch of her whispered of refinement. Grant sensed a weakening in the knees. This had to stop. He had to remind himself that he barely tolerated her. He held out the rose.

She said nothing but grasped the flower daintily with two fingers, being careful not to touch the thorns, and drank in its sweet fragrance. Her gaze lifted to his, and in that moment, no recollection of her exquisite features compared to the wide-eyed splendor before him. Never before had he noticed her flawless, creamy skin, or her pert little nose, or how her chestnut hair framed her oval face. If Rebecca grew up looking like this, he was in for real trouble.

"Thank you, Grant. The rose is beautiful," she said much too softly.

"Am I forgiven?"

"For what?"

"For not stopping by this morning with Rebecca to take you to church." He found himself increasingly ill at ease.

"My goodness. I believe you're right. Did you forget, Dr. Andrews?" She inhaled the rose again.

Was that a hint of teasing in her voice?

"No, ma'am. Rebecca and I spent the night at Morgan and Casey's ranch. We were caught in the thunderstorm this morning and couldn't make it back. I apologize and hope I didn't inconvenience you."

Jenny delivered a smile that could have rivaled a whole field of flowers. He was in a real pickle and too weak to run.

"It stormed horribly here. I dressed for church, but I truly didn't expect you to come by. Honestly, I used the time to write my parents."

"Don't they think you're visiting in Boston?" He willed his pulse to cease its racing.

"Yes, they do. I decided to tell them about Kahlerville—about visiting the cemetery and about Rebecca. I apologized for deceiving them about my whereabouts, but I needed questions answered about my sister and her child."

"Good. I'm proud of you."

"I didn't write them to obtain your approval."

A distressing moment of silence followed. He weighed his earlier decision to ask her for a stroll. "I didn't mean to imply otherwise."

She sighed. "I mean, what upset them the most about Jessica was her dishonesty. And I want to be truthful with them, even if it makes them angry."

Grant toyed with the felt brim of his hat. "I wondered if you'd enjoy a walk to the parsonage. I'm sure Mama and the reverend would appreciate a visit, especially since both of us missed church."

"Are you sure the reverend held a service this morning?"

"Oh, I'm sure." He laughed much too loud, and it sounded like a braying mule. "He always preaches on Sunday regardless of the weather or who is or isn't there."

Their gazes met briefly again, but Jenny quickly averted her attention. "Why do you go out of your way to be nice to me? I know you said before I was family, but I'm not really."

Any answer he might have formed left him. He scrambled for words with a prayer for guidance. "I'd like for us to be friends. You know I will not give up Rebecca, but I want her aunt Jenny in her life. I have strongly considered taking a trip to Cleveland so Rebecca could meet her grandparents."

She paused for a moment, and he knew she pondered his words. "Friendship? I'm not sure how to respond. To me, you have everything—a perfect family, friends, a lovely town. My life is not as content—for reasons I don't really care to discuss. Rebecca would make my world complete and give me, and my parents, happiness."

He wanted to tell her only God gave true happiness but refrained. "And what if she ended up just as dissatisfied as you are now?"

Jenny's face paled. "Surely not. I wouldn't permit it."

Viewing her wariness, he chose to abandon the topic. "Let's not talk of this right now. It wasn't my purpose to upset you."

She glanced away, then delivered a weak smile. "Thank you."

"But, Jenny, if we are to resolve this problem, we must be honest with each other."

"I agree with what you're saying, and I'll try."

"Shall we take a walk?"

"That sounds like a wonderful idea. Let's not quarrel today, Grant."

"All right." He started to say more, but once again words escaped him.

"I need to get my parasol. I'll only be a minute."

Before he could answer, she disappeared up the stairs. Grant glanced at Harold behind the registration desk.

"Heh, heh, heh. Doc, that gal's gotten under your skin, hasn't she?"

Grant frowned. "I don't know how you came to that conclusion."

"By simply watching the two of you."

Once Grant and Jenny made their way toward the parsonage, he remembered the shooting.

"Jenny, there's something about Aubrey Turner I need to tell you."

"If it's his obnoxious mannerisms, I'm fully aware."

"This is a more serious matter. He was involved in a shooting Thursday night—a dispute over a card game. A man pulled a gun on him, and Turner shot him."

"Goodness, will he recover?"

"No, he died."

She gasped and pulled her reticule closer to her. "Someone should run that man out of town."

CHAPTER  13

"Rebecca actually drank from the cats' milk pan?" Jenny laughed. "She doesn't even like milk." She and Grant's stroll to the parsonage had taken a delightful turn as he relayed what had gone on at his brother's ranch.

"That's why I was so surprised when I found her lapping it up," he said.

"Whatever did you say to her?"

"I considered joining her—"

"Grant, you didn't?"

His eyes sparkled, and she allowed the moment to relax the uneasiness of hearing about Turner shooting another man.

"No. I don't like warm milk."

"I wonder who's the child at your household." Jenny wondered if the heat had affected her mind. She had flirted with Grant like a naive schoolgirl and enjoyed it.

She'd been in Kahlerville such a short time, and already many of the values her parents had instilled in her had been questioned.

Grant knocked on the door of the parsonage. She took a deep breath and took in the sweet scent of roses climbing up a trellis on the end of the porch.

"Mama and the reverend will be glad to see you," he said.

Before she could answer, the door opened, and his mother welcomed them inside. "Ellen and Frank are here," she said.

"Should we come back another time?" Grant asked.

"Mercy, no. We've finished discussing all we need about the wedding, and we're just visiting."

"Good. I wanted Jenny to meet Ellen."

"I already have," Jenny said. "In fact, she invited me to her wedding."

He appeared to be a little taken aback, and Jenny offered her sweetest smile.

"Good," he said. "I should have handled the introductions before this."

"Actually, it was an accident. I happened to be at the general store, and we started a conversation."

Grant nodded and turned to his mother. "Do I smell a blackberry crumb pie and coffee?"

"You could smell a pie a mile away. It's still hot, and there's plenty for you—with lots of cream." Jocelyn led them to the dining room, where Ellen and a man twice her size ate pie and drank coffee.

Once the greetings were completed and Jenny had been introduced to the burly Frank Kahler, Jocelyn served up pie and coffee.

"Frank, are you ready to get married?" Grant laughed. "Aren't getting cold feet, are you?"

"Nope. Wish it was tomorrow." Frank smiled at Ellen as though they were the only two people in the room.

Jenny envied their obvious love. She and Oscar were to be engaged once she returned, but she didn't feel anything but friendship for him. Father had arranged it. Said it was good for Oscar's business.

"Well, in the years to come, I'm looking forward to delivering a dozen babies," Grant said. "I hear you're starting up a lumberyard."

"Sure am. Ellen and I are going to have a good life." He glanced at Jenny. "Are you two coming to the wedding?"

Jenny felt the color rise from her bodice to her cheeks. She wanted to say something for propriety's sake, but her rebuttal would be rude. Grant must have sensed her discomfort, for his gaze lingered on her warm face.

"Mimi, Rebecca, and I are going, and we'd like for you to join us," Grant said.

What else dare he say? He'd been pressed into asking her.

"And all the guests will be here at the parsonage for the celebration afterward," Jocelyn said.

"I plan to help," Grant said. "Another dishwasher is always welcomed."

Mother would have flown into a rage if someone had approached her about performing the duties of a servant. But she wasn't Mother. "I'd be delighted." Jenny wondered how one more time she'd acquiesced to the will of these people. She turned her attention to Ellen. "Is it appropriate for me to visit you at the store?"

"As long as we aren't busy, I can chat away."

Jenny needed to talk to Ellen about more than Jessica. She still needed someone to show her how to use the small revolver. Every time she considered approaching Mr. Snyder, he was busy.

After exchanging a few more pleasantries, Ellen and Frank bid them good-bye. Frank's family expected them for supper before church that evening.

Once the couple left, Jenny garnered the courage to ask about Jessica. "Reverend Rainer, do you mind telling me about my sister? I understand you were with her when she died, and I remember Jocelyn saying she'd been here to see you."

He appeared to think back to when he talked with Jessica. "Why don't I tell you about the discussions Jessica and I had when she expressed interest in learning about God? Then if you have more questions, I can answer them for you."

"That is probably best. I appreciate this."

"Would you like for Mama and me to leave you two alone?" Grant asked.

"Not at all," Jenny said. "Both of you know more about Jessica than I do." She turned her attention to the reverend, although Grant's presence and the sound of his voice distracted her. She had to push him away from her mind before he took root in her heart.

"Jessica attended two Sunday morning services and one in the evening," the reverend said. "After the Sunday evening service, she asked to meet with me. She raised questions about the gospel and what it meant for her. We agreed to talk as soon as I finished dismissing the congregation. Jessica visited with Jocelyn here at the parsonage until I got home. We spent the evening examining the Bible and discussing God's love and promises. She agreed to come the following Sunday. The next week, I noticed her absence and decided to pay her a call at the brothel."

Jenny raised an eyebrow.

"We are all God's children." Reverend Rainer spoke softly as though he understood her silent objection. "The moment I saw your sister, I knew something terribly wrong had happened since our last meeting. Jessica reluctantly confirmed she was expecting a child. She expressed her anger and bitterness toward God and her belief that He'd punished her for her wicked ways. In any event, she refused to see me any more after that. She no longer 'needed a God who issued judgments' such as the one given out to her. Jessica felt God's ways were cruel and heartless."

Jessica's response to the reverend sounded like the sister she knew. Jenny could almost hear Jessica's voice making the declaration about not needing God.

"I didn't have an opportunity to speak with her again until the night she died. When Grant determined that she wouldn't survive childbirth, he asked if she'd like to see me. Jessica agreed, and he sent Ellen to fetch me. When I arrived, Jessica lay extremely weak. In fact, she rested so still I feared she'd already passed on. I shared with her the goodness of God's love and how He really cared for her. She listened while I urged her to surrender her heart to a living God who wanted her to be with Him. The poor girl struggled with every breath, but she fought the inevitable long enough to ask God for forgiveness and to tell me about Grant's agreement to raise Rebecca as his own."

That part was not Jessica—her sister never needed anyone. Jenny took a deep breath and fought for control. Her sister had died alone, without family, because her family had failed her. What a miserable death for one so beautiful.

"Quite often when a soul stands on the brink of eternity, things once deemed unnecessary are seen in a different light," the reverend said.

Jenny felt as though Jocelyn and Grant had vanished and the reverend had read her mind.

"Jenny, have you made a decision for Jesus?" Long moments followed, and the reverend waited patiently for her reply.

"No." She toyed with the handle of the china cup.

"Would you like to do so now?"

Her eyes never left her hands. "No, sir. My father would disown me if he knew I even contemplated religious matters. He doesn't believe in God."

"Is he a happy man?"

Jenny lifted her gaze to meet the reverend's. "I never thought of my father as being happy. He's very intelligent. He believes science contains the answers to our questions about such matters."

"I see," the reverend said. "But your Grandmother Martin believed in God."

Jenny startled. "Jessica told you about Grandma Martin?"

"She did. Your grandmother was the only Christian Jessica ever knew. According to your sister, she was a happy woman."

Jenny stiffened. "I don't have any more answers regarding my father's views about life. Reverend, I really don't want to discuss my grandmother or my parents. Grandma is gone, and I have to manage with the way life is now."

He smiled. "My intentions are not to anger you. I merely wanted to point out their differences to make a comparison. One day, and probably soon, you'll have to select your own values and priorities. My door is always open."

"Thank you, sir." Jenny wanted to tell him not to waste his time, but the things he said stirred her heart. She definitely didn't want to be like her parents, and she desired the peace and contentment so clearly seen in Grandma Martin and the Andrews family. But why did she have to turn her whole life over to God? Couldn't she believe in God and not relinquish everything? Couldn't she keep some of herself?

Jenny trembled. Her fingers refused to wrap around the small revolver in her favorite beaded reticule. She'd never brought it out to display to anyone, and now she must learn how to fire it. The sound of birdsongs and insects calling out to each other in the secluded woods outside of Kahlerville should have set her mind at ease. But it didn't. Her heart thumped against her chest like a drummer boy in a parade. She should have thought this through before joining Ellen on the wagon ride here.

"Are you sure you want to go through with this?" Ellen asked. "You're shaking so that I'm afraid to load it for fear you'll shoot either me or yourself."

Jenny pulled the gun from her reticule and handed it to Ellen. "I have to protect myself." She reached inside again and drew out the bullets.

"From what? I don't mind showing you how to use this because I believe every woman needs to know how to use a gun. I'm simply wondering why."

Jenny swallowed hard. Dare she tell Ellen what she feared?

"From your pale face, I gather a man has frightened you," Ellen said. "Is it Turner? He's pompous, but I don't think he'd harm you. Besides, Ben is a good sheriff. He'll keep his eyes on Turner."

"I'm not sure how to reply."

"Frank told me why you came to Kahlerville." Ellen gasped. "Please, Jenny, tell me you're not thinking of taking Rebecca by force."

"No. Oh, not at all." Jenny glanced about. In the beginning she'd considered snatching Rebecca away from Grant, but she'd tossed that notion aside some days ago. The thought now repulsed her. "Yes, I did come to Kahlerville to find Rebecca and to take her back with me to Cleveland, but I want to do that with Grant's permission." She caught her breath. When had she changed her mind about her quest? "You're right. It's Turner. He does frighten me."

"Has he threatened you?"

Jenny refused to cry. The man didn't warrant her tears. Instead, she blinked them back. "He followed me from Cleveland. He said it was to find out about Jessica's disappearance."

"And you had no knowledge of this?"

"Not until I arrived."

Ellen looked at the gun in her hand. "Have you spoken to Grant or Ben about your fears?"

"Not that I'm afraid, only my concern."

Ellen looked beyond Jenny into the trees as though her thoughts had carried her far beyond the beauty of nature. She inhaled deeply. "I promised myself that I'd never be afraid of a man again, and neither will you be." She grabbed the revolver by the handle. "First of all, you need to get rid of your gloves. You need to feel the gun in the palm of your hand. This is a little bigger than a lady's derringer, but you can manage it with some practice."

Ellen pushed a small release lever, and the barrel seemed to break open. She dropped bullets into the chambers.

"It's that simple to load?" Jenny asked.

"Just be careful. To fire, cock the hammer." She used the thumb of her free hand to demonstrate what she meant. "Aim, pull back the trigger, and fire." Ellen aimed at a tree, and a *boom* startled Jenny. Gray-black smoke gathered.

"What is that horrible smell?" Jenny asked. "Reminds me of rotten eggs."

Ellen laughed. "If someone is after you, the smell won't bother you at all."

Jenny joined in the laugh, but nervously. "I guess not."

"I'm surprised you didn't ask Casey Andrews to show you how to shoot," Ellen said.

"Why?"

"Never mind. She's a good markswoman and a better shot than me. But I'm glad you asked me. Shall we practice some at that tree?"

Jenny nodded. She'd purchased extra bullets earlier. If she planned to stay in the Wild West, then she must learn how to handle herself.

"How often can we do this?" Jenny asked. "I want to be accurate and fast."

Ellen laughed until she held her sides. "What have I done? Turned you into the next Annie Oakley?"

"Sounds like a splendid idea to me. I may need a new source of livelihood by the end of summer."

CHAPTER  14

Grant believed he had the prettiest women in all of Texas sitting with him in the wagon. Rebecca wore a mint green and white ruffled frock with a matching ribbon encircling her waist and another woven in her curls. Jenny had chosen a lavender dress hosting wide, full sleeves, fitted below the elbow, and trimmed in pearl buttons trailing from a high neckline to her waist. A ribbon in different shades of lavender, green, and cream tied on a stylish hat.

He knew better than to stare. His heart raced unexpectedly at the mere thought. He quickly averted his gaze to Mimi. She joined them in an equally dazzling display of finery. His dear housekeeper wore a light blue ruffled blouse and a skirt and jacket of a dark blue. An ivory cameo trimmed in gold rested at her throat, and Grant noted just a hint of color to the older woman's cheeks. A huge, flamboyant hat with many shades of blue and white flowers intertwined with ribbon and feathers balanced atop her head.

"My, but you ladies look beautiful," Grant said as he helped each one of them down from his wagon at the Piney Woods Church. He didn't understand why women went to so much trouble, but today he appreciated it. "If I'm not careful, someone will think you three are the brides, and I'll be left all alone."

Mimi reached up and gingerly touched the plumage as though she thought the hat might topple to the ground. "You don't think my hat is too large?"

"Not at all." Grant suppressed a chuckle and waved his hands in a grandiose gesture. "It's perfect. Beautiful. All of you are rivals to a flower garden. I think, next to Frank, I'm the luckiest man in town."

Mimi fidgeted with the hat a moment more. "Well, if you're certain it's not too much. Oh, let's hurry inside. I don't want to miss any of this wedding." She gave the bow on Rebecca's dress one last touch of expertise.

Stifling his humor and still wondering if his housekeeper's hat might take flight, Grant bent to pick up his daughter.

Mimi gasped and clutched both hands to her bosom. "No, please. She can walk. It will wrinkle her dress."

Jenny giggled, a perfectly delightful sound. How could this vision of loveliness be so set on taking from him his most precious treasure?

"Mimi, you'd think Rebecca is getting married." Grant feigned his irritation. "She'll muss soon enough. May I remind you that our dear little girl didn't nap today?"

"Exactly." Mimi tugged on the fingers of her white gloves, which seemed to be a trifle too small. "I want to enjoy the perfection as long as possible."

Grant laughed and offered the older woman his arm. She re-adjusted her hat once more and snatched up Rebecca's hand. Jenny linked her arm into Grant's free arm and gave him a quick toss of her head that sent his heart straight to the top of his derby. They were ready to celebrate the marriage of Frank Kahler and Ellen Smythe.

"This will be grand. . .simply grand," Mimi said. "Frank and Ellen deserve the best wedding this town has ever seen. I knew the first time I saw them together that this was a match made in heaven."

Inside the church, sitting between Rebecca and Jenny, Grant became even more acutely aware of the young woman beside him.

The faint smell of lilac teased his nostrils. He recognized the intoxicating scent from last Sunday when he had complimented her on its fragrance and she had told him its name. She also had told him about a lilac tree that grew outside her mother's kitchen window and how she and Jessica had spent many hours beneath it. Grant imagined the two little girls playing with their dolls and tea sets. He inhaled again, catching another breath of her. What had happened to him? The man who loved the smell of the outdoors. . .hunting. . . working the ranch?

Frank's younger sister, one of Mimi's former piano students, opened the ceremony with a song Grant recognized, "O Perfect Love." Another one of Frank's sisters sang the melody. Grant glanced at Jenny. A tear slipped over her cheek. Perhaps she was thinking about Jessica and how her sister had missed seeing her best friend get married.

His mind slipped back to the conversation with Morgan and Casey at the ranch. At the time, his brother's suggestion of an attraction to Jenny had frustrated him, but whenever the idea flashed across his mind, he saw more hints of the truth. But for now, his emotions must be nothing more than friendship. More important, Jenny needed to find peace with God. Second, she must deal with the turmoil inside her about taking Rebecca from him. He sensed a part of the problem came from her parents. What little information Jenny had shared about her relationship with them did not sound warm and loving. So why expose an innocent child to such coldness? Not once did Grant believe she'd succeed with her plans. He'd give his life for Rebecca.

Piano music ushered the bride past a crowd of standing friends and family.

"Isn't Ellen lovely?" Jenny whispered.

One of Frank's uncles escorted her, and he looked as proud of Ellen in her pale blue dress as if she were his own daughter.

"Yes, she is." Grant leaned Jenny's way. "Look at Frank. He looks like he's about to bust out of his suit."

"That's love," she said.

Grant refused to comment.

The young couple took their place at the front of the church, and the crowd seated themselves on both sides of the aisle. Along with a Bible, Ellen carried a small cluster of red roses, no doubt from the Rainers' backyard. A closer study revealed moistened eyes, glowing cheeks, and a trembling smile. Grant felt a little strange noting female sentiment when he normally ignored such details, but he'd seen Ellen rise from the brothel to a beautiful bride.

Frank's family made up the majority of guests. All of the Andrews were there, too, and of course Mrs. Lewis sat in the front pew designated for mother of the bride. Grant thought the older woman beamed. She was so proud of her Ellen.

Reverend John Rainer instructed the groom to repeat his vows, and Frank's booming voice could be heard clearly all over the church, but Ellen wept through her pledge, smiling through the tears. Finally, the reverend gave permission for Frank to kiss his bride. He turned the couple to face the onlookers and raised his arms to hush them all.

"Ladies and gentlemen, I'd like to introduce to you Mr. and Mrs. Frank Kahler. As soon as ya'll offer your congratulations, there's food and drink for everyone at the parsonage."

Grant took a quick glance around at the well-wishers. Seated in the back was Aubrey Turner. He had no business being here.

A whoop and more applause exploded from inside the small church and snatched Grant's attention. Frank grabbed his wife's hand and hurried to the rear of the church for the reception line. Caught up in the gaiety of the festivities, Grant turned to view Jenny, who dabbed her eyes lightly with a lace handkerchief.

"It amazes me why women cry at the happiest occasions." He grinned.

Jenny wrinkled her nose at him and daintily tucked her handkerchief back into a reticule dangling from her wrist. The drawstring bag looked heavy, but who knew what women carried in those things? She pretended to ignore him, then his teasing coaxed a smile.

"You're incorrigible." She stood on her toes in an effort to see the new Mr. and Mrs. Kahler through the crowd of happy people.

Rebecca, standing on the pew, peered up at her father curiously. "Papa, what's corybil?" Her innocence prompted more laughter from Jenny.

"See what you've done," Grant said.

"Papa?"

He lifted his daughter's chin. "Sweetheart, it means your papa is. . .has. . .good manners."

"Excellent description, Doctor," Jenny replied. "But I don't think it fits the occasion."

They joined the greeting line, and once more Grant relished the closeness of the comely young woman beside him.

"I'm so happy for you," Jenny said to Ellen, grasping the bride's hand in hers. Both women were overcome with emotion.

"Our Jessica is smiling down on us," Ellen managed. "And I know she's glad you're here."

In the next moment, Jenny linked her arm into Grant's and started down the church steps. She startled.

"What's wrong?" Grant asked, although he guessed before she spoke.

"Aubrey Turner. Ellen would never have invited him."

"Anyone could walk in here, Jenny. But I have no idea why he's here."

"I don't trust him, Grant. Something about him isn't proper."

He saw her quiver, but Rebecca and Mimi hadn't heard their conversation, and he had no intention of it reaching their ears. "Ben is looking into it."

He ushered the women into the parsonage. A three-layer vanilla cake decorated in pink rosebuds not only looked good, but its delicate flavor called out for seconds. Frank frosted Ellen's nose with a sugared rosebud, and she iced his mustache. Late into the evening, laughter lifted and fell. The new couple was given gifts of food and household items, and children refused to give in to sleep. Not even the heat of a Texas summer night could dampen the spirits of the bride and groom or the wedding guests.

As the festivities carried on into a late hour, the reverend and Jocelyn insisted that Frank and Ellen bid everyone good night. The young couple voiced their concern over the condition of the parsonage, but many guests volunteered to stay and help. Shortly thereafter, the new Mr. and Mrs. Kahler boarded a wagon and headed for their new home.

Soon plans developed for a "serenading" to take place around midnight, when a boisterous band of singers arranged to visit the newly married couple. Grant hoped Frank and Ellen had enough food to feed the hearty group—or they'd never get rid of them.

The guests slowly disbanded, and Jenny and Grant gathered up punch cups to whisk them off to the kitchen for washing. Both of them wore aprons. His derby hat hung on the hall tree near the front entrance of the house, and her hat rested beside it.

Grant observed Jenny listening to a pair of ladies talking rather loudly near the punch bowl. She smiled politely and appeared to cling to every word.

"Can you believe Frank actually married that woman?" a matronly woman said.

"No, I can't, Sylvia," a second woman said. "Poor MayBelle and Pete have to face the humiliation of a daughter-in-law with a distasteful reputation."

Sylvia fanned herself vigorously. "Who knows what Ellen did to entice poor Frank into marrying her?" She raised her eyebrows. "It won't last a year. Mark my word. That woman will run off with everything Frank has. And my Lester agrees."

"Excuse me." Jenny smiled. "You two ladies aren't referring to the new Mrs. Kahler, are you?"

Both women exchanged horrified looks. Sylvia paled, and the other woman gaped.

"My goodness," Jenny continued. "I can see by the looks on your faces that I was sadly mistaken. Do forgive me, will you? I thought you two were speaking of Ellen Kahler. You know, she is such a dear, wonderful lady. I have never seen anyone so giving and loving. Don't you agree Frank made a wise choice?"

The pair hastily fled the room, reproof clearly written across reddened faces. Grant watched Jenny glare angrily after them.

"Very nicely stated," he said.

"I grew up with my mother making the same type of rude remarks. Ellen deserves a good life with Frank, but folks like those two 'proper ladies' will stop at nothing to make life miserable for them. Besides, Ellen could very well have been my sister."

Admiration swept through Grant. "Frank and Ellen are pretty strong people. In time, most of the folks here in Kahlerville will forget the life she once led."

"It can't happen soon enough." Jenny snatched up a stack of empty cake plates.

"I agree. Let's finish cleaning this up and get Rebecca home. I don't know how she keeps going."

Hours later, Grant crawled into bed. The day had been long, beginning with patients at seven this morning and ending with finally getting Rebecca into bed after the wedding. He had enjoyed every minute of the evening—more than he wanted to consider. Jenny's face floated across his mind, their lighthearted conversation, the scent of her. He had to stop thinking about her. But tonight with Miss Jenny Martin had been very close to perfect.

Her defense of Ellen surprised him, although he realized the improbable chance of ever predicting how Jenny would react to any situation. Morgan, Ben, and the reverend had warned him about the erratic behavior of women. Of course, growing up in the same household with a sister and mother did shed some light on the subject, but usually he ignored their moods. As a youth, he didn't try to understand women, not placing much importance on the matter, except for Casey.

In the darkness of his room, Grant questioned what God had in store for him. Casey Andrews had been the first love of his life and the only woman he'd ever tried to impress. Unfortunately, she fell in love with his brother, and Grant decided never to love again. A huge difference stood between his tall, auburn-haired sister-in-law who once rode with an outlaw gang, and the petite school teacher from Cleveland, Ohio, who probably didn't know how to ride a horse. But despite their apparent differences, both were spunky—and both would give the devil a run when they were angry.

CHAPTER 15

Winking at Mimi, Grant took a big gulp of coffee. "Wonderful breakfast, simply wonderful." He proceeded to spread strawberry jam between the flaky layers of a buttermilk biscuit.

"Don't you flash those green eyes at me, Dr. Andrews." She shook her silver head at his one-handed attempt to stretch the preserves over his biscuit. "Breakfast has nothing to do with your wonderful mood."

"Of course it does. It's Saturday morning," he said between bites. "There's a breeze blowing in through the window behind you. You've fixed my favorite scrambled eggs, sausage, gravy, and biscuits. I have my weekly *Houston Post* newspaper to catch up on all the news. . . ."

"You're avoiding the obvious." A twinkle lit up her midnight-colored eyes.

Grant popped the remains of the hot biscuit into his mouth, licked his fingers, and reached for another one. "Mimi, is something on your mind?" He spooned a generous amount of preserves between the layers of another biscuit.

"No, I was just taking note of your good nature this morning." She refilled his coffee and handed him the plate of sausage patties.

"And why is that?" he asked between mouthfuls.

"I believe it has something to do with the company of a certain young lady last night."

"Our Miss Mischief?"

"No, not our Rebecca. Who's left?"

He peered at the older woman in feigned bewilderment. "Surely you don't mean Jenny?"

"Love is blind, my dear boy."

"I'm not in love," Grant said. "I don't want to be. I refuse to be, and a woman doesn't fit into my life right now, especially the likes of Miss Jenny Martin. When it's the proper time, God will put a lady in my path. Besides, I may never get married."

"Who said anything about getting married? Or who said anything about love?"

"You were thinking it," he said. "Jenny and I may be approaching friendship, but that's all. It wouldn't surprise me if she was using my affections to get Rebecca."

"So now you have affections? But—" She raised a brow. "Sounds like you've thought it through." She took a sip of her coffee.

He reached for another biscuit, but this time he snatched up the honey. "I thought I had Miss Jenny in proper perspective until you brought up the matter. Remember, she's not a Christian. A courting relationship with her isn't sensible."

"I didn't know you were considering courting. Let me point out to you that the heart doesn't work on logic," Mimi said. "Neither does God. You both are too stubborn to see what is plain as day to me. And her heart is softening to things of God. I can see it." She stood and took her plate to the kitchen.

Grant heard her mumbling. "You aren't talking to yourself, are you, Mimi?"

"No, sir. It wouldn't be sensible," she said from the kitchen.

He gathered up the newspaper, chuckled, and took a gulp of coffee. He imagined his housekeeper tying a crisp clean apron around her slightly plump waist and bustling around the kitchen. How he loved every smoky-gray hair on her sweet head. "Would you come back in here so we can discuss this?" he asked, unable to put his mind at ease about Jenny.

Mimi exited the kitchen and sat beside him, folding her hands primly in her lap. "All right, let's discuss you and Jenny."

Her knowing smile frustrated him. "I changed my mind. I don't want to talk about her at all."

"Then read your newspaper while I clean up breakfast. My guess is Rebecca will sleep quite late."

"Don't you want to hear the latest news?" he half-questioned, half-implored.

She rested her folded hands on the table. "Of course, read to me. There's obviously something you want me to hear."

He combed his fingers through his hair and winked at her. "Let's see, there's more talk about admitting Utah as a state and Hawaii as a republic. Um. . .President Cleveland is facing opposition again. He can't make everyone happy when the country's coming out of a depression." He reached for his coffee, skimmed the article, then read on.

"Some folks don't like the way the president has dealt directly with the treasury rather than with mortgage foreclosures, business failures, and unemployment. Although he has been able to maintain the treasury's gold reserve." He lifted his gaze to meet hers. She yawned and blinked. She wasn't the slightest bit interested in the state of the nation's treasury, and at the moment he wasn't, either. But he needed a distraction from Miss Jenny Martin. "I have my own opinions on his methods, but it looks like the Democrats are criticizing him, too."

"Any *good* news?"

"Oh, you can always find good news," he said from behind the paper.

"Especially this morning." She laughed heartily only to receive a disapproving look from him.

He folded the *Post* haphazardly in his lap and proceeded to finish his coffee. He'd already resolved to keep Jenny at a distance. A woman didn't fit into the life of a busy doctor and father. Even so, it might be nice for her to settle in Kahlerville for Rebecca's sake. Providing she gave up that fool notion of taking his daughter back to Ohio. The town could use another good teacher, but Jenny still had a teaching obligation to fulfill beginning in September. Naturally, at the end of summer, his life would go back to normal—whatever that might be.

Admittedly, Jenny had touched on a protected area of his heart, a portion he wasn't quite ready to concede. Most important, she needed a relationship with the Lord. That was certainly a matter of prayer for him and the rest of his family.

The morning sped by quickly. He read the latest medical journal, saw four patients, and prepared a bank deposit. Rebecca awoke mid-morning, and her crabby disposition caused him to question his logic in keeping her up so late the night before, except she did have a very good time at the wedding. So did her papa.

During lunch, Rebecca fell asleep against his chest, a partially eaten sandwich in her hand. Grant thought seriously of joining her but decided to check on Mrs. Lewis instead.

Until yesterday, Mrs. Lewis had shared her home with Ellen. The new Mrs. Kahler fretted over the widow living alone, but the older woman refused to move in with the newlyweds. Just like Ellen, Grant planned to check on her regularly. Of late, he'd heard the widow's heart skip a beat more than once, and it worried him. She'd never complained about chest pain, but Ellen had voiced a concern over her lack of appetite and strength.

Grant decided to take his medical bag and walk the three-quarters of a mile to her house. Halfway there, the afternoon heat and humidity got the best of him.

I'm getting weak. He wiped the beads of sweat from his brow. He needed to get outside more, even help out at the ranch regularly.

Throwing his jacket over his arm, he endured the remainder of the walk. By the time he arrived at Mrs. Lewis's house, perspiration rolled down his forehead and into his eyes, stinging and blinding his vision.

The widow's front door stood wide open, and it surprised him. She prided herself in maintaining a neat, well-kept home, and he hoped this oversight didn't indicate a problem. He mounted the porch steps and called her name several times before apprehension settled over him like the calm before a twister.

Maybe she'd decided to take a walk, but he doubted that possibility in the middle of a hot afternoon. Cautiously, he stepped inside, still calling for her. The only reply came from a clock ticking on the fireplace mantel. The small parlor appeared to be in order. His gaze swept over faded shades of wine-colored upholstery and tapestry-covered chairs. A cherry buffet against one wall held the photographs of many cherished friends and family members. The drawers were open, but Grant dismissed them as indicative of Mrs. Lewis feeling poorly.

He turned his attention to the right, where he knew the woman slept. She'd contracted pneumonia last winter, and he'd made daily house calls until she responded to rest and medication. The widow had accused him of wearing down a path to her door. Unfortunately, she didn't recover well from the illness, and the weakness made it difficult for her to fight other sicknesses.

Grant gasped at the condition of her bedroom. Dresser drawers stood open, their contents thrown everywhere. A chair leaned on its back legs precariously in one corner, and its cushion lay in shreds on the floor. Sheets and pillows had been tossed from the bed, then rolled up into a rounded heap in another corner. Feathers from the ticking lay on every visible inch of the wooden floor. He picked up a pillow and saw that it and the mattress had been slashed in multiple areas by a sharp, pointed object. Finding no trace of Mrs. Lewis, Grant rushed past the parlor into the kitchen.

He instantly took in the open cupboard with broken dishes and shattered glass scattered across the floor. He stepped over a pine pie safe heaved upside down with such force that the doors were off the upper hinges. All the while, he searched the room for signs of Mrs. Lewis. He continued to call her name, not really believing she'd answer, but certainly not wanting to find her hurt—or worse.

Grant moved toward a second bedroom where Ellen had slept and found it in a more deplorable condition than the other: torn bed linens, slashed pillows, and broken furniture littered the once neat abode. Even the curtains had been yanked to the floor and the window cracked. Grant caught a glimpse of the widow's frail body in a hideous twisted form near the foot of the bed.

He bent to examine her but found no fluttering of a heartbeat or movements of breathing, only the pale gray pallor of death. Gently closing her eyes, he searched the body for signs of a struggle or violence. Finding no marks upon her, he surmised the widow died of a heart attack when someone broke into her home.

A surge of anger burst through his veins at the thought of someone frightening her into heart failure. Catching his breath in the midst of indignation, he knew he must fetch Ben and inform the undertaker. The latter might be difficult to locate on a Saturday, for he also owned the livery and traveled about as a blacksmith. Covering the body with a crumpled bed sheet, he mentally listed what he needed to do the remainder of the afternoon.

Poor Ellen. Mrs. Lewis dies of a heart attack, and her house is ransacked the day after the wedding. To the best of his knowledge, the widow didn't have a single possession worth stealing. Her treasures were memories and friends. Once when he called on her last winter, she had talked the afternoon away reminiscing of days gone by: children grown with families of their own and her heartfelt prayers for all of them. She had shared with him a precious box of treasures: an inexpensive brooch given to her by her late husband, a polished rock sent from back East by her great-grandson, a faded photograph of her mother, and pieces of yellowed lace from her wedding gown. Stepping back into Mrs. Lewis's bedroom, he saw that the small, carved wood box had not been touched.

Walking back into the room where the widow's body lay, he peered around, wondering why it had been damaged more than the rest.

Ellen had slept in that room, he reminded himself. The bedclothes looked like torn rags around the body. Why would anyone want to destroy the widow's home? What was the intruder looking for? A twisted thought grabbed hold of him. Could the intruder have been someone Ellen had known before she left the brothel?

Shaking his head, he hurried from the house to get help. With the intense heat, the odor from the lifeless body would rise profusely in a few short hours. He stopped long enough to write a note for any passersby before heading into town.

The sun beat down hard, and almost immediately, perspiration dripped onto his face, but this time Grant was too deeply engrossed in thought to be bothered by the heat. His emotions ranged from fury to grief. Why would anyone want to do this to a sweet old lady who had nothing but a gentle spirit? He'd seen how Mrs. Lewis and Ellen scraped pennies to sustain day-to-day living.

He dreaded telling Ellen. She'd be devastated and most likely blame herself for the widow's death. Grant had never considered himself vengeful, but this death provoked his normally controlled temperament. For certain, Grant didn't need to learn the name of the guilty person. This wasn't an accident.

CHAPTER  16

Grant stopped in front of the small, newly framed home that Frank had built for his bride. Glancing at the front door, not yet painted, he decided he'd rather do anything than tell them about Mrs. Lewis. Deaths were a part of his profession, but it didn't make the responsibility of telling friends about the passing away of a loved one any easier. He shook his head. Not quite one day into married life, Frank and Ellen were about to receive tragic news.

Stepping to the ground, he secured the wagon and listened for Frank's dog. Nothing. Good. Perhaps the infamous General Lee still resided with the elder Kahlers. Grant wasn't in any mood to confront the bearlike dog who had a reputation for not liking folks. Opening the gate, still too new to squeak—just like their marriage—he breathed a prayer for the two inside.

Frank answered the knock, a look of surprise clearly etched across his tanned face. "Afternoon, Grant. Come on in. What can I do for you?"

Grant attempted a half smile and sensed he'd failed. "Can I talk to you and Ellen?"

"Why, yes." Frank eyed him curiously. "Honey, Grant's here to see us." Glancing back, he frowned. "What's wrong?"

"It's Mrs. Lewis," he said quietly. "Ellen's going to need you."

The young bride appeared breathless and blushing. "Afternoon, Grant." She smoothed back her hair. Suddenly, Ellen's flush vanished. "What is it?"

"I sure don't like bothering you two today. Can we sit down for a few minutes?"

She led the way into the small parlor. Frank wrapped his arm around his wife's waist and urged her to sit beside him on the sofa.

"Tell me what's happened." She wet her lips.

Grant took a deep breath. He wanted the best for these two, and now they faced this. "I have some bad news, Ellen. Mrs. Lewis went home to be with the Lord. Most likely her heart failed."

In an instant, all the color washed from her face. Shock and grief moved her to uncontrollable weeping. She buried her head against her husband's chest, and when she could not be comforted, Frank lifted her up into his mammoth arms and carried her to bed. Grant followed.

"I don't normally do this for my patients," he said as Frank tried to console his wife. "But I want to give her a sedative. It'll calm her down and let her sleep. With all of the excitement the last few days, she's probably exhausted. Tomorrow she can deal with her grief."

Frank's eyes filled with concern. "I agree. And I'll not leave her. I know my Ellen. She'll be blaming herself for not insisting Mrs. Lewis live with us."

Grant chose not to share the details surrounding the old woman's demise in Ellen's presence. She'd learn soon enough. "I'll stop by in the morning after church. Fetch me if you need to." Bone-tired and more depressed than he'd been in a long time, he shook his head to dispel the frustration. To him, the widow's death bordered on murder. It wouldn't take long for the news to spread.

Frank trailed behind him to the door.

"There's more," Grant said. "Someone destroyed the inside of the house. Furniture is overturned. Pillows and mattresses are slit.

It's a mess. There isn't a mark on Mrs. Lewis, which led me to believe her death resulted from her failing heart."

Frank's face hardened. "Who would take advantage of an old lady like that?"

"I have no idea, but it makes me good and mad." Grant pointed toward the bedroom. "Ellen needs you now. Do you want to tell her about the condition of the house, or do you want me to come by later?"

"I'll tell her."

"I'm on my way to see Ben and the undertaker. And I'll stop by the parsonage, too."

Grant wearily put one foot in front of the other and walked toward town. He stopped at the undertaker first, then on to see Ben.

"Why, Mrs. Lewis looked fit as a fiddle at the wedding last night," Ben said after Grant told him the news.

"I think you should take a look at her house. Somebody ransacked it. Most likely scared her to death."

"That makes me downright mad." He shook his head. "I'm heading there now."

"Thanks. I'm heading to the parsonage before going home."

Grant spent several minutes with his mother and the reverend. The older couple made plans to see Ellen and Frank for the funeral arrangements. Strange how the evening before had been such a celebration.

He walked on home to tell Mimi about Mrs. Lewis. She took the news badly, and it grew dark by the time he tucked Rebecca into bed and made Mimi comfortable. Too tired to hitch up the wagon, he walked the distance to the boardinghouse. Once there, Grant waited in the parlor while Harold informed Jenny of his visit. She didn't need to hear about the incident from town gossip. As he sat, he remembered the two of them discussing how the widow perked up with the celebration. Was that only the night before?

She soon appeared in the doorway, and he stood until she seated herself across from him. To Grant, she looked lovely—rested, almost peaceful. He attempted to capture the excitement of the previous evening rather than immediately inform her about Mrs. Lewis, but it proved impossible. She clearly saw through to his preoccupation.

"What's wrong?" she asked.

Grant reached for her hand and managed a faint smile. "I guess I don't do a very good job of hiding things."

"Is Rebecca all right? Is Miss Mimi ill?"

"They're both fine. Well, truthfully, Mimi has been better. I have some unpleasant news to tell you, a matter I'd prefer you hear from me." Strange how the mere touch of her hand eased the misfortunes of the day. "There's been a death."

Jenny's face paled. "Who?"

"Mrs. Lewis. Her heart failed her."

Clearly stunned, she shivered as though the cold chill of death had affected her physically. "But Mrs. Lewis looked wonderful at the wedding. And she seemed to really enjoy herself."

"I know, and I don't like being the one to tell you, but disturbing circumstances surround her passing."

Her gaze lifted questioningly. "I was the one who found her," he said. "Looks like someone broke into her house and frightened her into what resulted."

Jenny gasped. "How dreadful. Goodness, what about Ellen? She must be inconsolable with the news."

"I believe she'll be all right. I gave her a sedative, but she only knows about the passing—nothing else. Frank plans to tell her later."

"Should I go to her?"

The Jenny Martin he'd met a few weeks ago would not have been so quick to come to Ellen's aid. Perhaps Mimi's observation was correct. "That's very thoughtful, Jenny, but she'll rest through the night. Perhaps tomorrow if you're still inclined to visit."

"Yes, I'll leave directly after church. I'll need to give my regrets to the reverend and your mother. I told them I'd be there for dinner."

"And I need to do the same. You're more than welcome to join me."

She smiled. "Thank you. I don't want to be an imposition."

"Quite the contrary. Another woman may be exactly what Ellen needs—so she can cry and talk about her memories of Mrs. Lewis."

"So you believe simply listening is best?"

"Exactly, the best medicine."

Jenny stared at his hand covering hers, as though noticing it for the first time. She slowly drew it back. "How is Miss Mimi handling this?"

"She and Mrs. Lewis were good friends. Had been for years." He hesitated. "I despise this whole thing, Jenny. Whoever caused Mrs. Lewis's heart attack should be horsewhipped."

"Do you have any idea who's responsible?"

He shook his head. "Not at all. After I told Ben, he planned to search the house. Maybe he learned something then. Only Ellen could testify to anything missing."

Jenny glanced into the hallway that separated the parlor from the dining room. He followed her gaze and for the first time noted Aubrey Turner observing them. The man sauntered past and tipped his hat at Jenny. She pulled her drawstring bag into her lap and stiffened, then returned her attention to Grant.

"Why don't you go on home," she said. "You really need to be with Miss Mimi and get some rest."

Her sweet words eased the sadness swelling inside him. "I suppose you're right, and it's growing late. Thanks for taking time from your evening to see me."

"Oh, and I appreciate your being sensitive to my feelings. I'm so glad you were the one to tell me about Mrs. Lewis. It's hard for me to believe she's gone when just last night we laughed together about something Rebecca said."

They stood together and moved into the hallway and entrance of the boardinghouse. "Will you be able to escort me to church, or should I make other arrangements?"

The closeness of her stirred his senses. If he wasn't careful, he'd look like a fool, but he couldn't help himself. "I'll gladly come by for you."

Without thinking, he bent and kissed the petite young woman on the forehead. He saw astonishment spread quickly across her face along with a slow rise of red from her neck to her cheeks. Immediately, he regretted his impulsive action. A weighted silence reigned over them. What had he been thinking?

"I'm sorry," he said, with one hand on the doorknob. "I–I'll see you in the morning."

She didn't utter a word, and he could not bring himself to stare into her face.

Grant mumbled good night before closing the door behind him. *Idiot* pounded into his brain. He reminded himself of a love-struck schoolboy who stammered and fell all over himself. In his next breath, he defended his impromptu act. A casual kiss on the forehead meant nothing in 1895. He'd affectionately kissed the cheek of Bonnie, Casey, Mimi, and his mother, but they were family. *I shouldn't have taken such liberties without Jenny's permission. It's a wonder she didn't slap me.* He reached the street, paused momentarily, and retraced his steps.

Inside the boardinghouse, he found Jenny standing exactly where he'd left her. He instantly thought better of his decision to offer another apology. Why did foolishness seem to walk with him when it came to her?

"Grant?" Her face resembled a ripe tomato. "Did you forget something?"

"I neglected to tell you about another matter," he quickly said. "I'll most likely be a few minutes early in the morning so I can visit with my mother before church."

"I'll be ready," she said, still evading his gaze.

"Again, good night." He wasted no time in leaving the boardinghouse.

As he once more headed down the street, he thought about the following morning. He wished he had a more stylish wagon. His worn-out buckboard looked unsightly and was assuredly rough on the ladies. He could well afford a fashionable buggy. Mimi had complained about it for a long time, but he'd ignored her. At the time, spending money on a new buggy wasn't important. Now it bothered him. Expelling a labored breath, he hurried his pace toward home.

His thoughts circled back to Mrs. Lewis. He considered the vagrants of the town who might be under suspicion, but none came to mind. A few older boys tended to be reckless and wild in their ways—after all, he'd been one—but none of the town's youth had ever committed a serious crime. Grant had a gut feeling Kahlerville was dealing with more than a break-in, and he didn't like any of it.

Long after the others in his household slept, Grant remained on the front porch beneath a starlit night. Mimi grieved for her friend, and he knew she wouldn't sleep well even though he'd brewed her a cup of chamomile tea. Repeatedly, his troubled mind contemplated the events of the day. He prayed for trust and guidance until he felt a loving hand lead him to a decision, and his resolution required the confidence of a man in whom he could trust.

Jenny hesitated in the entranceway of the boardinghouse. Had Grant actually kissed her? She swallowed hard and touched her hand to her chest. Indeed, he had. A light kiss on the forehead meant fondness—like a man felt for an aunt or his mother. He most likely observed that type of behavior often. Should she feel honored or offended? One moment the memory of the soft look in his green eyes tingled through her, and in the next instant the kiss infuriated her. The idea he considered her on the level of an old maid kindled a fire in her blood. And to think he'd apologized for the kiss. She should have reminded him about the propriety of a gentleman.

"Miss Jenny, are you all right?"

The insufferable Aubrey Turner. She pasted on a smile and turned to face him. "I'm fine, Aubrey. And yourself?"

He nodded. "I wondered if the doctor had upset you and if I needed to defend your honor."

She caught her breath. *Defend my honor?* What was he implying? "Not at all. I'm sorry I gave you that impression."

"You looked lovely at the wedding last evening."

"Thank you. Ellen was a beautiful bride."

"Dare a woman with her past be a beautiful bride?"

The anger she'd held a few moments before with Grant she now directed at the man before her. "Excuse me?"

He offered a thin-lipped smile. "I'm sure you understand."

"I don't think her past is any of your concern."

"I just wonder how your parents would feel about the company you're keeping, since they believe you're in Boston."

An alarm sounded in her mind. How did he know this? "My parents know exactly where I am. And that, too, is none of your concern."

"I distinctly heard you at the train station tell them of your plans to visit friends in Boston."

He observed me even there? Fear seized her like a high fever. She whirled around and made her way to the stairway. What about this horrible man attracted Jessica? Praise God, Rebecca did not belong to him. She inwardly gasped. When had she begun to consider the existence of a deity?

The evening had been trying: Mrs. Lewis's passing, Grant's kiss, and now learning another detail about Aubrey Turner's following her in Cleveland. Perhaps it would all look better in the morning. The light of day always made the things of darkness fade. Odd, she hadn't thought of that expression in years. Grandma Martin used to say it.

Jenny raised the window in her room and crawled into bed. Summer Texas days and nights were merciless. At least a tree grew outside her window, and at night a breeze often cooled the stifling heat. In the morning a few wasps always buzzed about, but she'd rather chase them down than be bathed in perspiration.

Her mind raced with thoughts of the day. Too many unanswered questions. Grant puzzled her. She repeatedly denied her attraction to him, and then he gave her a chaste kiss. What had entered his mind to do such a thing? Weary and confused, she soon gave way to sleep.

Startled, Jenny shot up from the bed. What was that horrible smell? Her mind and body struggled in a maze of confusion. Then she recognized the origin. A skunk. And its scent floated through her open window. She threw back the thin coverlet and hurried to close it. Voices outside captured her attention, and she recognized Aubrey Turner's.

"We'll both stand here and smell like skunks all night before I let you go," Aubrey said. "I asked you a question, and I want an answer."

"Look, I have no idea about Martha's finances. She handles her girls and pays the bills."

"You were supposed to find out if she came into money after the Martin girl died."

"And I told you nothing had been reported at the bank."

Martha's Place was the brothel where Jessica and Ellen had worked. Why was Aubrey interested in her finances? And who was the second man? She covered her nose and took a peek out the window. The shadowy figures of two men were directly across the street.

"If you value your reputation, you'll get me the bank records," Aubrey said. "I'd hate for you to end up like Howe."

The man he shot. She held her breath.

"Are you threatening me?"

Aubrey laughed. "You have a lot to lose if I go to the folks of this town with what I know."

"All right. I'll get your information."

Is this something I should tell the sheriff or Grant about? Jenny held her breath and continued to watch the two men part ways. Aubrey was dangerous—she sensed it deep in her bones. She eased the window down and crept back to bed. In the shadows her gaze drifted to her reticule where her revolver had taken up permanent residence.

CHAPTER  17

The following morning, Reverend Rainer announced Mrs. Lewis's sudden heart attack. The funeral services were scheduled for the afternoon. As soon as he dismissed the congregation, Grant and Jenny left Piney Woods Church to visit Ellen.

"I'm nervous about seeing Ellen," Jenny said. "I'm not very confident about what I should say or do. Listening doesn't seem to be enough, but what else is there?"

Grant wished she understood how God could be her strength, but he could only take comfort in the hope that she'd soon come to know the Lord.

"It's not so difficult." He observed her confusion. "I used to think the best way to help a person deal with tragedy was to get them thinking about something else."

"And it's not?" she asked. "Wouldn't dwelling on it make her miserable?"

Grant paused for a moment, remembering his own past thoughts about the matter. "For a long time I felt the same way, but the reverend told me it is for ourselves we mourn. Ellen knows Mrs. Lewis is happy and at peace with Jesus. Her tears are for herself and the guilt she wrongly assumes for the despicable way the widow died. She will miss the dear lady and their friendship. They were extremely close."

Jenny sat quietly, obviously contemplating his words. "You make sense. In fact, a month ago my response might have been completely different. My whole perspective on life has changed since I've come to Kahlerville." She shifted on the seat. "I'm afraid I'll cry with her."

"Then do so. Ellen won't be ashamed of her tears. You shouldn't be, either. Right now she needs a good friend, and I believe you two have enough in common for her to relax and speak her heart."

She stiffened and lifted her chin slightly. "All right. I'll do my best."

Grant silently struggled with his decision to take her along. Perhaps he should have taken Mimi or his mother. After all, could Jenny really be a solace when she didn't know the Lord?

At the Kahler home, Ellen greeted them at the door dressed in a simple dark skirt and blouse. Her eyes were red and swollen, but she fared much better than the previous day. "Please come in, and thank you so much for coming." Her lips quivered, and she took in a breath. "Jenny, you are a dear to take time from your day to stop by. And, Grant, I apologize for yesterday. I didn't mean to be such a bother."

"Nonsense, I was glad to help. I trust you slept last night?"

"Oh, yes. I'm ashamed of myself for sleeping so late that I missed church." Instead of escorting them into the parlor, Ellen pointed toward the kitchen. "We were just putting the food together for after the funeral. People started bringing things yesterday afternoon." She choked back a sob. "There's even wedding cake left."

"Let us help," Jenny said. "And I'll be here right after the funeral, too."

Ellen hugged her, bringing a fresh sprinkling of tears to both of their faces. "You are a jewel, and we won't refuse the help."

Frank met them in the hallway. In its narrow depth, he more closely resembled a giant in his overalls and chambray shirt. The two men shook hands.

Grant removed his jacket and rolled up his sleeves. "I'm ready to work. Just tell me what to do."

"Thanks. This town has always been good to me," Ellen said. "The people reached out and helped me when I had nowhere to go. Their kindness with Mrs. Lewis's passing is another blessing."

Grant observed Jenny from the corner of his eye. She appeared poised in every respect except for her reddened eyes. How were proper ladies supposed to conduct themselves in the face of such a tragedy? Did it really matter that she was here and attempting to fit into small-town life? But why?

Is she trying to prove to me that she can care for Rebecca better than me?

A week went by, and Ben failed to find any clues or suspects in the vandalism. Strangely enough, Ellen discovered nothing missing from the house. It served to frighten not only her but also the residents in and around town. Folks were nervous and cautious in their daily activities, unable to relax and go about their business. The idea of anyone willfully destroying personal property shocked and alarmed them. Men refused to leave their wives and children alone at night, and women barred their doors in the daytime.

Grant heard rumors of a similar happening in a town about forty miles west of Kahlerville. The authorities didn't find any clues or suspects there, either.

"Folks sure are jumpy," Mimi said on Sunday evening after Rebecca had gone to bed.

Grant frowned. "We haven't seen much violence in a long time. Oh, we have the occasional shooting, but few incidents involving innocent folks since those two outlaws shot it out on Morgan's ranch years ago. I heard a couple of old men at the general store say the outlaw's ghost was to blame for Mrs. Lewis's death. I despise folks speculating on ridiculous tales, so I told them that outlaw was dead and buried. After all, I was there."

Mimi picked up her sewing basket and one of Rebecca's petticoats to mend. "When do you think the gossip will end?"

He speculated for a moment. "I think time or catching the culprits, preferably the latter, should stop wagging tongues and settle down folks."

He wondered if the guilty persons would ever be found. He'd heard enough tall tales to last a lifetime. More presumed cases of heart problems than ever before came through his office. His patients were simply scared.

Concern for Jenny's safety nudged at Grant's conscience. He didn't like the idea of her living alone at the boardinghouse. The owners of the establishment were good people, but it didn't stop undesirables from renting rooms. His protective nature drew him closer to her, but he kept his distance with his heart. He still maintained his busy schedule and ruled out any thoughts of a romantic involvement. Jenny visited Rebecca daily, and Mimi often encouraged her to stay for meals. Outwardly, nothing changed between the two, but Grant sensed the pains of unapproachable love. What good did denying his feelings do when he desired her company?

❧

The musical bell above the door of Kahler's General Store sounded on Monday morning as Jenny stepped through and searched for Ellen. Her new friend's sweet smile always reminded her of flowers nodding in the sunshine. There she stood straightening the candy bin. Most likely Grant had been there, for the licorice jar was nearly empty.

"Good morning," Jenny called. "How is my friend's first week of marriage?"

"Perfect." Ellen's voice fairly sang. "Despite what happened afterward, God has blessed us with so much. I'm glad you're here. I wanted to ask you some—"

The bell tinkled again, and a matronly woman sashayed in. Dressed in a proper navy blue dress and a plumed hat, she took up the whole store.

"Good morning, Martha," Ellen said. "How are you?"

"It's Mrs. DeMott to you," the woman said. "And I'm not doing well at all."

"Why is that?" Ellen asked.

"I've heard rumors." Mrs. DeMott slid a dark gaze in Jenny's direction.

"What kind? I recently married. Was that it?"

Mrs. DeMott ran a finger of her glove across the top of the counter. She examined the finger, then sighed deeply. "I understand that you and Miss Jenny Martin here are planning to open your own business to rival my establishment."

Is this the owner of Martha's brothel? Jenny stopped short of gasping in horror.

Ellen's eyes widened. "I assure you that we do not have any such intentions."

"I was told you'd deny it until you stole away my girls."

Jenny felt as though her tongue stuck to the roof of her mouth. She could neither think of a response to the preposterous claim nor form the words to repudiate it.

Ellen folded her hands at her waist. She appeared calm, with no trace of agony or anger.

Where is Ellen's God in all of this? First Mrs. Lewis dies and now this horrible gossip? Jenny waited, her mouth agape.

"Mrs. DeMott," Ellen replied, "I am happily married. I help out my husband's parents here, and my Frank is starting a lumberyard. I do not have any desire to persuade any of your girls other than to enlighten them to the ways of the Lord and urge them to leave the life of prostitution."

"And I forbid you to come near my business again for any reason." Mrs. DeMott added a curse word to punctuate her meaning. "I've already lost another girl to your preaching. I have the means of destroying you, Ellen." She shook a gloved finger in Ellen's face. "I'd hate to have *your* Frank's lumberyard burn to the ground."

"There is no need to threaten me. Your source of information is wrong."

Mrs. DeMott swung her attention to Jenny. "True or false, heed my warning. Your sister gave me more trouble than she was worth, and I won't be duped by a pretty face and a clever word again. Do you understand?"

Jenny struggled with a response. "As. . .as Ellen just told you, we have no such plans."

Mrs. DeMott's menacing glare would have caused an outlaw to back away. "I already know all about you from someone who knows you better than anyone in this town." With those final words, she whirled around and made her way to the door. Her skirts swished, and her backside turned from right to left as though a hundred men gawked with plenty of money in their pockets.

Once she left, the silence seemed to roar in Jenny's ears. "Where did she get such vile information?"

Ellen crossed her arms over her chest. "Think, Jenny. Who despises us enough to gossip?"

Those two ladies from the wedding reception? "I'm not sure."

"There are plenty of women in this town who look down on me, but none is capable of such treachery. Normally, Martha is very proper in public, which tells me she is upset." Ellen paused. "She distinctively said to you, 'who knows you better than anyone in town.'"

"No one but Grant or. . .Aubrey Turner." She lifted her gaze to Ellen's face, clearly clothed in anger. "Do you think he did this?"

"Without a doubt. Grant has no dealings with that woman unless to tend to someone ill. Turner, on the other hand, has already established himself as a man who followed you here from Ohio and shot a man in a card game."

Jenny's stomach did the familiar churning. "Why?"

Ellen hesitated to answer. "I don't know, but I do know where the answers might be."

"Who should I talk to?"

"Jessica."

Irritated, Jenny thought this must be a part of Christianity with which she was unfamiliar. "But she's gone."

"Remember I said I wanted to talk to you about something? I have Jessica's journal. She gave it to me when she went into labor. I've kept it but not read a word. I would have given it to you sooner, except I wanted to make sure it was the proper thing to do."

"A journal? She used to write in one faithfully when we were younger."

Ellen nodded. "She continued. Can you come by on Wednesday morning? I don't have to work then. I'm worried that Turner may be dangerous, and if he's mentioned in Jessica's journal, we may find out more about him. Ben is working on the matter, but he may need specific information. . .information that may be in the journal."

Jenny took a ragged breath. Fear settled on her—as though an invisible army sought to do her harm. "I'll be there. Why haven't you read it?"

"Jessica said for me to keep it until you came looking for her."

"She said that?" For the first time Jenny realized her sister had known her far better than she ever comprehended.

Ellen stepped toward her and wrapped her arms around Jenny's trembling shoulders. "Jessica loved you very much. Forgive me for saying this, but she felt your parents had mistreated you. Jessica believed one day you'd break free of them and come looking for her." She shrugged. "I thought at the time her thinking was wishful. Our Jessica felt such loneliness—and bitterness for far too many things." Ellen paused. "Would you do something for me?"

"Of course."

"Please tell Grant about Martha's visit. The accusation is a delicate matter, and it may be difficult for you, but he may be able to persuade Ben to work faster. I'll do the same with Frank."

"All right. I'll go this very minute, and if he is seeing patients, I'll wait until he's finished. I don't want to put an undue burden upon him, but I'll do what you ask."

Grant sat across from Jenny beneath the cool shade of a live oak at the back of his house. Rebecca had fallen asleep during lunch and rested peacefully not far from them. A breeze picked up a chestnut curl and toyed with it before gently placing it on her forehead. If he could keep her innocence forever, he'd be a happy man. Did all fathers feel this way?

He pulled a black-eyed Susan from his hair where Rebecca had stuck it earlier. How odd he must look to Jenny—the town's doctor giving in to the whims of a tiny girl.

His gaze rested on Jenny. Ignoring his affection for her seemed to be a constant battle. She'd come to speak to him, and whatever the reason, paleness had taken residence on her face. Had she grown more beautiful since arriving in Kahlerville?

"What's wrong?" he asked. "Do you not feel well?"

She stood. "May we walk a bit?" She glanced at Rebecca. "I didn't want to say anything upsetting before she napped."

Grant joined her. His natural instinct was to question her further, but instead, he waited for her to speak. What if she'd gone ahead and hired a fancy lawyer?

"I visited Ellen at the general store today," she said. "While we were chatting, a woman came inside, a Mrs. Martha DeMott."

Grant raised a brow.

"She accused Ellen and me of starting our own—own. . ." Jenny's face changed from near white to rose-red. "A business like hers."

The thought caused a bubble of mirth in his throat, but he chased it away. "You and Ellen?"

She glanced away. "Yes, and of trying to steal her. . .her workers."

"She doesn't know either of you very well, does she?"

"There's more. We denied the accusation, but Mrs. DeMott insisted that her information was accurate. She told Ellen never to speak to her. . .her ladies again. I had no idea that Ellen visits there to persuade them to leave Martha's employ. Anyway, Mrs. DeMott threatened Ellen. She indicated something could happen to Frank's lumberyard."

Fury bubbled through Grant's veins, hotter than a Texas day in August. "She what? Have you talked to Ben?"

Jenny shook her head. "Not yet. I wanted to talk to you about it first. And Ellen intended to tell Frank." She hesitated.

"What else?"

"Oh, I'm thinking that bothering you with this is improper."

"Nonsense. Did Mrs. DeMott give you any idea who told her this?"

"No, but Ellen and I think it might be Aubrey Turner."

"Any particular reason why?"

Jenny rubbed her gloved palms together. "Mrs. DeMott said the person who told her was someone who knew me better than anyone else in Kahlerville."

"Aubrey Turner, the scoundrel," Grant murmured. "Excuse me, I shouldn't be judging him. However, I do think the man's capable of spreading gossip, but I don't know why. Could he be so infatuated with you that he's desperate?"

"I hardly think so." She shuddered. "I've never encouraged him."

Grant studied the petite young woman beside him. Like the grass beneath their feet swaying in the wind, she trembled. "You're frightened."

"A little. And I'm fearful for Ellen."

"Frank will protect her. Ben's been looking for a reason to run Turner out of town. I think the time has come for you to live someplace other than the boardinghouse."

"I'm perfectly fine there." She raised her chin.

"How can you protect yourself from Turner?"

She lifted her wrist that held her drawstring bag that she never went anywhere without. "I have a revolver in my reticule."

He stopped dead still in his shoes. "You what?"

She glanced about as though someone might hear. "I have a revolver in my reticule."

"Is it loaded?"

"Yes."

"Do you know how to use it?"

"Ellen showed me how to load and fire it. I've been practicing."

"Mercy, Jenny." If the situation hadn't been so serious, he'd have burst out laughing. What was it about him and Morgan that caused them to fall for gun-totin' women? "You can't carry a weapon on you like a piece of armor."

"Why not? I believe he can be dangerous."

"This is nearly the twentieth century. Ben's a good sheriff. Looking out for folks is his job. What if you accidentally shoot yourself?"

"I hadn't thought of an accident."

Obviously. "Please give me the gun, and let's go talk to Ben. He may even have found information to run Turner out of town or arrest him."

"What about your patients?"

He narrowed his brows. "Would you wait for me?"

She smiled and nodded. "I think I'd like to sit on the blanket with Rebecca. I love watching her sleep."

Grant should have felt secure, except he wasn't certain she had abandoned her plan of taking his daughter from him.

"You don't trust me?" Irritation laced every word.

"I didn't say that."

"But you were thinking it."

"Would you? I mean—" He stepped back and inhaled deeply. "If she were your daughter, would you leave her alone with someone who wanted to take her from you?"

Her eyes widened, reminding him of smoke signals. "Thank you very much, Dr. Andrews. I'll keep my gun, and I'll take care of Aubrey Turner and Mrs. DeMott without your assistance." She stomped away.

"Jenny, wait. Let's talk about this. Be reasonable."

She whirled around and nearly fell. "I am being reasonable."

What a stubborn woman. "I will be at the boardinghouse when I finish with patients."

"I'm not seeing callers."

"Fine. Then I'll go see Ben."

"I'm on my way there now."

"You aren't getting rid of me easily," he said.

"You. . .you impossible, horrible man. I thought that is what you wanted."

He paused for a moment to catch his breath. "It isn't. Not at all."

"You make absolutely no sense. How ever did you manage your way through medical school?" Jenny flung her words like stones, then turned and stomped toward the house, flinging her arms like Rebecca's rag doll.

Jenny was right. He made about as much sense when it came to her as he would if he stayed awake all night to see if he snored.

CHAPTER  18

Jenny toyed with the envelope in her hand. Her gaze took in the familiar handwriting and the postmark. Memories of the massive brick home, its rich, dark decor, and the sullen maids and creative gardener crept across her mind. Heaviness weighed on her as though she'd been forced to carry a load of bricks.

She shivered. Apprehension mounted the longer she held the missive in her hands. The letter came from home.

Outside her open window on this late Tuesday morning, sounds from the busy street continued uninterrupted: the *clop-clop* of horses, the shout of one man greeting another, a dog barking, and a child's infectious laughter. But nothing pulled her attention from the letter in her hand. She hoped the contents indicated her parents were satisfied, even pleased with her, but deep inside, she knew otherwise. In an attempt to perceive what was right and wrong, Jenny had conveyed to them what she'd done and begged for them to understand her desire to learn more about Jessica's death and the particulars of her sister's illegitimate daughter.

Jenny had taken great pride in her description of Rebecca and the doctor who had adopted her. She told them about his close-knit family and how kind they'd been since her arrival.

Distressing recollections of her father's domination flooded over her. She recalled his lectures that went on for hours. Once when she was twelve, he demanded she sit perfectly straight on the piano bench for four hours while he lectured on the value of practicing. Another time when she and Jessica were in their teens, they were forced to stand for eight hours until they could recite a large portion of *Hamlet* word for word. He ruled his household harshly with moments of rage and great excitability. Father valued education and discipline above all other things in life, and he measured success by money and power. To him nothing else mattered—not personal relationships, friends, or family.

And Mother never disputed his word. Jessica alone defied his strict directives. Jessica and Father's arguments resembled more a fierce thunderstorm than a father-daughter difference of opinion. Listening to them verbally battle often made Jenny physically ill. She'd done anything to seek her parents' approval and agreed with them no matter how badly it hurt her sister. Were those times so long ago?

With a sigh, her thoughts returned to the present. The envelope smelled faintly of vanilla, her mother's favorite stationery used only for special occasions. *At least my reply warranted her best stationery.*

Familiar trepidation whirled around in the pit of her stomach. For a moment she feared a repeat of what the train ride from Cleveland had done to her. Did she really want to read the contents of the letter? Her hands shook so badly that she nearly dropped it. Taking a deep breath, Jenny used a hairpin to release the seal.

Dear Jennifer,

Your father and I are greatly distraught by your missive. We both assumed your unescorted trip to Boston would be of importance in strengthening your independence and thus ensuring the stability necessary for your role as Mrs. Oscar Watkins. We also believed you intended to visit friends and your

*arrangements to leave school without completing the year were
warranted. Now we learn by your own admittance that you
deliberately deceived us and embarked upon a foolish journey to
locate your sister's child.*

*Your father and I have discussed your impudent behavior
and have concluded your character more closely resembles that of
your late sister. This audacious nature of both of our daughters is
most disheartening. It appears that you, like Jessica, take great
pleasure in rebelling against us. Neither Jessica nor you have
any appreciation or respect for the sacrifices your dear father and
I have made on your behalf.*

*We have no desire to hear, see, or receive any information
concerning this alleged granddaughter. Jessica's memory
vanished when she left our home with the rogue who led her
astray. I dare say the two were well suited for each other. And I
venture to say the good doctor who adopted her baby is probably
the father and did so for conscience' sake. We do not recognize
such a disgrace. Even if Jessica had lived, we would not under
any circumstances be in contact with her or the child.*

*In addition, we find it deplorable of Jessica to have
chosen her grandmother's name for her illegitimate offspring.
Grandmother Martin may have been eccentric in her actions
and fanatic in her religious convictions, but she did not deserve
the shame of a namesake through a misbegotten child.*

*Jennifer, as your mother, I beg of you to come home and
reconcile with your father. Already he speaks of disowning you.
He has spoken of your behavior to Oscar, who remains your
devoted friend and insists you must be ill to have endeavored
upon such a furtive journey. Oscar is anxiously awaiting your
response to his proposal. He has yet to receive any correspondence
from you.*

*I personally feel Jessica's influence upon your character
tainted your excellent upbringing. We hoped you would escape*

*her impulsive behavior, but evidently our desires did not
enter your thoughts. My heart is greatly grieved with this
present state of happenings. Of a certainty, our position in the
community is under great scrutiny as some of our friends are
beginning to ask questions about your whereabouts. Please, I
implore you, leave those common people and come back home
where you belong. It is still not too late to save yourself from the
same fate as your sister.*

Mother

Jenny wasn't aware of holding her breath until she finished reading the letter. Exhaling deeply, she meticulously refolded the vanilla-scented stationery, placed it inside the envelope, and laid it on the bed. She rose to her feet and stepped in front of the dresser mirror, eyeing herself critically.

I look like the same person who left Cleveland.

Turning her hands over to view her palms, then back again to examine her slender fingers, she realized she'd played the piano but a few times since her arrival in Kahlerville. Nevertheless, the ability existed. Nothing about her physical appearance had changed.

But she felt different.

Jenny couldn't recall when the transition had happened, but she realized that just beyond her reach was more happiness than she could ever hope to find. Decidedly so, the whole process had begun the moment she had stepped down from the train in Kahlerville. The kindness and acceptance of new friends shattered her original thoughts and plans. The child she desired for selfish reasons had reached out and touched her with love and joy. No longer did she yearn to rob Grant of Rebecca—even though she was furious with him about his reluctance to leave her alone with the little girl. She could no more follow through with such a loathsome scheme than deny her love for Jessica. . .or the secret fondness she carried in her heart for Grant.

Without the influence of her parents, Jenny sensed a newfound freedom that exhilarated her very being. Something was lacking in her life, like a piece missing from an intricate puzzle. Many nights she wakened to find herself no longer afraid of the future, feeling an unmistakable anticipation taking precedence over the old loneliness.

The answer lay in the precious people of Kahlerville. Perhaps Jessica had felt the love of God in them. When she walked in their midst, had she sensed their goodness and peace wrap around her like a down comforter on a cold night? Had she felt this warmth in Grant when the agony of her unborn child's future weighed heavily upon her heart?

Jessica, I wish I knew what you were thinking those last few days before giving birth. I can't bring you back, but I desperately need to understand why you came here and why you stayed. Were you mad, as our father often claimed? Or were you merely misunderstood?

Jenny determined to read the journal in hopes of learning more about Jessica. The mystery behind Aubrey's relationship with her sister and why Jessica came to Kahlerville tormented her. She recalled a portion of last Sunday evening's sermon. Reverend Rainer had stated that mercy meant reaching out to meet someone else's need. Grant and his family had followed those instructions for Jessica— and now for her. Yet life would be more pleasant if she and Grant ceased to quarrel.

She realized God wanted her to step into His embrace, but the thought of a commitment left her confused and fearful of her parents. She glanced at the letter on the dresser. Mother and Father were angry and threatening to disown her. What was left to fear from them? Yet she couldn't turn her life over to God. What if He demanded more than she could relinquish? Her music and teaching were an important part of her life, and He might ask her to forsake them. Would she suddenly possess love, mercy, and forgiveness for others, or would it be a long process?

The teachings were impossible.

Not wanting to deliberate the matter any further, she focused on her pangs of hunger. Hopefully, Aubrey had eaten earlier, but if not, she'd take the food to her room. Snatching up the key and her reticule with the loaded revolver, she locked the door and descended the stairs to where the enticing smells of chicken and biscuits beckoned her. Seeing Aubrey might unleash the anger simmering for what she believed he'd said to Mrs. DeMott. Jenny smiled. She'd welcome the opportunity to give him a taste of her temper.

An array of people bustled about the dining room. Some were boarders, and others were townspeople who relished the cook's mouth-watering dishes. She inwardly smiled. Cleo Ann was not the cook—her few attempts had been disastrous. But the woman always wore a smile. Jenny never noticed things like that in Ohio.

"Won't you sit with us, dear?" said an elderly lady, Mrs. Benson.

Jenny saw only one available chair at the table and quickly accepted. Now she could enjoy her noon meal in pleasant company without the threat of Aubrey. The three ladies present were widows who met once a week for a quilting afternoon. Midway through their meal, one of the women turned to her.

"Miss Martin, you certainly have put a smile on our doctor's face since you came to town." Mrs. Benson's clouded eyes twinkled.

"Oh, I don't think it has anything to do with me, and do call me Jenny." She sensed the warm glow of a blush creep up her neck. Mrs. Benson would think differently if she'd heard their latest quarrel the day before.

"Fiddlesticks," said Mrs. Cropper, a pencil-thin woman. "He needs a wife—makes a man complete."

Jenny took a deep breath. "You see, Rebecca's mother was my sister. The child is why I came to Kahlerville."

Not one eyebrow lifted closer to their gray heads.

Mrs. Cropper smiled. "Ah, now I see why you and the little one look so much alike. Yes, must be a match made in heaven."

"Now, ladies," Mrs. Benson said, striking an authoritative pose.

"Tsk. Tsk. We're making Miss Martin feel uncomfortable, and I was the one who asked her to join us. We need to hush and let her eat in peace."

Jenny offered her sweetest smile to Mrs. Benson. While their topics of conversation moved to other things, she sorted out her ever-growing fondness for Grant, realizing she felt more than mere admiration or friendship, but not knowing exactly when that change had happened.

Yesterday he'd been furious about Martha DeMott's accusation, but then he'd made Jenny furious with his caution about Rebecca. Up until that time, he'd been quite concerned about her safety and well-being. She contemplated their harsh words for a moment. She really couldn't blame him. Perhaps she should apologize. He'd tried to see her, but she'd refused.

Would Grant take such an interest in her unless he had deeper feelings? But she hadn't done anything to deserve his favor. Noticeably, she'd done quite the contrary.

Jenny sipped her tea. She felt the whole world could see her discomfort around Grant. When those encounters occurred, she vowed to gain control of her heart. But the resolve lasted only until the next time she saw him.

After politely excusing herself from the ladies, she mounted the stairs to her room. Fortunately, Aubrey had been nowhere in sight.

Jenny read the afternoon away, a wonderful novel by Jane Austen entitled *Emma,* and later took a walk through town. Always the letter fixed foremost in her mind. This afternoon it took precedence over Grant and Rebecca. Back in her room, she reflected on what tomorrow might bring with Jessica's journal. Her gaze rested on the outline of the letter on the dresser.

She lit the kerosene lamp and reread the contents in hopes she had misinterpreted her mother's words. This time she mulled over every one, twisting and turning each thought. When she finished, Jenny carefully creased the folds until it looked as though it hadn't been removed from the envelope.

Oscar deserved an explanation, and she intended to write tonight and tell him she could not accept his proposal. He had always treated her with the utmost kindness, and this was not his fault. She clearly took the blame. But for right now, the proper words to communicate to her parents escaped her. She lived in a state of confusion and unrest amid the most wonderful people in the world. How would Mother and Father interpret that? They had given her the best of everything: education, fine clothes, social status, and an honored name in the community. She loved and respected them for all the things they'd done for her, but she disagreed with their views about Jessica, the people of Kahlerville, and even God. Her mother and father lived in a melancholy state. She doubted if they were conscious of it. Grant was right—she didn't want to subject Rebecca to that life. Why hadn't she told him those very words yesterday?

With the scent of her mother's favorite stationery in her nostrils, Jenny pulled the chamber pot from under the bed and tossed the letter inside. Gasping, she immediately regretted the impulsive act. She hadn't discarded her parents—only their words.

CHAPTER  19

Grant finally closed the door to his office shortly after five. He'd had a steady stream of patients all afternoon, which had kept his mind off the confrontation with Jenny the previous day. That woman could perplex a saint. He simply lost all manner of logic the moment she cast those big brown eyes his way. Maybe he should have shot that deer long ago and established himself at the ripe old age of twelve as a grand hunter. Then maybe he wouldn't fall slave to those doelike eyes of hers.

Not likely. I was the prey the moment she came to town.

To make matters worse, a sickly child bothered him, a four-year-old little boy who'd weighed barely five pounds at birth. He was now the same size as two-and-a-half-year-old Rebecca. Grant realized he might lose him, and he sensed a helplessness that depressed him. Ofttimes he questioned God's wisdom when children perished needlessly. Parents grieved and wished their own bodies lay still in the grave instead of a precious new life. Grant prayed that some day medicine would help more children to survive. The thought of living without Rebecca tormented his soul. Praise God, she rarely became ill, and he kept a watchful eye on Jenny's activities to make sure she didn't snatch his daughter away. Life held more blessings than he took the time to acknowledge.

He made his way into the kitchen, where he inhaled a tantalizing beef roast. Mimi had the garden bucket in her hand, and Rebecca played with her favorite doll on the floor, chatting away like a magpie.

"Do I have time to see Ben before supper?" he asked Mimi.

She glanced about. "I believe so. I haven't started the biscuits, shucked the corn, or picked a few peppers and cucumbers. Rebecca and I helped your mother can tomatoes today, and we were late getting home."

At the sound of her name, his daughter smiled from her position on the floor. "I helped Grandpa in the church."

"Good. You are my angel." He picked her up and planted a kiss on her peachy cheek. "Sure smells good in here," he said and stared hungrily at the stove.

Mimi eyed him curiously. "Did you and the lady quarrel again?" she asked.

"A little."

She shook her head. "I thought so."

He didn't ask her why for fear she'd want to know the details and give her opinion about how to resolve the matter. "I might try to see her before coming home."

"Are you going to see Aunt Jenny?" Rebecca asked.

I've got to watch more carefully what I say. "I might see her if I get finished with Uncle Ben soon enough."

"Can I go?"

Those dark eyes were hard to resist. "Not this time, sugar. Miss Jenny will be back to see you soon."

"She'll be here early tomorrow morning for a baking lesson," Mimi said with a laugh. "Although I'd rather hear her play piano. When she touches those keys, sounds like all of heaven stops to listen."

Rebecca smiled and wrapped her arms around his neck. "Goodie."

If only making Jenny happy could be this simple. He grabbed his hat and headed to the sheriff's office.

~~~

"What do you think about Martha's threat to Ellen and Jenny?" Grant asked.

Ben stood outside the sheriff's office and glanced down the street toward the town's eyesore. The church sat farther down the road than the brothel. "I'd like nothing better than to shut her down, and she knows it. But some of the town's money is invested there. Every time I try to put her and her girls on a train, I get stabbed in the back with politics." He blew out an exasperated sigh. "Believe me. She'll get a good tongue-lashing from me about it. After all, Ellen is my sister-in-law, and I'm proud of her."

"Do you think Ellen and Jenny are overreacting to the idea that Turner put Martha up to it?"

"Probably not. I keep wondering why he's hanging around. If he was engaged to Jessica and she left him before she came here, why is he so interested in Kahlerville now?"

"And why did he follow Jenny?"

"I'm not turning up a thing on him. If he's wanted, he's using a different name."

"That's reassuring."

"And I can't do a thing unless he breaks the law." Ben broke into a fit of coughing.

"When are you going to see me about that cough?"

"It's nothing. A little summer cold."

"It's getting worse."

Ben frowned. "Look, I'll talk to Martha. Once Frank hears about this tonight, he'll be ready to burn down her brothel before anyone gets the chance to burn his lumberyard. Sure would hate to put my own brother in jail."

Grant peered into Ben's face. When had he grown so pale? "And I'll expect you to stop by the house so I can give you some medicine for your cough."

Ben waved him away. "I'm too busy for such nonsense."

"How—"

"Please. I've got too much on my mind right now with the baby coming and this business with Turner."

Grant understood. When Ben felt so bad he couldn't work, then he'd come see the doctor. "Let me know what I can do."

Ben simply nodded. "I'll stop by after I talk to Martha."

No eye contact. No smile. The glazed look in his eyes indicated a fever.

Jenny took a deep breath and knocked on Grant's front door. She hadn't seen him since their argument on Monday, and neither had he tried to contact her again at the boardinghouse. He must be furious with her, just as she'd been with him. The more she pondered the matter, the more she realized Grant had no reason to trust her. She'd been trouble for him since the day she fell off the train and greeted him with vomit on her dress and a treacherous plan in her heart.

As difficult as it might be, she needed to apologize. If only the proper words would magically come to mind to set her heart at ease. But if she truly had abandoned her desire to take Rebecca, then she should leave Kahlerville soon. A deep yearning surfaced. She never wanted to leave. She wanted to stay in this town forever. How foolish. How very foolish. Not even her teaching position or friends tempted her to return to Cleveland.

The door creaked open, interrupting her musings. Jenny breathed relief when Mimi welcomed her inside.

"I hope I'm not too early," Jenny said. "It's not even dawn, but I wanted to take a loaf of our bread to Ellen's this morning."

"Nonsense. I'm always up and about at this time. And we do want your bread to rise nicely."

Jenny peered about.

"He's in his office. Most likely talking to God. You should do the same."

Jenny reddened.

"You and Grant must still be in a tiff. Land sakes alive, girl, can't you two see what the rest of us already know?" Mimi stared into her face with wrinkled wisdom and insight that sent Jenny's heart into a whirlwind of emotions.

"What are you saying?" Jenny asked.

Mimi placed her hands on her ample hips and waddled down the hallway to the kitchen. "Let me tell you a story."

Obviously, Mimi planned to enlighten her about the whole matter whether she wanted to hear the story or not.

"There's a man who comes to see Grant real regular. Don't know why. He's healthy as a horse. He and my husband, God rest his soul, were best friends. Whenever Jake comes by, he always stops to see me. I always act like I'm too busy and put-out with him interfering in my day. But the truth of the matter is, the moment I know he's here, I bustle about the kitchen making fresh coffee and tidying up myself."

"I don't understand."

"I pretend he's the last person I want to see when he's really the only one I want to see."

Jenny gasped. "I think you must be wrong. Grant and I—"

"Grant and I what?"

Jenny swung around to see the object of her bewilderment.

"Good morning. You're here early. I thought I heard my name."

Jenny would like nothing better than to sink through the floor. What had he heard? Best she ignore his comment. "Mimi and I are baking bread this morning."

He smiled. Avoiding him might be easier if he had a mole on

the end of his nose. . .or smelled bad. . .or his eyes weren't such an incredible shade of green.

"I'm sure Rebecca will be thrilled to see you."

But you're not? "We'll have a good time. I'm sure of it." She hesitated. "Do you have a minute to talk privately?"

"Of course. We could step outside."

She followed him while her heart pounded faster than a hummingbird's wings. The predawn darkness hid her flushed face, for which she was thankful. A dose of a potion guaranteed to calm her shaking limbs would be most appreciated.

"I want to apologize for my behavior on Monday." The words gushed out like a boiling pot overflowing the brim. "I understand how you couldn't possibly trust me." She sucked in a breath, then added, "When I've never given you a reason to think I'm trustworthy."

The imposing silence shattered what little poise she had remaining.

"I've given up on taking Rebecca back to Cleveland. She belongs here with you. I can see that now." She willed her heart to cease its incessant pounding.

Grant pointed toward the east, where shades of purple, pink, and orange slowly spread across the horizon. "Would you look at that? Absolutely beautiful. I was awake most of the night pacing the floor of my room with too many matters on my mind. I talked, and God listened. Everything looked black. And when I went to my window, there wasn't even a star in the sky. Here is the beginning of a new day, and it nearly takes my breath away." He turned toward her and reached for her hand. "Thank you, Jenny. I believe it's going to be a grand day."

Confused to the point she might not recognize her own name, Jenny allowed him to take her arm and walk back inside the house. What a strange response to her confession. Of course, she'd been confused since the day she met him.

CHAPTER  20

Jenny stood alongside the white picket fence of Frank and Ellen's home and admired the charm of the small, newly built home. She smelled paint and noted the sparkle of dark green shutters, wet and shiny in the midmorning sun. Two large clay pots of red geraniums rested on each side of the front steps, and purple and white petunias bordered a red brick walkway. A welcome sign from the gate beckoned her to lift the gate's latch and walk inside. Her gaze swept over a porch swing and on to a display of green plants and a huge hanging fern. The scent of honeysuckle drew her attention to the far end where a white trellis supported a climbing vine filled with tubular deep orange blooms. She hadn't noticed the home's charm on the day of Mrs. Lewis's funeral. But the vision this morning was like a scene lifted from a painting.

"How lovely," she whispered.

The low growl and fierce bark of a dog sent tremors up her spine, and she remembered Grant cautioning her to be wary until she made friends with the Kahlers' animal. A long time ago she'd been chased by a huge dog, and ever since then, she feared all of them. With a sigh of relief, she realized the ominous sound came from inside the house.

She climbed the steps and lifted the metal door knocker. Her gaze rested on a walnut-stained plaque engraved with the words of Joshua 24:15: "Choose you this day whom ye will serve. . .but as for me and my house, we will serve the LORD." She tipped the rocker beside her and watched it gently sway back and forth.

Jenny wanted this day to be a time to deepen her friendship with Ellen. The journal had seized Jenny's interest, and she longed to read it, but the prospect of a true friend also lifted her spirits.

The door opened, and the strawberry blond, dressed in a gray skirt and white beaded blouse, met Jenny with open arms. "I'm so glad you came. Your last visit here was not a happy one. Do come inside."

A huge golden dog growled at her waist, and Jenny's pulse quickened.

"General Lee, hush." Ellen gave Jenny a reassuring smile. "He won't bother you. Actually, he's very well behaved."

Jenny lifted an eyebrow and glanced nervously at him.

"Really, he is. I can put him outside if he scares you."

She took a deep breath. "No, please. I'm perfectly fine."

Ellen bent to the dog's side and lifted his chin. "General Lee, this is Miss Jenny, and I expect you to be sweet." Immediately, the pet wagged its tail.

Masking her fear, Jenny stepped inside and presented a small basket covered with a red-checked towel. "I brought you a loaf of bread."

Ellen lifted the corner of the towel and inhaled the aroma of the warm bread. Her nose wrinkled, accenting her abundance of orange freckles. "It smells wonderful and freshly baked, too. How thoughtful, and the basket is so pretty."

Jenny felt herself flush with the compliment. "Thank you. Miss Mimi has been teaching me how to cook, and this is the morning's lesson. I hope it tastes all right. Some of my things have been, well, rather unusual." Jenny laughed. "If it tastes terrible, you won't hurt my feelings by feeding it to your dog." He brushed against her skirt. She stiffened, but the animal didn't growl.

"Nonsense. I'm sure the bread is as delicious as it smells, and I certainly wouldn't give it to General Lee."

"Miss Mimi says a good cook never visits empty-handed. I may not be a good cook yet, but I try."

Ellen tilted her head. "Your mother didn't teach you how to cook?"

"Oh, no." Jenny giggled at the thought of her mother in the kitchen. "My parents have servants to do those kinds of things."

"So proper ladies don't spend time in the kitchen?"

"You and I are proper ladies, and we cook." She followed Ellen into the sparkling new parlor. "Your home is simply lovely. I thought so the first time I was here, but we were so busy that day. What a wonderful job you've done."

"Frank is an excellent carpenter, and he is creative, too. He built this before we were married, and together we've worked on making it our home. We still have much to do, but most of the fun is in the planning."

They began their conversation in the parlor, but Ellen suggested they move to the back porch with its two massive elm trees to keep them cool. The lure of sunshine and a gentle breeze promised a perfect day.

Moments later they sat in two rocking chairs, drinking cool lemonade and enjoying sugar cookies. General Lee followed them outside and curled up in front of the back door. He slept until a noise from the road perked his ears and sent him running to investigate, but Ellen called the dog back to her. Jenny was amazed at how well General Lee obeyed her soft commands.

The rear of the yard hosted a variety of flowers: red and purple petunias, white daisies, and towering sunflowers. A fenced area in the far left-hand corner held a vegetable garden. The couple definitely shared a love for growing things.

After much talk about the happenings in Kahlerville, Ellen took on a more somber expression. "I promised you Jessica's journal." She leveled her gaze at Jenny. "Before you read it, I want to caution you about the contents."

"I understand. Some of it may be shocking."

"She wanted you to have her journal. As I told you before, she believed you'd come looking for her. Someday. . ." Ellen paused. "Someday I'll tell you what happened those few days before she died. But not today."

Jenny wanted to learn it all now, but respect for Ellen stopped her insistence. "When you feel the time is right, I'll be ready to listen."

"I can't help but look at you and see Jessica. Being with you and sipping lemonade is like chatting with an old friend. Unfortunately, she was never as happy and content." Ellen took a breath, and her eyes revealed painful memories. When she spoke again, a smile played upon her lips and her hazel eyes moistened. "She died at peace with God. It's such a comfort to know she lives in heaven."

Uneasiness swept through Jenny. Discussing God was not why she came. Although she sensed her spirit growing closer to Him, she couldn't bring herself to discuss religion.

Ellen inhaled deeply before speaking. "When she died, I was devastated. I know now that it was a blessing in disguise. Neither one of us would have received Jesus as Lord without the birth of Rebecca. When Grant walked out of the brothel with Jessica's baby girl, I went with him and never looked back. The reverend and his wife took me in and told me about Jesus."

A knot formed in Jenny's chest. Had Jessica felt this uncomfortable with talk about God?

Ellen stepped across the porch and down to the grass where a bench rested under one of the trees. She gestured for Jenny to join her. General Lee rose from his resting spot and descended the porch steps to rest his head in Ellen's lap.

"She often talked about you," Ellen said.

The knot tightened in Jenny's chest. "This is all so confusing to me. We didn't get along very well. I always sided with our parents and openly condemned her rebellion. I treated her horribly simply because I feared angering our parents."

"I know love is a very powerful emotion, and she dearly loved you. She even told me what you looked like, about your music, your desire to teach, and your mannerisms."

"I had no idea she cared so much." Jenny fought the inner turmoil. She'd been such a poor sister.

"Jessica spent hours telling me about your lives as children and growing up together. Her favorite memory was of the many hours you played with your dolls beneath a lilac tree." She stopped abruptly and placed her hand over Jenny's. "Wait here a minute. I'll go get the journal."

Jenny wanted to go with her. At the very least, have her take General Lee.

With one hand on the doorknob, Ellen turned and smiled. "I think I'll slice us a piece of your bread. I churned butter this morning while Frank painted the front shutters."

"Can I help?" *Please, don't leave me alone with your beast of a dog.*

"No need. I'll only be a moment, and I wouldn't want to deny you this lovely breeze from the trees."

Jenny kept one eye fixed on General Lee. He moved closer. How did one dog grow so large? What did it eat? She trembled.

The beast growled, and she clutched her hands together. He rose on his haunches and stared at the road. A moment later a wagon passed, and he settled back down.

Jenny nearly choked in the dog's presence. General Lee moved closer. Dare she ask Ellen for help? The dog turned his massive head her way. Why, it was bigger than her head.

General Lee barked, sounding like the roar of a powerful locomotive moving down the tracks. She jumped and feared fainting. His face was so close that she could smell his breath. And it wasn't pleasant.

Please, Ellen, hurry back before I'm ill or he eats me.

Jenny could not move her head. If she did, she'd touch the dog's snout. How much longer could she endure this? She squeezed her eyes shut. Something wet swept across her cheek.

"Oh, my, General. Miss Jenny may not appreciate your kisses." Ellen gasped. "You are deathly pale. Are you afraid of my dear pet?"

Jenny nodded and forced the bile back down into her stomach. "I've always been fearful of things."

"I'm so sorry. General, come up here on the porch. You've frightened the wits out of Jenny." Ellen made her way to the bench with the bread and a book tucked under her arm.

General obeyed.

Ellen handed her a small navy book neatly tied with a faded blue ribbon. She set a small plate with a slice of bread and the butter beside Jenny on the bench.

"Would you like for me to leave you alone?" Ellen asked. "I can take General inside with me."

"Not at all. I can read this later at the boardinghouse." Tracing the textured cover with her index finger, Jenny repeatedly turned it over in her hands. She longed to open it.

"I asked Jessica if I could mail it to you in Ohio, but she refused. She said I must put it into your hands myself. I've never read it or even lifted its cover. To the best of my knowledge, this has not been opened since she last wrote in it a few days before Rebecca's birth. I firmly believe the secrets of her life before she came to Kahlerville are inside. I'm hoping you learn about Aubrey Turner there. Your sister was cautious of something or someone. Always studied new faces at Martha's." She stopped. "My advice to you is to read it all first and then, if necessary, share it with a person you can trust."

Jenny shivered. She held the very words Jessica had written. . . for her. Again, she turned the journal over in her hand. Her sister had left a genuine legacy: Rebecca and the words written in the navy book. A deep desire to read and memorize every word rose inside her. Beneath these pages she could once more acquaint herself with the sister of her youth.

"Thank you." Jenny peered into Ellen's face. Her hazel eyes reflected love and compassion, and her smile gave Jenny the reassurance that no one was to blame for Jessica's death.

Her friend stood and strolled a few feet beyond the shade, and in the sunlight her strawberry blond hair glistened as though she wore an angel's halo. "I'm not sure I understand my own words." She laughed softly. In the next moment, she grew melancholy. "At times, Jessica got an odd, somewhat frightening look about her, but she wouldn't discuss it. About a month before Rebecca's birth, she told me she was in danger. Refused to say why. Didn't want me to fret. Anyway, she told me about the journal shortly thereafter and asked me to keep it safe for her. The times she needed to record things, she'd ask for it, then return it to me for safekeeping."

If only I'd been a loving sister. . .and friend. "This means more to me than you can ever imagine. I am so ashamed of my attitude toward her and the way I treated her."

"We all have regrets," Ellen said. "There's nothing we can do about them but learn from our mistakes and go on."

"My life is so much richer since I've come to Kahlerville. There are days I don't ever want to leave."

Ellen's sweet smile warmed her fragile spirit.

"I'd love for you to settle here, and I know all of Grant's family is fond of you."

"And I'm devoted to them," she replied, avoiding Ellen's eyes for fear she'd ask about Grant.

The young women spent the rest of the afternoon sharing and laughing about their experiences with Jessica. Ellen told her about Jessica's pranks, and Jenny revealed her sister's antics in their younger days. They exchanged stories until near suppertime. Ellen begged Jenny to stay, but Jenny insisted Frank needed to spend the time with his new bride. The women promised to get together again very soon.

Jenny hurried back to the boardinghouse with the treasured journal tucked under her arm and her revolver resting inside her reticule. She thought of walking outside of town far enough to practice, but she had an even greater urgency to read the journal.

Goodness, Ellen hasn't even read this herself. I'm not so sure I could have been so resolute.

Still, she marveled at Jessica's sensitivity—and at the love she professed for Jenny. What kind of danger could she have detected? Who could have been so evil as to threaten the life of a young woman with child—unless it was one of her past customers or Rebecca's father? Nevertheless, tonight Jenny intended to find the answers to all her fervent questions, for she planned to read the journal in its entirety.

CHAPTER  21

At the boardinghouse Jenny carried a dinner tray of chicken and dumplings to her room. She didn't want to waste a single moment of the evening. Already the sun had begun its descent, and amber shadows danced across the faint light from the window.

Pulling her chair close to the small nightstand, she lit the wick of the kerosene lamp and positioned herself comfortably for the hours of reading ahead. Mindful of the task before her and with an air of solemn reverence, she lifted the journal's cover and examined the inscription. The pages were ivory in color and the lettering in royal blue ink. Instantly, she recognized her mother's handwriting:

> Given to: *Jessica Kathryn Martin*
> Date: *22 January 1888*
> From: *Mother and Father*

Cautiously, Jenny proceeded to the second page:

22 January 1888
Today is my eighteenth birthday. I wonder why Mother and Father gave me this journal. They must believe I will

record my deepest thoughts, and when I am not at home, they
can read it. I do plan to record everything about my life, but
this journal will always be with me. It will be my friend and
companion, for I have neither one. No one understands or even
dares to know me.

Sometimes I think even Jenny is fearful of me, and I cannot
blame her. I even loathe myself. For certain, she is afraid of our
parents. Father continually lectures her, and she cries more than
she laughs. That too is probably my fault. I wish I understood
why he treats her so harshly simply because her school marks are
not the same as mine. Perhaps he fears she will become like me.
How could she when she possesses a much gentler spirit?

I am so miserable with myself. . .and with Mother and
Father. I despise the things I do, but I cannot stop them. My
heart and mind tell me to be kind, but my actions do otherwise.
Perhaps I am a monster. If I thought someone cared, I would
gladly try to resist this senseless defiance and find meaning in
my life. Although I believe my greatest rebellion is within me.

What if I never change? Even if I placed my whole being
into the purpose of rearranging Jessica Kathryn Martin, who
would care? Does anyone fathom the destruction of my soul? I
have ruined any notion of a relationship with everyone I touch.
And dear Jenny. . .oh, how I love her.

A demon lives inside me. I'm convinced of it. An ugly
creature that derives some sort of morbid satisfaction in hurting
others. I've spent the afternoon debating this very issue within
me. Perhaps the only solution is to do away with myself, but I
am a coward. Death has such a sweet call. It whispers my name
in the darkest of hours. And as the night beckons me into the
shadows of shame, my heart longs to be at rest, to sleep peacefully
without wild thoughts pulling and tugging at me. How
merciful is the song of death when my heart aches to be free of
this troublesome world.

Jenny abruptly shut the journal. She covered her mouth in horror at her sister's statements. A steady stream of liquid emotion dripped from her eyes. Never, no, never, had she perceived the intensity of Jessica's tormented mind. Taking a deep breath, she once more began to read.

The journal shifted from dismal days of gloom to ones of uncontrollable excitement. She wrote every day—the journal truly did become her friend and companion. During a time of almost maddening exhilaration, Jessica decided to take the step from innocence into womanhood. She discovered by using her body she received favors from men who walked all roads of life. She used them as they used her, but soon this no longer provided a challenge or an escape from her misery.

She acquired a taste for liquor, but the telltale odor on her breath infuriated her parents. They attempted to curtail her activities, but she always found a way to escape their watchful eyes. Weeks and months passed, and Jessica sank lower into depression.

Jenny glanced about her. She'd found such contentment in Kahlerville. If only Jessica could be with her now. Together they'd work through her dear sister's agony.

Suddenly, new people, new sights, and new sounds stirred Jessica's mind into a frenzied whirl of euphoria. Her behavior followed a pattern of utmost joy followed by prolonged tears. For nearly two years the cycle repeated itself. Each time the melancholy threatened to take her life. However, the moods evened when she met a particular captivating gentleman:

I met the most delightful man tonight. Oh, but he is handsome. I have never gazed into such deep violet eyes, and his thick blond hair looks as though it were kissed by the sun. His name is Robert, Robert Jacobs, and his words are as rich as fresh cream and flow from his lips like sweet honey. He is a man of many talents—an actor by profession. Mother and

Father would be appalled. But I don't care. I am in love.

Jenny paled in the twilight of her room. Robert. . .Robert Jacobs. He fit the same description as Aubrey Turner. In the heat of the summer evening, she pronounced judgment. Aubrey Turner and Robert Jacobs were the same man. But why had he changed his name? He admitted to being Jessica's fiancé. Jenny focused her attention on the pages before her:

> *Robert enjoys gambling. I stood behind him tonight and watched him play cards with remarkable expertise. I did exactly as he instructed: masked my face with no emotion and drummed on his shoulder a code of what the other gentlemen held in their hands. It was such fun! He won, of course, and the profits were grand. He gave me three hundred dollars for acting as his assistant, and later we went to his hotel room to celebrate. I barely made it home before dawn. Tomorrow I shall see him again.*

Jenny read on and discovered how Jessica formed an instant alliance with Robert. She accompanied him to his card games and took great delight in helping him secure winning hands. His smooth speech and extremely good looks drew Jessica ever closer to him, and he became her shining knight, the one designated to save her from herself. She attempted to change her habits to please his every whim and successfully covered her troubled emotions in his company, but then she unleashed them in full force upon returning home. The lies and deceit mounted. Nothing mattered to Jessica but Robert, and she treasured the earth beneath his feet. When he asked her to pose as his wife and travel with him, she eagerly accepted.

In the beginning their relationship blossomed. They enjoyed the gambling, and their clever cheating brought in more money than the two could conceivably spend. Jessica continued to hide her old ways until she could no longer keep the demon captive. When Robert began experiencing Jessica's moods, he responded violently, and she tasted his frightening temper. Together their passions ruled selfish and cruel:

> *Today, Robert killed a man on board the* River Queen. *He said the man accused him of cheating. It terrifies me to think that he enjoyed the gunplay, especially since the man's accusation proved correct. . . .*
>
> *This is not enjoyable anymore. I am frightened, but there is nowhere to go, no one to help me.*

On another day, Jessica wrote:

> *Robert takes all of the money and gives me little to survive. It is impossible to save a thing, and he knows it. He is not sane. I am sure of it. Oh, we are a matched pair with our madness. Tonight, he told me I was nothing without him, and later he told me he loved me. I cringe at his affections. I only want to be free.*

A week later Jessica's pain had increased:

> *My life is more wretched than ever. Robert is vicious, and I think he enjoys hurting me. He takes on the stage characteristics of his most villainous characters until I wonder who he will become next. My only refuge is to feign a nap each afternoon—to think and plan a way out of this nightmare.*

Jenny gasped in recalling Aubrey Turner's comment about Jessica's naps.

Days later in the journal, Jessica's tone had changed:

I have devised a scheme to free myself. I know where he keeps his money. It will work, if I can just endure a few more nights with him.

Robert is deplorable, repulsive. I cannot bear for him to touch me, but I must. He must not suspect what I plan to do.

Jenny felt her sister's fear but was astonished by what Jessica wrote just two days later:

Today, Robert asked me to marry him. He wants to travel to San Francisco and purchase a theater and gambling house. Acting is what he loves best, and he promises not to hit me again. Perhaps I should consider his proposal. He might truly change. . . .

Jenny shook her head, convinced that if Robert was the man she knew as Turner, he would not have changed. Her fears were confirmed as she read an entry a few pages later in the journal:

I wanted to write Jenny and tell her about the upcoming wedding, but Robert became furious. I can no longer bear his beatings. He has become an expert in hurting me where the bruises do not show. I have to get away.

Several entries later, Jessica wrote from San Francisco:

At last I am free—finally free, and I did not have to marry him. I vow to do whatever is necessary to earn a living. Any pride and self-respect I might have had is gone, but I will never allow a man to rule over me again. Most of the money is hidden away until I find a safe place to live.

Jenny learned how Jessica had stumbled into the town of Kahler-ville. Prostitution was not new to her, and she lost no time in seeking out the town's brothel.

> *Must everyday be the same? If only these men would do something else besides satisfy their physical needs. I deplore them, or maybe it is myself I long to destroy.*

Days of deep hopelessness followed. Jessica's life brightened when she met Ellen. For the first time, she found a true friend:

> *This afternoon I told Ellen about Jenny and Grandma Martin. Both are so dear to my heart. I remember how Grandma always said "Goodness" when surprised or excited. When Jenny was four years old, I heard her use the same expression. At the time, Jenny and I were playing dolls beneath the lilac tree, and she said, "Goodness, Miss Suzanne has a frightful cold."*
> *My precious Jenny and Grandma, I miss you both so very much. I wish I had told you how much I loved you. I really wanted to be a good girl like I promised Grandma. My life has been a squander.*

The entry for the following Sunday elaborated on what Jenny had already learned from the Rainers:

> *I visited Reverend Rainer this afternoon. He says that God loves me just as I am, and He will stay by me forever. I wish I could believe those words. It is simply impossible, too difficult for me to even conceive such an idea. The reverend says God sent His Son to die for my sins, just like Grandma used to tell me. Maybe for someone else, but not for the likes of me. Nothing could ever make me feel clean enough for God.*

But I'd like to think so. I truly would.

Jenny felt her sister's fear and despair as she read the entry from two days later:

> *I must be pregnant. It has been over two months since my time. I have no idea who is the father. There are so many. I thought I had been careful, taken the precautions. How stupid of me. How could I have sunk to such lowness? Surely God has punished me for all the horrible things I have done. If He truly loves me, then why this curse?*

Jessica wrote in her journal faithfully every day of her pregnancy. She tried to be fit company for Ellen's sake, but the lowest of depression settled upon her. Near the end of her confinement, an unusual entry captured Jenny's attention. It was a letter:

> *My dear sister,*
> *I have a strange feeling that giving birth to this baby will cause my death, and I welcome it. I'd never be a fit mother. Why should I subject a babe to a mother who cannot control her behavior? Some days I fancy it might change my life and cure this madness, but I think not. I would rather die than subject my own flesh to this insanity.*
> *I don't know what will happen to my child, but I am sure Ellen will see the baby receives a proper home. She has been so good to me, priceless—much more than I deserve. I hope she leaves this sordid life and finds real happiness. Never mind my rambling, Jenny. I need to tell you about crucial matters.*
> *I have carefully explained to Ellen that she must give this journal to you. I hope, in reading this, you will see I truly wanted things to be right between us. If there is a God, I pray He will press upon you to find this town. I know you will come.*

I must believe it.

I desperately tried to be like you. You are so pretty, so smart, and you found it easy to be obedient. How cruel of me to leave you to the mercy of Mother and Father, and I have regretted it a thousand times. I should have been stronger and stayed for your sake. For this I am truly sorry. Please forgive me.

Within the pages of this journal are the means of locating a large sum of money. Yes, it is the money taken from Robert, but he obtained it through ill means. It is for you and my dear baby, and I know you will do the best with it.

Please make sure my baby is loved and cared for, and please remember I love you. We had such good fun playing dolls beneath the lilac tree. Remember playing school and how I vexed you with my obsession with numbers? Remember the tea parties and the days of innocence? I believe those days were true paradise— no madness, no regrets, and no concerns about the morrow.

Jenny lifted her tear-glazed eyes from the journal. The hour chimed long past midnight. She ached from mental exhaustion and the pang of her sister's troubled mind. The truth about Aubrey Turner or Robert Jacobs, whatever his true name, made her tremble. She clearly understood why he'd followed her to Texas. He wanted his money and thought Jenny knew of its whereabouts. He lied to her and Ellen about his love for Jessica in an effort to secure his funds. No wonder Ellen kept her distance from him. She felt his evil, too.

Tomorrow she must talk to Ben about Robert Jacobs and the connection to Aubrey Turner. She also wanted to ask Grant to help her decipher Jessica's journal. She didn't want the money for herself—Grant could keep it for Rebecca.

My dear Jessica.

I was not a sister to you in life, but I promise you I will do my best to fulfill your dying wish.

CHAPTER  22

Ben scooted his chair closer to his desk, scraping the legs across the bare wooden floor. He wrote the name Robert Jacobs on a piece of paper and stared at it. "And Jessica said he posed as an actor and a gambler?"

"Yes, sir." Jenny pressed her lips together to keep calm. Her gaze swept across the sheriff's small office. Although tidy, it smelled a bit like her chamber pot in the mornings. Must have been the occupant locked up in the back. Smelled like a whole gang of them.

"No need to be nervous, Jenny. This information is just between you and me." Ben coughed. The sound seemed to come from his boots.

"Are you all right?"

"Yes, of course. Just a little tickle in my throat." He turned his head and coughed again. "Back to business here. Other than the man having a temper, did she make mention where all of this happened?"

"Only Cleveland and San Francisco."

"Anything else I should know?"

"He shot and killed a man in a card game on board a boat called the *River Queen*." Jenny took in a breath. "I understand he did the

189

same thing here. Since I learned he hurt my sister, I'm a little afraid for myself and Ellen, given that Jessica stole money from him."

"I'm sure Ellen has already told Frank."

"Oh, no. I read that part in the journal. Ellen isn't aware of the stolen money."

Ben leaned back in his chair. "I'll go to work on this. With this information, it shouldn't take long before we have a few answers. Did your sister's journal mention any other names that he used?"

"No. How soon can you arrest him?"

"I can't unless he's broken the law."

Indignation rose up in her. "Are you saying he could continue to frighten Ellen and me, and there's nothing you can do?"

Ben offered a smile that she assumed he meant as reassuring. "As long as I'm sheriff, no woman in Kahlerville will ever be afraid. I have no problem escorting him out of town if he even bends the law."

She nodded. Relief flowed warm through her veins. "Good. I wonder. . ."

"What are you thinking?"

"Should I confront him with what I know? Tell him I have no idea where Jessica hid the money?" She hesitated while a memory danced across her mind. "I just remembered something. One night at the boardinghouse I awoke to a horrible smell—a skunk. When I arose from my bed to shut the window, I heard Mr. Turner—or whatever his name is—speaking harshly to another man. He wanted to know about the finances at. . .Martha's Place and if she came into any money after Jessica died."

Ben leaned forward. "What was the response?"

"The man claimed to know nothing."

"Did the man have a name?"

"I didn't hear it spoken."

Ben made more notes. He glanced up and studied her. "Do you understand what this means?"

"I think so. Aubrey Turner is an evil man."

"In case you have any doubts, Turner must believe you or Ellen has his money."

"But we don't."

"If he was convinced of that, he wouldn't be wasting his time here in Kahlerville."

"What can I do?"

"Be very careful. Is there somewhere else you can live besides the boardinghouse? I don't feel comfortable with you staying there in the same establishment as him."

She shook her head. "The boardinghouse is fine. I have a lock on my door, and the men stay in a different section."

"Do you trust me to make a few inquiries regarding your safety?"

"What do you mean? Find me another place to live? I refuse to be a burden to anyone. I'll stay at the boardinghouse until I decide to return to Cleveland."

"I advise you not to attempt the journey back until I can get to the bottom of this mess with Turner."

"All right. But I won't live in fear." A surge of courage swept through her. Or perhaps it was a wave of pride from the knowledge of the revolver in her reticule. "I won't be confined to my room like a frightened child."

"I understand your sentiments. Just be wary of where you are and what is going on around you. One more thing. Grant needs to hear all of what we've discussed today."

"Why?"

Ben laid the pen on his desk and folded his thin hands. "Two reasons: One, he has a concern for you, and two, he is raising Jessica's daughter."

"Surely Mr. Turner wouldn't harm an innocent child."

"Frankly, Jenny, if he followed you from Cleveland and committed the other crimes we suspect, do you think he'd hesitate to use a child to obtain his money?"

Jenny left Ben's office with a slightly dizzy sensation. She had insisted there was no need for an escort, but now she wished someone supported her. The conversation had been overwhelming, and the future looked bleak as long as Aubrey Turner stayed in town. The startling revelation about the potential danger to her, Ellen, and precious little Rebecca left her shaken. And what about all of the Andrews family and the Reverend and Mrs. Rainer? And Miss Mimi? For a moment she believed her knees would not hold her legs.

I can be a strong woman. I won't cower in fear.

She must tell Grant about the journal. If he disliked her before, he certainly would when he learned Rebecca might be in danger. She hated to tell him what she'd learned, not because she wanted to keep the truth from him, but because the news would sadden him. Dear Grant. All he ever wanted was to raise his daughter in peace. Then Jenny came along and disrupted his world.

And he had disrupted hers. How sad to love a man she'd hurt so badly. She'd known him but five weeks and realized her heart was smitten, and she'd been friends with Oscar for two years. Never had she felt any of the insurmountable feelings with Oscar that she experienced with Dr. Grant Andrews. Unfortunately, he would never give her a single thought with all the trouble she'd brought his way.

She peered about as though Turner might try to speak with her on the street—or demand what belonged to him. Where was his money? Jessica had indicated the clues to the whereabouts were within the pages of her journal. But Jenny had read it from cover to cover, and nothing was revealed.

The perplexing notions about Jessica and her world were more than she could bear, and with this knowledge came a pounding headache. Guilt for all the trouble she'd caused crept over her. If she had not promised Ben to tell Grant this instant about the journal, she'd walk back to her room.

Grant spied Ben and Frank in the corner of the churchyard after Sunday morning services. He wanted to talk to both of them together about Turner. The man had become a burr in his saddle. No one stood with the two brothers. Most likely, they were discussing the same matters weighing heavily on him.

"I need to talk to Ben and Frank," he said to Mimi. "Would you keep an eye on Rebecca?" He smiled at Jenny, regretting the tug at his heart and the anger in his soul for all that her coming to Kahlerville had caused. And to think he'd just finished worshiping God.

"We'll chat with the other ladies until you're ready." Mimi reached for Rebecca's hand. "Jenny needs to get better acquainted with the other fine women in this town."

Grant offered another token smile and made his way toward the Kahler brothers. The conversation he'd shared yesterday with Jenny made him a little dour. He feared for her safety and expressed it, but deep inside was a heavy dose of resentment.

The closer he walked toward Ben and Frank, the more he realized the two weren't happy. He turned around to give them their privacy. In his present mood, he almost welcomed a good argument.

"Grant, come on back. This affects you, too," Ben said.

So they were discussing Turner. He wasn't so sure he wanted to get involved with feuding brothers. He and Morgan had seen their share of disagreements, but those were years ago. He retraced his steps and was suddenly thankful for the slight breeze under the oak tree. Frank had a line across his forehead deep enough to plant potatoes. Ben looked pale. His flesh seemed to be falling from his body. This was no summer cold. Grant prayed his suspicions of a chronic lung condition would prove false.

"I'm ready to run Turner and Martha DeMott out of town," Frank said.

"My, brother, you sure are wearing your Christian hat this morning," Ben said.

Frank stuck his finger into Ben's face. "It's not your wife who was threatened, and it's not your lumberyard looking at a match."

Ben's face softened. "You're right. It's not. But arguing about what to do isn't going to make the problem disappear. I should have some answers about Turner this week or the next. I sent wires to lawmen, U.S. marshals, and the Pinkertons. Besides, I think Martha is harmless."

"As in Turner put her up to it?" Frank asked.

"I think so. She was real polite when I confronted her. Said she was angry about the rumor but wouldn't tell me where she heard it." Ben focused on Grant. "What's your opinion about all of this?"

As in I should have put Jenny on a train back East weeks ago? "I think if Turner is wanted somewhere, we're all better off."

Frank slowly nodded. "As mad as I am, I have to agree. Can't figure out for my life why he's so bent on learning more about Jessica. The woman's been dead almost three years. Makes me wonder if he thinks she's still alive."

Grant knew what kept Turner in town, but he wasn't about to tell Frank. That was Ben's job.

Ben scratched his chin, then coughed.

"What are you not telling me?" Frank asked. "And when are you going to see Grant about that cough?"

Ben finished up his spell. "In answer to your first question, Jessica stole money from Turner, if he's the same man mentioned in Jessica's journal—a Robert Jacobs. The answer to your second question is none of your business."

Frank's eyes widened then hardened. "Suit yourself. Are you thinking he's after Ellen and Jenny for the money?" He paused. "Of course he is. Why else did he follow Jenny here from Cleveland?" He slammed his fist into his palm. "This means my Ellen and—" He slid an alarmed look Grant's way. "Jenny could be in danger."

"I just learned about this, too," Grant said. "And don't forget my daughter."

None of them said anything for several long moments.

"Let me work with the law," Ben finally said. "We're jumping to conclusions when the answer may be simple."

"Where's the man's money? If Jessica stole it, then we'll return it." Frank crammed his hands inside his pockets.

"We don't know," Grant said. "No one has any idea where it might be or how much is involved. To the best of my knowledge, Ellen doesn't have any idea about Jessica taking his money."

"I'm sure of it," Frank said. "She would have told me. As it is, she isn't sleeping well. The situation is worrying her because she's frettin' over Jenny. But I need to tell her this so she's more careful."

"I'd like to see Jenny living somewhere besides the boardinghouse, but she won't hear of it." Grant glanced back at a group of laughing children. Rebecca called out to him, and he waved. Jenny stood beside her with Mimi. His favorite ladies.

"I tried, too, but she refused," Ben said. "I thought you might have better luck."

"Are you kidding? Most of the time we're fussing about something."

"Ellen and I started out that way," Frank said. "Took me a long time to see the reason why she riled me so was because I loved her."

Grant's face reddened. "Don't think that's the case here." Then he remembered how Casey and Morgan had battled until they admitted their love. "We're talking about another matter here today."

"I sure hope the Lord is listening this morning," Ben said. "Leave it to an Andrews to make my job a little more difficult."

Grant grinned. "Hey, that's what we do best." But his thoughts raced back twelve years to when Casey was being chased by a band of outlaws and to the resulting blood bath on Morgan's ranch. One tragedy in a family was enough.

CHAPTER  23

Jenny waved at the sleek black surrey approaching her. Casey had invited her to spend a day at the Andrews ranch, and she had been thrilled with the prospect of time away from the boardinghouse. Jenny had been ready long before the arranged meeting with the expectation of developing one more friend. As the surrey slowed to a halt, she admired the brass mountings and the fine horse pulling it. Beneath a green and black fringed canopy, Casey sat with Daniel perched beside her.

"I'm your driver," Casey announced. "And I have a helper."

"I see you do," Jenny said. "I'm amazed that you manage this all by yourself." She offered her hand to the small boy. "How do you do, Mr. Daniel?"

He turned shyly and hid his round face in Casey's skirt. All she could see of him was a mass of auburn curls.

"Daniel, do be polite," his mother said.

He peeked around with one eye and mumbled a good morning.

"As you can see, Mr. Daniel tends to be a bit shy. He's not at all like his cousin Rebecca," Casey said. "Both of them are the same age, but she is months ahead of him. Climb on up, Jenny. I've been looking forward to spending the day with you for a long time."

Jenny tugged at her skirt and clumsily attempted to board the surrey. When her foot refused to secure a firm hold, Casey offered a hand.

"Goodness, being short can be a problem," Jenny said and seated herself beside Daniel. She leaned his way. "Your mama rescued me."

The child wordlessly clung to his mother, and she soon realized this was the little boy's typical behavior.

"Oh my, I do apologize," Casey said. "I have nightmares of him being thirty years old and still tugging at my skirts."

The two shared a laugh, but Daniel didn't budge or squeak a word.

"What do you have planned for us?" Jenny asked as the surrey rolled out of town.

"I'm not quite sure. Last week I put up peas and sweet corn, and yesterday I made pickles, so we're free to do as we like. It's much too hot a day to spend in the kitchen. We'll just have a wonderful time doing whatever we please. Perhaps a tour of the ranch would be in order?"

"Splendid. I know absolutely nothing about ranch life, so this will be something I can relate to my students."

"Chad and Lark could give you a wealth of information specific to children their age, but Chad is spending the day riding fence with a few of our hands, and Lark is visiting her grandparents."

Disappointment needled her, but Jenny didn't show it. Chad and Lark displayed excellent manners, and their inquisitive minds were a delight. At times she missed her students back home.

Casey laughed. "They'll be back for dinner. Do you plan to journey to Ohio before the start of the school year?"

"Oh, yes. Sometime around the first of September." Jenny didn't want to delve deeper into her life in Cleveland, especially when her future there looked uncertain.

"I'd imagine your parents miss you. I certainly fuss over my children, even when they are fussing at each other." Casey gave her a sweet smile.

Jenny hesitated, not quite sure how to respond. "I'm sure my parents would like me home again." After tasting independence, she had no desire to step back under the domination of her parents. Last night's efforts at writing them had resulted in one crumpled sheet of paper after another. How could she ever make them understand her feelings without sounding rebellious and unappreciative of all they'd done? Hopefully after spending the day with Casey, the right words would flow from her heart and her pen.

The beauty of the thick green countryside was breathtaking. Each little bend in the road was dotted with pastel wildflowers, and a grove of trees offered a breezy serenity of its own. Jenny wished she knew how to paint so she could capture the color and vibrancy on canvas and take it back to Cleveland for the long months ahead.

Casey pointed to a small hill ahead of them. "This marks the beginning of our ranch. You can see cattle and horses grazing in the distance."

Jenny shaded her eyes to view the animals. "It's so grand. What do you call it?"

"The Double H after Morgan's father, Hayden. Jocelyn used to refer to their homestead as Hayden's Heaven. Later they shortened the name to the Double H for branding purposes."

"What happened to Mr. Andrews?"

"He died of a rattlesnake bite just as the ranch began to flourish. Jocelyn took over the hundreds of acres, determined to make a success of their dream. She purchased cattle and horses, built and mended fences, acquired more land, and did whatever else she deemed necessary. All the while raising their children alone."

"How courageous. So Mrs. Rainer originally ran this ranch. This is definitely a story I'll want to share in my classroom. You must be proud of her legacy."

"The hardest part of her marrying the reverend was turning over all of the ranch's management to Morgan and me." She laughed. "Now she says it was easier to maintain the Double H than to keep

LANTERNS
LACE

up with the reverend's schedule."

Jenny could tell Casey loved every inch of the land. She gave a lengthy tour in the surrey, since Jenny had never ridden a horse. She introduced Jenny to all the ranch hands and proudly displayed a breed of cattle that Jocelyn and Grant had developed years before. Beautiful dark brown horses lifted their heads when the surrey passed. She laughed at the spring colts frolicking about the green pastures as though they were the owners. They visited barns and rode along a narrow river winding through their property. Genuinely impressed, Jenny asked questions and discovered Casey displayed excellent business skills, far more than any woman she'd ever met.

At noon both women assisted the cook—a rather hard-looking fellow. They filled plates of roast venison, potatoes, and carrots for the ranch hands. Afterward, the two women and Daniel ate their meal under a huge elm tree. Soon the small boy crawled up into his mother's lap and slept while she stroked his cheek. The tender scene reminded Jenny of the first time she'd viewed Rebecca and Grant.

"You have such a beautiful home," Jenny said. "So quiet and peaceful. I think Jocelyn gave it a rightful name."

"God has been good to us," Casey said. "We've been able to add on to the original home and furnish it nicely as we've seen a profit. But it takes a lot of hard work."

"It must be easy for you to feel grateful. Your whole life centers on God."

"Not always."

"Goodness, your life couldn't have been as dismal as mine," Jenny said, somewhat indignant. "Shall we compare?"

"You go first."

Jenny took a quick breath. All of the emotions about Jessica, Aubrey Turner, and her miserable life in Cleveland surfaced, and she fought for control as she slowly unveiled the tale of her unhappy life. "So I thought if I brought Rebecca back to Cleveland, my parents would look at me more favorably." Finally, she took a ragged breath.

"How foolish I've been. My niece belongs with Grant. Why ever did I think I could subject a little girl to such cruelty?"

She couldn't tell Casey about the journal and the stolen money. Maybe another time. Maybe never, for Jenny hadn't come to terms with the realization her sister had not only worked as a prostitute but had also stolen money.

Casey nodded solemnly before speaking. Her pale blue gaze lifted in understanding. "I can see why you don't speak of home. I'm sorry life has been difficult for you." The lovely woman paused, and a pained look swept over her face before she quietly began her story.

"I rode with an outlaw gang from the age of thirteen until I was twenty-one. By the time I reached my fourteenth birthday, my face was on wanted posters all over the West."

Jenny gasped, bewildered. "I had no idea. . . . How horrible."

"For me? Or for the life I led?"

Jenny opened her mouth to speak but abruptly closed it again.

"Both?" Casey patted her hand. "I understand the revulsion. I'm not proud of it, either."

Jenny forced a smile, too embarrassed to comment.

Casey glanced down at Daniel, who slept peacefully. "I want to tell you about my life. It shows the wonder of God's grace and His love and forgiveness for all of us. Perhaps then you will better see how Jessica was able to embrace God."

In the stillness of the warm summer afternoon amid the hum of busy insects and a napping little boy, Casey unfolded the early years of her life.

"My mother died when I was barely thirteen. My father drank night and day and took to beating my older brother, Tim, and me. Tim soon had enough of the abuse and decided to strike out on his own. He even went so far as to arrange for me to live with a local storekeeper and his wife. Well, I'm pretty stubborn, and I dearly loved my brother, so when he left home, I stole Pa's horse and trailed him for three days before I let him know about me.

"Oh, Tim was furious. He threatened to beat me worse than our pa ever had. I begged and pleaded, and in the end he allowed me to go with him. He outfitted me in boy's clothes and made me pile all of my hair up under a hat, and off we went to see the world." She paused, and the look in her eyes wove together regret and sorrow.

Jenny remembered Ellen speaking of Casey's ability to shoot well and understood others in Kahlerville knew the story. How ever did she bear the shame of it?

Casey glanced back at Jenny and nodded as though she'd resolved whatever had pained her in the past. "My brother taught me how to shoot, and it wasn't long before I could outshoot him. . . . Little did I realize I would live to regret my speed and accuracy."

"I'm so sorry for you," Jenny whispered. "I can't imagine what you've been through."

"That was just the beginning. Tim joined up with a band of outlaws, led by Davis Jenkins. And I, acting as his little brother, did the cooking and whatever chores the outlaws chose not to do. Well, I stuck to Tim like a pesky fly, and he looked out for me. Our masquerade lasted two weeks before Jenkins discovered I was a girl. Do I have to tell you what that meant?" Not a single sign of bitterness creased her face.

Jenny sensed her own cheeks growing warm. She willed it away, but still it lingered. "I understand."

"Unfortunately, Jenkins complained that I didn't do enough to earn my keep and demanded I ride with them on the next job just to hold the horses. They planned to rob a land office in Billings, Montana, and needed me to watch their mounts, to signal any trouble, and to be an extra shot. I'd never been so frightened in my entire life, afraid of the gang's lawlessness and afraid of making a mistake. About the time my nerves got the best of me, the gang burst through the building with exploding gunfire and smoke everywhere. A man aimed for me, and I shot him. I thought I killed him, but many years later I learned he survived." Casey glanced down at her sleeping son and planted a kiss on his cheek.

"You don't have to tell me this," Jenny said. "You've told me enough to realize how selfish I've been."

"No, hear me out." Casey took a deep breath. "Morgan and I have prayed about telling you our story. We believe God wants you to hear this. Maybe you know why. . .and it will help." She brushed her hand back over her auburn hair, neat and perfectly pinned atop her head. Jenny couldn't picture Casey ever riding with a band of outlaws. She more resembled a proper lady with delicate features and a smile to rival any field of wildflowers. As she deliberated the matter, she couldn't picture Ellen or Jessica working as prostitutes, either.

"The news traveled fast, and before long I had quite a reputation. The sad part about it was I didn't do any of the things the law credited to me except the shooting in Billings. I hated the gang, but Jenkins threatened to kill Tim if I left. I realized Jenkins gave the orders, and Tim made sure the men followed through. I wanted a better life, a respectable life, one I could be proud of. I wanted to be something more than a face on a wanted poster or another outlaw hanging from a noose."

Jenny cringed with the vivid picture. "So you came to Kahlerville?" *Like me, looking for answers?*

"Not exactly. One day while the outlaws were gone, I packed up my belongings and rode out. Jenkins and the whole bunch came after me. I got trapped in the snow-covered mountains of Utah when Morgan walked into my campsite, took my rifle, and ordered me to follow him. He was gunning for Jenkins and thought he'd use me for bait. Unfortunately, Jenkins did catch up with us. Morgan tried to help me but was seriously wounded in the process. I remembered my mother used to pray, so I asked God to spare his life. Only by His grace did I get Morgan to a doctor. Soon after, I left him with the doctor, fearing Jenkins would find us and finish off Morgan."

The story seemed to grow worse. How had Casey survived the ordeal?

"I spent the following months running and hiding. I recalled Morgan suggesting I settle in Texas. Partly because I didn't know where to go and partly because I had fallen in love with him, I came to Texas. Along the way, God put special people in my life who helped me get closer to Him. My life certainly didn't become any easier, but I no longer had to carry on by myself. Once in Kahlerville, I accepted what God had done for me. He became my peace and my strength."

Casey clasped Jenny's hand. "God is so good. He led me right here to Kahlerville. As God works things out for our good, I discovered Morgan lived here, too. I used another name to secure a job nursing Reverend Rainer's dying wife and finally revealed the truth. But I still lived in fear of Jenkins and the law. I'd been a part of an outlaw gang, and someday I needed to pay for what I'd done. Life was rough—real rough, and I simply had no choice but to put my trust in God. I found out that Jenkins had murdered Morgan's wife, and Morgan had not been the same since. God not only worked out the problems between us, but He allowed me to receive a full pardon from the governor of Texas and the president of the United States by helping federal marshals locate other outlaws."

Jenny felt like a child hearing a story with uncertainty. "And the outlaw Jenkins. What happened to him?"

"He caught up with me." Casey gestured toward the porch. "I was sitting right there with Jocelyn and Bonnie when he surprised us. He had plans to kill me, but my brother surprised him." She swallowed hard. "Tim was killed trying to save me. Morgan arrived before Jenkins finished me, too. He was arrested and later executed according to the law."

Jenny blinked back her tears. She couldn't speak the words she longed to—words to commend Casey's strength. . .and her faith.

"Jenny, you've heard my story. Someday I'll have to tell my children." She stroked Daniel's face. "It's a loathsome tale, yet I'm proof of God's love. He seeks us out to be His very own. My life had been so horrible, but it all changed when I surrendered to Him. It's the most important decision that you'll ever make, and I pray you will soon understand the power of God's unconditional love."

"Unconditional?" She'd never heard this word describe God.

"Yes, Jenny. God loves us as we are, but He also loves us too much to let us stay in our sin. That's why He sought out me and your sister. God doesn't care what roads we've traveled, only that our roads turn to Him."

The words to respond to Casey never surfaced because Jenny couldn't utter a sound. Tears filled her eyes, and the hopelessness of her life poured over her face.

"Tears can be good," Casey said. "They can cleanse us from our misery."

Jenny nodded. Finally, she felt she could speak. "God seems so far away."

"Does He? Have you noted the splendid display of wildflowers? Have you listened to a child's laughter or watched a sunrise or a sunset? Have you seen peace on a person's face when they should be utterly miserable?"

"I–I have. And I've seen a look in Reverend Rainer's eyes that draws me to a place I don't deserve."

Casey smiled. "I want that for you. I want you to be able to face every moment of the day knowing God loves you."

A quickening in Jenny's heart nearly frightened her. Yes, she wanted God in her life, and she wanted to thank Jesus for His sacrifice for her. "Can you help me, Casey? Can you show me the way?"

CHAPTER  24

Early the next morning Jenny grasped the brass knocker and lightly rapped on Grant's door. She could barely contain her excitement. She, Jennifer Elizabeth Martin, was an official child of God, and she felt grand. Simply grand. She'd read a Bible Casey had given her until nearly four this morning.

The Psalms were like fine poetry, and the Gospel of Luke reminded her of the stories Grandmother Martin used to tell her and Jessica. Except they weren't stories. These were true, historical accountings. Jenny's toes wiggled in her buttoned shoes. She had to tell Grant the news before she burst.

Maybe she'd come too early. She blinked to ward off the sleepiness while invisible slivers of wood held her eyes open. The hour couldn't be much more than seven o'clock. But she'd been here before dawn when Mimi gave her cooking lessons. Of course, Mimi expected her then. She refrained from pounding too hard for fear of waking Rebecca. The last thing she wanted to do was to annoy Grant or Mimi. A feeling of foolishness crept over her as though she were a child excited about a new adventure. She turned to walk back to the boardinghouse, but the big door slowly opened.

"Jenny?" Grant asked, obviously surprised to see her at the early hour. He stood with a steaming cup of coffee in one hand. "Is something wrong? Are you ill?"

She smiled broadly. "No, something is very right."

He swung open the door, and she saw a grin spread across his face. He looked much like a sleepy little boy, his hair still tousled. . . rested. . .much too handsome.

"And what is very right?" He gestured for her to come inside.

"Do you want to guess?"

He hesitated and studied her face. "From the glow on your face, I think our prayers have been answered."

"They have, Grant. I've come to Jesus."

"Praise God. . .praise God!"

Both of them began laughing, and her merriment brought dampness to her eyes once again.

"When did all of this come about?" he asked.

"I spent yesterday with Casey, and after hearing her story, I realized God brought me here for a special reason. She prayed with me. I never knew I could feel so peaceful."

Grant's smile extended to his voice. "And you look utterly radiant."

Jenny took a deep breath to control emotions that threatened to drown her words. "I have another important piece of information for you." Her pulse quickened with what she must say.

He closed the door behind her, and they walked toward the dining room with its rich oak furnishings.

"I'm waiting," he said. "But I don't think it can be any better than the news you've already given me."

A blend of sadness and seriousness sped through her body. "I've said this before, but I want to say it again because I mean it with all my heart. I don't want to take Rebecca from you. Not now or ever. I'm truly sorry for all of the heartache I've caused you, Mimi, and everyone else."

"And I apologize for upsetting you all those times," he said. "I despised the quarreling. Truthfully, I never thought I had a temper until. . .recently." His green eyes were soft, tender.

She covered her lips to muffle a laugh. "I have a bit of a temper myself. Goodness, I've been incredibly selfish, but I will try so very hard not to put myself before others. I'm afraid it will take some time."

"There's a lot I liked about the old Jenny. I'm a firm believer that the small things in life are what we learn to appreciate the most."

Jenny felt a peculiar sensation as she contemplated his words. She didn't really think it had anything to do with her lack of sleep or her newfound faith. But for now, she'd be content to wait. She hoped that wasn't too difficult to learn considering her upbringing contradicted everything she'd just adopted as her own.

"Do we have a visitor?" Mimi bustled into the dining room with a huge bowl of oatmeal and plopped it on the table. "Good morning, Jenny. My, aren't you up early."

"Yes, I guess so. I have something to tell you."

"She has wonderful news," Grant said.

Mimi struck her familiar pose: tilting her head and resting her hands on her hips. "Well, Jenny, you certainly look happy."

"I gave my life to Jesus."

Mimi hurried around the table and hugged her close. "Oh, we've been praying for you." Tears flowed freely between them. "Now, you must stay for breakfast."

"I really couldn't impose. I've done enough of that."

The older woman shook her silver head. "Nonsense, of course you can. We have cause for a real celebration this morning."

"I agree." Grant laughed. "You could help me get Rebecca up, and after breakfast I can walk you back to the boardinghouse." He paused for a moment. "Which reminds me, I do want to discuss a matter with you."

Jenny took a deep breath and hoped the news was good. Perhaps Aubrey had been apprehended. "All right, I'll stay. But I insist on helping you with Rebecca and Mimi with breakfast—as long as I don't have to cook anything."

"Amen," Mimi said.

The three laughed, and for the first time, Jenny understood the delightful sensation of belonging to a circle of friends. It was most pleasant indeed.

After breakfast Jenny and Grant took a leisurely stroll to the sound of singing birds and the gentle brush of a southerly breeze, not yet the stifling heat sure to come. A light, almost dizzy sensation attached to her heart.

"Jenny?" Grant began.

"Hmm, yes?"

"Would you consider moving in with Mama and the reverend?"

She glanced up and met his gaze. She laughed. "Absolutely not. I don't mind the boardinghouse." She refused to mention Aubrey Turner's name. The day was too glorious to ruin it with a questionable character.

"I know, but living at the parsonage would be homey—and safe."

She nodded, thrilled at the sound of his caring voice. "I don't doubt that living there would be wonderful, but I've already paid for my room through July." She glanced up at a cloudless, crystal blue sky. "It's really all right. I don't venture out in the evening, and I keep a careful watch for anything suspicious. Soon Ben will have the situation resolved, and I do have my revolver."

Lines creased Grant's brow. "I worry about you. Turner could easily take it, and then where would you be?"

"Thank you for your concern. But I'm perfectly contented."

"We must plan a time to examine Jessica's journal."

She'd nearly forgotten the money. "Of course. I don't want the money for myself. In fact, I'd like for it to go to Rebecca."

"You are much too generous."

Grant's unexpected words warmed her heart.

"Thank you."

"I'd still like for you to consider moving in with Mama and the reverend."

She giggled, so totally unlike her with all of the proprieties of a proper lady. "I'll think about it, but I already know my answer. Now if God wants me out of the boardinghouse, then I'll go."

Grant nodded, but the tiny lines around his eyes and a slight frown stayed for the remainder of their walk.

Once Grant left Jenny at the boardinghouse, he made his way to Ben's office. A thought had occurred to him this morning—a wary thought. But before he approached Ben on the subject, he wanted to simply enjoy Jenny's news. His prayers had been answered, and with the news came another realization. He was free to pursue her without any guilt or thoughts of displeasing God. All of the crazy dreaming and lingering on images of Jenny now had meaning. They could share picnics and long walks, plan for the future, and have a purposeful life. He was free to tell her of his growing love. In fact, he could tell the whole world if he felt like it. But according to Mimi, everyone knew anyway.

My word, but he and Jenny could someday have more children who'd have their mother's huge dark brown eyes. What a magnificent life they'd have. With all the frightening events going on in Kahlerville, he could protect Jenny for as long as they lived. Love had cast a peculiar spell on him. Some days he floated on clouds, and other days he wore gloom like a pair of spectacles.

Grant drew in a deep breath. Mindless dreams had taken over him. She no more cared for him than a cat took to swimming. To make matters worse, the idea of courting Jenny scared him to death.

I'm a fool. Never did have much sense when it came to love.

He shook off the pesky thoughts and opened the door to the sheriff's office.

"Take a walk with me," Grant said to Ben.

"A walk? We have privacy right here in my office. It's already near a hundred degrees out there."

"But I do my best talking when one leg is firmly planted in front of the other."

"What's this all about?"

"Our friend Turner and dear Mrs. DeMott."

Ben's brow rose. "For that I'll concede to a walk in this heat."

Grant forced a smile. Another reason why he wanted Ben out of his office was to observe how weak he'd become. With Bonnie due any day with their third child, maybe Ben would look into his failing health. If it wasn't already too late. He wondered how his frail sister would manage on her own. But he didn't want to dwell on that at the moment. God had the power to heal, and his was a praying family.

"What's got you all fired up this morning?" Ben chuckled. "I saw you walking Jenny. Are you feuding less and lovin' more?"

"Very funny. If you have to know, she found the Lord."

Ben startled. "That *is* good news. I'll be sure to tell Bonnie."

"How is she doing this morning? When I saw her yesterday, she complained from the moment she walked through my door until she left."

"Big as a barn and anxious for this baby to get here. But you didn't haul me out here to talk about Bonnie."

"No. I have a few serious things bothering me."

The two men walked toward the opposite end of town—away from Martha's Place.

"I'm ready to listen," Ben said. He started to say more, but the nagging cough interrupted him.

Grant would not comment on the cough. It would only rile Ben. "Remember when Jenny said that late one night she heard Turner and a man talking outside her window?"

"I sure do. A skunk woke her up. Do you have an idea who that man was?"

Grant nodded. "And I think you do, too."

"I could about swear on it."

"Have you talked to him?"

"Started to yesterday when I was at the bank, but Sylvia showed up."

Grant jammed his hands into his pockets. "I've seen him with Martha plenty of times when I've treated the girls—and that's just between you and me. I wonder how he's kept it from Sylvia all these years." He shrugged. "She probably ignores it."

"If it leaked out, Sylvia would kill him."

"I imagine so. Do you think Turner knows more about Lester than that he's keeping company with Martha?"

Ben tipped his hat at a passing wagon. "My guess is yes. But I've got to figure out what."

"Besides destroying his marriage, losing his position as deacon at church, and folks taking their money to the next town, what do you think it could be?"

"Something big enough for him to take up with the likes of Turner," Ben said.

"Enough to burn down a man's business?"

"Possibly. I've considered Lester's gambling, his fancy house and clothes, the trips he takes by himself. . .and Martha's boys."

"I delivered those children."

"Was Lester around?"

"What do you think?"

"He and Sylvia don't have any children," Ben said as though thinking aloud. "Martha is a demanding woman."

"And Lester is a demanding man. I think I should talk to her, since I know those boys belong to Lester," Grant said.

"What do you know about the law?"

"About as much as you do about doctoring, but I figure I have a brother-in-law who could tell me what I need to ask. And Martha likes me more than she does you."

Ben laughed. "We both know the truth in that. Martha despises me, so it's a deal."

What a web of deceit existed in their small town. The admittance both saddened and angered Grant. Before, he had ignored Martha and Lester's business, but in the event of Turner creating one mess after another, he'd have to do what he could to stop it.

CHAPTER  25

Grant looked forward to Thursday's Fourth of July almost as much as Christmas. The celebration shifted the lingering uneasiness of the townspeople from Mrs. Lewis's death to one of games, good food, and firecrackers. Every year, the citizens of Kahlerville met at Piney Woods Church for a community picnic and games. The festivities began late morning and ended at nightfall with firecrackers.

The day before the Fourth, Jenny arrived to help Mimi with food preparation. She'd been there nearly an hour when Grant walked through the dining room and overheard their conversation.

"What can I do now?" Jenny asked.

"Hmm," Mimi said thoughtfully. "You could remove all the pinfeathers from those chickens."

Silence.

He heard Jenny walk across the kitchen. "Mimi?"

"Yes, dear."

"What are pinfeathers?"

"Mercy, child, who cooked at your house?" Mimi asked.

Jenny sighed. "The cook. She did everything. Jessica and I weren't permitted in the kitchen except for meals until we acquired proper etiquette to eat in the dining room."

"How were you supposed to learn anything?" Mimi blew out an exasperated sigh. "I'm not upset with you. It's just for the life of me, I can't figure out the sense of not showing a woman how to be a woman."

"We weren't allowed to learn any of the domestic skills. Mother detested kitchen work, and she believed a young lady should learn social graces, poise, and the arts."

"That's fine and dandy, but what about the things that matter as a wife and mother?"

Jenny hesitated. "She said housekeeping and cooking would never attract a rich husband."

"And did you get a rich husband?"

Grant muffled his laughter. Leave it to Mimi to speak her mind.

"No, ma'am," Jenny whispered.

Grant bit his lip to keep from letting the women know of his whereabouts and peeked around the corner.

Mimi perched her hands on her hips. "Well then, it's high time someone told you the way to a man's heart is through his stomach. That's the best way to land a husband. A pretty face like yours is just fine, but when you get to be as wrinkled as me, other things are more important. Like fried chicken. Let me tie an apron around you, and we'll get busy."

"I want to learn to cook, Miss Mimi, but I don't want a husband." Jenny whirled around to see Grant spying on them. She turned brighter red than the tomatoes ripening on the kitchen windowsill.

Seeing the humiliated look on Jenny's face, Mimi's gaze flew to the dining room. "You get on out of here, Grant Andrews. This is women's business."

Breaking into a peal of laughter, he stepped into the kitchen and snatched up Rebecca. But with another seething glare from his housekeeper, Grant promptly kissed his daughter and set her back on a chair before hurrying to his office.

Shortly after lunch, Mimi caught him alone.

"I will never, ever again offer to teach a grown woman what she should have already learned from her mother." Her dark blue eyes darted about. "All the expensive books and education at Jenny's fancy university didn't help her at all to learn what God intended for every woman to master."

"Well, Mimi, some folks may not agree with you, but I surely understand how you feel. I like to eat!"

By Rebecca's bedtime, the chickens were fried, strawberry and custard pies cooled on the kitchen table, fresh vegetables were washed and ready to cook, and hot rolls disappeared as Grant came and went from the kitchen. Jenny looked pleased and excited. Mimi claimed she was ready for bed.

The following morning, Grant gathered the food and his favorite three ladies into the buckboard and headed for the church grounds. The day promised to be hot, but thankfully the church and parsonage were embraced by numerous pine and oak trees. A handful of folks had assembled early to lend a hand, and the reverend immediately put them to work gathering up supplies for the various events and activities.

Grant looked out over the grassy area separating the church from the parsonage. Tables constructed of long wooden planks on sawbuck legs stood ready to support the huge amounts of food beginning to arrive. As quickly as the men placed the tables alongside the church, Mimi, Jocelyn, and Jenny covered them with colorful cloths.

As the food appeared, the women arranged each item on designated tables. The first one held the meat dishes: platters of fried chicken, beef and pork roasts smothered in onions and gravy, smoked venison, thick fried steaks, and pork chops. A second table hosted the vegetables and such. It bowed slightly under the weight of the potato dishes, baked beans, corn custard, fresh sugar peas, snap beans and bacon, tender greens, deviled eggs, wilted lettuce, coleslaw, tomatoes, cucumbers, green peppers, onions, and jars of pickles and relishes. On one end of the third table sat corn bread, biscuits, sliced warm brown and white bread, muffins, and baskets of rolls. Beside these the women displayed freshly churned butter, jars of apple butter, honey, sorghum molasses, and every kind of jam and jelly imaginable. They filled the last table full of desserts—layered cakes; fruit, custard, and pecan pies; cobblers with thick sugary crusts; and huge cinnamon cookies. Each family brought their own dishes and eating utensils, but the deacons' wives provided plenty of tea and sweet lemonade to drink.

Grant stared hungrily at the feast before him. He'd already walked the length of the tables twice. He felt like an impulsive young boy ready to snatch a chicken leg and run to eat it behind a tree where no one would see him. In fact, no one would miss a little piece of chicken.

The reverend tapped him on the shoulder. "Can't eat until we've said the blessing, and I know exactly what you're thinking."

Grant took a quick look around, determined to fill his stomach at the next opportunity. "Yes, but I'm starved. I delivered a baby boy this morning and missed breakfast. I'm beginning to sound like Rebecca—whining when things don't go my way."

"Can't have the town doctor starving." The reverend's soft gray eyes glistened in the sun. "I'll gather folks together so we can do God the honors."

Any other time, Grant would have protested, but he'd risen before three, and his stomach growled. The reverend's deep voice echoed across the grounds. Soon the crowd formed around him.

"Let's bow our heads. Heavenly Father, we thank You for a beautiful day of celebration and for our country's freedom to worship and grow closer to Thee. We humbly ask that Thou wouldst be with each and every one of us throughout the day as we enjoy time with our friends and family. Keep us safe in Thy tender care. Bless all of this wonderful food and the hands that have prepared it. In Jesus' name, amen."

Lines on each side of the tables formed. Everyone would have an opportunity to throw horse shoes, participate in three-legged races, enter a watermelon seed-spitting contest, race their best horse, show off their muscles to the ladies in a tug-of-war, and just plain visit. Grant watched as the younger men picked out the prettiest girls to impress with their feats of glory and each girl pointed out to her favorite beau exactly what food item she'd prepared. He thought again of Jenny's attempts at cooking and laughed. Maybe he should warn these good folks.

Grant lost no time in grasping Rebecca's hand and finding a good spot near the front. Searching the crowd for Mimi and Jenny, he all but knocked into his short, plump housekeeper.

"I've saved you an excellent position in line," he said.

Mimi glanced around as if embarrassed. "Grant, you're near the front."

"I know." He teetered on his heels. "I'm famished."

Jenny covered her mouth to keep from laughing.

"This should be for the elderly and those with children," Mimi whispered, leaning into him.

He hooked his free arm into Mimi's. "Guess I'm all set. Jenny, you take Mimi's other arm."

Jenny tried to muffle her laughter, but Mimi shot both of them a disapproving glare. Grant filled Rebecca's plate and piled his own two layers high. Reluctantly, he turned from the dessert table. His plate didn't have a speck of room. Selecting a perfect spot for the entire family under a broad-limbed oak, he and Rebecca claimed it and anxiously waited for the other members to arrive. Shortly thereafter, all of the Andrews clan joined him. Jocelyn and the reverend carried an extra pitcher of lemonade.

A few feet away, Frank and Ellen Kahler waved in the midst of their own family.

"Oh, they seem so happy." Jenny sighed.

Casey turned to wave at them. "Yes, extremely happy."

"Frank's smile will fade once the honeymoon marks a month,"

Morgan said, lifting a glass of lemonade to his lips.

Casey punched him playfully, but Morgan retaliated by giving her an affectionate kiss on the cheek. "You are so beautiful today, my dear," he said. "I declare your loveliness rivals the sun."

Bonnie laughed until tears rolled down her cheeks. "If ya'll don't hush, this baby will come this afternoon."

Grant stole a glance at Jenny. Her cheeks glowed a healthy shade of pink, and her brown eyes fairly danced. She caught his gaze, and he noticed a slow blush. It satisfied him tremendously to realize he caused the extra color in her face.

"You look absolutely beautiful today, too," he said, barely loud enough for Jenny to hear.

"Thank you," she replied in the same hushed tone. "But my dress isn't green. It's blue."

"Who says you have to be dressed in green?" Grant searched his thoughts, somewhat bewildered at her statement.

"No one. All I have to do is look at Rebecca." A dimple in her left cheek deepened—the same as his daughter's.

"Have you considered Mimi may have a fondness for green?"

Jenny laughed again. "She favors blue." And Grant noted Mimi's pale blue blouse with her deep navy blue skirt.

"All right. I confess. Green is my favorite."

They both turned their attention to Rebecca, who was dressed from head to toe in her father's favorite color.

Jenny giggled and brushed a wayward chestnut curl from her face. "Rebecca's first word must have been green."

"It was 'Papa,'" he said in feigned annoyance.

A shout from the road caught his attention. A young boy raced a mule bareback toward the church. "Doc Andrews!" He jumped from the animal and glanced frantically about.

Grant stood and signaled for the boy's attention.

"Who is it?" the reverend asked with the familiar look of concern on his brow.

LANTERNS
LACE

"Timothy Detterman." Grant shielded his eyes from the sun. He reached for his hat on the ground and walked toward the dark-headed boy.

Timothy tied his horse to the hitching rail and ran toward Grant. "Doc Andrews," he said breathlessly. "You gotta come fast."

Grant gently took him by the shoulders. "Slow down. What's wrong?"

Taking a deep breath, Timothy tried again. "It's Aaron. He fell out of the barn and hit his head. Ma sent me to fetch you. He's just lying there, Doc. He ain't movin' nothin', and his leg's all twisted."

"Calm down, son. I'm coming. I've got my bag with me, but I need to stop at my house and get a few other things. I'd best take the wagon in case I need to bring him back." He swung his gaze to Mimi. "Will you mind Rebecca?"

"Yes. Don't worry about a thing."

Jenny instantly rose and faced him. "Please, let me go with you. Maybe I can help."

He didn't want to take the time to argue, just dissuade her. Aaron's condition meant more than contemplating whether she could be a help or hindrance. "I don't know what I'll find, and I have no idea when I'll be back."

"It doesn't matter. I'd like to go."

He reluctantly agreed and met the reverend's gaze. Quickly, a look of understanding passed between them. Sam Detterman was a hard man, and he despised doctors. While Timothy raced for his mule, Jenny and Grant hurried toward the buckboard.

"You go on back and tell your ma and pa I'm on my way," Grant called to the boy. "I won't take long to fetch my other things."

Timothy shook like a brittle leaf, and Grant stopped long enough to show him that several folks were standing to watch them leave. The reverend had announced Aaron's unfortunate accident, and the crowd stood to pray.

"Prayer is the best medicine," Grant said. "I'll be right along."

Grant stepped up onto the buckboard and gave Jenny a hand up. He said nothing. He needed to think through Timothy's description of his brother's condition. Finally, he wet his lips. "I sure hope Aaron had his eyes closed because of the pain in his leg and nothing else."

"A broken leg and a head injury sound serious."

"Have you ever seen a dead person?"

Jenny sucked in a breath. "My grandmother passed on in her sleep, and Mrs. Lewis."

"This isn't the same. It's not too late to change your mind. Besides, the injuries are only half the problem."

Jenny's confused glance flew to his face. "What do you mean?"

"Aaron's father doesn't believe in doctors." He pulled the horse to a halt in front of his house. "This is your last opportunity to change your mind."

"No. I'm going. You can tell me about the boys' father while we're on our way."

Stubborn woman. Makes me wonder if I've met my match. He raced up the front walk and returned a few moments later with splints and straps along with a handful of cloth strips. As soon as he stepped onto the buckboard, she asked about Mr. Detterman.

"A few years back, their oldest son died when a mule kicked him in the head. I couldn't save him."

"So he blamed you?"

Grant nodded and rounded the curve near his home. "Yes, and still does. The man swore he never believed in doctors in the first place. It doesn't really matter since I'm the only one in town." He slapped the reins over the horse's back. "Hold on tight, Jenny. This is going to be a wild ride."

She gripped the side of the wooden seat. "I'm ready."

What transformed Miss Society into a small-town girl with spunk? He liked this side of her. He liked it very much.

For the first time since the picnic, he turned and gave her a reassuring smile. "That's my girl," he said, as much to encourage himself as the young lady seated beside him.

"What can I do there to help?" Jenny bounced along on the wagon seat. If the situation hadn't been serious, he'd have teased her.

"Let me see what mood Sam is in first. My guess is that his wife will be very upset. If Aaron is unconscious, it'll bring back bad memories."

"I'll wait for your instructions. Hopefully his mother will allow me to comfort her—maybe keep her away from her son so you can tend to him."

Maybe she'd be a help after all. "That's a good idea. Just pray his father will let me close enough to help him."

CHAPTER  26

Grant gripped the reins as he directed the fast-moving horse and wagon. He prayed for guidance and wisdom in dealing with the Detterman family and for God's healing power to touch the boy. The memory of Sam's temper and his bitterness over the oldest son's tragic death flashed vividly across Grant's mind.

That was more than three years ago, which means Aaron must be around fifteen. He most likely recalled his brother's death—clearly. Surely the youth didn't hold a grudge like his father did. Until this very moment, Grant hadn't considered resentment from Aaron. Uneasiness settled in the pit of his stomach. What if Aaron didn't want Grant to tend to him?

Silently, he prayed for a softening of Sam's resolve and an end to the bitterness. Perhaps Grant had been given a second chance to show Sam the compassion and commitment with which he treated all his patients.

"I'm praying for you," Jenny said, breaking into his thoughts. Her brown eyes were warm and sincere. "I'm new at talking to God, but I wanted you to know that."

"Thanks. I don't mean to be ignoring you."

"I know." She returned his smile. "You have a lot on your mind."

And he suddenly realized that having Jenny beside him made him feel. . .complete. He wondered how she felt about him.

In a storm of dust, they arrived at the modest farm. Sam and his wife were bent over Aaron, but Grant couldn't tell if the boy was conscious. Upon further survey of the area, he believed Aaron must still be in the same position as when he fell. Three other boys, including Timothy, and two girls huddled together on the front porch several feet from their parents.

Sam Detterman, a stocky, hairy man known for his strength, stood to face Grant. He waved his fist in the air, and a stream of obscenities broke through the still, hot summer day.

"Go home, sawbones. We don't need your help." The red-faced farmer stomped toward the wagon.

"Your boy's hurt," Grant said, much more calmly than he felt. He stepped down from the wagon, his left hand firmly wrapped around the handle of his medical bag. "This isn't going to be easy," he whispered to Jenny. "It might be best if you join the children on the porch."

Alarm flashed across her face, and she nodded. Taking her along went against his better judgment. She didn't need to witness any of this. *The reverend may have a funeral tomorrow—the town doctor's.*

"I need to take a look at Aaron," Grant said. A trickle of sweat slid down his face.

"I already told you to go home. You won't be killing another one of my boys."

"Sam, please." Mrs. Detterman, a thin, pale woman, touched her husband's arm. "Timothy didn't go after Doc Andrews on his own. I sent him. We need him to set Aaron's leg."

"I said no." He shoved her hand from his arm with such force that she sprawled backward into the dirt.

Grant continued to walk toward them slowly, steadily—praying with each step. Seeing Sam lash out at his wife disgusted him, but Grant vowed not to succumb to anger, no matter how much he wanted to. He contemplated wrestling Sam to the ground and tying him up until Aaron's leg was set.

"I came to treat your son, and I'm not leaving until I do," Grant said.

"You'll have to come through me first."

Mrs. Detterman knelt at Aaron's side. "Sam, let him set Aaron's leg. It won't heal right if he doesn't." She wept and stroked her injured son's face.

"Is he conscious?" Grant asked the tear-stained woman.

"Yes." She continued to gaze into Aaron's blanched face. "He's hurting real bad."

"Shut up." Sam's voice echoed around them. "I'm the head of this family, and I say he ain't touching my boy. Have you forgotten what happened to Edgar?"

Grant didn't hesitate in his pace toward the big man. With each step, he became more determined to tend to the youth.

"Sam, I'll fight you if that's what it takes. But one way or another, I'm looking after Aaron." Grant eyed Sam Detterman squarely. Without saying another word, he set down his bag and rolled up his sleeves.

"I'm bigger and stronger than you." Sam's threats mounted with each word.

Grant didn't doubt him. The man stood more than two inches taller, had broader shoulders, and worked hard physically every day of his life. Grant knew his own best defense came from his faith and reliance upon God.

"Most likely you'll beat me up good, but I'm not afraid of you. I didn't kill Edgar. Your son died when the mule kicked him—before I even got here. It doesn't make sense to blame me."

Sam swung his right fist toward Grant's face, but Grant blocked it with his left hand and pushed the big man back. The intensity and surprise of Grant's defense knocked Sam into the dirt. Swearing, Sam quickly regained his balance and landed a punch to Grant's jaw.

The impact stunned him, and he tasted blood. For a split second he questioned the sensibility of fighting this mountain of a man.

Grant drew back his left hand and laid into Sam's stomach, doubling him over. Sam, in turn, used his head and body to hit Grant's midsection. The pain sent the doctor to his knees, gasping for breath.

"Stop, please." Mrs. Detterman attempted to pull her husband back, but he shook off her grip.

A little girl cried out for her papa.

Jenny said nothing while she waited on the porch with the children.

The two men continued to brawl in the dust and dirt. Sam's strength only surpassed his rage, and Grant feared he was losing the struggle. With each blow to his body, he felt himself weaken. It wouldn't be long before he'd be stretched out beside Aaron. The youth moaned above the sounds of the others, strengthening Grant's efforts. If Sam succeeded, his son would limp for the rest of his life.

Sam began to show signs of tiring, but Grant felt his own strength wavering, too. He knew he'd more than held his own, and he thanked God for allowing him to endure the blows thus far.

Instantly, Grant received another closed fist to his right eye, which didn't hurt nearly as badly as the first time—apparently it was numb. Finally, he managed to throw his entire body into the larger man, knocking him to the ground. It gave Grant the needed advantage, and he pinned Sam to the rock-hard earth. They both knew the fight was over. Even so, Grant grappled with whether to release him or not.

"I need to tend to your boy," Grant said between ragged breaths. "Before I let you go, I need your word that you won't interfere."

Sam's face had already begun to swell, and blood trickled over his chin. He nodded.

"I also need your help in setting his leg. It will go faster if the two of us work together."

Sam glared at him, but Grant increased the pressure on his arms.

"Pa," Aaron whispered within a few feet of them. "Please, help the doc set my leg. I don't want to be a cripple."

Sam's body relaxed beneath the hold, and Grant released him. He prayed for wisdom. He hurt all over, yet he needed a clear head and steady hands to treat Aaron.

"Mrs. Detterman, I need some clean strips of cloth, warm water, soap, and the straps and splints from my wagon. I have a few cloth strips there, too, but it might not be enough." He took a deep breath between words and wiped the blood from his mouth. The woman hurried off into the house, and Timothy called for his brothers to help him with the items in the wagon.

For the first time since he and Sam had exchanged blows, Grant caught sight of Jenny sitting on the porch with the other Detterman children. She smiled encouragingly. She hadn't shed a tear, and he hadn't heard her scream.

"I'll help Mrs. Detterman." Jenny lifted her skirts and disappeared into the house.

Grant bent over Aaron. He gingerly examined every part of the boy's body. Aaron's eyes were alert. Internal organs were not abnormally tender, but a huge bump rose from the side of his head where he had fallen. A few ribs appeared to be broken along with the right femur.

"He looks pretty good except for his leg and a few bruised and broken ribs." He glanced over at Sam, who knelt on the opposite side of his son. "Have you ever set a leg, Sam?"

"No. Watched a time or two but never tried it myself." Sam's left eye was nearly swollen shut.

"Well, it'll hurt him. I'm going to give him a shot of morphine, but he might still pass out. Be better if he does. Aaron is going to fight me, and that's where I need your help. If you'll position yourself above his head and hold him still, I can work fast to get the bone into place."

He sighed deeply. "I'll do it."

Mrs. Detterman returned with the requested supplies. Grant wiped the blood trickling down from his lip and scrubbed his hands. Meanwhile, Timothy returned and watched Grant's every move, obviously intrigued with the whole process. As Grant administered the painkiller, he remembered the days when he had observed others being treated for injuries and ailments. Grant wondered if Timothy shared the same interest for medicine.

Grant took a fleeting glance at Jenny. She looked to be telling the children a story. What a blessing. Those kids were probably scared to death.

Giving Aaron his full attention, Grant took a deep breath to steady his hands. A drop of blood dripped onto his arm, and Mrs. Detterman wiped it off. "Aaron, I know you hurt powerfully bad, but I need you to look at me."

Aaron's cloudy gaze silently begged Grant to remove the pain.

"Good. Now, I want you to listen carefully. Your pa is going to help me set your leg. It's going to hurt worse than it does now. I want you to go ahead and holler all you want. Don't be a hero. If you feel like passing out, give in to it. I promise I'll work fast, but we've got to straighten out the bone in order for you to walk proper again." Grant touched his forehead. "Do you have any questions?"

"No, sir," Aaron managed. "I–I don't want to be a cripple."

"We're going to make sure your leg heals straight as a tree trunk. You're a brave young man, and I know your parents are proud of you."

Mrs. Detterman wiped the beads of sweat from Aaron's face, and he forced a tight-lipped smile for her. Grant looked up at Timothy, who still seemed interested in everything that was going on.

"Timothy, I need you to take your ma over by your brothers and sisters with Miss Jenny. Please keep her there until your pa and I are finished," Grant said.

Mrs. Detterman looked tearfully at her husband for direction. Sam nodded, and Timothy complied with Grant's wishes.

"All right, Sam," Grant said in a low tone.

The big man firmly held his son's arms and silently signaled for Grant to begin. Quickly, Grant twisted and turned Aaron's broken leg into its original position. The youth sank his teeth into his lower lip until it bled, and when his father shouted for him to scream, he let out an ear-piercing cry.

"It's set," Grant said in the next moment. "The worst is over."

He worked diligently wrapping the cloths around the leg and splints, then bandaging Aaron's ribs. Grimacing in pain, the boy used all of his strength to lift his head and view the set leg.

"You're the best patient I've ever had," Grant said.

"Thanks, Doc. It looks straight, doesn't it?"

Grant smiled. "I'll be racing you next year at the Fourth of July picnic. You can tell all the girls what happened and how brave you were."

Once finished, Grant studied Sam. Blood oozed from various cuts on his face, and his left eye sat enclosed in a ring of black and blue. "Do I look as pitiful as you do?"

For the first time, Sam grinned. "Worse." He held out his hand, and Grant grasped it firmly. "Thanks for helping my boy. I was wrong about. . .everything."

"That's all right. A good fight makes a day entertaining." Grant wasn't about to admit he ached all over.

"Well, I've been spiteful. I never got over losing our firstborn, and deep down, I knew it wasn't your fault, most likely mine for not getting rid of that crazy mule. What I mean is I'm sorry." He met Grant's gaze with a look of respect.

"You had no way of knowing what would happen to Edgar. You can't blame yourself."

Sam wiped the tears filling his eyes and focused on Aaron. "Guess your brothers will be doing your chores for quite a spell, son. Nigh on to harvesttime."

Aaron nodded wearily, visibly exhausted. "I'm going to be cranky and bored, but I won't be a cripple."

Sam touched his son's face before another tear spilled from his own eyes. He brushed it away. Even so, emotion rested on his father's face.

"Thanks, Pa," Aaron whispered. "Doc couldn't have fixed me without your help."

"Is it still hurtin' bad?" Sam asked.

"Yeah, pretty bad."

"I can leave him something for the pain," Grant said. "What do you say we get him into the house?"

Sam called to his wife, who sat obediently with her other children. "Ma, this boy needs to come inside. Are you ready for him?"

❧❧❧

Grant didn't want to take the Dettermans' money for his doctoring, but he knew that refusing payment would have injured Sam's pride. The man insisted Grant clean up and stood by while Jenny dabbed a wet cloth over the cuts and bruises. Much to Grant's surprise, once Jenny completed her nursing, she turned to Sam and gave him more attention than Grant had received.

Good. She understands Sam's pride took a beating today.

Mrs. Detterman pressed Grant and Jenny to stay for supper. Grant had felt the hunger pangs earlier, remembering the unfinished plate of food at the picnic. Jenny appeared exhausted, and she, too, admitted to hunger.

The couple stayed long past sundown, laughing and talking with the family. Grant found several licorice sticks for the younger children, for which they thanked him repeatedly. Mrs. Detterman remarked how horrible both men looked. In fact, she couldn't decide whose face had the most cuts and bruises.

"You know," Sam began, passing a plate of fried chicken to Grant, "the mark of real friendship comes from a good fight where both men win."

"Oh, but we'll be hurtin' tomorrow," Grant said, and the family laughed.

Once dinner was over, Grant checked Aaron again to make sure he had received no other injuries. "Thank you for the fine meal, Mrs. Detterman. I guess we'll be heading toward town, but I'll be back day after tomorrow." He turned to Sam and grasped his arm in a firm shake. "I look forward to seeing you on Saturday. It'll be best if Aaron's not moved until I get back."

Grant helped Jenny crawl up onto the buckboard and sensed a new injury to his right shoulder. The ride back to town proved slow, not like the whirlwind trip earlier in the day. Truthfully, he hurt all over, and the soreness guaranteed tomorrow and the next day would be worse. Still, he felt a sense of satisfaction, or rather gratefulness, that God had used him to unite this family again.

Sam had been a bitter man, and he'd often taken it out on his family. His wife and children weren't the only part of his life that he'd turned his back on. Before Edgar's accident, Sam had been active in church and a real witness to God's power and grace. Perhaps now the slow healing process could begin. It would be wonderful to see the Dettermans in church again.

In the faint shadows, Grant stole a glimpse at Jenny. An array of stubborn curls circled her face, and she'd long since given up on trying to tuck them inside her hairpins.

"You were a real help today," he said. "Thank you for giving up the Fourth of July celebration."

"I wanted to come, remember? You were magnificent."

"I got into a fight," he said. "Not sure how God feels about that."

"You made sure Aaron wouldn't be lame."

"I did my best." He hesitated. "Are you as tired as I am?"

"If you're tired enough to sleep in the back of this wagon, then I guess so." She reached up and pulled the pins from her hair. "And this will help my headache."

In the pale light cast from the two lanterns lit on both sides of the wagon, he saw a cascade of thick brown curls fall softly around her shoulders. Framed against a half moon, her hair looked to have streaks of gold woven throughout. The sight took his breath away.

Grant didn't have a firm hold on what he should say, but a mere "thank you" hadn't seemed like enough. His awkwardness brought a siege of silence. Finally, he decided to speak from the depths of his heart. If only he could see her eyes.

"Jenny," he began. "I thought Sam and I would battle in words today, not with our fists. Sorry you had to see it. Not once did I hear you scream or cry out. Instead, you gathered up the children and kept them occupied. And I didn't have to say a word about Mrs. Detterman. You comforted her like you two had been lifelong friends. You're a strong, courageous woman, and I don't know anyone else I'd rather have had with me today."

Her hand lightly brushed over his. "I'm glad I went with you, and I'd do it again."

"Let's hope not too soon. My body couldn't handle it."

They both laughed despite the gravity of the day's events.

"Too bad you're a teacher. I think you'd make an excellent nurse." He hoped his praise didn't reveal what lay in his heart.

The closeness of the young woman caused him to wish he didn't smell of sweat and look twice as nasty as what hit his nostrils. It didn't seem fair that even in the dim light of the kerosene lanterns, Jenny remained lovely. . .radiant. She took up so much of his thoughts lately. Why, he found himself thinking about her before he went to sleep at night and before he opened his eyes in the morning. Each time he saw his daughter, an image of Jenny took over his senses. They looked too much alike. It distracted him more than a Christian man should allow. What happened to his resolve about not needing a woman? Didn't being a father and a doctor take up all of his time? What about the slip of paper in his Bible listing all of his requirements for a wife? Besides, this woman couldn't possibly. . . .

"Jenny?"

"Yes?"

"Have you ever been kissed by a sweaty, dirty, black-eyed, bruised, and beaten doctor?"

"No. Can't say I have."

"Good." He pulled the horse to a halt. "You may want to hold your nose," he said with a halfhearted attempt at humor.

"I don't think so," she said.

Wrapping his arms around her small shoulders, he drew her close to him. She trembled in his embrace as he lifted her chin. In the darkness, he envisioned those huge, endless pools of brown, feathered in the longest lashes he'd ever seen.

Slowly he descended upon her lips, gently tasting. The softness increased his desire for more. She seemed fragile to him, like a porcelain doll, but real—and in his arms.

Hesitantly, he pulled back. He wanted to say something, but the words refused to come. What he'd yearned for in a kiss had now manifested itself, and it shook his senses.

Without a doubt, Grant realized he was in love.

CHAPTER  27

Grant opened the door of Martha's Place shortly before noon. The quiet hit him as such a contrast to the raucous sounds that began after the sun set. He'd been there a few times amid the off-key tunes of the battered piano, the smell of liquor, and the mask of counterfeit happiness. Unfortunately, some of the patrons had a tendency to become violent, and that's when the knives and guns took over. But today the residents were apparently asleep, except for Martha. She rarely slept.

A strange woman, Mrs. Martha DeMott. No one had ever met Mr. DeMott. Grant doubted if one existed, especially given the relationship she shared with the town's banker, Lester Hillman, which had resulted in two young sons.

Glancing at the gaudy red and gold decorations, Grant considered the contrast of the church a scant half mile down the road. So much sadness dwelt within the two-story building inappropriately referred to as a "pleasure palace." Drunkenness, loneliness, unwanted pregnancies, diseases of the trade, and physical abuse all continued while the citizens of Kahlerville looked down their noses and closed their minds to the despair.

Grant called out for Martha. He knew her ways—she'd keep

him waiting until she decided to venture into the front area with a sweet look of surprise. He pulled out the newspaper from under his arm and began to read.

"Grant, what a pleasure." Martha strolled into the room, looking as grand at midday as she did at midnight.

With an inward smile, he folded the paper. "Can you spare me a moment?" he asked.

She tilted her head and batted her eyes. "For you, I can spare an hour."

He laughed. "Now, Martha. We'd set the town's tongues wagging."

She nodded, almost sadly. He often wondered if she regretted her profession, even if she was the richest woman in town. "Best we talk in my office." She whirled around, and he followed.

Oh, the role he played to pacify this woman who made money from the sinful pleasures of men. But how would she ever see Jesus through condemning eyes and wagging tongues?

"I won't waste your time, Martha. I want to know who told you that Ellen Kahler and Jenny Martin had plans to open a brothel."

She frowned. "Why?"

"Because it's not true. Ellen is happily married, and Jenny is only visiting."

"My, you do draw the Martin girls, don't you?"

He swallowed the sarcasm he itched to unleash. "What if the person who lied to you was more interested in causing trouble than in telling you the truth?"

Martha leaned in closer. The neckline of her dress needed. . . adjustment. Grant glanced away.

"Tell me more," she said.

"I don't have any more to say. I have a hunch all is not as it seems."

Martha wrapped her slender fingers around a cup of coffee. "Life is seldom what it seems, Grant. A trusted person told me about their plans."

"Know what I think?" Grant studied her face.

Before she could respond, the door opened, and two small boys raced inside. The endearing smile on Martha's face confirmed Grant's belief that she loved those boys with all of her heart.

"How are my sons?" she asked and drew the younger one into her lap while tousling the hair of the other.

"Very good, Mama," the older boy said.

Martha kissed them both. "Can you go play for a few more minutes? Then I will join you."

"Yes, ma'am," the older one said and took the hand of his brother. A tear coursed down the younger boy's face. "It's all right. Mama will be with us soon."

Deeply moved, Grant saw in Martha's sons the affection he and Rebecca shared. A penetrating thought settled on him. Martha would do anything for her children. He also had seen the fondness she and Lester shared. The relationship was wrong; nevertheless, the feelings between them were strong.

Once the door closed, Martha turned her attention to him.

"Those are fine boys, Martha," he said.

"Yes. They are. Thank you for keeping their father a secret."

He nodded. *But Ben knows.* "Is someone trying to blackmail him?"

She gasped—a rarity considering her otherwise guarded emotions. "Whatever for?"

Grant paused. He needed to put himself in Martha and Lester's shoes. "Someone could have learned about the boys. Someone who didn't care who they hurt. Someone who was clever and wanted something from you."

She stared at him, her eyes gleaming with something akin to revulsion. "You don't know what you're talking about, Grant. No such thing is going on."

He hadn't expected her to respond any differently, but the truth glared back at him. If Turner had traveled all this distance to recover his money, he'd most likely find a way to compensate for his efforts in another devious way.

Grant listened intently to the rhythmic sounds of Jake Weather's heart. Satisfied that it beat strong and steady, he moved the stethoscope across the chest to his lungs. Deep, even breathing provided additional proof of the old man's remarkable good health. Excellent hearing, keen eyesight, and a sharp mind kept him the envy of men half his age.

"Jake, you'll outlive me." Grant picked up Jake's faded blue shirt and assisted him in putting on the garment.

"The Lord's smilin' on me." A wide grin spread across the wiry old man's face.

"He must be," Grant responded, "but I don't see how you do it. You smoke too much, drink your own whiskey, work like an ox, and never miss a church service. According to my records, you must be eighty-four years old."

The old man chuckled. "I think eighty-six. Doesn't matter nohow. I'm old, real old. So, I'm fine, Doc?"

"Excellent. Your heart and lungs are good. Your skin's a good color, and your only complaint is aching bones. I figure you'll live to be a hundred at least."

Jake laughed until his skeletal body shook. "I'll double your fee for that report." He pulled a wad of bills from his pants pocket and slapped them on the examining table. "Believe I'll see how Miss Mimi is doing before I leave."

The two ambled into the kitchen, and Grant noticed his chubby housekeeper suddenly found a tremendous amount of energy, for she immediately listed what all needed to be done before lunch. Her hustling and bustling about the kitchen soon caused her face to flush pink. Grant excused himself, leaving Mimi alone with old Jake.

Before Grant had the opportunity to record Jake's examination into his file, Ben called from the front hallway. "Grant, the baby's coming." He broke into a coughing spasm.

Grant knew better than to question the respiratory problem and his brother-in-law's failing health. In the past when he had expressed concern, Ben had lectured him on borrowing trouble.

"How far apart are Bonnie's pains?" he asked once Ben caught his breath.

"Two minutes, and her water broke. I came as fast as I could."

Grant remembered his sister's last baby had arrived within an hour after her labor started. Lifting his medical bag from the examination table, he hurried toward the kitchen. "Bonnie's baby is on its way, Mimi. I'll be back as quickly as I can."

"Do you want to take your lunch with you?" she asked, her cheeks a bit pinker than before.

"No, thanks. You can let Jake have it."

The old man eased up behind her. "I'll look after Mimi and the little one while yer gone."

"I knew I could count on you." Grant winked at Mimi's seething face. Suddenly, guilt took over his practical joking. "Tell you what— if I'm not back in an hour, go on home. Mimi and Rebecca are used to my absence."

Outside, the two men climbed into Ben's buggy for the short ride to the Kahler home. The stylish house stood about two miles east of town on nearly three hundred acres. The home boasted elegance and grandeur unlike any other for miles around. A decorator from Dallas had advised Bonnie on the interior furnishings, and most of the furniture had come from back East.

Ben owned a profitable cattle ranch and had made several wise investments while working as the town sheriff. The Kahler family did well in this town, and Ben's family lacked for nothing. Grant always wondered why he stayed on as the town's sheriff. But Ben insisted he found tremendous satisfaction in keeping the town safe for its citizens.

His brother-in-law started to speak, but the coughing halted his words. This bout lasted longer than the previous one.

"I don't want Bonnie having any more children," Ben finally said.

Maybe now Grant would learn the truth. "Why not? She's healthy and hasn't had any trouble with the other two."

"Bonnie isn't the problem. I don't want her raising more than three children alone." He lifted his hat and wiped the sweat from his brow with a starched white handkerchief.

Grant hesitated. "Ben, you don't know that for sure."

"I saw a doctor in Dallas about a month ago. I hope you don't mind, but I couldn't talk to you about it after I'd lost my temper. Pride has a way of doing things to a man."

Grant nodded. "I'm just glad you sought medical attention. What did the doctor say?"

He paused and took a deep breath as though fighting off another coughing spell. "Either move to Arizona where it's dry and I might get better, or settle my affairs," he said with a labored breath. "I believe the Bible phrases it as 'putting your house in order.'"

Although Grant had long suspected the advanced stages of a lung sickness, the news devastated him. "Have you told Bonnie?"

"No. At first I didn't want to bother her with it until after the baby came, but now I don't think I'll tell her at all."

"Arizona is a fine place."

"Maybe so, but I'm not uprooting my wife from her family and friends. You know your sister. She's lived a sheltered life. Emotionally, she couldn't stand leaving Kahlerville. It might do more harm than good."

"So you'd rather die a premature death?" Grant studied Ben's pale skin and cavernous eyes. "You think it'd be easier for her to handle being a widow with three children to raise on her own?"

"Don't preach to me." Ben started coughing again. "I'm sorry. Look, Grant, this is the best way for all concerned. Bonnie and the children will be with family, and she won't have any money worries.

My finances, or rather, my affairs, are in order."

"Promise me you'll pray about this," Grant said. "There are fine hospitals back East."

"I have been, and I'll continue. But I'd appreciate it if you'd keep our conversation to yourself."

Grant nodded. "I'll not say a word, but I want to talk more about this later. Right now let's get your new baby born."

He shrugged his thin shoulders. "Who knows? I might get better. God may see fit for me to watch my children grow up."

Grant chose to change the topic of their conversation. "Remember how upset Bonnie was when she went into labor the first time?"

"And do I. She wanted a midwife, not her brother."

"I didn't think my little sister could argue and go through birthing pains at the same time."

Ben nodded. "She was so embarrassed with the thought of her brother delivering her baby. If I hadn't insisted upon it, she'd never have consented."

"I understood her modesty. We grew up together, scrapping like brothers and sisters do. But when I delivered Zach and then Michael Paul, she trusted me as her doctor, not as her teasing brother."

"I just love her so much."

Hearing those words, Grant realized Ben would die a premature death before upsetting his beloved Bonnie with the news about his health.

Within the hour, Bonnie gave birth to a healthy little girl. From the moment she opened her eyes and wailed her first announcement into the world, Grant saw she seized her father's heart. Without a doubt, she looked every bit like her mother—big crystal blue eyes, a pert little mouth, and an oval face.

"Just look at that bald head." Grant chuckled. "She'll be a blond for sure."

Ben smiled and leaned over his wife. "What are we going to name her, sweetheart?"

Bonnie sighed happily, although exhausted. "I like the name we talked about—Lydia Anne."

"Perfect," her husband whispered, and planted kisses on both of his girls' foreheads.

While Bonnie slept, Ben went after the reverend and Jocelyn. Remaining behind at his sister's bedside, Grant's thoughts flew back to the newly acquired information about Ben. This was not the first time he'd been asked to keep a patient's diagnosis confidential, but this man was family.

Then again, he didn't need to be reminded about his brother-in-law's protective nature when it came to Bonnie. Since the day they'd met, Ben had guarded her from anything unpleasant and showered her with everything money could buy. Even their father before he died had spoiled Bonnie, and later Morgan fell into the same habit. Their mother and Grant had been united in their endeavors to force Bonnie to take on responsibilities, but their efforts were futile when it came to Ben.

Now Grant feared his sister wouldn't be strong enough to endure her husband's impending death, and there were three children to consider. He commended her mothering abilities, but could she bring up those children alone?

If only his brother-in-law's fears were unfounded, but he'd observed the changes in Ben for months—and Morgan had expressed concern when the man failed to perform routine law matters. But God performed miracles. Grant saw His divine mercy and grace every day within his own profession. . . . Yet sometimes God called for a man to alter his mind-set—even a stubborn man like Ben Kahler.

Grant lightly touched Bonnie's cheek, his beautiful sister, asleep with a new baby resting in her arms. Was she ready to deal with the harsh realities of life? He wanted desperately to believe so. Smiling down at his tiny niece all wrinkled and pink, he was reminded of his Rebecca. Birth always prompted a sense of awe in him. Silently Grant gave the matter over to God, determined not to worry about

Ben and Bonnie but recognizing his own flaws of perfectionism and determination to be in control. God on His mighty throne knew the needs of them all, and Grant must rest in that assurance.

He retrieved his Bible from the medical bag and turned to a familiar passage. He really didn't need to look it up, for he'd memorized the words. Finding Philippians 4:6 and 7, he closed his eyes and allowed the scripture to be his earnest prayer: "Be careful for nothing; but in everything by prayer and supplication with thanksgiving let your requests be made known unto God. And the peace of God, which passeth all understanding, shall keep your hearts and minds through Christ Jesus."

Dear Lord, thank You for this new birth and for seeing Bonnie safely through the delivery. I'm worried about Ben, and my fears have taken form. I'm torn and broken inside. Ben's a good man, and he loves You. Must he be taken home so soon? Can't he watch his children grow? Help me to trust in Your divine wisdom. I give it all to You. In Jesus' name, amen.

Tucking the Bible back inside his bag, his thoughts turned to Jenny—another continuous object of his prayers. He'd given his growing affections for her to God, but still the thought of her going back to Ohio plagued him. And Turner kept him wary of the future. He'd seen fear in Martha's eyes, and Grant suspected Turner had his hand dipped in far too many unlawful happenings in Kahlerville.

Oh, God, how frustrating we humans must be to You. I pray for Ben to take his family to Arizona and for Jenny to stay in Kahlerville. Seems like we're never content with the way things are. Not sure how to pray for Aubrey Turner, but You do. What a sad world we live in. And You know that, too.

CHAPTER 28

"A girl." Jenny's eyes widened. "Oh, Grant, what wonderful news. Thank you so much for stopping by to tell me. Is Bonnie all right? Who does the baby look like? What did they name her? How do the boys feel about a baby sister?"

"Slow down." Grant waved his hands in defense at the onslaught of questions. She reminded him of Rebecca when all of her little-girl thoughts and questions spilled out at once. But the sound of Jenny's voice had a different effect on him—it flowed over his heart like a lazy river.

"I'm sorry," she said, but the sparkle in her eyes could not disguise the excitement. "Please tell me everything, and I promise to listen quietly." The two strolled along the side of the quiet street.

"How long can you wait?" Grant asked. "Too bad I'm not a gambling man. We might make a little wager."

"Heaven forbid, Dr. Andrews." She laughed lightly. "How long must I sit in anticipation?"

"Ah, but I could take a bribe."

"How shameful, but name your price."

He'd like a repeat of their kiss on the Fourth of July, but they hadn't discussed their relationship—if there was one. And he had no idea if she had feelings for him—or had simply felt sorry for him that evening. "Cooking lunch for Rebecca and me on Saturday, and then a long wagon ride. We might even go see the new baby."

Jenny sighed deeply as though the task were too arduous. "I suppose I could manage a few hours away from my busy schedule, and you are including my favorite Miss Mischief. What about Mimi?"

"She has plans with her grandchildren. . . . So do you agree?"

She glanced away, then back at him. Flirting, the ladies called that kind of behavior, and he loved every minute of it.

"I'll manage, Doctor," she said. "Now, may I hear everything about Bonnie and Ben's baby girl?"

Grant leaned forward and whispered, "Do I detect the faint twinge of a whine?"

She attempted a somber face but failed as the corners of her mouth lifted. "I think so, but I'm very curious."

"I know, but for you, I will refrain from any more teasing." He winked before he began. "Miss Lydia Anne Kahler arrived this afternoon at three fifteen. She weighed five pounds and is a fine, healthy baby. She looks like her mother, except she's bald, which leads me to believe she'll have the same color of hair as her mother and grandmother. Bonnie is doing well, just tired." He drummed his fingers on the table. "Let's see—Zachary and Michael Paul held their new baby sister, and Ben is thoroughly smitten. Did I answer all of your questions?"

"Is your mother staying with her?"

"Yes, and I will take you for a visit on Saturday if the food is good."

A strange look passed over her delicate features. "Mimi will have to give me a review. I do have an idea, though."

"For us to eat?"

Jenny shook her finger as though reprimanding an impish school-boy. "No, a gift for the baby. You'll have to settle for fried chicken, green beans, and blueberry cobbler. Mimi has given me more cooking lessons."

Have you learned what pinfeathers are? And the way to a man's heart? Grant grinned. "Deal."

❧❧❧

An unexpected downpour on Saturday crushed any expectations of a wagon ride. Grant heard the *pitter-patter* of rain on the roof in the early morning hours. By the time daylight broke over the horizon, heavy drops pelted against the windowpane of his bedroom. Midmorning, he checked for signs of sunlight and diminishing rain, but it continued to drench the earth.

Again Grant considered the purchase of a buggy so he and his passengers could stay dry. When he thought about the many times he'd been soaked while checking on patients, he realized the necessity of a fine carriage.

"There goes your afternoon," Mimi said, her round face downcast. "And Jenny worked hard on the food yesterday."

And he'd looked forward to spending the day with her and Rebecca. Grant peered at the rolling thunderclouds. "What about your plans to visit your grandchildren?"

"Oh, I can do that another day." She shrugged. "Why don't you three have a picnic on the back porch?"

He stepped through the kitchen and examined the roofed area. The wind hadn't blown the rain inside. In fact, it was quite pleasant.

"Good idea. I'll go get Jenny as soon as it lets up a bit, and I'll not forget the umbrella." He wrapped an arm around her waist. "And you can nap or whatever you want."

"Mercy, Grant. That sounds real inviting."

"Can I go, Papa?" a small voice asked from behind him.

Grant swooped up Rebecca into his arms. "So you want to ride with me to fetch Aunt Jenny?"

The little girl nodded, her dark brown curls bouncing. She hugged his neck and planted a rosebud kiss on his cheek. "Pease, Papa. I not get wet."

"We will see, sweetheart. You can go providing it stops raining. I don't want my little girl sick." The mere words reminded him of Ben's illness, but he shook away the gloom.

"I not get sick. I don't yike medicine." She shook her head with two vigorous tosses.

Within the hour, the sun peeked through the clouds, and at least momentarily, the rain subsided to a few sprinkles. As promised, Grant took Rebecca to fetch Jenny before another downpour. Mimi decided to read in her room after asking Rebecca to make sure Papa and Aunt Jenny behaved.

Jenny finished their noon meal preparation with more ease than Grant expected. For a moment, he allowed his thoughts to stray. What a threesome they'd make. . .if Jenny agreed to be his wife.

The two spread a blue gingham tablecloth over the porch floor as the rain began again. She set the dishes and eating utensils for three while Grant retrieved the food from inside the kitchen. Soon fried chicken, roasted potatoes, buttered corn and beans, warm bread, and blueberry cobbler tempted the trio. Grant asked the blessing, making sure to ask God to bless the hands that had prepared their food.

"This is certainly not like the last picnic I attended." Jenny watched Rebecca fight sleep until she could no longer sit on the hard porch and leaned her head into Jenny's lap. She kissed the little girl's cheek and brushed a wispy curl from her face.

"You mean the Fourth of July?" He buttered a slice of warm bread and recalled the kiss. "Tell me about it."

Jenny blushed, and he laughed.

"It's quieter today," he said.

"You are truly incorrigible," she whispered.

"Guilty. Would you like for me to carry Rebecca upstairs? I could help you clean up, and perhaps we could discuss Jessica's journal."

"I'd like that." She glanced down at her hands. "I'd like to tell

245

you something about my sister, and when you take me back to the boardinghouse today, I want to give you her journal to read."

"Any particular reason why?"

"Some things about Jessica were rather peculiar." She moistened her lips. "Would you mind taking Rebecca to bed first?"

A little confused, Grant picked up his sleeping daughter and carried her upstairs. When he returned, Jenny had not moved from the porch.

"I'm ready," he said. "From the look on your face, this must be serious."

Jenny turned to face him. "Before you read Jessica's journal, I need to explain a few things about her. Jessica's behavior was very strange. According to my parents, she had these tendencies from birth. She displayed either extremely happy or extremely dark moods, rarely even-tempered. I remember times when she refused to sleep for up to three days in a wild state of elation. Then she'd retreat to her room with such melancholy that I feared she might harm herself."

As Grant listened to Jenny explain her sister's oddities, he sensed a growing fear swell in his mind. He thought back over Rebecca's behavior, and thankfully, she did not exhibit any of her mother's strange mannerisms. If he truly examined his daughter's personality, he saw that her temperament more resembled Jenny's.

Grant had studied mental disorders in medical school and had kept himself informed on the mysteries of the mind. During his practice, he'd seen more than one case that involved the unexplainable. As he further pondered Jessica's behavior, he remembered Ellen telling him about Jessica blocking out labor pains by counting flowers on the faded wallpaper in her room. At the time, he didn't dwell on Ellen's statement, but now he understood. She'd most likely seen Jessica's bizarre behavior on more than one occasion. Poor Jessica. Her troubles went far deeper than rebellion against her parents or a lack of faith in God.

"I'm sorry to be the one to tell you the truth about my sister,"

Jenny said. "But I wanted you to hear it from me, not read it in her journal."

"I appreciate that. Praise God, Rebecca doesn't show the same tendencies. I'm really blessed with my little girl. . .and with you."

Jenny awoke to the sound of the grandfather clock downstairs chiming three o'clock. She groaned at the early hour, especially since she'd not fallen asleep until nearly midnight. Even then, nightmares had plagued her—nightmares about Aubrey Turner looking for his money.

She had given Grant the journal last evening. She felt as strongly as ever that he needed to know everything about Jessica. Perhaps he could find the clues to locate the money. Although she wanted the money for Rebecca, Jenny would gladly give it to Turner and have him gone from her life and the lives of those she loved.

Perhaps I should leave town. Ben asked me to stay until the matter was settled, but the thought of these good people in danger because of me is wrong. Selfish. How long can I continue to keep them in harm's way?

The idea of journeying back to Cleveland left her ill at ease. She loved teaching, but she loved Kahlerville more. She loved her new friends more. Jenny sighed. Back in Cleveland she'd have to find a place to live. A second letter from her parents had confirmed that she could no longer live with them. She'd have to face her future as it should be, not she desired. With God's help, she'd find a place to live in Cleveland and continue teaching.

Jenny closed her eyes and heard Rebecca's sweet giggle and Grant's deep voice. She saw Rebecca's eyes in a sweet doll of nearly three and the sea-green gaze of her dear papa. Yes, she must leave them soon for fear he'd learn the truth about her feelings for him.

A bell pealed out through the night. Jenny startled. The bell continued to ring. Its clamor shouted the words she heard in her next breath.

Fire!

Jenny threw back her bed sheet and stumbled to the window.

"It's the brothel," a man shouted.

"At this hour, it's full," another man said. "Looks to me like God is bringing down judgment on Martha's Place."

"We still need to get those folks out of there," said the first man.

Jenny shrank back from the window. Frank had threatened to burn Martha's Place when the woman had accosted Ellen at the store. But surely he hadn't actually done so.

Have I caused this, too?

⁂

Grant's arms ached from hauling water up and down the bucket brigade in an effort to save the building from burning to the ground. Men, women, and children worked side by side to destroy the fiery monster. Those within Martha's Place had escaped, some wrapped in bedclothes to hide their nakedness. A couple of men slipped into the shadows, no doubt making fast tracks home before the whole town learned where they'd been.

No one seemed upset about the brothel's demise other than making sure to douse the flames before any other buildings caught fire. No one expressed regret except the girls who worked there and Martha, who stood off to the side by herself with one babe in her arms and the other clutching her hand. Dressed in her evening finery, Martha didn't offer a picture of motherhood, but Grant knew her heart.

With the building in smoldering ashes, Grant made his way to Martha. Lester had battled the blaze like the rest of them, men and women alike. Now the town's banker stood with the others—no move toward the soiled doves who shed tear after tear or the woman who'd born him two sons—Lester's only children.

"Martha, we need to find a place for you and the girls to stay," he said.

She lifted her gaze to meet his. In the darkness he sensed her sadness. He was certain she'd heard enough of God bringing an end to the sin in their town. Why would any of these women search out Jesus after the way they were treated?

"Look around you, Grant. Which one of these citizens is going to step forward in Christian love?"

He glanced about and saw his mother and the reverend talking with the girls. His mother placed an arm around one of them. "There, Martha." The four girls trailed after his mother and the reverend. He turned back to Martha. "You and the boys come home with me. Mimi and I have plenty of room."

"Grant, some of the townsfolk already claim these boys are yours. Why ruin your reputation?"

He chuckled. "Have you ever known an Andrews to run from a little bit of gossip?"

"No, I guess not."

He sensed a presence beside him. "Ellen, good to see you," Grant said.

"Frank is watching the ashes to make sure it's all out," she said.

"That's right nice of him considering he threatened to burn my establishment." Martha's voice echoed over the night air.

"You and I know he didn't do this," Ellen said. "He was with me."

"I wouldn't expect you to say anything differently," Martha said.

Grant knew Martha's temper. "Ladies, we're all tired. Let's go home and get some rest."

"I wanted to see if Martha and the boys had a place to stay," Ellen said. "Our home is small, but we'd be glad to make room."

Bless you, Ellen.

Martha had a rare moment of silence. The younger of the boys whimpered, and she bounced him lightly in her arms. "Doc Grant here offered us to stay there."

"I see. If you need anything, let me know." Ellen bent to the little boy tugging at Martha's skirts. "Your boys are beautiful. I'm so glad all of you are all right."

She stood and touched Grant's arm. "Jenny helped us carry water. She headed back to the boardinghouse a few minutes ago." She nodded at him and walked back to where Frank stared into the flickering red embers.

"Frank and Ellen are good people," Grant said. "He didn't do this tonight."

Martha shook her head. "Men do strange things when they love a woman. Sometimes it makes them act in madness. I've seen it all." She sighed. "I don't expect Ben to question or even arrest him. It'll go down with folks as an act of God while a model citizen hides his matches."

Grant found no purpose in stating the list of what could have caused the fire. She'd not hear it anyway; she grieved the wealth buried in the cinders. Desperation clung to her like the smoke buried in the folds of her clothes.

He grasped the hand of the older boy and glanced up at Martha. "You and these children don't need to look at this one minute longer."

"I sure wish I hadn't made the statement about Martha's Place needing to be burned to the ground," Frank said.

Ellen wrung out a rag and gently wiped the black soot from his forehead, cheeks, and neck. Her beloved Frank had worked hard this evening. His arms had been singed, and a few sparks had destroyed the front of his shirt. As he sat at the kitchen table, she tried to comfort him about the fire. "Honey, you were angry at the time. No one would ever suspect you."

He glanced up. "Martha would. She'll probably see Ben tonight."

"I don't think so. I saw Grant lead her and the boys toward his house. I offered our home to them, but she wasn't interested." Ellen sighed. "And I would have taken any of the girls, too."

"You have more of a Christian heart than most of the folks in this town." He laid the wet rag aside and wrapped his large hands around her waist, pulling her into his lap. "I am the luckiest man in the world."

"No, I'm the luckiest woman in the world."

"We have what few folks ever find," he whispered. "I wish I was a poet so I could read to you what's always on my heart."

"You do just fine, Frank. All I have to do is look into your eyes, and I see your love for me." She paused and recalled the frightened stares of Martha's girls tonight. "I hope the girls at Martha's never go back to that kind of work. I'm going to try real hard to help them."

"They'll listen to you before they listen to anyone else." He kissed her lightly. "And Martha, too. Makes me wonder what she and those little boys will do."

"She's a smart woman, Frank. She could open a fine, respectable business."

"What about the father of her children?"

Ellen considered telling her husband what she suspected but thought better of it. Gossip didn't please the Lord. "Maybe she doesn't want his help."

CHAPTER  29

"Afternoon, brother." Morgan's eyes sparked a teasing glint.

Boyhood days crept through Grant's mind, memories and times he never wanted to forget.

"Not enough sick folks today, so you're out looking for some?" Morgan asked.

"Not exactly. My house has been corralled by three little people under the age of four. Mischief is in the air."

"You haven't been around mine for a while." Morgan leaned back in his chair and rested his head in his hands. "I saw the remains of Martha's Place when I rode into town this morning. Mama told me you took in Martha and her boys. How is she faring?"

"Angry. Bitter. I wish she'd see how much God wants to help her through this. But as long as folks turn up their noses at her, she isn't interested."

"I heard she accused Frank of burning the brothel to the ground."

"She's convinced of it."

"Who knows with all the goings on there what actually sparked the fire?" Morgan rubbed his jaw. "I'd like to think Martha might consider a different profession than rebuilding."

"She's a good mother to those boys. Maybe that will influence her."

"Why do I think you came here today to talk about something other than the fire?"

Grant seated himself on a chair across from his brother's desk. "I need help sorting out a few things."

"A certain Jenny Martin?" He smiled wide. "I think she has you hooked and on the line."

"Maybe. Not sure yet. We started out despising each other."

"So did Casey and I. Love seldom makes sense."

Grant took a deep breath. "That's not the reason why I'm here."

Morgan narrowed his eyes. He pulled out a pad of paper, picked up his pen, and dipped it into the inkwell. "Ready. I'll do what I can."

"Thanks." He paused a moment to organize his thoughts. "Jenny came to town with the purpose of snatching up Rebecca and learning what happened to her sister. Turner followed her from Cleveland. My guess is he'd been watching her for a long time. According to Jessica's journal—"

"What journal?"

"Ellen gave Jenny a journal from her sister. In it she describes Aubrey Turner, but he used the name Robert Jacobs. This man had a violent streak, including murder."

Morgan glanced up. Lately, a few more lines had been etched around his eyes.

"He tried to get Jenny interested in him, but she refused. He also tried to strike up a friendship with Ellen, but she ignored him. Then Mrs. Lewis died, and no one knows why."

Morgan rested the pen beside the inkwell. "I know where this is going, and Ben is working on it. I'm sure it will be worked out soon." He paused. "How sick is Ben?"

Grant despised the thought of lying to his brother. "He hasn't been to see me."

Silence as heavy as a boulder settled in the room.

"I see you can't tell me a thing," Morgan said. "But when you can, I want to know. Bonnie's my sister, too."

"I'll do all I can."

Morgan dipped the pen once more into the inkwell. "So give me more of your thoughts about Turner."

Thank you, Brother. "Martha accused Ellen and Jenny of starting a brothel. She also threatened to burn Frank's lumberyard, and he in turn let her know what business in Kahlerville should go up in smoke. I talked to Martha about Ellen and Jenny not being interested in opening a business. She acted peculiar." He hesitated, making sure his thoughts were in order. "In the journal, Jessica wrote that she stole money from Jacobs."

"Then last night the brothel burns." Morgan sat back. "I wonder where our man was during all of this?"

"I have no idea."

"All when a sweet little lady came to town." Morgan shook his head. "I didn't mean that like it sounded. I imagine Turner eventually would have made his way here once he learned this is where Jessica died." He lifted his pen from the paper. "Is that it?"

I can't tell you what I know about Martha and Lester. "What pieces are missing?"

"Evidence to lock up Turner. The same as Ben would tell you. Can't arrest a man unless you have proof he's broken the law."

Grant tapped his finger atop the desk. "I think he and I will have a friendly chat."

"Be careful, little brother."

"He has no reason to suspect me of digging into his life. He thinks my only interest is in Jenny."

"Don't be so sure of that. With your brother as the town's lawyer and your brother-in-law, the sheriff, he has no reason to trust you with spit."

"Maybe his cocky attitude will be his demise." Grant stood from the chair. "I'm going to find out."

After promising his brother to be careful in his dealings with Turner, Grant set out for the boardinghouse. Lately, his feet headed in the establishment's direction without much thought. How could one little lady turn his life upside down and leave him dangling like a schoolboy from a tree limb?

His thoughts of Jenny rose and fell as he considered how much he cared for her in one breath and how she planned to return to Ohio at the close of summer. He swung open the door of the boardinghouse and nearly collided with the young woman in question.

"Excuse me, Jenny. I wasn't expecting anyone on the opposite side."

"I'm fine." She blushed, and he warmed.

"Mimi wondered if you would join us tonight for supper," he said. "Martha and her two boys are staying with us after last night's fire. Would that be a problem for you?"

"Not at all. I'll come early and see what I can do to help."

"Can we talk about the journal later? I've read it and want to discuss my findings."

"Certainly," she said. "I'm on my way to see Ellen. She told me after the fire that it was time to tell me what happened when Rebecca was born."

I'd have told you. "I suppose you'll have a lot of questions answered."

She smiled. "I hope so. We may even be able to figure out the contents of the journal."

"I'll look forward to this evening."

Grant tipped his hat and held open the door for her. He realized he'd have a difficult time concentrating on the rest of the day. A mixture of love for her and fear for her safety—and the safety of others—kept him after Turner like a bloodhound.

I'd marry her tomorrow if I thought I could keep her safe. Right now is not a good time to tell her how I feel. She has enough angst without me clouding her mind with a marriage proposal. Especially when I don't know how she feels.

What a fool notion anyway. Turner had plans, and Grant had a feeling he'd stop at nothing to find his money. Marrying Jenny wouldn't end the turmoil any more than destroying Jessica's journal.

How much had Jessica taken to cause Turner to pursue the matter for more than three years? Grant made his way to Harold's desk and, after polite conversation, asked to see Turner.

"He checked out," Harold said. "Claimed to have had enough of this town and was heading back to Ohio. I felt sorry for the man. Didn't seem to have many friends. Every morning he walked to the cemetery to visit Jessica Martin's grave. Love must have had a strong hold on him."

Gone? He hadn't known Turner to be amiable, but obviously Harold had found more compassion for the man than most of the town. Guilt nibbled at his conscience. He should have tried harder to befriend the man. But he couldn't help but be relieved that Kahlerville was finally free of Turner's torment and unrest. A stirring in Grant's soul alerted him that maybe the town hadn't seen the last of Turner.

∽∾⟨ℰ⟩∾∽

Jenny studied Ellen from the small settee in the newlyweds' parlor. Her blanched skin and darting gaze said more than words about her emotional unrest.

"Ellen, don't torture yourself this way. It's not necessary for me to hear what happened when Jessica died." Jenny's claim shook the foundations of why she'd originally come to Kahlerville. Slowly, her selfishness had dissipated, but the reasons why she'd originally journeyed to this town plagued her night and day. "She died a believer, and that's what matters most."

Ellen straightened. "I want to tell you the whole story because it's important to me, too. I've never told anyone all of it, and I should. I need to."

Jenny placed her hand atop Ellen's. "We loved her, yet we understand she fought a league of demons with her troubled mind."

"I fret about Rebecca."

"I've never seen a trace of Jessica's behavior in her. In fact, I told Grant the same."

Ellen lifted a tear-glazed face. "Good. Very good." She glanced at the hand resting atop hers. "You love him, don't you?"

Jenny wrestled with her answer, for to lie went against everything she now believed. "We haven't known each other very long."

"The heart doesn't wear a clock."

At that moment, the clock on the mantle struck the hour of ten o'clock. They laughed, and it broke the tension.

"Never mind. It will all work out," Ellen said.

"Will it? How, when I've caused so much pain? I ought to go home and give all of you a little peace."

"Maybe this is home." Ellen's gentle smile pierced the heart of Jenny's dreams.

"So you know the truth," she finally said. "You saw through my best-kept secret."

"I remember when I realized how much I loved Frank. I felt so vile with all I'd done. But he made me feel like a princess, something from a children's storybook. When I think about it all, I see that Frank is a picture of Christ for me." She laughed. "Understand, my Frank isn't perfect, but he is very close. He loves me unconditionally, just like the Bible says. I'll go to my dying day thanking God for Frank. I want that for you, Jenny. I've seen the way Grant looks at you, and the love is there."

Jenny remembered the kiss on the Fourth of July. She wanted to believe it was real. "It's hard for me to consider a relationship with him after the trouble I've caused—am still causing." She refused to dwell another moment longer on her and Grant. Love between them was impossible—he deserved someone better.

"God is in the miracle business. Just wait and see. Are you ready to hear about your sister?"

Jenny nodded. Anything to rid her mind of her ragged sentiments about Grant. "I want to know what happened. Every word."

"In the beginning, the pains seized Jessica without relief, and she expected the delivery to come quickly. We both did. Hour after hour, she cried out for relief until she feared her life had come to a dreadful end. I was afraid that she'd not make it, but I couldn't convince her to let me fetch Grant. Her screams clamored throughout the second floor of the brothel and echoed in the corners of the first-floor parlor.

"I'd been around women giving birth, but with your sister, it seemed like a paralyzing force seemed to grip her body, one that held her captive. She'd endured the pains for more than three days, and still the babe hadn't come. Jessica wondered if her child warred against life itself or its mother, who didn't know the identity of its father."

Ellen tilted her head, and Jenny knew she recalled every moment. "So many things come to mind about that day. The odors of unwashed bodies fused with perspiration prevailed in the small, cramped room. An open window ushered in a cool breeze on that January day, as though mocking her suffering. An invisible knife seemed to twist inside her body, but her screams sounded more like pitiful whimpers. She had no strength left to fight. Jess closed her eyes and told me she was going to dream away the agony. I understood completely. Any pleasant thought helped drown out the ritual sounds of sordid laughter, the clinking of glasses, and the jingle of men's money at Martha's Place. All had contributed to her unwanted child."

Ellen stood from the settee and walked into the hallway. She touched the petals of a daisy. Jenny said nothing. She saw the torment on Ellen's face. Too many things left unsaid between her and Jessica, like picking berries before they were ripe. Yesteryear crept to the present, and Ellen transported her mind to the nightmare of Jessica's impending death. . . .

"You'd be better off to work more on your backside than find yourself and this baby in a pine box." I dipped a rag into a basin of tepid water and gently pressed it against Jessica's face. "Let me fetch Doc Andrews. I'll help you pay him."

"I can't," Jessica said. "All I can think about are my past choices. They cling to me like cobwebs, and now I'm afraid." She grasped the bed sheet and yanked it from the sides of the bed. Her knuckles bleached white as a scream poured from her lips.

A moment later, Jessica licked parched, cracked lips and closed her eyes. "Go get him then. I can't go on much longer."

"Doc Grant will come," I whispered. "He always comes to help us. He treats us like real ladies."

A wave of anguish passed over Jessica's face, and I swallowed a sob. "I'll hurry."

The door closed behind me, and I scurried down the hallway and the steps. How I hated leaving Jessica suffering alone with no hope.

Grant came immediately. With his long strides, I had to run to keep up with him. Finally, we were at the brothel, up the stairs, and in Jessica's room.

"You shouldn't have waited so long." His voice full of compassion should have calmed Jessica, but it didn't. He examined her while I held her hand. She squeezed it until I bit my lip to keep from crying out.

"The money," Jessica managed through a ragged breath.

"Nonsense. You know me better than that," Grant said.

I knew Grant's payment was to attend a church service. Jessica and I had tried that, and the cruel stares from all those "decent" ladies drove us to never return, although Jessica did try a few more times than I did.

Jessica's body revolted in torment. Would it ever end?

"I need to turn the baby," Grant said. "The little rascal wants to come out feet first."

Jessica nodded and gripped my hand even harder. When the pain grew unbearable, Jessica fled to blackness, and for a moment her body relaxed. An hour later, she gave birth to a tiny baby girl. Grant attempted to lay the infant in Jessica's embrace, but she was too weak to hold her. The bloodied towels beneath her told a grim story.

He lifted the baby above Jessica's eyes. "A beauty," he said softly. "A real beauty."

"Thank you." Tears trickled down her cheeks. "I know I'm dying. . . . What will happen to my baby?"

He glanced up at me. I remember his sad eyes as though they grieved, too. "Life is in the hands of the Father. You need to simply rest."

"I know the truth." She glanced toward the open window where a threadbare curtain barely moved.

I wondered if this was how life passed from one hell to another.

"Is there anyone for me to contact?" he asked.

Jessica shook her head. "Surely you understand." She peered up at me. "No family. No one that matters but. . .Ellen."

I started to mention you but thought better of it. Jessica had her reasons.

"I understand." Grant's deep, soft voice comforted even me.

"My baby," she said. "Will you. . .take my baby? If she stays here, she'll be working by the time she's eleven."

"Of course," Grant said. "I'd be honored to find a home for her."

"No, please." She searched for strength. "I want you to have her. I'm giving my baby girl to you."

Frustration stole across his face. "I can't raise a baby. I'm not married. There's no one to tend to her."

Pale, weak, and trembling, Jessica fought for strength to continue. "Please. . .promise me." Her eyes never left her baby's face.

"You don't know what you're asking."

"Because I'm a whore?"

"Absolutely not." Long moments followed, heavy as though the thoughts going through Grant's mind swung like a pendulum. He stared at the infant's peaceful face. "If you don't get better, I'll adopt and raise her as my own daughter."

Using one foot, he pulled a chair to her bedside and sat with the baby partially in his arms yet resting near Jessica's heart. "She is so very beautiful."

Jessica smiled. She seemed to marvel at the tiny turned-up nose, rosebud mouth, and the long, thick lashes curling up from sleepy eyes. Oh, and she had that thick dark hair then, too. Such an exquisite creature, so delicate, so perfect.

"Her name is Rebecca," Jessica whispered.

"A lovely name." Grant's gaze swept over Jessica's face. "Do you know Jesus?"

She closed her eyes. "Jesus has no use for the likes of me. It's too late now."

"No matter what happens, it's not too late. Would you like to talk to the reverend?"

She took a deep breath and hesitated. Finally, she nodded.

He turned to me. "Would you mind going after the reverend? He should be at the parsonage."

I hurried to find the reverend just as I'd done earlier to fetch Grant. The tall, white-haired gentleman did not hesitate. As always, he had the undeniable look of caring on his lined face. Within moments, we joined Jessica, the baby, and Grant.

"Thank you," Grant said to his stepfather and laid tiny Rebecca at Jessica's side. "Do you want Ellen and me to leave?"

"No. Please, stay with me," she said.

Reverend Rainer took her hand and eased into the chair beside her bed. His soft gray eyes extended a rare kind of love.

"I'm dying," she said simply. "Help me. I'm scared."

I swiped at the tears. I was losing the only friend I'd ever known.

Ellen walked back to the settee and sat on the soft cushion. "She found life in Jesus and allowed Him to take her home. That's the story. So sad, yet it had a beautiful ending."

Jenny blinked back her tears. "Rebecca has a fine father and a beautiful family, and. . .I would never have known a fine woman like you."

Ellen smiled. "Grant had a rough time of it in the beginning. Folks believed he was the father. I stayed with the reverend and Jocelyn; then I found a place to live with the Widow Lewis. Grant's mother and the reverend helped him with the baby, but he wanted to do it all himself."

Jenny remembered Grant telling her about those early days with a new baby.

"So he bought a big house, and Miss Mimi came to live with him and Rebecca."

Jenny's mind spun with the story. The truth had been bittersweet. Perhaps the time had come for her to go home to Cleveland. These people had endured enough of life's interruptions. They needed peace.

CHAPTER  30

"Higher," Rebecca squealed while Jenny lightly pushed on the rope swing in Grant's rear yard.

"You'll be touching the limbs soon," Jenny said.

"No, I not," Rebecca said, her cheeks flushed with excitement. "Higher, please."

You are Miss Mischief. "I can't, sweetheart. It's dangerous for you to swing so far. I love you too much to risk your getting hurt."

Rebecca puckered up to give her finest pout, but Jenny ignored the protruding lower lip. Instead, she hurried around the tree and faced the little girl on the opposite side of the swing.

"I've got you!" She lifted Rebecca from the wooden seat into her own arms. "Now I have a little butterfly, and she can't ever fly away."

Rebecca squirmed and giggled, her brown curls bouncing. "Let me go. Me a butterfly."

"Whoa, there," Grant said from the doorway. "What's going on out here?"

Jenny laughed, not once taking her eyes from the little girl's angelic face.

"My butterfly is trying to fly away."

He walked toward them and pressed his lips tight—no doubt to conceal a smile. "We will have none of that. Shall I find a cage? No loose butterflies at this house."

"Oh, yes, a cage is a splendid idea." Jenny caught a glint in his eyes. Her pulse quickened, and she hastily glanced away.

"No cage," Rebecca said between laughs.

Jenny pulled her down into the soft green grass. At first the little girl didn't mind being held, but soon she wiggled free and ran to the swing.

"Swing me, Papa." She held on to the rope with both hands and tried futilely to jump onto the wooden seat.

"I will later. I promise." Grant bent to her level. "I need to talk to your aunt Jenny. Why don't you visit Mimi? She's in the kitchen baking an apple cobbler, and I think she needs your help. In fact, she wants you to help stir."

Rebecca raced inside with her chubby little legs working so fast that she nearly stumbled.

"Am I in trouble?" Jenny hoped her words masked what being alone with him did to her heart.

"No, ma'am." He peered around. "Where are Martha and the boys?"

"The baby grew a little fussy, and the older boy didn't want to stay with me."

"How is she today?"

Jenny hesitated, wanting to form the right words without sounding frustrated. "Sad. Very sad. I asked her if I could do anything to help, but she said no." *You and your sister have caused enough trouble.* "I think it's time I boarded the train back to Cleveland."

Grant frowned. "Why?"

"Your town needs to go back to the serenity it enjoyed before I came."

"You've made some wonderful friendships here."

What about you? "True, I have. But I need to leave before long. I have a teaching responsibility."

"I understand." He paused and stared at her intently, but she couldn't read the strange, faraway look in his eyes. "I learned something earlier today and thought you might be ready for some good news."

"And what might that be?"

"Aubrey Turner left town." Grant stuck his hands in his trouser pockets and leaned against the oak tree housing the swing.

Could it be true? Startled, Jenny could only wring her hands. "Does this mean he's given up on finding the money?"

"I guess so. Harold said he checked out of the boardinghouse and planned to head back to Cleveland."

"Cleveland?" She'd be no better off at home than here, except those she treasured would be safe.

Grant shook his head. "I don't know what I was thinking. Turner will be there when you get back, most likely causing more trouble than here." He palmed his fist into his hand. "You can't go home now. It's not safe."

His words played over in her mind. Did he truly care, or was she reading something into his words that didn't exist? "I'll contact the local police when I return." She glanced up into the tree holding the swing. "He may be very tired of dealing with the Martin sisters." *As you are, I'm sure.*

As the evening wore on, Jenny went through the motions of a gracious guest. Her mother would have been proud. The children were a grand distraction from the animosity she felt from Martha, and Grant kept himself occupied with keeping everyone civil. After supper Jenny helped Mimi tidy up the kitchen before slipping out the back door to the boardinghouse. She left without saying good-bye to Grant or Rebecca, and she doubted if Grant realized her absence.

Misery took every step with her. A peculiar feeling, or rather an inner sensation, urged her to make a decision. The inclination had needled her for days. The guilt of selfishness had reached its climax, and she must act soon. If she stayed much longer, she'd find herself so hopelessly in love with Grant that everyone would know.

Grant's gestures and mannerisms were a part of her forever. Even his fondness for licorice lingered. She nearly laughed aloud as she recalled him dipping the black candy sticks into coffee. As it was, she might never recover. Neither did she want to. The splendor of simply existing in the same room with him brought her pulse to dangerously high levels. Sometimes the mere thought of him sent her emotions soaring like a flock of birds that kept climbing higher into the clouds.

Never seeing Grant or Rebecca again wrenched her heart. The ache of loving both of them hurt beyond belief. How foolish of her to dream about the three of them becoming a real family. She could make a multitude of excuses to stay, but it wasn't fair to any of them. She'd uprooted their lives with her foolish notion of taking Rebecca back to Cleveland, and then that wretched Aubrey Turner had followed her, causing more unrest.

Unsettled affairs did bring some uncertainty, particularly deciphering Jessica's journal. But Grant was brilliant. He'd easily solve the riddle and recover the money. If Turner was indeed wanted for unspeakable crimes, Ben would alert the authorities in Cleveland.

Dear Ellen. Already Jenny missed her treasured friendship. They'd grown so close—the friend Jenny had always wanted. The more she prayed about the matter, the more leaving seemed to be the best choice, and it must happen tomorrow or her resolve would weaken. Knowing that all those dear to her heart would be safe and content lifted her spirits. Reverend Rainer had said God would always walk with her, even in Cleveland, where she didn't know a single Christian. But she could find a church and start life anew.

Lighting the kerosene lamp on the dresser in her room, Jenny lay across the bed and picked up pen and paper. Her mind drifted back to the first time she had met Dr. Grant Andrews. Oh, my, she'd been so ill at the train station. On and on the memories flowed until stinging tears brought it all to a peak. Drying her eyes, Jenny determined to stop prolonging the inevitable and write the letter. Dipping the pen into the inkwell, she began pouring out her heart.

Dear Grant,

By the time you receive this, I will be on my way back to Cleveland. I can no longer stay here in Kahlerville in good conscience. The time has come for me to give you and your dear family and friends much-deserved rest and peace.

Words can never express what you, your family, and friends have done for me. Even as I write this, I weep for those faces I will never see or touch again. Believe me, I now have beautiful memories of those who will always hold a special place in my heart. Most important, I now have Jesus, and I know that someday I will see all of you again in heaven.

For me to say "thank you" sounds so insignificant for all you have done for me—not just your outward hospitality, but also your encouragement and prayers. Please let everyone know I will never forget their goodness, and I will always keep them in my thoughts and prayers. I found a true friend in Ellen. She is so dear to me.

Grant, you are indeed the best father God could have provided for Rebecca. Jessica must have recognized your wonderful traits even as she lay dying, and I saw it each time you were with your daughter. I love every inch of Rebecca, and I know with your guidance and love she will grow into a godly young woman.

As for the journal, I want you to have it for Rebecca. Someday when she is grown, she will want to read about her mama. When you are able to locate the money, I want it for your and Rebecca's welfare, as we discussed previously. If there is any left over, I'd like a fund established to help those girls who formerly worked at the brothel.

I am so sorry for all of the trouble I caused. I only wish I could have found the Lord earlier and spared you my dis-agreeable temperament. Truly believe me, Grant, my heart aches for the sorrow I inflicted upon you. I really was a self-centered, impetuous woman, and I am deeply ashamed of my actions.

I could not leave Kahlerville without telling you the most important reason why I must go home. You have been to me what no man has ever been before. From the very beginning, you welcomed me and took care of me while I plotted to destroy everything you loved and cherished. Even then, you reached out in a special friendship that I grasped like a child. For the first time in years, I was a student again, and you were the teacher. No matter what I threatened, you responded in a manner that I later learned was Christlike. But then I fell in love with you. There, I said it, and I've lived with this knowledge for so many days. Goodness, I certainly did not intend for it to happen, but you see, it does not matter any longer. I am on a train traveling as fast as I can away from you. Your life can now go back to normal. I wish you well, the best our Lord can give.

I plan to write Ellen and Mimi a letter tonight, too. Mimi was better to me than my own mother. She loved me through so many horrible cooking experiences and such ignorance about life. I'll miss her stories and her gentleness.

Please give Rebecca a hug and kiss for me. I miss you both already. You cannot find me in Ohio. Ironically enough, I don't have an address. It is better this way, you know. Just forget the summer, but remember those days will be with me forever.

I love you and Rebecca more than life itself. Take care and God bless you.

Jenny

She reread the letter twice. With a heavy sigh and a muffled sob, she gently folded it over and slipped it inside an envelope. Not really satisfied with the contents, but not quite sure how to phrase all the secrets of her heart, Jenny set it aside and wrote the others.

Tomorrow morning Mr. Snyder's son would carry her trunk and bags to an awaiting wagon. She'd graciously thank Mr. Snyder for all of his kindness and settle the bill. She'd entrust the letters to him and board the Union Pacific Railroad on the way back to Cleveland, Ohio. The people of Kahlerville would never again be troubled because of her.

CHAPTER  31

Ellen patted General Lee's head as he nestled up against her lap in the parlor that evening. She relaxed in a moment of quiet reflection after a busy day with this overgrown animal that followed her about like a puppy. She laughed at his awkward appearance: large, pointed ears, huge feet, and a flat nose like a pig's.

No one had intended for General Lee to be a part of their home, but the animal displayed such fierce loyalty toward her husband that the elder Kahlers hadn't had much choice. When the couple married, the dog sulked and refused to eat until Frank's father delivered him to the newlyweds. Strangely enough, General Lee extended his affections and guardianship to Ellen. Right from the beginning of Frank and Ellen's courtship, the dog had sensed Frank's devotion to her and quickly made friends. The dog's loyalty gave rise to family jokes, but Frank claimed he had the best guardian angel in town. When work kept him away from home, Ellen was safe. Folks still felt squeamish since Mrs. Lewis's passing, but not Ellen. She had General. How she loved that dog, the first pet she'd ever had.

"What is it, General?" Ellen asked the dog for the second time.

The dog lifted his ears and growled at the front door. She reached over and patted him, noting the tense muscles across his shoulders and back. Feeling a twinge of alarm, she glanced at the clock on the mantel.

Shortly after supper, Frank had gone back to the feed store to catch up on some bookkeeping. He and Ellen planned to take a few days to themselves in another week, and he wanted to make sure the plans for the lumberyard were in order. Since the day they had been married, the two had worked from before dawn until after sunset at their regular positions and then picked up paint brushes and tools to finish their home at night. Both were looking forward to a few days together.

"Is anyone there?" The sound of her own voice was laced with a hint of trepidation.

General Lee bolted from the rug near her chair and leaped to the door. He snarled and barked fiercely. Breaking away from Ellen's hold, he planted himself firmly at the entrance. She watched the dog's actions with growing apprehension, and her gaze bore holes into the door until she finally stopped shaking long enough to rise from the rocking chair.

"Is someone there? Frank?" She drew in a quick breath, keenly aware that General would not attack his own master. They lived on the outskirts of town, and she feared a cry for help might not be heard.

The door handle turned. Ellen's heart pounded so hard against her chest that it hurt, and the sound rumbled against her ears. General Lee bared his teeth and crouched low to spring on the intruder. *Sweet Jesus, I'm afraid.*

Her gaze darted helplessly around the room in a frantic search for a weapon. Frank's shotgun rested against the wall in the kitchen. He didn't keep it loaded, but she knew where he stored the shells.

She rushed into the kitchen and fell against the corner of the table. Snatching up the shotgun, she stumbled to grasp the box of shells from the kitchen cupboard. In her haste, they tumbled to the floor, rolling everywhere. Ellen scooped up a handful and dropped them into her apron pocket. Her shaking fingers fumbled so that she couldn't load the gun.

The front door slowly swung open.

General Lee growled and sprang from his stance only to be silenced by the sharp crack of a handgun. His body twisted and plunged to the floor.

A scream escaped her lips. Devotion cost a dear price.

She stepped back into the living room and clumsily hoisted the heavy shotgun to her shoulder. "Get out, or I'll blow a hole right through you." Her voice sounded hollow, or perhaps her terror spoke more bravely than she truly felt.

"It's not loaded," said the calm, quiet voice of Aubrey Turner.

"Yes, it is. I should kill you for what you did to my dog."

"It's Frank's dog, my dear, and your pocket is full of shells. You haven't had time to load that shotgun, and I doubt if Frank keeps it loaded."

Ellen raised the weapon higher to reinforce her threat, but he only laughed. His obvious confidence sent a chill to her fingertips. "Frank will be home any minute." She glared into violet eyes, the ones Jessica had feared and hated. "You'd best get out of here."

"I beg to differ. I saw him enter the feed store about a half hour ago, and his habit is to work at least two hours." He moved closer, stepping over General Lee's still body.

"Not tonight. He only needed to pick up something." She waved the gun toward his face. If only it were loaded, she'd gladly pull the trigger.

"You should have killed me before I got inside."

She glanced at General Lee lying in a pool of blood. His head lay twisted to one side where the bullet had torn into his neck. He hadn't even whimpered. Her shoulders ached from aiming the shotgun at Turner, but before she could contemplate another thought, he snatched the weapon from her trembling hands.

"Frank will never let you get away with this. What do you want?"

Hysteria rose from the pit of her stomach.

"He'd have to find me first. In case you didn't know, I left town. The train conductor will vouch for me getting on board." He tossed the shotgun aside. The crash echoed across the small home.

Ellen realized she faced the same end as her dog.

Turner's features twisted into something more distorted and vile than anything she'd ever seen. His malevolent eyes penetrated deep inside her, radiating evil.

"What do you want?" she asked again, although the words barely choked out.

He reached out to seize her, but she instantly shrank back. Her only escape from his clutches was through the back door.

"I want my money." And for every step she took back, he moved closer.

"What money?" Maybe Frank had enough cash there to pacify him.

Picking up a kitchen chair, he threw it out of his way and continued edging his way toward her. "You know what I mean—the money Jessica stole from me."

Ellen shivered in the late July heat. Panic seized every part of her body.

"I loved that woman! I loved her with my soul, and she robbed me."

Ellen lifted her chin in a futile attempt to calm her raging emotions. "I don't know anything about your money. Jessica never mentioned it."

He grabbed her chin sharply and savagely pulled her face within inches of his. "Liar, you know exactly what I'm talking about. If you value your life, you'll tell me where it is."

She tasted the acidity of terror. "I swear I don't know a thing about any money. All Jessica told me was that she left a man when they didn't get along."

Turner's hands tightened around her jaw. He slid his fingers to her throat. "If I have to squeeze it out of you, I will. I have nothing to lose by killing you or Jenny. And I know you have it, or Jenny wouldn't have come to this godforsaken hole."

"I know nothing," she whispered as his hands slowly cut off her air.

"Then why did you have her sister come all the way out here?"

"I didn't."

His crimson face blazed fire. "Liar. You two planned to split my money. I'm sure of it." With the intensity of each word, his hold tightened around her neck. "Tell me where I can find my money, and I won't kill you."

When she failed to respond, he slapped her soundly across the face with his other hand. Madness reigned in his eyes—a wild, uncontrollable rage. *O God, help me.*

"Tell me," he said through clenched teeth. Ellen knew if she could utter a word, it would be to no avail. His anger soared beyond reason.

Ellen's knees buckled against the force of his body. She fell to the floor. A sharp stab of pain ripped through the back of her head. The pressure of his hand tightened around her throat, and she felt herself struggling desperately for air. A wicked grin spread across his face, one of triumph and control. Pain and blackness threatened to engulf her, and she resisted until the prevailing darkness finally swept her under its control.

Hours after Jenny had walked home from supper without telling Grant good-bye, he still wondered why she'd left without telling him or Rebecca good-bye. He'd been busy with the children, but he'd have gladly walked her home. Perhaps Martha had upset her or she was concerned about the news of Turner heading to Ohio. Even now, Grant berated himself for his stupidity. Jenny needed to agree to stay here and marry him. He wanted to ask her tonight—this instant—

but the words would flounder from his mouth like a fish out of water. She may very well despise him, but he thought he'd seen something akin to love in her eyes.

He crumpled another sheet of paper and tossed it into a metal can beside his desk. The receptacle was nearly full. Jessica's journal tormented him worse than a case of chicken pox in July. Tonight he'd spent every spare minute searching its pages for the secrets hidden between its cover, and he'd become obsessed with finding the answers. Frustrated, Grant didn't know if his fixation lay in finding the money itself or in the fact that Jenny had placed it into his hands, confident he could unravel it.

His mind lingered on Jessica's instability. For certain, he'd not let a single symptom appearing in Rebecca slip by him. *Lord, keep my little daughter safe and free from the demons that besieged her mother.*

Grant opened the heavy double doors to his office and made his way through the darkened house to the kitchen. He refused to go to bed until he solved the riddle of the journal, but he needed some coffee to help him stay awake. His stomach ached from eating far too much licorice while he worked tonight. He, the doctor, should have shoved the bag back into his desk drawer. His lips were probably the color of coal. With a sigh, he rekindled the cookstove, and soon the fresh coffee's nutty aroma filled the kitchen.

Mimi would be proud of me taking care of myself. His housekeeper had retired to her room shortly after the two of them had tucked Rebecca into bed.

His little daughter seemed troubled this evening. She said Aunt Jenny had gotten dirt in her eyes and it made her cry, so he and Rebecca prayed for her. To Grant, that explanation sounded like Jenny had been avoiding telling Rebecca the truth. What had happened to make her cry? He ran his fingers through his hair. Martha's dislike for Jenny flashed across his mind. Irritated, he intended to speak to Martha in the morning—should have done so tonight. The woman may have escaped a tragedy, but that did not excuse ill treatment of

Jenny. His Jenny. Shaking his head, he grasped the handle of the coffeepot with a towel and carried it back to his office.

Grant pulled the opened journal from the top of his desk and reread the last entry. Always his attention focused on this short passage. Surely her words of money for Jenny weren't written to confuse her sister—or an ugly joke contrived during one of her maddening episodes. Well, he couldn't discount the validity of Jessica's words until he exhausted all of his efforts.

Flipping through the pages, he looked to see if anything was missing or torn. Every page appeared intact. The key to resolving the issue lay in mathematics, but what form or how?

Grant took a huge gulp of his hot coffee and sputtered as it burned his tongue. Upset with himself for not figuring out the code and upset with Jessica for creating it, he set the coffee down and pulled out a blank sheet of paper from inside his middle desk drawer. Leaning back in his chair, he closed his eyes. What if he were a child playing school and fancied arithmetic? How might he present a numbered code to a younger sister?

First, he looked to see if Jessica's birthday, January 22, 1870, corresponded to pages one, twenty-two, eighteen, or seventy in the journal. When Grant saw nothing that looked unusual, he released a heavy sigh.

In attempting to recall Jenny's birthday, he remembered Jessica had written something special to her on that day. After leafing through several pages, he found the date: November 12, 1873. He turned to the matching journal entries of eleven, twelve, and seventy-three. Again, his hunch proved wrong.

He drummed his pen habitually on the desk, aggravated at his own inability to decipher Jessica's code. Nevertheless, it challenged him, and he couldn't put it aside.

Lord, if You want me to solve this riddle, please show me. I don't know what to do with it. I'm frustrated, but I don't feel that You want me to give up.

A thought occurred to him. Grant wrote the alphabet across the top of his paper. Beneath each letter he assigned a corresponding number, with the letter *A* receiving a one and the letter Z, a twenty-six. For the next hour he matched up Jessica's name, Jenny's name, Cleveland, Ohio, Kahlerville, Texas, and many other words and phrases that might provide a clue, but none of it made any sense. He found the letters could repeat themselves and yet form nothing sensible.

This idea isn't any better than the others. I'm a fool to keep working. I should give up, at least for tonight.

Taking a deep breath, he studied the last page of the journal one more time and smiled at the mention of the lilac tree. It seemed to be a favorite childhood memory for both girls. . . . He sat straighter in his chair. Unless Jessica wrote about it for a specific purpose. A renewed enthusiasm drove him back to the journal.

Grant copied "beneath the lilac tree" atop a clean sheet of paper. He assigned the letters with matching numbers. His original method hadn't made sense, just as before, but this time he couldn't bring himself to destroy his work.

Beneath had seven letters. Page seven of the journal revealed nothing. Grant totaled the numbers given to each letter of the word; it added up to fifty-five. He turned to that entry. A tingle of excitement spurred him. The word *first* was underlined. Nervously, he totaled the numbers of the letters in the word *the*, and it equaled thirty-three. On page thirty-three he saw the word *national* with a distinct line under it. *Lilac* added up to thirty-seven, and on that page he saw the word *bank* in a different color ink. Taking a deep breath, he totaled the word *tree*, and on page forty-eight, Jessica had faintly selected *Houston*. First National Bank of Houston. Grant silently repeated, *First National Bank of Houston.*

"I've figured out the journal," he whispered. "I can't believe it, but this is the code." Glancing at the clock on his desk, he saw the hour approached ten. Realizing the lateness required a certain amount of silence, he instantly hushed. His findings must wait until morning. Jenny would be so pleased. She had claimed he could decipher it, but he really had his doubts.

Thank You, Lord. He leaned back in his chair and allowed satisfaction to roll over him. Not that Rebecca would have money for her future, but that Jenny believed he could decipher the journal.

Grant lifted the coffee to his lips. Jessica's method of concealing the money had been nothing more than child's play. Yet both he and Jenny had found her code nearly impossible. Now, finding the name listed on the account should be easy, certainly simpler than where the money had been hidden.

Propping his feet on the desk, he felt decisively wonderful—and pleased. Turner had left town, and Jenny needed to stay. Perhaps she not only feared for herself but for her parents, too. Grant couldn't offer her much of a future if he couldn't place the root of her fears in jail. First thing in the morning, he'd visit Ben and Morgan. Hopefully, one of them had turned up something on Turner. Afterward he planned to stop by the boardinghouse and present Jenny with the journal's findings. The wording of a marriage proposal flashed in and out of his mind.

The sound of someone frantically shouting his name broke his reverie. Alerted, he sprang from his desk and took long strides toward the entrance of his home. This could only be an emergency.

CHAPTER  32

The pounding at Grant's door sounded like someone was kicking it in. He flung it open to find Frank carrying the limp body of a small woman.

"Someone broke into the house while I was gone," he said with a gasp. "She's hurt real bad, Grant. Oh, dear God, please don't take my Ellen."

Grant reached for her, but Frank shook his head. "No, I'll lay her wherever you want."

Pointing to the examination table in his office, Grant lit the lamps while Frank placed Ellen gently on the table. Her ashen face and faint breathing revealed the tell-tale signs of her attack. Who could have done such a thing? Purplish-blue finger marks pressed in around her throat, and her face was swollen and beginning to discolor.

Lord, it's a miracle that she's still alive. Touch her, I beg of You, with Your healing power. Guide my hands. Give me wisdom, and let all the glory be Yours. Amen.

"She's a fighter," Grant said. He carefully felt her bruised neck, face, and the back of her head. A large bump rose beneath his fingers but there was no blood. Had she fallen, or had someone struck her head? "We know God can pull her through this."

Frank's powerful chest rose and fell with the gravity of the situation before him. "It's all my fault. I was a fool to leave a dog to protect her. She was no match for whoever did this."

"You had no way of knowing."

Frank buried his face in his hands. "The house was turned upside down by some wild man—like Mrs. Lewis's."

Suspicion stole inside Grant's mind that Turner might have attacked Ellen, but he kept silent. "We'll let Ben deal with it later. Right now I need Mimi." He kept his attention focused on Ellen. "Would you go upstairs and knock on the second door on the right for me? And pray, Frank. Keep praying."

"I am. I will." His boots thundered against the steps, sure to wake the entire household.

But Grant didn't have time to fret over trivial matters. Ellen's unresponsiveness scared him. *Who did this?* blared across his mind. An old customer who couldn't bear the fact she'd married, or Turner? Before he could contemplate the question further, Frank bounded back down the stairs.

"She's on her way. No matter what happens with my Ellen, I'll always be grateful for your help." Pulling a handkerchief from his pants pocket, he wiped his face and nose. "I'll stand back in the corner and hush so you can tend to her."

Soon Mimi appeared in the doorway wrapped in a long robe. "Grant, I'm here." Her voice was strong, in control. Grant needed that right now; so did Frank. "What do you need for me to do first?" she asked.

"Could you prepare the upstairs room? I'd like to get her into a comfortable bed as soon as I can. There's not much I can do but treat her injuries." He glanced into Mimi's lined face. "I appreciate your getting up."

"What's happened?"

Martha's grating voice served only to irritate him. How long before all the kids were up? He needed quiet to care for Ellen.

"Ellen Kahler was attacked at her home tonight," Mimi said.

Martha sucked in a breath. "When will it end? One tragedy after another."

"We need to let Grant do what he can for her," Mimi said.

"Did she say who did this?" Martha asked.

"She's unconscious." Frank's voice was infected with anger and bitterness. "How could she tell me anything?"

"Frank, I never wanted this for her. Not Ellen," Martha said.

Before Frank could respond, Mimi took Martha by the arm. "I need you to help me upstairs." A moment later, the office door closed.

"Would you go after Ben?" Grant lifted Ellen's arm. He feared it might be broken, but it was only bruised.

"All right." Frank drew in a ragged breath. "Do you think she'll make it?"

"That's up to God and the skill He's given me." Grant lifted his gaze to Frank's face and reddened eyes. "I'm doing everything I can." He focused his attention back on cleaning the cuts on Ellen's face and throat.

"I think I'll stop at the parsonage, too. Have to go right by there."

"Good idea. We need everyone praying. Take my horse. It's stabled in back."

Once Frank left, Grant had more time to think. He couldn't do much more for Ellen than wait, but Frank needed things to keep his body and mind busy. He examined her again, still questioning if her arm had been broken. At least she'd not been molested, which minimized the probability of her past life being the motive for the assault.

Grant didn't believe in coincidences. Until the journal had come into his possession, he wouldn't have had such strong suspicions about Aubrey Turner. But now he felt strongly that one certain individual stood behind all three calamities—Mrs. Lewis's death, the fire, and now Ellen's attack.

Ben and the reverend arrived with Frank within the hour. The three men met in Grant's office. The only sound was Ben's hacking coughs, reminding Grant of yet one more critical situation.

"How is she?" Frank asked. "Who would have done this?"

"No change. But she isn't worse. I haven't taken her upstairs yet."

Ben coughed, then cleared his throat. "Hey, brother, do you feel like answering some questions for me? I remember you said she was at the house while you were working."

"That's right. And I'll do anything to help find the one who did this."

"I understand," Ben said. "Have you made anyone mad or had problems at the store or the lumberyard?"

Frank's misty eyes never left Ellen's face. "No, business is good, and I haven't had any trouble."

Ben's gaze darted about, appearing reluctant to ask the next question. He hesitated, paused, and finally began again. "Could a man from Ellen's past have done this?"

Frank came out of his chair with both fists clenched, but Grant grabbed him. "He has to ask questions. It's his job." Grant turned his attention to Ben. "Although he could have waited on that one. If your investigation is going to upset Frank, then it can wait until morning. Ellen needs my full attention."

"I'm sorry." Ben pushed back his hat. "Just tryin' to figure out why someone would've attacked her."

"I want to know, too," Grant said. "But not at the expense of my patient or Frank. If you're going to ask any more questions tonight, make sure they're reasonable. I have no intention of breaking up a fight between you two. Seems like I've done that most of my life." He didn't need to add his last comment, but exasperation ground at him.

Ben nodded. "I suspect you have. One more thing is puzzling me. What about General Lee? Why didn't he attack the intruder?"

Frank closed his eyes. "The man shot him near the front door. That tells me he had to be someone who knew General's fierce nature."

"Mind if I stop in at your place and take a look around?"

"No, go ahead. As upset as I am right now, you probably should go on over to the house now."

Hours later, Grant quietly closed the door to the room where Ellen slept and where Frank and the reverend kept a constant vigil. Descending the stairs, he mentally listed the items he needed to do first thing this morning. Ellen had made it through the night, and the worst was over. Every bone in his body ached after the all-night ordeal, but he praised God for bringing Ellen through her brush with death.

Anger and a yearning for revenge needled at him despite his oath to protect and preserve human life. He knew God reserved the right to judge men by their deeds, but Grant wanted the crimes of late ended.

He hurried through the house looking for Mimi. She'd been up most of the night with him, and soon Rebecca would be out and about. He'd already heard Martha's boys. Wearily, he shook his head in an attempt to dispel a hammering pain across his brow. He didn't dare consider rest until his errands were completed and Ellen had responded to his care.

Mimi moved slowly about the kitchen. She looked pitifully tired, her normally clear eyes clouded red and puffy.

"Thanks for helping me last night," he said.

"Nonsense." Already she had an apron tied about her chubby waist, and the aroma of biscuits rested pleasantly in the air.

He sensed a gnawing hunger, but food hadn't made it on his list. "I take advantage of you far too often."

"Helping you and caring for Rebecca gives me more joy than you'll ever know. So you hush about it right now."

"It's still not right. One of these days, I'm going to make all this up to you." He hesitated. "I need to see Ben, then stop by the boardinghouse. I won't be long, maybe an hour. Ellen is sleeping and shouldn't stir for some time. Frank and the reverend are with her."

Guilt clung to him like flies on sugar for leaving Ellen if only for a little while.

She poured a cup of coffee and handed it to him. "I'm glad you're on your way to see Jenny."

"I'm hoping last night will prove to her the importance of moving into the parsonage."

She sighed. "I don't know what this town is coming to. With Mrs. Lewis's heart failure and this horrible attack on Ellen, it's simply not safe for any woman." She wiped her eyes with a corner of her apron. "It's downright frightening to think there's someone living in our town who's mean enough to harm defenseless women."

Grant wrapped his arm around her shoulders, which were trembling from the weight of her anguish. "I'm sorry, too, Mimi. If it makes you feel any better, I may have a lead, which is one of the reasons why I'm stopping in to see Ben. Frank needs to know there's a suspect. It won't undo what happened to Ellen, but we'll all feel better when the man's caught."

"Has Ellen spoken yet?"

"No, and I don't want her talking for a few days. We can communicate with her by writing notes. I'm sure she knows who attacked her. Frank says shotgun shells were strewn all over the floor. She must have tried hard to protect herself."

"It's a wonder their dog didn't tear the person to pieces," Mimi said and smoothed back her smoky-gray hair.

Grant hesitated. He'd rather Mimi heard the details from him than someone else. "Someone shot the dog. When Ben left here last night, he planned to stop by their house to remove the dog and the bullet."

His housekeeper grimaced. "This is just so awful. And I thought Texas had settled down." She took a handkerchief from her apron pocket and blew her nose. "I know God had His hand on Ellen last night. How else could she have survived what happened to her?"

"I agree. He brought her through a rough night."

Mimi attempted a smile. "You run along and get your things done. I'm all right, really I am. When you see Jenny, please tell her I need help. That should get her here in no time at all. You know—"

"What?"

"Martha was very upset last night. She must have liked Ellen more than we thought."

Or she knows who attacked her. "I'm glad she helped you." He squeezed her shoulders again. "I'm sure as soon as Jenny hears about Ellen, she'll be fussin' with Frank about who'll take care of her."

"I plan to take some breakfast up to him and the reverend."

"Good idea. Last night was a close call—too close." Gently grasping her arms, he pushed her back and peered into her deep blue eyes. "You are exhausted. Once Jenny is here, I'd like for you to lie down. Can't have my best girl sick."

She pursed her lips stubbornly. "Maybe this afternoon. Right now I'm too upset to sleep."

"I understand." He turned to leave, then whirled around. "If Ellen does waken while I'm gone, let her have only a little water. And remember, don't let her talk. Frank knows that, too. I don't know how much damage has been done to her throat. She may not be able to speak for a good while, so we'll need to take one step at a time."

His housekeeper patted his hand. "Go ahead now. Time's a wasting."

He headed back to his office, snatched up a folder of papers, and stepped out into the morning air. Deep in thought over the happenings of the night, he picked up his pace and hurried down the long stone walkway from his home.

The attacker couldn't be anyone other than Turner, and Grant believed the journal proved his theory. Turner had to be the one who frightened Mrs. Lewis into a heart attack and probably instigated the fire—although he couldn't piece together why. Without a doubt, Turner wanted his money and would do whatever was necessary to get it. Thoughts of Jenny's safety lay heavily on Grant's mind. She might be Turner's next target.

Once he reached the street, Grant pulled out his pocket watch: seven o'clock. Jenny might not be out and about, but this was important. She'd be shattered with the news and most likely terrified.

He considered Turner's all-too-obvious announcement of his departure from Kahlerville. It must have been designed to throw off any suspicion of involvement in the crimes he planned to commit. *I know it's him. According to the journal, he has motive plus a history of violence.*

He could hear Morgan's words now. "A man is innocent until proven guilty." Grant knew he wanted to blame someone and have the matter cleared up. In fact, he wanted that very thing today. He felt secure in his accusations, but still he needed definite proof. He hoped that between Ben and Morgan they could put an end to Turner's reign of lawlessness.

Grabbing the doorknob to Ben's office, he took a deep breath to calm his troubled mind.

"Morning, Grant." Ben yawned, his dark hair uncombed. He must not have gone home. "How's Ellen?"

"Much better. She'll make it. I'll send word as soon as she's able to let us know the details of what happened. I'm in a rush this morning, but I wondered about the bullet from Frank and Ellen's dog."

Ben pointed to the bullet on his desk. "Looks like it came from a small revolver, probably a Remington. The same type of gun that killed Howe."

Grant glanced down at the unopened mail and watched Ben thumb through it.

"I've been looking for some reason to arrest Turner for days," Ben said. "Now that he's gone, the information I need is probably right here." Using his pocketknife, he carefully slit an envelope and pulled out its contents. "Let me skim over this first." Ben breathed deeply while absorbing the words before him. "Turner's a professional gambler all right, and he uses an assortment of names. . .one of which is Jacobs. He's wanted for two counts of embezzlement and three killings."

"Do you really think he left town?"

"Just covering his tracks. My guess is he's hiding out. Still looking for his money. In any event, I'll swear in a couple of deputies and start looking for him. You and I both know he's behind the crimes that have hit our town." He raised a brow. "Have you talked to Jenny?"

"I'm on my way. I'm taking her back to my house if I have to carry her screaming through town."

"She's been afraid of Turner, and rightfully so."

"I figured out where the money is. Later on today I'll get Morgan to check out my findings. At least it's in a place where Turner can't get his hands on it."

"I'll send a wire to Houston, Dallas, Austin, and San Anton' in case he leaves town for a few days. I'll also alert the railroad. Anything you want me to tell Morgan? I'm on my way there now."

"He doesn't know about Ellen. And would you ask him to contact the First National Bank of Houston? See if there's an account under Jenny's or Jessica's name."

"Sure thing."

Should Grant reveal his suspicions about Martha and Lester somehow being involved with Turner? *Not yet. I don't have any proof.* He reached for the door. "Thanks, Ben. I need to get going. Like I said before, I'll send word about Ellen as soon as I can." He frowned. "Turner had better not show his face in town."

"What did you say?"

"Oh, nothing. I'm beginning to have more apprehensions than an old spinster. I'm wondering if we shouldn't tell anyone that Ellen survived the attack."

"I'd been thinking that very thing."

"I'll tell those at my house as soon as I get back not to let anyone know that Ellen survived the attack." He shook Ben's hand and left the office.

Stepping out onto the street, he noticed how tired he truly felt—not necessarily physically spent, because fatigue walked hand in hand with his profession, but mentally worn. *I want Turner stopped.*

If Jenny refused to move into the parsonage, then he'd propose. They could marry today, and he'd make sure Turner never laid his filthy hands on her.

Once inside the boardinghouse, Grant stopped at the front desk to greet Harold.

"I'd like to see Jenny," Grant said.

"Something tells me that you haven't heard the news." Harold peered down his long, pointed nose. "Miss Martin checked out early this morning. She left on the early train to head back home. In fact, she asked me to hand out a few letters. Here's one for you. Oh, here, take them all."

Stunned, Grant mumbled a thank you, not really sure if he wanted to read the letter there or wait for the privacy of his home. Shock and concern paralyzed his senses. An urgency overcame any need to be alone. He wanted to know what the letter said—now.

Grant took the missive and seated himself at a single table in the dining room. Staring at it for a brief moment, he carefully lifted the flap.

His gaze consumed every word. He simply refused to believe Jenny had gone back to Cleveland and purposely not left an address for him to find her. He read her heartfelt words of love for his family, Ellen, and most of all for the Lord. A mixture of anger and helplessness wove through his weary heart. He read on.

She didn't have to apologize to him. Neither did she have to leave town without so much as a word. Now he understood why Rebecca had seen Jenny crying. She'd already decided to leave and masked her feelings by saying she had dirt in her eyes.

His reading took in the most important reason for her leaving Kahlerville. He reread it to make certain he hadn't been mistaken. *She left here because she's in love with me?* Bewilderment and frustration captured his mind. Why hadn't he told her how he felt sooner? His stupidity might cost him a dear price.

His thoughts drifted back to moments, glances, and words left unspoken. What a fool he'd been. He thought her kindness and gentle ways were from the Lord beginning to direct her life. Those endearing traits were heaven-sent, but the love she spread around her had been intended for him in a very special way.

How could I have been so blind? Address or no address, he'd find her and bring her right back where she belonged. God had given him a woman to love, and he didn't intend for her to get away.

Suddenly, Grant realized the other implication of Jenny's letter. Did Turner know she had left Kahlerville? Had he still been watching her? Instantly on his feet, Grant rushed out of the boardinghouse and back to Ben's office.

Jenny had no inkling of the possible danger.

CHAPTER  33

Mimi opened the front door just as Grant reached for the outside knob. "Ellen's awake. It's a miracle, a real miracle. She tried to talk, but Frank stopped her just like you said. Then he asked if she knew who attacked her."

Grant's heart raced. "And she does?"

"Yes." She blinked, no doubt to keep her wavering tears from drowning their conversation. "So I've been sitting with her while Frank went to fetch Ben. The reverend headed back to the parsonage before Frank left. I rushed downstairs when I saw you coming up the front walk."

Grant glanced at the staircase. "Praise God. Maybe now we can get to the bottom of this." He started up the stairs, then turned heel. "Mimi, how is Rebecca faring in all of this?"

She smiled faintly. "Martha has kept her busy playing with the boys."

"Good. I don't want her overhearing anything that might scare her. Ben doesn't want anyone to know that Ellen survived until we find out who attacked her."

"I'll do my part and tell the others. Is Jenny on her way?"

He stopped midway. "No. . .she's gone."

"I don't understand." Mimi's face drained of color. "Where is she?"

He hesitated to reply and, in his indecision, gripped the handrail. The magnitude of the troubles facing him and those he loved mounted with each fleeting moment, and his normal, orderly pattern of handling matters threatened to crumble. With one hand he squeezed the hand of God, and with the other he shielded himself and those he loved from the grim occurrences around them. Breathing a quick prayer for strength and trust, he viewed the confusion and shock written clearly across Mimi's face. It took only seconds to reach her.

"Jenny boarded the train this morning for Ohio."

"Why? Did you two quarrel? She never said a word about leaving. No good-bye. Nothing."

He shook his head, torn between the needs of his patient and those of his housekeeper. "She wrote several letters. One is addressed to you." He reached inside his jacket. "All I know is what she wrote in mine."

Her gaze darted nervously about. "Did she say why she left? Sorry, but I have to ask. I mean, I know you need to see Ellen."

He paused. "Please keep this between us, and we'll talk as soon as Ben leaves. Jenny is gone because she feels responsible for all the things that have happened in Kahlerville and because she's in love with me."

Grant reached out to take her hand. "It's not over yet, so don't you cry. I'm not letting Jenny get away. I know God intended for us to be together, and I'm going to find a way to overcome that stubborn resolve of hers." He released the older woman and watched her dab her eyes.

"Go take care of Ellen." She shooed him away with her soggy handkerchief. "I need to have another good cry and pray God's protection over Ellen, Jenny, and. . .and everyone else."

He bent over and kissed her cheek. "Ben always says that God's in control. He knows the outcome, and we simply need to have faith."

With an encouraging smile, he left Mimi to see his patient. Once inside the room where Ellen lay with her eyes closed, Grant viewed the purplish-red and blue-black bruises extending from above her eyes to the visible area of her neck. Anger soared again with the realization that this dear lady had suffered needlessly at the hands of a brutal man.

"Ellen," Grant whispered, but she didn't stir. He sat down beside her and decided to wait a few minutes until she awakened again. Had it been only a few hours ago that he thought Frank carried a dead woman? Ellen's breathing had been so shallow, so faint that he had to feel her chest for its rise and fall.

With the night behind all of them and the knowledge of Jenny heading back to Ohio, Grant desperately needed to know for sure who attacked Ellen. She opened her swollen eyes through narrowed slits and stared at the empty chair where her husband had sat. Her questioning gaze flew to Grant.

"He went to fetch Ben," Grant said. "They'll be here shortly."

Something terrifying captured her attention, and she tried to raise herself from the bed.

Grant eased her back onto the pillow. When she could not be consoled, he produced paper and pen. "Can you write it down? I need to know what's upsetting you."

She reached for the pen with shaking fingers, and Grant assisted her in scribbling one word onto the paper. It read "Jenny."

Outwardly, he kept his composure, but his mind and heart weighed heavily with fear. "Jenny left on the morning train back to Ohio," Grant said.

Heavy footsteps and the voices of Ben and Frank came up the stairs. Grant didn't turn to greet either man but kept his attention on his patient. "Is Jenny in danger?"

A fresh array of tears streamed down her face. Instantly, Frank bent to his knees at her side. A smile of understanding passed between them.

"Ellen," Grant said. "Did Aubrey Turner do this to you?"

Her anxious gaze flew from Frank to Grant and back again.

Frank lightly brushed the strawberry blond hair from her face. "Give Grant and Ben the answer, sweetheart. Nobody's going to hurt you again. I'm right here."

Grant marveled at the big man's infinite tenderness. He ached for Jenny. *Dear God, she has to be safe.*

Finally, Ellen nodded affirmatively. Pain etched her features, and Frank lifted her hand into his.

"Was he looking for something?" Ben asked.

Again, Ellen wordlessly agreed.

"Money?" Ben leaned in next to his brother. The animosity between the two men about Ben's questioning had vanished. But that was the way with brothers.

Ellen nodded.

"Did he find what he was looking for?"

She shook her head no.

"Did he plan to go after Jenny?"

She nodded and blinked back the tears.

Grant clenched his fists to dispel the rising anger. "We need to let Ellen rest." He exited the room with Ben to speak privately downstairs. More than enough evidence had been obtained to issue a warrant for Turner's arrest, but Grant wanted more. He wanted the man behind bars now.

Ben coughed—that nagging perpetual cough. "I'll wire all the towns where the train is scheduled to stop and ask them to be on the lookout for a man fitting Turner's description. I'll also ask them to detain Jenny until one of us can talk to her."

"That sounds better. In the meantime, I'm going after her myself. I simply can't stay here and do nothing."

"What about tending to Ellen?" Frank asked.

"I've already sent word to a doctor in Montgomery County to send a nurse to help Mimi. Ellen's going to be all right, but she needs good medical care. In the meantime, I'm sure Mimi and my mother will sit with her."

Ben frowned. "Tell you what—I'll swear in Frank and make him a deputy until this mess is cleared up. That way he can protect the women and children here while you're gone."

"Thanks. That makes me feel better. I want that murdering thief found before someone else is hurt." He could say no more. Turner had been successful in completing two of his attacks, proof of his clever planning. What else was he capable of doing?

"Ben, let's talk downstairs," Grant said. "I have a few things I want to tell you about Turner."

The two men slowly made their way down the stairs.

"Grant, Ben, I need to talk to you." Martha met them at the bottom of the stairs. "For once in my life, I'm going to do the decent thing."

"We can talk in my office," Grant said. Could he be right about Turner on this point, too? He hoped not, but it made sense.

"Fine. Mimi is watching the children. This is going to be hard, very hard, but I have to tell you about Aubrey Turner. I really think he's the one who hurt Ellen."

Grant gestured her into his office, and she sat stiffly. He and Ben exchanged glances. Curious. Hopeful. But could Martha be trusted to tell the truth about anything?

"What is it, Martha? I'm hoping you know something about Turner that can help me throw him in jail," Ben said.

"I do. That and more." She lifted her chin. "Turner is a professional gambler. He boasted about a colorful past, and from what he's done here, I'm sure it's true. He learned from one of my girls about Lester and me." She peered up at Grant, then at Ben. "I trust you to keep this confidential, but Lester is the father of my sons.

"Grant, you were nearly right that day. All the time Turner played up to me and the girls, he was scheming. He took the information and went to Lester's wife with the truth. You see, it's her money invested in the bank, and when she found out her money was supporting the boys, well, she didn't take it well. My sons look just like Lester, so there wasn't any point in him denying who they belonged to. Turner threatened to take the news to the whole town unless the three of us agreed to help him find the money that Jessica supposedly stole from him. Sylvia Hillman is not a bad person. She could have said a lot of things to me but didn't. Anyway, we were all forced to do whatever Turner demanded."

She glanced down at her folded hands in her lap. "Sylvia was supposed to spread rumors about Ellen and Jenny—anything to discredit them. I did my job that day in the general store. Lester searched through all the records at his bank in an effort to find the money, but he found nothing."

"Did Turner set the fire?"

"I think so. When I refused to set up another card game, he said he'd get even."

"Why did you refuse him?" Ben asked. "You have card games there all the time."

"He cheats, and I didn't want someone else killed." She stiffened. "I do have my own morals. Looks to me like Jenny Martin is in danger, especially if what happened to Ellen is any indication of what Turner will do next. I never learned how much money was at stake, but it must be a tidy sum." She stood from her chair. "I've said my piece. In the next few days, I'm leaving Kahlerville with my sons. No point in staying here any longer."

"Martha, are you afraid of Turner?" Ben's soft tone was what Grant appreciated about his brother-in-law. Compassion for the downtrodden.

"Normally, I'm not afraid of much, but I have my sons to consider. Now you can arrest him, right?"

"Ellen identified him as her attacker."

"We have to find him first," Ben said. "He supposedly left town."

Grant glanced out the open window of his office. No breeze

today. Just the stifling heat that caused tempers to soar and strong men to grow weak.

Jenny, are you safe?

Jenny watched the countryside disappear as the train passed by tall, spindly pines and green, rolling hills dotted with colorful foliage. The steady click of the train wheels against the track took her farther and farther away from the people and the town she loved. Her lace handkerchief rested damp in the palm of her hand from wiping away the many tears. Each time she recalled a special moment with Grant, Rebecca, the Andrews family, Miss Mimi, or Ellen, her eyes flooded again. All that she had left from the summer rested in the fond memories forever embedded in her heart.

"Miss, is there anything I can do for you?" a kindly porter asked.

"No, thank you."

The porter smiled. "I'll check with you again later."

Jenny brushed away the wetness only to have her eyes water again. Pleasant recollections drifted by, much like the miles, leaving a landscape of beauty far behind, never to be forgotten and never to be recaptured again. She knew no regrets in coming to Texas. How could she? For there in that country town she had found the meaning of love and a real relationship with Jesus Christ. Without a doubt, she knew her trip had been the result of divine intervention. This fact alone comforted her as the train chugged along.

Little Rebecca would grow into a fine young lady. Jenny wanted to remember her niece on special occasions with small sentiments. After all, she didn't really want Rebecca to forget her aunt Jenny.

How could I ever have thought she would be better off with Mother and Father or me? A permanent lump seemed to have settled in her throat. How selfish she'd been when what she really needed was to experience God's unconditional love.

Images of Grant crept into her thoughts once more. She wondered how long before he forgot her—how long before he began escorting another woman to church. Oh, how she loved Kahlerville's young doctor. His green eyes flashed vividly across her mind. If only he'd loved her in return, then she might be there today. But Grant knew all her ugly traits: how she had tried to steal his precious Rebecca. Nothing good could come from a love begun in deceit.

Pushing the summer from her mind, she envisioned teaching school and going on with her life without her parents' influence. She whimsically hoped for a softening of their spirits, even though she knew such a feat was impossible. They had little use for Christianity or those who professed such beliefs. Of course, not so long ago, she had shared in their opinions. They could be touched by God, too.

She had ignored their disapproval of her activities and continued to write cheery letters in which she spoke of the people and events going on around her. She needed for them to see she was happy and content, more at peace than she had ever thought possible. Jenny smiled in guessing her mother's reaction to the news of her daughter learning how to cook.

Jenny sensed a special closeness to Jessica, and someday she planned to instill in her own children the value of telling them how much they are loved. A twinge of regret nibbled at her in the decision to leave the journal with Grant. She'd reread many portions of it, enough to memorize the treasured entries so dear to her. How grand if she'd discovered where Jessica had deposited the money and then presented it to Grant for Rebecca and the young women from the brothel. Nevertheless, she felt Grant would have no difficulty in deciphering its contents.

She looked around at the few passengers. Two men sat several seats in front of her. From time to time, they talked quite loudly and smoked foul-smelling cigars. She remembered how the smell had made her stomach retch on her trip to Texas, and she shuddered at the thought of the sickness returning. The older couple opposite her appeared deeply engrossed in a newspaper and spoke in low whispers. No other passengers were on the train.

She couldn't help but feel ashamed and embarrassed about her first train ride to Texas. It didn't matter that she'd been ill. She'd still treated people horribly. Jenny hoped she might see some of those same faces again so she could apologize for her previous behavior.

She wanted to do so much for Jesus, to have her life count for good, and to touch people's lives the way she'd been touched by Him. Jesus rode with her on the lonely train back to Ohio. She knew He understood her sadness and the pain in leaving Kahlerville.

Little time remained before school started, and she needed to prepare herself for the new students. Already she intended to use hymns in her piano lessons and to utilize the optional opening time at the beginning of the school day for prayer and devotions. Once she had ignored it, but no longer. Bible verse memorization and student-read scripture would benefit not only the students but also the teacher.

Her mind swept over Cleveland's familiar streets and the churches solidly built on their corners. Finding a suitable church home might take awhile.

A man sat down beside her, interrupting her reflections.

"Good morning, Jenny."

She gasped, alarmed with the instant recognition of the man. Caution and control fought to keep her steady. "Aubrey, what a surprise."

"I gathered you'd feel that way." He flicked a bit of dust from his jacket.

"I thought you'd left town earlier."

"A bit of unfinished business brought me back." His violet eyes looked menacing, and she noted his smile and charm from past encounters had vanished.

The handsome features that once had attracted her to Aubrey Turner now filled her with morbid dread. The revolver lay in her reticule. She'd use it if he refused to leave her alone.

"I certainly hope your business is pleasant." She searched for the porter.

"It all depends upon you, my dear," he said.

"I know you mean well, but I really need this time to be alone." She despised the game she played with this vile man.

"I'd planned for us to engage in some delightful conversations."

Aubrey opened the left side of his jacket and revealed a small handgun. Before she could fully acknowledge the danger, he neatly slipped it from a strap around his shoulders and shoved the barrel into her ribs.

"Do not utter a sound," he said. "Let me explain a peculiar fact about this type of handgun. It has a short firing range and sometimes misses the target entirely, but at this distance I believe accuracy isn't a problem. You are mine, dear Jenny, to do with as I choose."

CHAPTER  34

Grant saddled his spotted mare at the livery. He filled a saddlebag with extra bullets and strapped a holster around his waist. It had been a long time since he'd tied on a gun, and it felt foreign, uncomfortable, out of place. He'd been an expert marksman at one time, but that was years ago. Using violence to settle differences was against everything he believed in, but, then again, so was murder. His mind crept back to his fight with Sam Detterman; this wasn't the same. With a deep sigh, he checked to make sure he'd included two canteens of water. The sun beat down hard—hot and relentless.

"Don't you go looking for trouble," Ben warned, watching him make ready. "You best let the law handle this."

He ignored the warnings and tightened the cinch.

"Grant, why don't you stay here and let us handle this business with Turner?"

"While you let him go after Jenny? I don't think so. Not that I doubt your capabilities, but you stated what you could and couldn't do." He yanked on the girth. "Just wire those train stops for me. Maybe the law can get their hands on him or keep Jenny safe until I get there."

"But—"

He shook his head. "Look, Ben, you know when I set my mind

on something, nothing changes it."

"All right. I've already sworn in Frank, so don't be worrying about your family. And I'll be praying for you."

The sound of an approaching rider captured Grant's attention. In an instant, he recognized his brother. Morgan had stopped by the house earlier, and the two had argued about Grant taking out after Jenny. This time his brother rode one of his prize stallions: a sleek animal, all black except for a white star above its eyes.

"Is this a send-off party?" Grant asked. "Or are you offering me one of your best horses?"

"Neither," Morgan said. "I'm riding with you."

"No, you're not. This is too dangerous for a family man."

"You have a child, too, little brother. I'm not letting you go after Jenny or Turner alone. No point in arguing with me. I'm the oldest."

Grant's temper simmered hot, and he wondered how to get rid of Morgan. "We haven't had a good fight in years, but I'm in the mood for one now."

"Might not set well that the town's doctor and lawyer were brawling in the street—good Christian men that we are. Besides, I saw how you and Sam Detterman looked after the Fourth of July." He narrowed his eyes. "My mind is set on going with you." He pushed his hat back and revealed a receding hairline.

Grant glared at him. "I don't need your help."

"You don't have a choice in the matter."

He expelled a deep breath, realizing his brother definitely was the expert in debate. "And how does Casey feel about this?"

"She's fighting this one on her knees."

Grant swung up into the saddle. "Your wife has more sense than both of us. If you're coming, let's get going. Time's wasting."

The longer Jenny sat, the more she battled the nausea churning in her stomach. Aubrey Turner had trapped her. Unspoken words between them, linked with the journal's truth, caused her to shiver uncontrollably. She wanted to leap across him and shout for help, but instead she sat numb with fear. At least she still had her reticule within her fingertips.

"And if you decide to go ahead and scream, I also have a revolver that could easily eliminate the passengers or employees of this fine Union Pacific coach." Aubrey smiled candidly, tilting his head as though engaging her in an intimate chat.

She breathed a prayer for deliverance. "What do you want from me?"

"I believe you already know the answer, being the smart young woman that you are. My money, please. After all, that is why you traveled all this way."

She fought the rising panic. "I have no idea what this is all about. I came to learn about my sister."

Aubrey stared at her, his eyes emotionless. A slight smile played upon his lips. "You came to Texas to recover the money Jessica stole from me. I don't think I'm mistaken when I say you and Ellen were in this scheme together."

"What money?" The words of the journal scrolled across her mind. "If my sister stole money from you, I don't know where it is." How quickly could she retrieve her revolver? Would he actually hurt these innocent people?

"You sound as ignorant as Ellen."

"Ellen was Jessica's friend, and now she's mine. I came to Texas to visit my niece and learn what I could about my sister's death. I had never met or heard of Ellen until Grant Andrews told me about her." Jenny feared she was losing control. Hysteria twisted and rose like a vine that threatened to choke the life out of her.

"And you have no idea where Jessica put my money?"

His face slowly turned crimson. Father often grew angry this way, but his temper did not trigger the fear that this man evoked. "I swear to you I have no idea."

"Ellen insisted the same thing." He jabbed the gun barrel deep into her side. "Right up until I finally had to kill her. Her begging scratched at my nerves—just like that old lady where she used to live."

Jenny's mouth grew dry, and the words refused to form. "Ellen. . . you killed Ellen? And Mrs. Lewis?"

"And you'll end up just like them if you don't tell me what I need to know."

She feared the terror would overcome her sanity. "If I knew where Jessica hid your money, then I'd tell you." She licked her parched lips. "You can go through my trunk and see for yourself."

He chuckled and gave her a foreboding grin. "I intend to go through everything you own, and if that doesn't bring me any satisfaction, then I'll search every inch of you. The latter may be quite enjoyable. At least your sister always took pleasure in that sort of thing."

"I'd rather be dead." Instantly she regretted her words.

"I can accommodate your wishes."

"Please, listen to me. Would I willingly offer my trunk and bags if I had anything that belonged to you?"

He turned in his seat to face her and smiled as though filled with unwavering devotion. The small gun pierced her ribs. "Possibly. The fear of death brings about strange behavior in most people." He caressed her cheek. "I detest the thought of soiling your pretty blue traveling attire. No matter. I'll get my money from you with or without your assistance."

She shuddered. Casey would have been smarter than this. She'd have out-thought this disgusting animal.

Aubrey picked up her trembling gloved hand and kissed it lightly before placing it back in her lap. "There's a stop scheduled in a few hours, pretty lady. You and I will get off there so I can continue my questioning."

"But there's nothing to find."

"Well, looks like I'll need to dispose of you, doesn't it?"

Her pulse quickened. "Then you'll have three murders on your hands."

A slow, hideous smile spread across his face. "It will be one of many."

Jenny chilled to the bone. The vine of desperation tightened. "I can't give you what I don't have."

"I'm positive you know more than you indicate, so relax and enjoy the journey until we get to the next town. I've already informed the porter to have your belongings ready. And I'll take your reticule. There may be something of interest there for me." He reached for her bag. In the next moment he chuckled. "Clever girl. I'd never have guessed you had a gun. You do surprise me. Your sister detested them. You have amazed me on more than one occasion, like boarding the train to this forsaken dirt hole without your parents' knowledge."

Jenny sank back into the seat, terrified and unable to sort through her thoughts to think, to plan. She couldn't even pray properly. Turner had killed Ellen! Precious, dear Ellen, whose only crime was friendship.

My dear sister, I know you never intended for those you loved to be killed over Aubrey's money. I wish I had the journal. I'd gladly give it to him so he could figure it out for himself.

But Aubrey *didn't* know about the journal. He couldn't link any of this to Grant, and that might guarantee his and Rebecca's safety.

Perhaps she might gain permission to excuse herself for a moment of discretion and find someone to help her. Surely the conductor had a weapon to protect the passengers. Railroads were supposed to be prepared for emergencies. Folding her hands primly, Jenny decided to sit quietly and concentrate on every prayer she'd ever heard. In a little while she'd plead her situation and hope he'd not be cruel enough to deny her a moment of privacy.

As Turner had stated, a few hours later the train screeched and began a slow halt. Jenny watched Aubrey carefully study two men standing at the railroad station. Both of them wore badges. Her spirits lifted. Surely the lawmen could free her. Her previous plan of seeking help failed when he refused her the necessary room.

Thank You. Hope lifted her spirits. Aubrey had said they must prepare to disembark from the train. She relaxed slightly. They would pass right by the two men wearing badges.

Oh, Lord, help me to break away from him, and please don't let any innocent people get hurt.

"We're departing from the rear," Aubrey said and grasped her elbow. "I'll have someone from the hotel get your trunk."

Before she had a moment to contemplate his decision, Jenny found herself pushed along the aisle and out the rear door. Her feet barely touched the ground as the train still moved along its track.

If only those men could see that she was in danger. But if she called out for help, Aubrey might shoot one of them. No one here knew he had murdered Ellen. No one knew he'd threatened her. Her hope was futile.

Aubrey hooked her arm into his, and together they strolled into the noisy hotel. She held her breath, repulsed when he signed the hotel register as *Mr. and Mrs. Charles Windsor.* Pulling a silver dollar from his pocket, he flipped it to a youth standing nearby.

"Here, boy. Fetch my trunk at the train stop. There will be another one for you when you bring it up to our room. The name is Windsor, Charles Windsor."

The excited youth sped from the hotel lobby, banging the door behind him and irritating the matronly hotel clerk. Jenny glowered at Aubrey, but he pressed a kiss against her cheek and smiled, clearly displaying his milky-white teeth.

"I loved Jessica," he said. "She was the one woman who could have had everything I own. The mere sight of her took away my breath."

He reminded her of an oleander—handsome but deadly.

The matronly woman warmly welcomed the two and handed him the keys to a second-floor room. Together Jenny and Aubrey mounted the stairs, and he ostentatiously complimented her loveliness. Once inside the room, she found the courage to challenge his obvious foolishness.

"And how will you get my trunk using the name of Charles Windsor?" The question held more daring than she felt.

Obviously annoyed, Aubrey removed his jacket and laid it fastidiously across the back of an overstuffed chair.

"I am far cleverer than you give me credit for," he said and pulled off his gloves, finger by finger. "Once I saw you at the train station in Kahlerville, I purchased a ticket under my new name, disguised with a wig and a beard. My past as an actor has never failed me. Once we were gone from that dreadful town, I tearfully informed the conductor that my new bride had deserted me and I must do whatever was necessary to win back my wife. He allowed me to change the name on the list of passengers to Mr. and Mrs. Charles Windsor, which included replacing the name on your belongings. So you see, my dear, there was no Jenny Martin on the train. You don't exist."

Jenny fought panic while her heart pounded against her chest like a frightened bird. She couldn't escape him; no one knew where to find her. She'd written to her friends that she planned to leave by railroad. Except now the train didn't have her listed as a passenger.

A new thought occurred to her, and with it came a strange sensation of peace. God knew where Aubrey held her captive. He stood right beside her. Whatever happened, He would help her endure the hours ahead. And Grant knew what she'd done because of the letter she'd left with Mr. Snyder.

Shortly thereafter, a knock sounded at the door, signaling the youth's return with her things. Aubrey spent the next hour rifling through every article of her belongings. He tucked her revolver inside his jacket and laughed again.

"Even Jessica in her insanity never tried to shoot me," he said.

Finding nothing, he began slitting the hems and seams of her dresses, jackets, undergarments, and then the trunk itself, looking for his money. When he had exhausted every possible means of hiding any valuables, he turned on her savagely. Grabbing her shoulders, his fingers pressed deep into her flesh.

"Please, you're hurting me," she cried. "I know nothing about your money."

He struck her soundly across her cheek. It stung, then burned hot. Jenny held her breath. The sharp crack of his hand against her skin seemed to incite him even more. He squeezed her upper arms until she felt herself collapsing to the floor in excruciating pain. Snatching up a torn petticoat from the strewn pile of clothes, he tied her hands behind her back. He shoved her to the floor and grabbed up another ripped garment, wrapping it several times around her ankles. When she protested, he gagged her tightly.

"I'll give you until tonight to tell me where to find my money." He towered over her. In that instant, she feared he might kick her. "I'm a generous man. I'll give you some time to remember where you hid it." He hastily replaced his jacket and left the room. Jenny heard the key turn and click, ensuring her imprisonment.

All afternoon the sun played shadows across the small quarters. She wept until she could shed no more tears. Prayers were wordless— her heart spoke silent grief and sorrow. The peace she'd experienced earlier slowly dissipated as light faded around her.

God is with me, she repeated. *I shouldn't be afraid, but I am.* As if to prove her trepidation correct, fear ripped through her body. Had she abandoned her new faith? She tried not to listen to the sounds outside the door, instead focusing on what she knew of the Lord. No means of stalling Aubrey existed, and no point existed for conjuring up a story to delay the inevitable.

Her reflections turned to dying. Was this whole journey designed to bring her closer to God so she would die with the blessings of heaven?

She must have faith that God would lead someone to find her before Aubrey ended her life.

CHAPTER  35

Morgan and Grant rode through a small Texas town along the train line, much like their own Kahlerville. They peered from side to side, scrutinizing every figure and looking for anyone who resembled Jenny or Turner.

Morgan lifted his hat and wiped the sweat from his forehead with a damp bandanna. "This heat reminds me of the time when Davis Jenkins held Casey captive."

"That's a comforting thought." Grant blew out an exasperated sigh. He didn't relish the memory of those days when he nearly lost Morgan and Casey.

His brother leaned against the saddle horn. "Did I ever thank you for taking a bullet in the shoulder?"

"Yes, Morgan, many times," Grant replied. He wasn't usually so irritated at his brother, but concern over Jenny dominated his thoughts. "You even thanked me on your wedding day."

"Well, that bullet is why I'm here."

Frustrated, he glanced at his brother. "How do you figure?"

"It's the same thing all over again, except this time it's Turner after Jenny."

Grant shook his head to keep from demanding that his brother find another topic of conversation. "So, are you wanting to be best man at my wedding?"

"I didn't know you'd asked her."

"I haven't, but I'm the reason she left Kahlerville."

Morgan replaced his hat. "What did you do?"

"Caused her to fall in love with me."

His brother laughed—the first bit of humor they'd exchanged all day. "The poor girl is in for a lot more trouble than Aubrey Turner."

"Save your comments for after the wedding, providing she accepts my proposal."

They rode slowly down the street, both searching the townsfolk for a petite woman with chestnut curls or a tall, blond man.

"Grant," Morgan said, his focus intent on their surroundings.

"Yeah?"

"I'm glad you're my brother, and I'm praying for you and Jenny."

Grant half grinned despite the solemnity of the circumstances. His brother had a difficult time expressing sentiment to Grant, and when he did, it sounded profound. "Thanks. I appreciate your prayers and that you're riding with me today. It's hard for me to hold onto the hand of God when I'm the type of person who wants to fix everything for everybody. I'm the town doctor, supposedly with healing in my fingertips. Right now, I'm scared to death."

"I understand."

The two men rode the remainder of the street in silence. Both knew the train had already passed through for the day, and they realized the slim chance of Turner being apprehended by the law. Grant didn't want to consider that Turner might have already found Jenny.

"Think I'll check out the train station," Morgan said. "What about you?"

Grant knew exactly where he was headed. "I'll stop by the sheriff's office. It's hard to say if they would have received a telegram before or after the train stopped here."

The two soon discovered that neither the train station nor the sheriff offered much hope. They talked of riding on to the next town.

"Let's go back and see that lawman," Grant said, standing beneath a shade tree near the railroad depot. "He's a bit cocky, and I'm not so sure he even met the train."

As Grant expected, the sheriff didn't appreciate being questioned again, especially by two dust-ridden men. "Hate to disappoint you, but there wasn't a young woman traveling alone on the train. I searched it myself."

"She had to be on it. She boarded it in Kahlerville." Grant glared at the young man—in his opinion too young to wear a badge. He didn't even look old enough to shave. What was this country coming to? Grant's persistent headache and lack of sleep had ushered in a short fuse. "Do you have a list of passengers?"

The younger man spat a mouthful of tobacco juice onto a spittoon. "Sure do, but wait a minute. Who are you two, anyway?"

"I'm Dr. Grant Andrews from Kahlerville, and this is my brother, Morgan. He's a lawyer there. And who are you?"

"Sheriff Nelson. Got any identification?"

Morgan grabbed Grant's arm, apparently sensing the anger that searched for a spot to land. "Yes, we do," Morgan said, reaching inside his shirt pocket.

Moments later, the sheriff opened a narrow desk drawer and shuffled through some papers before producing the list of the train's occupants. "Two cattlemen headed for Dallas, an old couple on their way to their son's farm in Arkansas, and a young married couple."

Rubbing his chin, Morgan stared at the sheriff. "What did the couple look like?"

"Don't know. I didn't see 'em." He spat again, and the sound of it smacking against the pan rankled Grant beyond comprehension.

"You just said you searched the train yourself," Grant said.

"The conductor told me the couple wanted to be alone. Seems as though they were having a tiff, and the husband was trying to smooth things out."

"What were their names?" Grant asked.

The sheriff glanced down at his piece of paper. "Windsor, Mr. and Mrs. Charles Windsor."

"Did they leave on the train?" Grant leaned over the desk, eyeing the young sheriff critically.

"Naw, don't think so 'cause a boy from the hotel fetched their trunk and a few bags."

Within moments, Grant raced toward the establishment.

Dear God, don't let me be too late. Calm me down, and help me think clearly.

∾≈⊙⌒∾

Jenny attempted to twist her body into a less painful position. Her shoulders and legs throbbed, and her cheek hurt where Aubrey had slapped her. Watching the fading light disappear from the room and shadows dance across the walls, she awaited his return. Her vision blurred, and her mouth tasted acrid.

She wanted Aubrey to simply finish what he'd threatened. She had nothing to tell him. The sound of a man's boots echoed down the hall and stopped abruptly outside the door.

Her heart pounded fiercely. Out of sheer desperation, she scrambled through her mind for a plan or a diversion, something to stall for time. Aubrey would see through any fabrication. She couldn't fight him, and she couldn't escape. No matter what she might consider, others could be harmed.

I don't want to die.

The dull ring of the key tapping against the metal lock sounded the approach of her execution. She watched the knob slowly turn, hysteria stealing her prayers. Slowly, the door swung open. If she could have screamed, she would have gladly alarmed every person in the hotel.

Jenny squeezed her eyes shut for one more prayer before Aubrey entered the room. It took all of her might to look at him, but she wanted to project some sense of bravery.

"Jenny, it's me."

She blinked. Grant. Had he found her, or was she dreaming? Had she lost her faint hold on sanity?

He kneeled at her side and untied the makeshift gag. His eyes softened. "I'm so sorry. You shouldn't have left Kahlerville. Don't you know I love you?"

Tears of relief and exhaustion welled up in her eyes. *Love me?* "How did you ever find me?"

He gathered her up in his arms. "I prayed and God led me here. I had to find you before Turner attempted another murder. Morgan's with me, too. He's at the sheriff's office."

A wave of sickness swept over her. "Aubrey will be back any minute. He'll kill you. He killed Ellen."

Grant pushed away the torn garments wrapped around her arms and legs and held her close. "Ellen is alive. He thought he killed her."

She attempted to think more clearly as he massaged her wrists and ankles. She wanted to say so much, be courageous, but the words refused to come.

"Can you stand? We need to get out of here." Grant helped her to her feet. When her legs buckled, he lifted her up into his arms.

The ordeal had left her weak and utterly shaken.

"Put the little lady down." Aubrey kicked the door shut. He aimed his revolver at Jenny. "I won't hesitate to shoot either one of you, so put her down easy."

"The sheriff's on his way." Grant slowly set Jenny on her feet.

She held onto his arm for balance, not once doubting Aubrey's threat.

"You're lying." Aubrey smirked. "Take off that gun belt and toss it this way." He steadied his aim at her while Grant released his weapon. "Join me, dear Jenny, or the doctor will be mending his own wounds."

She stepped forward, but Grant pulled her back. "She's not going anywhere with you, Turner, Jacobs, or whatever your name is. You fire that gun, and half a dozen men will be climbing those stairs. You won't have a chance."

"I'll take the risk." He raised his revolver.

"Wait, I'll come with you." Jenny tried to shake loose of Grant's hold, but he held her firmly. "I'll go with you, Aubrey, and do whatever you say. Just don't hurt him."

Aubrey narrowed his violet gaze. "Your devotion repulses me. Have you forgotten Ellen's fate?"

"She isn't dead," Grant said. "And she identified you this morning. Warrants are out for your arrest."

"I don't believe a word. When I kill somebody, they stay dead."

"Not this time."

"They'll have to catch me first."

Grant shook his head. "Why don't you give up now before you add another killing to the list?"

"Save your pious words for someone else, Doc. And you know, I might consider behaving myself once I have my money, providing Miss Jenny cooperates. She could be taught how to behave." He glared greedily at her.

She wanted to spit on him. Drag her fingernails across his face.

"I can take you to your money," Grant said, his words controlled.

"I'm smarter than that. Why would she be heading back to Ohio if she didn't know where Jessica hid it?"

Grant's gaze bore into Aubrey's face. "I tell you, I know where it's located. Jessica left it for Rebecca's care."

Aubrey waved the revolver in front of Grant's face. "You're a bad liar, and I've heard enough of your gallant tales. In fact, I've heard all I need to shut you up for good."

"Aubrey, please," Jenny whispered.

The hammer clicked on the revolver.

The door flew open. Morgan burst into the room.

The gambler whirled around and fired. The booming sound, the smell of rotten eggs, and the grayish smoke were not the thrill Jenny experienced when she practiced firing her revolver. She never wanted to go through this horror again.

Morgan fell back against the wall with a spurt of blood gushing from a hole in his shoulder.

Jenny screamed, and Aubrey pulled her from Grant and then squeezed a second shot. The bullet whizzed narrowly above Grant's head, but he yanked his own revolver from Aubrey's grasp and fired into the man's right thigh. The sharp crack of Grant's gun echoed across the room.

Jenny twisted free of Aubrey's hold, giving Grant time to pin the man to the floor. Within seconds, the sheriff appeared.

"Someone send for the doctor," the sheriff said. He yanked on Aubrey's arm. "I'll take this one with me."

"I *am* a doctor," Grant said and bent down to examine his brother. "But I need antiseptic and instruments to pull out this bullet." He peeled back the burnt cloth embedded in the gunshot while Jenny tore strips from the remains of her petticoat to hinder the flow of blood. When she handed the cloth to him, their gazes met.

"You could have been killed, and now Morgan is hurt," she said.

For a brief moment Grant allowed his attention to sway from his brother. "I had no choice," he said. "I simply couldn't sit back and wait for the authorities to find you when I knew Turner had plans of his own." He made a bandage from another piece of cloth. "Morgan, how are you doing?"

"I think we're even," Morgan said.

"Even?" Grant smiled. "I guess so. You're going to be just fine."

Jenny had no idea what they were talking about. Perhaps Grant would tell her later. Relief settled through her entire body. Aubrey was under arrest. Ellen was alive. Grant was close enough for her to touch him. And he loved her.

Grant finished tending to Morgan and wiped his hands on a

strip of torn petticoat. They waited for the town's sheriff to return.

"I was so scared," she said. "When he told me about Ellen and Mrs. Lewis. . .I wanted to give up, but I kept praying."

"Ellen simply needs rest, and I'm sure Frank will dote on her every minute of the day." He drew her to him. "I love you, Jenny Martin." He swiped at the wetness beneath her eyes and lightly kissed the bruise darkening her cheek. He frowned and shook his head. "I kept finding excuses for not telling you how I felt. I'm sure a prideful fool. Thought I had my life just where I wanted it, and to think I nearly lost you by not speaking my heart. I don't ever want to let you go."

For once, Jenny didn't cry. Joy filled every inch of her heart. "I meant every word of my letter."

"Then I need to do this right." He gently pushed her away, then lifted her chin to meet his ardent gaze. "Jenny, I'm a slow learner, so I hope you'll have patience with me, but I love you with all my heart. God put us together for a reason—to spend the rest of our lives together. What I'm saying is. . .will you marry me?"

"Oh, yes, Grant. If you will have me, I will love you forever."

"Save it for later, you two." Morgan moaned. "You have an injured man in your midst, and I plan to be best man."

EPILOGUE

Jenny laid her pen aside. While the ink dried, she stared dreamily out the window facing her and Grant's backyard. Their lives were good and definitely blessed, and even the bad times brought them closer to God and each other.

Sadly enough, Ben had passed away last Christmas after a fierce battle with a lung ailment. Bonnie seemed so lost, unhappy, and lonely.

Morgan and Casey were busy expanding the ranch to include more horses—always busy and working together.

Mimi didn't seem to age or slow down. In fact, she just added more projects to her list of things to accomplish. Jenny didn't know what she'd do without the widow, who was so much a part of their family.

Jenny smiled at the thought of Ellen and Frank's news. They were expecting a baby in a few months. Such a blessing for two good people.

Grant and Jenny's prayers had been answered about her parents. Shortly after the wedding, they had taken Rebecca to Cleveland. At first her parents had refused to see them, but then something had changed their minds. Her parents claimed it was precious Rebecca. Jenny smiled. *God changed their minds.* At first the meeting was very uncomfortable, especially when Grant prayed at dinner.

"Mr. Andrews, we do not pray in our home," her father had said.

"We have no use for such nonsense."

"Sir, my family is a praying family," Grant said. "Have you read the Bible?"

"No. I haven't. Never saw a reason to." Her father's face reddened, and Jenny feared a display of his temper.

"Then I challenge you to read and study it. I, too, have studied the sciences—even read Darwin's views on the origin of life. We could conduct a discussion of both books through letters."

Grant's suggestion sparked a challenge, and Jenny's father agreed. After much debate and many letters, her father wrote Grant and Jenny of his desire to attend church. Neither he nor her mother had found salvation in Jesus Christ, but they were in church and reading scripture, and Grant and Jenny continued to pray for them, convinced that God would continue to draw her parents to Him.

Jenny's eyes trailed down to her letter. Guess she'd read it one more time before posting it:

Dear Mother and Father,

I am so excited to write you this letter. We have a new addition to our family. A week ago, Grant and I presented Rebecca with a precious baby sister. I cannot say who is prouder. Grant tells me she looks just like Rebecca did as a baby. Big sister is doing quite well with her new role, and Grant and I are working diligently to make her feel important and needed. She acts so grown up at age four and wants to help with everything about the new baby.

We named our new daughter Rachel Kathryn, and she is beautiful—lots of dark hair, and eyes so blue they are nearly black. I imagine they will be brown.

We are so looking forward to your visit at Christmas. It will make our holiday perfect. May God bless you both.

Love,
Grant, Jenny, Rebecca, and Rachel

Award-winning author DiAnn Mills launched her career in 1998 with the publication of her first book. Currently she has nineteen novels, fifteen novellas, a nonfiction book, and several articles and short stories in print.

DiAnn believes her readers should "expect an adventure." Her desire is to show characters solving real problems of today from a Christian perspective through a compelling story.

Five of her anthologies have appeared on the CBA best-seller list. Three of her books have won the distinction of Best Historical of the Year by Heartsong Presents, and she remains a favorite author of Heartsong Presents' readers. Two of her books have won Short Historical of the Year by American Christian Romance Writers for 2003 and 2004. She is the recipient of the Inspirational Reader's Choice award for 2005 in the long contemporary and novella category.

DiAnn is a founding board member of American Christian Fiction Writers and a member of Inspirational Writers Alive, Chi Libris, and Advanced Writers and Speakers Association. She speaks to various groups and teaches writing workshops. She is also a mentor for the Christian Writers Guild.

She lives in sunny Houston, Texas, the home of heat, humidity, and Harleys. In fact, she'd own one, but her legs are too short. DiAnn and her husband have four adult sons and are active members of Metropolitan Baptist Church.

SOME OTHER BOOKS BY DIANN MILLS

Texas Charm

Nebraska Legacy

Footsteps

When the Lion Roars

Leather and Lace

AVAILABLE WHEREVER GREAT
CHRISTIAN FICTION IS SOLD

Visit DiAnn's Web site at www.diannmills.com